Praise for Nalini Singh, "the alpha author of paranormal romance" (*Booklist*), and the Psy-Changeling Novels

"Once again immersing readers in a richly imagined world . . . Singh's third Psy-Changeling Trinity novel (after *Ocean Light*) delights with lovingly drawn characters."
—*Publishers Weekly*

"Another Psy-Changeling page-turner from the brilliant Singh."
—*Kirkus Reviews*

"Another hands-down winner that expands Singh's brilliantly conceived world."
—*Library Journal* (starred review)

"Nalini Singh pulled out all the stops in this heart-pounding novel. . . . Highly recommended."
—*Harlequin Junkie*

"Whatever you are looking for in a book that will hold you captivated, *Wolf Rain* has it."
—*Fresh Fiction*

"*Wolf Rain* [is] a wonderful addition to an already wonderful series."
—BookBinge

"If you have not read Nalini Singh, you are missing such a gem of an author."
—The Reading Cafe

"The alpha author of paranormal romance."
—*Booklist*

"A must-read for all of my fans."
—#1 *New York Times* bestselling author Christine Feehan

Berkley titles by Nalini Singh

A MADNESS OF SUNSHINE

Psy-Changeling Series

SLAVE TO SENSATION
VISIONS OF HEAT
CARESSED BY ICE
MINE TO POSSESS
HOSTAGE TO PLEASURE
BRANDED BY FIRE
BLAZE OF MEMORY
BONDS OF JUSTICE
PLAY OF PASSION
KISS OF SNOW
TANGLE OF NEED
HEART OF OBSIDIAN
SHIELD OF WINTER
SHARDS OF HOPE
ALLEGIANCE OF HONOR

Psy-Changeling Trinity Series

SILVER SILENCE
OCEAN LIGHT
WOLF RAIN

Guild Hunter Series

ANGELS' BLOOD
ARCHANGEL'S KISS
ARCHANGEL'S CONSORT
ARCHANGEL'S BLADE
ARCHANGEL'S STORM
ARCHANGEL'S LEGION
ARCHANGEL'S SHADOWS
ARCHANGEL'S ENIGMA
ARCHANGEL'S HEART
ARCHANGEL'S VIPER
ARCHANGEL'S PROPHECY
ARCHANGEL'S WAR

Anthologies

AN ENCHANTED SEASON
(with Maggie Shayne, Erin McCarthy, and Jean Johnson)

THE MAGICAL CHRISTMAS CAT
(with Lora Leigh, Erin McCarthy, and Linda Winstead Jones)

MUST LOVE HELLHOUNDS
(with Charlaine Harris, Ilona Andrews, and Meljean Brook)

BURNING UP
(with Angela Knight, Virginia Kantra, and Meljean Brook)

ANGELS OF DARKNESS
(with Ilona Andrews, Meljean Brook, and Sharon Shinn)

ANGELS' FLIGHT

WILD INVITATION

NIGHT SHIFT
(with Ilona Andrews, Lisa Shearin, and Milla Vane)

WILD EMBRACE

Specials

ANGELS' PAWN

ANGELS' DANCE

TEXTURE OF INTIMACY

DECLARATION OF COURTSHIP

WHISPER OF SIN

SECRETS AT MIDNIGHT

Wolf Rain

A PSY-CHANGELING TRINITY NOVEL

NALINI SINGH

JOVE
New York

A JOVE BOOK
Published by Berkley
An imprint of Penguin Random House LLC
penguinrandomhouse.com

ISBN: 9781984803610

Berkley hardcover edition / June 2019
Jove mass-market edition / February 2020

Printed in the United States of America
3 5 7 9 10 8 6 4

Cover art by Tony Mauro
Cover design by Rita Frangie

Wolf Rain

Awakenings

THE SILENCE PROTOCOL fell with a crash heard around the world.

For the first time in over a hundred years, the Psy were free to feel.

Free to love, free to hate, free to laugh, free to hurt.

Free.

Telepaths and telekinetics, foreseers and psychometrics, the weak and the strong, all were free to step out of their emotionless cages and into the sunshine of a life lived without boundaries.

The empaths, their abilities linked inextricably to emotion, gained far more than freedom. No longer considered defective. No longer hidden away, their abilities deliberately and cruelly suppressed. No longer failures. Now, in the heart of winter's cold kiss in the year 2083, empaths are the glue that hold their shocked and shaken people together, millions of lives balanced on their fragile shoulders.

But empaths weren't the only ones who woke with the fall of Silence.

So did a power that should've lain dormant forever.

And that dark power . . . it screams.

EXTRACT FROM
THE MYSTERIOUS E DESIGNATION:
EMPATHIC GIFTS & SHADOWS
BY ALICE ELDRIDGE (CIRCA 1972)

The E designation has no official subdesignations. That, however, does not mean those subdesignations do not exist.

Unofficially, a large percentage of Es tend to put themselves in various subgroups. E-med Psy, for example, work well with the ill and the physically wounded, while E-com Psy are more geared toward commerce.

Regardless, argument continues to rage in the empathic community about whether such inclinations are powerful enough to be considered subdesignations. A small but vocal percentage of empaths believe it is all a matter of differing personalities leading to differing paths, that E is a designation devoid of subdesignations.

I do not have enough data to formulate an answer to this question.[1]

---

1. As a point of interest, I have been unable to find any data whatsoever on the rumored E-sigma, a subdesignation of empathy said to be so dangerous for the E involved that the E's only option for survival is to deliberately suppress their own strength. No E interviewed over the course of this study would explain the E-sigma's divergent abilities to me. Any mention of the subdesignation resulted in both a flash of fear on the faces of my subjects—and in a sudden and implacable shutdown in communication. Either the E-sigma are a shared dark myth, a kind of empathic ghost story . . . or the Es are so afraid for one of their own kind that they protect them against all outsiders.

Chapter 1

The Psy hid their evil in the snow. Watch. Be vigilant. Do not allow such heartbreak to happen again.
—Letter from Aren Snow,
opened in the aftermath of her death in 2059

GRIEF HIT HIM with the force of a backhanded punch.

Alexei stumbled, came to a halt under the driving rain—and immediately realized the soul-shredding pain wasn't his. His eyes burned and his throat threatened to clog, but both the man who ran under the rain and the wolf inside him understood that this grief came from the outside.

Alexei's own grief remained locked up tight in an airless box, where it stayed except for bleak midnight hours about once a month when he could no longer hold it inside. Those nights, he ran in wolf form, howling up at the cold moon in pure fury and ignoring the wolf song that responded to his.

His grief was primal, angry and aggressive and stubbornly determined to be a private thing. His packmates didn't know the meaning of "private" most of the time, but in this, everyone except the toughest, most stubborn wolves held back. Likely because Alexei would growl them right back inside the den. His grief had claws.

The grief he could sense today . . . it was raw, without shields, naked and defenseless. It was a wounded animal with its paw caught in a cruel trap. A broken creature in a place without light, alone and afraid. A sentient being who had lost all hope.

Both parts of him strained at the leash to find the grieving one, attempt to assuage their grief. He was a dominant predatory changeling, a deep protectiveness toward weaker packmates built into his blood. This person wasn't pack, wasn't wolf, but his instincts didn't make the distinction when so close to such terrible anguish.

Alexei had to force himself to pause, *think*. Such an overwhelming emotional storm, the roar of it thunder in his blood, it could come from only one type of being. An empath. And not just any empath. A *powerful* empath who was broadcasting on all bands with no thought to who their pain might hit.

Alexei had only ever met two empaths. The one he knew best had laughed during their meeting and he'd felt the ripple of her happiness in the air, but it had been akin to catching a distant scent on the wind. *This* was a deluge, but there was no attempt to confuse his own senses.

The E was broadcasting so loudly that he couldn't help but feel their crushing grief, his already battered and bruised heart aching, but he knew the grief wasn't his own. The E wasn't targeting him or making any attempt to hack his mind. The waves of emotion were too uncontrolled and chaotic for that. As a wolf might react at the loss of his mate, throwing back his head and howling his rage and grief up at the sky, uncaring of who else might hear.

This was no Psy trick or trap.

Alexei ran in the direction of the torrent of pain.

Only moments earlier and regardless of his wolf's edgy need to run, he'd been considering turning back. The sudden rise in the strength of the wind worried him, and the rain had become a pitiless silver sheet that threatened to turn into shards of ice. Though heavy snow yet shrouded the higher elevations, including thick patches in his current location, it had been cloudy but otherwise fine when he left his pack's central den in California's Sierra Nevada mountains.

Now, turning back was not an option.

The fallen pine needles and snowy leaf litter were fleeting touches under his booted feet, the water that ran over him frigid. Tall green firs thickly dusted with white speared into the granite-colored sky at the start of his run toward the E, but five minutes of loping over the landscape with wolfish speed and the forest giants began to feather out in favor of smaller trees.

Those, too, disappeared not long afterward.

It could get bitingly cold at this elevation even in the summer months, the mountains less than hospitable to large foliage. But they'd had an unseasonal warm snap over the past two weeks. Grass had begun to poke its sharp blades through the snow, and in between the huge shattered rocks that thrust out of the mountain, he spotted tiny rain-bedraggled wildflowers that would raise their hopeful faces to the sun after the storm was past.

The wind slapped at his skin and the icy rain ran down his back, but he didn't slow, driven to find the empath suffering so terribly that she was threatening to crush his heart.

She.

Yes, the "taste" of the presence he could sense was categorically female. It was as if she were broadcasting part of herself with her pain. As if the slamming waves of emotion held a scent his wolf could catch.

His heart thundered, his lungs expanding and collapsing in a harsh rhythm. Inside him ran the wolf that was his other half—a half without which he could never be whole. Alexei and his wolf, they were one . . . even when it came to the curse that haunted his family and had taken his brother. Primal wolf and changeling heart, Alexei accepted who he was—and the price it demanded.

He ran on, the hunt in his blood.

His packmates didn't often wander this way—the power substation he'd promised to look in on during this run was a half hour to the west and could be approached from multiple other directions. It was possible no one had spent time up here for months, maybe longer.

In any other part of the pack's territory, such a gap would be highly unusual. SnowDancer as a pack didn't take territorial security lightly—but things got complicated in this particular section of their land. When Alexei had mentioned his intended route to his alpha, the other man had narrowed his ice-blue eyes. "I haven't been through there in too long." A tension in Hawke's muscles, his jaw working. "My wolf's fur always stands up the wrong way there."

Alexei's claws had pricked the insides of his fingers at the unspoken reference to the nightmarish past. Hawke had been a child of twelve, Alexei barely four when the Psy attempted to savage the pack with cowardice and stealth. A fringe group of scientists had abducted wolf after wolf, then broken their minds and souls beyond repair, the scientists' aim to poison the pack from within.

Hawke's parents hadn't survived.

His strong, highly trained father had gone missing up here during a routine patrol. Tristan had been found a week later, badly wounded from an apparent fall. No one knew the Psy had twisted his mind until it was far too late and he lay bleeding out on the snow.

Hawke's gifted artist mother, Aren, had tried to hold on after Tristan's death, but her heart had been broken into so many pieces that she couldn't put it back together again; she'd simply gone to sleep one day and never woken up.

It was hardly surprising that Hawke preferred not to roam here.

Odd, however, that other packmates avoided it, too. Even pragmatic Elias had shuddered when he ran into Alexei as Alexei was about to leave that afternoon. "Area gives me the creeps," the senior soldier had muttered. "Can a mountain be haunted? 'Cause I'm pretty sure that particular section is."

The E's grief was a crushing vise around his heart by this point, nails that threatened to puncture his lungs. Gritting his teeth, he continued on, uncaring of the sharpness of the rain, the danger of the uneven and rocky terrain. He was a wolf. He was a lieutenant. He was a SnowDancer. And this was wolf land.

The grief reached a screaming crescendo . . . only to begin to fade as he ran on.

Halting, he backed up until the pitch grated and scraped and told him he was right beside her.

Only there was no one within sight or scent. Rain or not, his vision was acute enough that he could see a hell of a long way at this treeless elevation. The only things in his line of sight were patches of snow, exposed juts of rock, the odd area of grass-speckled earth revealed by the recent warm spell, and, over in the distance, a falcon riding the powerful wind.

A changeling bird. It was too big to be a natural falcon.

But the falcon was no concern. The WindHaven falcons had an agreement with SnowDancer that permitted them flight paths over SnowDancer land. Plus, the falcon was far distant and heading in the opposite direction, nearly a dot by now, yet the pain, the pain, it continued to rise and rise and *rise*.

Her heart, it was breaking.

His wolf clawed at the inside of his skin. The primal urge rippling through his blood, Alexei's human hands sprouted claws as he began to hunt among the nearby rocks, on the impossible chance that she was curled up hiding behind one. Impossible because there weren't many rocks large enough. And because how could she *be* here? This area was so deep in SnowDancer territory that you'd have to be a teleporter to get in without being spotted.

A teleport-capable empath?

Alexei had never heard of that combination of psychic abilities, but that didn't mean it couldn't exist. There was a lot changelings and humans didn't know about the Psy. The psychic race had kept a wall of cold Silence between themselves and the rest of the world for over a hundred years.

The protocol that had stifled emotion among the Psy race had also severed their bonds with those outside the PsyNet, the sprawling psychic network that connected all Psy on the planet but for the defectors and renegades. For more than a century, the Psy had focused on icy perfection. They had regarded the other races as lesser, as primitive beings driven by basic animal urges.

Things had changed in recent times, and Alexei's alpha was mated to a deadly cardinal Psy, while one of Alexei's closest friends was a telekinetic former assassin. But even his Psy packmates and friends didn't know all of their race's secrets—Psy leaders had kept the truth from their own people, too. Hidden monsters and predators and psychopaths.

For it was only the pathologically emotionless who'd *truly* thrived under Silence.

Where was she?

He growled deep inside his chest, his wolf rising to the surface to alter his vision. Had anyone been looking at him, they'd have seen his gray eyes turn a shockingly pale amber shot through with shards of gold, his pupils pinpricks of black.

The effect was startling because of his dark eyelashes and eyebrows—quite unlike the "sun-gold" of his hair—as described by his aunt. Even wet, it didn't darken much. Thank God the color didn't translate into his wolf's pelt; his packmates would've never let him live down being a fucking yellow wolf.

Agony, such agony.

Clenching his jaw, he tried to pick up *any* scent that denoted a living being. He caught hints of a small woodland creature and of a wild bird, but that was it. Only sodden vegetation, snow, and rock.

Hauling himself over a large jut of rock as the rain became a raging waterfall, he dropped down into an easy crouch on the other side. He found nothing but a thick pile of snow protected by the shadow the rock would throw in sunlight. Glancing absently back at the rock he'd scaled, he stilled at the sight of the jagged crack in the stone. Once, as a pup, Alexei's brother had found a small cave behind a crack just like that one and turned it into their secret hiding spot.

Brodie had always been generous with his kid brother. Maybe because he'd somehow known that, in the end, it would come down to the two of them. Except it hadn't worked out that way.

Could the empath be curled up in there?

He took extreme care as he went to explore the possibility. That he still couldn't scent even a hint of her told him his search was apt to be futile, because as far as he was aware, no one yet discovered a way to cloak their scent from changeling noses. The closest people had come was to soak themselves in a scent that echoed their surroundings, but rain and wet was too subtle a scent to be counterfeited.

Far more likely was interference by the raging wind, the scents ripped away before he could catch them. Not that it applied to the cracked rock—this close, there was no way he'd have missed anyone.

The gap in the stone was barely large enough for his body, even though he turned himself sideways. He knew before he entered that there was no living creature directly beyond. The only smells he'd caught had been of cold and dirt.

Cold had a scent; any wolf could tell you that.

Snow cold was different from dirt cold. And dirt cold was different from night cold.

Grumbling silently in disgust when a lump of snow fell on his face from some ledge it had been hiding on, he wiped it off before managing to squeeze through the narrow opening. His eyes adjusted quickly, his night vision kicking in. The space inside the cracked stone was nothing much; if he tried to spread out his arms, he'd have to stop with his elbows bent at ninety-degree angles. The area wasn't much deeper, either . . . but there, in the ground.

What the hell?

Alexei crouched down to stare at a depression in the dirt that was oddly square. Water dripped from his body and hair to darken the dirt. No way that was a natural shape, not unless nature had begun walking around with a tape measure and a slide rule.

Taking care not to make sounds that would carry, he began to push the dirt away using his claws. It was hard, compacted. As if it hadn't been disturbed in years. No question now—there had to be a teleporter involved in this somewhere.

His claws scraped against what felt like iron.

Slowing down, he worked with grim focus until he uncovered what he'd expected: a trapdoor. It was bolted down securely from the outside, the lock twisted in a way that had to have taken telekinesis. Nothing and no one would ever again open that lock. Rust crawled over it, as it did the solid metal hinges on the other end and the thick strips of iron that formed the body of the trapdoor.

The thing was old, possibly old enough to be from the time that had left SnowDancer badly wounded, many of its strongest lost.

Grief, rising and falling, rising and falling. Piercing his heart.

He shook his head to clear it of the empath's overwhelming pain, his wolf snarling inside his chest. Strands of hair fell across his forehead to drip water down his face. He shoved them roughly back. Despite his rage at finding a living being trapped in a fucking hole in the ground, he didn't immediately begin to hunt for a way to open the trapdoor. Instead, he sliced his claws back in and took out his satellite-linked phone.

The signal was weak, but his message got through. Should anything happen to Alexei, another wolf would find the grieving empath. And if it *was* a clever trap to capture a wolf, then his packmates would be warned and armed. He also sent a second message telling SnowDancer not to mobilize until he'd scoped out the situation—no point in more wolves coming out in this ugly weather if there was no lethal threat to the pack.

A return message lit up the screen as he was examining the hinges on the trapdoor: *We don't hear back from you in twenty, we head out.—H.*

Putting the phone in a side pocket of his black cargo pants, Alexei focused all his attention on the hinges. They were the weakest point in the entire construction.

And a predatory changeling wolf of Alexei's size and training was strong.

Far, far stronger than the Psy who'd probably built this thing.

Yeah, it could've been a changeling or a human who'd put this trapdoor in place, but he didn't think so. Such a thing couldn't be built in so small a space; it had to have been brought in, and no human or changeling could have ever traipsed through wolf territory carrying a trapdoor, or pieces for its construction, without being spotted. Not even at their weakest had SnowDancer let its borders fall to that extent.

Psy, then.

Nearly all Psy underestimated changeling strength by a large margin.

Only one problem though—there was no way to get leverage anywhere near the hinges. No gap through which to insert his claws. No twisted or warped area to provide even a minor entry point. He could leave it, ask his packmates to come up with tools, but he'd have to be a psychopath himself to abandon the E. Her crying had become quieter inside his head, even more lost.

She was breaking his heart and he wanted to growl at her to stop it, even knowing his response was irrational. Another part of him wanted to gather her in his arms *while* he growled at her—Es had that in common with changelings: they liked touch, hurt without it. So he'd promise to cuddle her if she'd just stop hurting.

Wiping away water from his face, he switched focus to the lock.

No way to open it, but the part where it was attached to the main body of the trapdoor was bolted down into rusting metal. Teeth bared, Alexei grabbed the entire lock mechanism and wrenched.

His biceps bunched, his abdomen clenching.

One pull. Two. Three.

A metallic groan as part of the attachment tore away from the base. It only took one more pull to break it fully off. Dropping the entire mass of cold and rust to the side, he inserted his fingers through the small warping in the iron where the lock had been bolted and used that grip to lift up the trapdoor.

It came away with a loud creak.

He halted, but the waves of emotion didn't stop or blip. No audible alarms went off. No voices rose in a shout. And no new living scents hit his nose.

Opening the trapdoor the rest of the way, he propped it up against the opposite wall. He wasn't afraid of it falling in. With the lock gone, he could push it open from the inside with only minimal effort.

Blackness greeted him when he first looked inside the space exposed by the opening. But his night vision didn't let him down and he was able to confirm the floor wasn't a dangerous distance for a jump.

He dropped down into the hole without further delay, landing silently in a hunting crouch.

A second later, a high frequency hum had the tiny hairs on his arms rising, his wolf flashing his canines. He shook it off, but made a note of what it represented: you didn't get that hum with newer lights, only the old ones that occasionally flickered and failed. Dust drifted around him, the motes caught in the extremely faint light emanating from some distance away. He followed that light, followed the grief.

A door stood in his way, barred and bolted from his side, with iron padlocks at the end of each bolt.

A cage.

His wolf ready to kill by now, he looked at the door and saw it was wood. Heavy wood that would've stopped most people.

Alexei slipped his claws in under the hinges and pulled.

The first pull created enough space for true leverage. The second gave him room to properly grip the wood.

He wrenched.

The grief hitched at last. The empath had heard him this time . . . but there was no spike of fear, no terror, a worrying flatness under the grief. Not a lack of emotion. A numbness caused by constant pain.

Maybe he'd try not to growl at her. It'd be difficult since he'd been in a bad mood for twelve months, but scaring an E wasn't a thing to be proud of—it'd be like stomping on a kitten.

Heat building in his muscles as he worked, Alexei kept going until he'd created enough weakness in the door that he could tear it off its hinges.

It hit the exposed stone wall of the tunnel with a hard thump.

Light poured out, muted and cold.

He walked in.

Chapter 2

Empaths are uniformly seen as good, but no sentient being is a two-dimensional caricature. We all have our light and our shadows—this truth is a core reason why I titled this book as I did. Because even Es aren't without darkness. How can they be? They often deal with the grimmest and most violent emotions of them all.

—Author's Note, *The Mysterious E Designation: Empathic Gifts & Shadows* by Alice Eldridge (Reprint: 2082)

SHE STARED AT him from where she sat crumpled on the floor, her tight black curls a wild and matted mass and her dark brown eyes huge and tear-reddened in a triangular face with a pointed chin and lush lips. Her skin was a pallid brown devoid of the glow that came from the heat of the sun, and her clothes hung off her frame: faded blue jeans, a large black sweater, and old canvas sneakers.

Her scent was soap and salt and an intrinsic bite he couldn't name.

In her arms, she held the body of a gray cat from which Alexei could scent the tiniest edge of decay. Ragged thin fur, a sense of fragility—the cat had been old when it died. A creature that had gone when its time had come, not one whose life had been stolen. The E held it with infinite care, and when Alexei did nothing to approach or startle her, she bent her head over her dead pet and cried again, her grief like waves crashing against his skin.

She wasn't afraid of him, was too lost in her pain to see the predator in the room. Or perhaps she did . . . and didn't care.

And he *knew*: that cat had been her only connection to the world, to *life*.

Alexei fought his need to go to her, offer her comfort. Before anything else, he was a SnowDancer lieutenant, and their pack had been hurt by the Psy one too many times.

He did a quick but thorough reconnaissance of the entire bunker. It didn't take long. He found a bedroom, neat and tidy, though the clothes in the freestanding wardrobe made his hand tighten on the wardrobe door. He barely stopped himself from wrenching off the door and breaking it to splinters. A large cat-size basket sat to one side, complete with what looked to be hand-knitted toys and a blanket. A half-full bowl of water rounded out the items.

No food bowl, but he had a feeling the little E with the big eyes must've hand-fed her elderly pet soft foods. She must've been so scared as she watched over her pet, knowing that every breath could be its last.

Hands fisting at his side, he carried on in his recon.

The toilet and a tight cubicle shower flowed off the bedroom. Across the narrow hallway from the bedroom was a room that held a small kitchen on one side, and a sofa on the other. The sofa faced a comm screen set to entertainment-only. The communications module, he saw at a glance, had been manually removed.

The kitty litter box sat at the far end of the hallway, close to the door he'd torn off. It was a model that turned the waste into small, odorless pellets that could be disposed of in the trash.

The trash receptacle was similar and connected to a chute that must have been put in place when the water was plumbed in. It didn't emerge on the outside or SnowDancer would've discovered it. Likely, it went to a small recycling or compacting unit concealed behind the wall, a unit that a teleporter could 'port out and put back when it reached capacity. And since the temperature in the bunker was mild instead of freezing, there was probably a heating and cooling system hidden beside the recycling unit.

It wouldn't need to be big to service an area this size.

He'd also spotted signs of a ventilation system. It was clearly an excellent one—the air was fresh, with no stuffiness to it. He'd put his money on the intake and exhaust valves being hidden higher up the mountainside. If they were small enough, no one would notice, not among all the shattered rocks.

The original work must've been done during the period decades earlier when SnowDancer didn't have the resources for satellites or the people to run regular patrols up here—the Psy who'd built this must've come in with precision plans, done the work at speed. Of course, having teleporters on the team took care of most of the risk.

The entire setup was perfect for a prison the warden didn't often visit.

And that was it.

No other doors to the outside world. No light but that thrown by the old-fashioned battery-powered strips that hummed and irritated his ear and had nothing in common with natural light. No sign that anyone but the empath and her pet had ever lived here.

Yet this place was old. *Much* older than the empath. That information was visible in the fixtures and panels used to build the place, and in the wear and tear on the walls, along with the age of the built-in appliances in the kitchen.

Whoever had put the E in here hadn't constructed the place. But it was the perfect hole in which to imprison a living being. No one would hear you scream, not even a changeling standing right on top of you.

Alexei would've either gone mad or broken every bone in his body trying to slam through the only door. The woman he'd seen was nowhere strong enough to have caused even minor damage to that door.

The E hadn't moved while he prowled around, her tears silent as she hugged her pet to her heart. As a wolf, Alexei wasn't much of a cat person—the only exceptions were a newborn SnowDancer who promised to turn into a leopard, and her mother. Little Belle would be the only cat with "dual citizenship" in a wolf pack. But no matter his views on cats, Alexei understood what it was to love a pet who'd been a loyal companion for years, and he understood what it was to grieve the loss of that pet.

That the cat had died a natural death didn't mean the E's pain would be any less.

Crouching down across from her, at least a foot of distance between them, he tempered his driving urge to haul her into his arms. She wasn't a wolf. More to the point, he was a large, strange male.

Act civilized, Alexei.

His wolf took a step back while the human half of him tried to look smaller and less like a very dangerous wolf with sharp teeth. At least his eyes were human again. And while he was generally annoyed by his face—he was far too fucking *pretty* for a SnowDancer lieutenant—it might come in handy here.

The first thing he needed to know was if the teleporter who'd put her in this place was apt to return—and if that teleporter could lock onto faces or just locations. Barking out that question, however, was a bad idea.

"What was your cat's name?" he asked with every ounce of gentleness he possessed.

The empath went motionless, her body stiff and her shoulders raised as she hunched protectively over her pet's body.

Alexei realized then and there that he couldn't hope to gain this trapped woman's trust rapidly enough to keep her safe; trust took time, took patience. "I'm Alexei, a Snow-Dancer wolf, and I need to get you out of here," he said, switching tactics with the speed of the predator that lived under his skin. "I'm assuming it's a teleporter who brought you here. Can that person lock on to your face?" The latter was a rare ability among teleport-capable telekinetics, but he could assume nothing.

A long silence from the E, followed by a jagged shake of her head.

"Then we move." He could take care of himself, his bones tough enough to handle being thrown against a wall by telekinesis. She didn't have that advantage—and a teleporter could grab and leave with her while he was out of action. There was a reason the now-defunct Psy Council had co-opted telekinetics into their ranks; the fuckers were tough opponents.

Alexei rose, went into her bedroom—to return with the knitted blanket from her cat's basket. "You can wrap your pet in this." He knew without asking that she would never agree to abandon the body, not even to save her own life. "We'll give him a burial as soon as we're safe."

No response.

Barely stopping the urge to bare his teeth at her, his wolf wanting to get her to safety *now*, he said, "You don't move, the teleporter comes back, you stay in this prison." When she didn't stir, he went for the jugular. "So does your pet."

A burst of ragged motion at his rough words devoid of softness or apparent care. But regardless of her intent, she struggled to get to her feet with her pet's body in her arms, as if she'd been in that position so long that her legs didn't work quite right anymore.

"I'm going to help you up." Alexei waited and, when she didn't twist away, placed his hands under her upper arms.

He all but lifted her up.

Her bones were like a bird's. He'd seen food in the kitchen, so her captor wasn't attempting to starve her—but trapped creatures often gave up on eating. Jaw clenched, he made sure she was stable, then stepped back and spread the blanket over his arms. Her lower lip quivered as she put her pet on it before quickly reclaiming the blanket-wrapped body from him.

Alexei took a second to grab a metal chair he'd seen in her lounge.

He didn't have to ask her to follow—she did so without a word. Once under the trapdoor, he put the chair directly beneath, illuminating the area using the light from his phone. She didn't have a wolf's eyes, couldn't see in the dark. "I'm going to stand on this," he told her. "I need you to climb up close to me and allow me to lift you up through the hole."

He held out his arms for her pet's body, sorry for this wild creature that may have spent its entire existence in a cage; the only mercy was that it appeared to have been deeply loved. "I'll pass him through after."

Her eyes flicked up to the trapdoor, an unexpectedly ferocious determination suddenly vivid on her features. Instead of handing him her small burden, she put it down on the ground with tender care. Alexei used the opportunity to shrug off his jacket so he could give it to the E. He'd looked for her own coat when he'd grabbed the blanket, but hadn't spotted one. The sweater she was wearing appeared to be her thickest item of clothing.

As it was, he didn't need his jacket for survival; he'd only put it on because the pack's very pregnant healer had silently held it out with a "wear this or feel my wrath" look on her face. Alexei wasn't scared of Lara's wrath, but neither was he about to stress her out when she was growing a pup inside her. He'd put on the damn jacket and had been glad of it when the freezing rain pelted down.

Even wolves didn't enjoy being drenched to the bone.

Waterproof and thickly lined, the jacket should keep the E from hypothermia while they were outside. "It's icy out," he said when the E hesitated. "You can't escape if you're too cold to function."

She took the jacket, pulled it on, then did up the zipper. He had to help her roll up the sleeves and did so quickly. That done, he got on the chair and hoped it would hold their combined weight. He only needed it to do so long enough to get her out. He had other ways of hauling himself up.

She climbed up to join him, her movements jerky but her jaw set and her eyes raised up toward freedom.

"One, two, *three*." He lifted her with his hands on her waist. "Get your arms over the top of the trapdoor."

She did it in one go, this woman who weighed less than nothing but whose empathic power was a storm; even quiet, her sadness swirled around him. He gave her another lift up to help her out, waited to catch her should she fall. She didn't. Instead, her small face looked down at him from the trapdoor, her large eyes fathomless.

Dropping to the floor, he picked up her pet, then got back on the chair to lift the small blanket-wrapped body up to her. She leaned in so far he thought she'd slip, but she managed to take hold of the cat without disaster. Yet she didn't pull back. "Hurry." It was a rasped whisper that ruffled his wolf's fur, made it prick its ears. "He likes to hurt people."

Yeah, she was an empath, couldn't help looking after others even when her own life was at risk. Like the healers in his pack—who he made a point of avoiding. Sometimes a man just wanted to brood in peace. How Lara had caught him today, he had no idea: his wolf was of the opinion that she and the maternals in the den were in cahoots, probably had a secret comm network.

Today, he had to get this little healer to safety. The predator in him would like nothing better than to lie in wait and tear her teleporting coward of an abductor to shreds, but his priority had to be the E. Stepping off the chair, he repositioned it slightly before moving back all the way to the broken door. A punch of speed, his wolf taking control of his movements as he used the chair to launch his body skyward, slammed the sole of one foot against a wall . . . and grabbed the lip of the open trapdoor.

The E had jumped back when he erupted toward her, watched him in breathless quiet as he hauled himself up. Soon as he was out, he closed the trapdoor before grabbing a large piece of rock he'd noticed in the corner, and weighing the trapdoor down. The weight wouldn't stop a teleporter, but whether that teleporter had any visual coordinates that would permit him to teleport *outside* the bunker was a good question.

Alexei couldn't take the risk, had to move the E away from this location.

"It's stormy and the rain might've turned to ice," he told the E afterward. "You'll get wet and cold."

No flinch, nothing but a steady stare that might've been disconcerting if he hadn't been aware that she couldn't get into his head unless she was a powerful telepath who wanted to smash his mind open. The latter idea just didn't sit right—not with the depth of the grief she'd broadcast, and not with how gently she held the body of her aged pet.

Alexei had also never heard of an E who went around doing violence except in self-defense—and even then, they had to be pushed to the furthest edge—so he was going to play the odds and assume she wasn't an enemy. The whole enemy operative angle made no sense in any case—the "trap" required far too much time and patience with no guarantee of success.

Pulling out his phone, he sent a message to Hawke: *I have the E. Taking her to the substation.* It was the only secure shelter around for miles. *She's no threat.*

The response was immediate. *Are you sure, Lexie?* Not stated but understood was that the Psy race might've left Silence behind, but many of them continued to believe they were the master race, changelings and humans their inferiors to be manipulated and used.

I'm sure, he assured his alpha. *She's more afraid of me than I am of her.* The strange flatness was gone; he could taste the sharp bite of her fear below the grief—and yet she'd warned him to hurry when she could've tried to run the instant she was out. *I'll message again from the substation— we'll be slow.*

He secured the phone in the side pocket of his cargoes. "We can't carry your pet's body far," he said quietly, very conscious of their relative sizes and making an effort to sound nonthreatening. Before his world fell apart, he hadn't been apt to growl or snarl except when pushed to it—he tried to channel that distant Alexei. "We have to walk at least a half hour." No, that was wolf speed. It'd be much longer at her pace.

She clutched her pet closer, but nodded. "In the open." A whisper. "Under the sky."

Blood hot with a need to go for her captor's throat, Alexei nodded. "Under the sky." Promise made, he exited first to ensure it was safe outside.

The rain was relentless, but it hadn't turned into snow.

The E came quickly after him, and though the rain soaked her within seconds, she stood staring up at the turgid gray sky with a radiant look on her face, her hair an electric halo that seemed to crackle under the energy of the storm. At that instant, she was the essence of freedom.

His wolf watched her in primal approval. "Let me." He held out his arms for her pet. "It'll slow you down and we need to move."

A glance around at the rocky and inhospitable terrain before she accepted his offer. Her lips were pressed tight and he was sure tears mixed with the raindrops on her face.

Alexei might eschew the type of intimate skin privileges his packmates loved and craved, but he'd never stopped holding packmates who needed touch. It was part of being a dominant, part of being a SnowDancer lieutenant. The E was crying out for comfort—but would likely scream if he engulfed her in his arms. Even the wolf understood they had to go gently.

Gritting his teeth, he hauled his instincts into line.

"Follow me," he said. "Step where I step."

The E's movements were jagged and ungraceful, but she had control of her limbs. He knew she had to be weak—she was too thin and moved with too little coordination for it to be otherwise—but though he kept an eye on her, he didn't halt until ten minutes later.

He'd taken them on a route that put a slight rise between them and the hidden bunker. No one would spot the two of them unless they came over the same rise. "Here?" He'd stopped at a spot that would be under full sunlight on a clear day.

Her breathing uneven, she nodded and picked up a broken piece of stone, then began to dig. Placing her pet's body on the ground, Alexei used his claws to accelerate the process. Her eyes widened slightly, but she didn't stop her movements, and they worked side by side under the chilling rain.

The tiny grave didn't take long to dig.

She put her pet's body inside it with gentle hands. Her tears fell like rain as she pushed the dirt back to cover the hole.

When she began to pick up other pieces of stone with fingers that shook from the cold, he realized what she was doing and helped her build the cairn. He made sure it was solid, but before they placed the last stones, he deliberately nicked his finger using a broken stone shard.

The E made a small sound.

"It's to make sure no animals disturb your pet," he told her as he rubbed his blood on the inner stones, placing it in enough crevices that the rain wouldn't wash it away. Every other creature in this area knew that the SnowDancer wolves were the apex predators. The merest hint of wolf scent and any scavengers or curious ramblers would give the cairn a wide berth.

"He'll be safe," Alexei told the E while the rain pounded down on both of them. The tangled mass of her hair had lost its buoyancy under the weight of the water, was limp enough that it highlighted both the dramatic bones of her face and the lack of flesh on those bones.

Silently—and with painful care—she put the last stones in place. "Bye, Jitterbug." A husky whisper, one hand on the cairn. "Thank you for being my friend."

Tenderness and pity crashed inside Alexei. The depth of the empath's grief, paired with the way she appeared so broken, it told him too much, none of it anything but enraging.

Giving her the only privacy he could, he kept his gaze on the rise over which they'd come until she was ready to leave her pet behind. *Jitterbug.* A name that conjured up a tiny, fast kitten who bounced and played and probably made her laugh.

That cat hadn't been a kitten for a long, long time.

Shrugging aside the hot burn of his anger, he led the E in the direction of the substation. The Sierra Nevada den was powered by solar energy harnessed by miniature panels scattered throughout their territory—partly to utilize the sun's energy across the day, but mostly so an enemy couldn't take out one area and cripple them.

A few of the larger panels hadn't yet been replaced, but the vast majority were now so small they could be hidden among the rocks on the high slopes of the mountains, could even be placed on tree trunks that got kissed by sunlight at a certain point in the day. Thousands of tiny cells working together to create a jolting current.

The solar grid hadn't ever let the den down, but Snow-Dancer also had a small hydro station as backup just in case, and it was this hydro unit the substation serviced.

Beside him, the empath stumbled a third time, almost cracking her knee against a slab of stone. He caught her as he had before, but this time, he closed his hand around her smaller and colder one while holding eye contact. "We'll get to safety faster this way."

Her fingers didn't curl around his, but—despite the acrid bite of her fear—neither did she pull her hand away, and they continued on. He didn't much feel the chill; changelings had far better cold tolerance than humans or Psy. He'd be even more resilient in his wolf form and could move like liquid through this environment. But the E couldn't follow the wolf and he had no idea how she'd react to his other form.

Human or wolf, he could tear out a throat with little effort, but non-changelings found it easier to ignore that truth while changelings like Alexei were in their human form.

The E's hand began to shiver in his not long after they left Jitterbug's grave. The two of them were under the canopy of the trees now, the rain no longer as hard on their bodies and the snow more manageable, but the weather hadn't let up at all. In fact, it looked to be getting worse.

Clenching his jaw as he fought the urge to tuck her against him, share his warmth, he kept her hand in his and tried to stay under the canopy as much as he could. When the wind whistled in, he used his body to shield hers. His frustrated wolf grumbled the entire time; the human side of Alexei agreed with the grumbling.

This would go much faster if he could just pick up the E and run.

Only he had a feeling she'd panic and fight . . . or go motionless and stiff. The latter would be worse, revealing bone-chilling terror. Alexei wasn't about to traumatize her that way, not after some bastard had already put her in a cage.

To his surprise, she kept up with him the entire way. He wasn't going fast, but neither was he pausing to let her rest—the weather was too cold for her to survive if she stopped; he'd worried she'd collapse partway. But she kept going, one dogged step after the other. Unfettered respect wiped away his earlier pity, his wolf looking at her with new eyes. *This* was how she'd survived in that bunker.

The woman beside him was a fighter.

The last part of the route to the substation meant crossing an empty field that, in the summer, was a favorite resting ground for wild black bears. Currently, it was full of snow turned into slush by the rain, the substation door barely visible in the gloom caused by the storm and the oncoming night. The gale-force winds almost bent them in half as they crossed that final stretch and, this time, he did put his arm around her. She didn't attempt to break away, and he got them both to the substation.

As with all the buildings SnowDancer had built in their

territory, it was designed to blend into the environment. Dug out of a small hill, the door was cleverly camouflaged with paint that echoed the surroundings, then hidden under trailing foliage. While the empath waited next to him, her bones all but clattering from the cold, he opened up the concealed entry-panel and used his palm print to unlock the door. He nudged her inside the second the lock snicked open.

She froze, a stone statue glued to the earth.

A *scream* of pure emotion hit him with vicious force.

Chapter 3

The ability to broadcast powerful emotion *at* a changeling mind appears to be a rare skill, and is currently limited to Sascha Duncan, possibly because of her mating bond with a changeling*—though the critical factor may be that Sascha also has a child who has genetic heritage from both races. Sascha's mate and child are also connected to her on the psychic plane.

Further data is required before we come to any conclusions; at present, any inference we make would be no better than a blind guess.

*DarkRiver Leopard Alpha, Lucas Hunter
    —Manuscript of *The Mysterious E Designation:
    A World Beyond Silence* by Alice Eldridge with
    research assistance from Sahara Kyriakus and
    Jaya Laila Storm (Work in Progress)

ALEXEI'S WOLF GROWLED, cold and wet and wanting out of this storm—but mostly wanting *her* out of it. About to pick up the damn tiny E with the huge mental voice and get them both inside, he suddenly realized what was going on.

Alexei Vasiliev Harte, you're an idiot.

Opening up the panel again, he input an administrative code, then took her fisted hand in his—it was stiff, unco-operative. "I'm adding you to the system," he said, a growl in his voice that came from untrammeled fury directed at the person who'd done this to her. "Put your palm on the panel."

The E didn't move, her breath coming in rapid gasps.

Her lips were beginning to turn blue. Alexei ran out of his already strained patience. Claws pricking the inside of his skin, he put one arm around her waist and literally lifted her up until he could get her fist on the panel.

"Spread open your fingers," he said when her fist remained closed tight. God, he was ready to *bite* her. Didn't she realize how close she was to hypothermia?

"I'm trying to give you a key." He couldn't help the snarl in his next words, all thoughts of being civilized and gentle forgotten. "Or would you prefer to freeze to death outside? I'm sure a snap-frozen E would delight your captor. He could just pick you up and put you back underground."

Emotion slapped at him: a blast of raging fury. She flexed her fingers open, pressing her palm flat on the screen of the reader. On the back of her index knuckle was a ridged white scar that might've come from a childhood cut that hadn't healed well, and her nails were ragged at the tips. Not as if she bit them, more as if they'd broken and caught on things and she hadn't cared to smooth out the damage.

Alexei initiated the scan while continuing to hold her up with one arm around her waist. Her silent fury bared its teeth at him. So, his E had anger within her. It made the wildness inside him open its mouth in a devious smile. If infuriating her was what it took to break through her trauma and panic, Alexei would push every button he could. There was a reason his alpha considered Alexei one of the best strategic minds in the pack—and why his friends had banned him from the poker table.

The scan complete, the screen flashed.

Putting the E down, he input a second authorization code, then scanned his palm again to lock in the change. He turned to see that she was staring at the panel and at his hand. He'd been careful to angle his body so she couldn't see the authorization codes—not that she could do anything without his living palm on the screen to confirm any changes—but the lieutenant part of his brain noted her intense focus.

It was likely a symptom of her need for freedom, but until he knew more about her, he couldn't discount an ulterior motive. "You can come and go at will." He'd given her local access only and he'd revoke it as soon as the two of them left the substation.

With that, he scanned the door open a second time. But this time, when she didn't enter, the tactical center of his brain told him to shrug and act unconcerned—despite his feral protectiveness toward this small, bedraggled creature he'd brought this far. "Not my job to babysit lost Es," he muttered loud enough that she'd hear. "If having your eyelashes freeze and break off while your face turns a nice shade of blue is your thing, enjoy."

No whiplash of emotion against his senses, but he was sure he spotted a spark of fire in her eyes before he stepped into the substation. He'd let that anger simmer, heat her up. His aunt Clementine was a talker, unlike the E, but when she got *really* mad, she'd go quiet and fume.

Like that time Alexei and Brodie had decided to skip school for no reason except that they were pissed at the world. *That,* Aunt Min would've forgiven, but that they'd been asshole boys who'd taken off without a word and stayed "lost" for two days? Yeah, she'd stripped their hides for that.

Alexei had been only twelve, but he'd figured he deserved it.

He'd also learned that, sometimes, when a woman got quiet, her anger was all the darker and deeper for it. It could fill her up, make her bigger, stronger. Though if his E didn't come in soon, he'd have to force the issue. The thought made his muscles knot—he didn't want to force her inside, have her see this safe place as another cage, but she'd die of cold if she stayed out much longer.

He made himself walk into the substation; he'd give her as much time as he could.

Unlocking the door had turned on the lights, and he had to blink a couple of times to adjust to the sudden change in brightness, his pupils yet dilated from the storm-gray dullness outside. After checking that the entrance area was devoid of any equipment, he shook himself off. It felt much better when he did it as a wolf, but it wasn't yet time to be a wolf. The care he took to balance out the two sides of his nature was about survival and about the choices a man had to make to retain his sanity.

Inside him, his usually irritable wolf stood motionless in solemn agreement.

The two parts of Alexei's nature were never at odds on this one thing.

A stirring near the door as he thrust both hands through his hair to push it back from his face. The strands were getting a bit too long for his liking. Once, when things had been different, when Brodie had still been alive and Alexei had been a younger brother to someone, he'd worn his hair long enough to tie back.

He hadn't felt young since he put his big brother in the ground.

The E stepped inside.

Wolf acting nonchalant inside him, Alexei made a show of removing his sodden boots and socks and placing them to one side of the entrance. Only after he was done did he glance back. The E was staring at the door, which was beginning to close.

"Automatic timer," he told her. "To stop the rain, wind, wild animals from coming in and damaging the equipment on the off-chance one of us forgets to close it."

The door shut.

Her shoulders stiffened, her hands fisting bloodlessly tight by her sides. Panic beat against his skull, the weight of the spiny and discordant emotion a hammer. And how was she *doing* that in the first place? He knew Sascha Duncan had learned to unleash her empathic abilities against people of all races, used them as a defensive measure when under attack, but it had taken her time and effort to work out the technique.

No other E could assault changelings in such a way.

Most empaths could take away pain and soften the edges of emotional trauma in Psy, humans, *and* changelings, but drenching others in powerful negative emotion? That was a whole other story.

Yet this skin-and-bones E was blasting at him, no holds barred.

Shaking his head in an attempt to dispel the barrage, he growled loud enough to fill the space. The emotional storm screeched to a halt; the E froze, then sent him a wary glance . . . with an edge of that delightful fury he intended to stoke into a fire.

He pointed to the panel on the inside wall. "You have the key," he reminded her. "Stop punching me with emotion or I might decide to eat you."

From the way she stared at him, it looked as if she was trying to decide whether to take him seriously or not. Good enough for now. At least it had stopped the howl of panic and fear that'd caused his wolf to bare its fangs. "I'm going to see if I can find us dry clothes."

He walked off—but his hearing was plenty sharp enough that he caught the click of the door opening only seconds later, followed by the rustle of the E slipping out. Cold and wet swept inside. He squeezed his eyes shut for a second and told himself to count to ten. "Calm," he gritted out through clenched teeth. "Be calm."

Regardless of his yearlong black mood—a mood that had led his denmates to get him a mug emblazoned with the image of a singularly unimpressed feline—he remained one of the most patient wolves in SnowDancer. However, even he had a limit—if the E went mad and decided to run off into the snow and rain, he'd drag her back in.

The idea of it made him want to kick the walls.

Caging a wild bird never had a good outcome. Either the bird would break all the tiny bones in its body crashing into walls as it attempted to get out, or it would stop flying and starve to death. A wounded wild creature had to decide to trust, decide to stay.

"You're a goddamn wolf," he grumbled to himself after the ten-second count was over, not that he was any less frustrated. "Most sensible people are scared of wolves. Let her be."

Except that he'd rescued her, muttered the mutinous wolf inside him. Surely that should've shown the E that he wasn't *actually* going to eat her. The wolf that was his other half growled at him for making that stupid threat and Alexei accepted he'd been an idiot. No more threatening the tiny E with his razor-sharp teeth.

He kept his ears open as he sent a quick message to Hawke to confirm they'd arrived safely; that done, he prowled around the substation. It had been a while since he'd been up here, but he remembered it well enough from when he'd helped with the initial setup. All of SnowDancer's soldiers had a qualification aside from their physical dexterity, tactical ability, and strength training. Alexei was a sniper and trained others for the pack, but his civilian training was in computronic engineering with a focus on the tangible rather than the programming end of things.

These days, his duties as one of Hawke's ten lieutenants—spread out across the pack's massive California territory—kept him too busy to do much in that area, but he'd always liked putting puzzle pieces together to create something useful. When at his own satellite den, near the border with Oregon, he joined in with projects where he could. The den's official computronic engineers were good sports about him nosing into their projects to put in the odd hour here and there.

It kept his skills sharp, and they never complained about his work, so he couldn't be too bad. It had been some time since he'd done anything as complex as this substation, however. To his left was a bedroom with a couple of bunk beds for any technicians who had to stay the night. On the other side of the small hallway were the shower and toilet.

The kitchenette was at the opposite end from the entry. A locked door stood on the right side of the kitchenette area. All of the tech that ran the substation was in a climate-controlled room downstairs. The access he'd given the empath wouldn't permit her to go into that section.

The wind cut off.

She'd finally shut the door again—and she was standing on this side of it. The look she shot him was defiant even though her bones rattled from her shivers. Alexei was fascinated by this small, angry woman who dared meet his gaze as if she were a lioness under the skin—female lion changelings had a reputation for being ornery and stubborn. Alexei had met three over his lifetime and all had proven that reputation to be well deserved.

Submissive wolves never met a dominant's gaze in so challenging a fashion.

His wolf didn't snarl at her. It was too astonished by this small creature who thought she could defy him. It was like being told off by a gnat. His currently habitually grumpy wolf nudged at Alexei to walk over there and investigate further, maybe use his teeth to grip the side of her neck to see what she'd do.

It wouldn't be about hurting her, more about learning her dominance.

Alexei shrugged off the aggressive impulse. The E, he sternly reminded both parts of his nature, wasn't changeling. Different rules applied. She had no idea that such direct and sustained eye contact with a dominant of Alexei's power and rank in the pack was a challenge. In all likelihood, she was probably just watching him because she thought she was in danger of being eaten.

Chest rumbling at the idea of being seen as a threat by a defenseless E—next he'd hear he kicked kittens for a hobby—he stalked into the bedroom and opened the cupboard. Thick towels in different colors sat stacked in neat rolls on the top shelf.

One of the maternals must come up here every so often and tidy things up. It wasn't that the rest of them were slobs, but no substation engineer or maintenance person would've rolled up the towels like colorful sushi, or left something inside the cupboard that made everything smell crisp and clean. That was a maternal wolf thing, those small touches that turned any place into a home.

His mother had been like that. Calissa Harte would cut his lunch sandwiches in the shape of a star because he'd liked astronomy. Once, he'd come home from school to find she'd used stencils to paint small dragons all over Brodie's bedroom. Alexei and his big brother had been speechless with joy, especially when their mom gave them both paintbrushes so they could add individual touches to the dragons.

He drew in a deep breath, and it fucking hurt, broken shards stabbing into him.

His sweet, soft, gentle mother was gone.

His adrenaline-junkie and blood-loyal big brother was gone.

His sardonic prankster of a father had been lost long before he died.

Of their small, tight pack-within-a-pack, only Alexei remained. Even Aunt Min couldn't change that, no matter how hard she tried. What drew a subtle line between Alexei's lost family and that of his devoted, loving aunt's was the curse that ran in his paternal line. Aunt Min's blood was thankfully untouched by the darkness responsible for the loss of her sister, brother-in-law, and nephew.

Maybe he should've mentioned to the E that he had a sweetheart of a twelve-year-old cousin who he babysat twice a month so Aunt Min and her mate could have the night out. His wolf snorted. Alexei had to agree with its skepticism: he'd blown his shot at a cuddly and nonintimidating image the second he ripped her bunker door off its hinges.

Then he'd threatened to turn her into dinner.

Great. Just great.

Guess the charm's working overtime today, huh, little bro?

Gut tightening at the phantom echo of Brodie's laughing voice, the teasing words exactly the ones Brodie would've spoken had his big brother been standing here, Alexei took a couple of towels out into the hallway. He threw a thick green one toward the empath. Her movements might be jerky, but there was nothing wrong with her reflexes. She caught the towel, but didn't start to dry herself.

Instead, he felt a brush of emotion that was . . . delicate.

Like someone patting gently at his fur.

He blinked. "Are you trying to pet me?"

The sensation disappeared, frown lines forming on her brow before she turned her back to him and began to dry herself.

Not quite sure what had happened but certain it hadn't been a threat—nothing that gentle and hesitant could be a threat—he opened out the dark blue towel in his hand. Maybe the E hadn't been petting him at all; maybe she'd been poking at him to see if he'd react with bared teeth and rage.

His wolf's fur brushed against the inside of his skin, the crabby creature reminding the human half once again that it was his fault the E thought she might get chomped on at any moment. Probably with hot sauce for extra flavor.

Alexei scowled under the towel.

After wiping off his face and his hair enough that it was

no longer dripping, he went back into the bedroom and rummaged around in the large trunk he'd spotted in one corner. As he'd expected, it was full of T-shirts, sweatpants, and sweatshirts of various sizes. About half were well washed and soft with wear, others newer, but everything was clean.

"Maternal," he muttered when a dried rose petal fell out of a T-shirt he'd picked up.

He curled his lip at the idea of smelling like roses. Hell, he was already "pretty"—his wolf shuddered at the reminder of the horrible description people kept using for his human face. All he needed now was to smell like a freaking rose petal.

A whisper of a different scent reached him. When he looked up, it was to find that the E had crept into the doorway, was watching him. Her scent was unlike any other in his mental database. There was an edge there, along with an unexpected touch of an intense darkness that he couldn't name.

What he did know was that after their recent close proximity, he could now track her.

"Dry clothes." He indicated the trunk. "The pack keeps this kind of stuff around for when we come in as wolves." Alexei wouldn't be the first SnowDancer to take shelter here, and loose-fitting stuff like sweats could be utilized by nearly everyone. The items might swamp a percentage of his packmates, and be a little short or tight for others, but in general, you could make do.

Having dug down to the very bottom, he pulled out the smallest sizes he could find. "Not too bad." The supply crew must've stocked the trunk for when the juveniles came up on training runs. Not that he didn't have petite adult packmates, but the E was on the tiny end of even that sizing. Still, he'd found her a pair of sweatpants, a T-shirt, and a sweatshirt. The sweatshirt was definitely too large, but that wouldn't matter if the pants fit well enough.

He passed her the items, then pointed to the other side of the hallway. "Bathroom's in there if you want a hot shower."

She held the clothing carefully away from her wet body. Water still dripped from her hair despite the fact that it was frizzy in places from her attempts to rub it dry.

"Wait." Grabbing a thinner towel from the sushi roll shelf, he handed that to her, too. "For your hair. Be easier to wrap around your head than that green one." Despite his recent state of mind, he wasn't feral; women generally liked him and he'd been around enough of them, both as a lover and as a friend, to pick up certain things.

The empath stared at him, those fathomless eyes searching his face for some indefinable thing. Man and wolf watched her as intently in turn, attempting to figure out this lost E who had claws hidden under her skin. The wolf was of the opinion that it might like a skinny would-be lion with psychic claws who dared meet its gaze.

Then she shivered.

Pointing to the shower, Alexei growled. "Warm up. *Now*."

A slight—very slight—narrowing of her eyes that made him want to snap his teeth at her. But she shivered again at that instant and it seemed to decide her. Turning on her heel, she walked through into the shower.

It shut; he heard the lock click, then the shower come on.

Alexei released a harsh breath.

He had *not* been looking forward to picking her up and dumping her under the hot spray—that would've well and truly eliminated any wary trust she had in him. Though . . . being an obstinate and testy lioness type under her chilled skin, she might well have kicked him in the family jewels while blasting his mind with fury.

Alexei grinned, cheered by the thought.

Deciding he could warm up without the shower, he stripped, then picked up his suspiciously sweet-smelling towel and sniffed at it. Fuck it, he *was* going to smell like roses. Wolf and man resigned to the ignominy, he rubbed vigorously, until his skin was pleasantly warm from the friction and his hair damp but not wet.

At least none of his pack were here to rag him about his floral bouquet. Brodie would've—

His stomach tightened, his heart a stone in his chest.

Hauling the door to the substation open after unlocking it, he stepped outside, shut the door behind him, then threw back his head and howled up at the thunderous black sky. The sound was whipped away by the wind and the rain, his throat raw in the aftermath. But the pain and anger, they were bearable again.

He could think of his big brother again without wanting to break the world. "Fuck you, Brodie." His chest hurt, his claws stabbing at his skin. "*Fuck* you."

This time, he heard no echo of yesterday, no laughter from a ghost. Just the rain and the thunder as lightning cracked the sky.

Chapter 4

Abstract: A study of changeling rogues. Prevalent only in the predatory changeling population. Not subject to any academic study or paper since Dr. Menet's *Rogue Genetics* (1989). Shame, fear, grief, are all part of the reason for changeling reticence on this subject.
    —*Changeling Rogues: Broken Minds & Broken Families*
        by Keelie Schaeffer, PhD (Work in Progress)

BACK INSIDE THE substation, Alexei dried off a second time, then pulled on a pair of black sweatpants and a gray T-shirt that hugged his pecs and biceps. He wasn't the biggest male in SnowDancer, but he was muscled enough through the shoulders and chest that this had been the best option in the trunk. He'd have to let the supply team know clothes were running low for the larger sizes—should Matthias come up here while he was visiting the main den, he'd be shit out of luck.

Alexei's friend and fellow lieutenant was built like a tank.

The ordinary thoughts, the ordinary business of being part of a thriving pack, it steadied him. He could never forget that Brodie was dead, had been executed, but he could function again as a SnowDancer lieutenant, as *Alexei*. Not the Alexei he'd once been, but the man he'd salvaged out of the ashes of his brother's betrayal.

He didn't feel the need for a sweatshirt. The substation was kept at a comfortable temperature for his changeling body. Picking up his wet gear and the towel, he placed them in a neat pile outside the bathroom. There had to be a container inside in which he could carry dirty laundry down to the den.

Because he'd learned *that* lesson a lifetime ago.

His lips kicked up at the unexpected memory.

Aunt Min had blistered both his and Brodie's ears when, as teens, they'd begun to drop towels on the floor. "Do I look like your maid?" Crossed arms, her booted foot tapping on the floor. "I'll answer for you—no, I do not. I look like a goddamn SnowDancer soldier who will boot you up the backside if I come home to this mess again."

Harsh words, but Aunt Min's discipline had always been meted out with a ferocious love that engulfed them and kept even Brodie from going off the rails—Alexei's brother had taken up doing dangerous hoverboard stunts and racing dirt bikes on deadly trails, but when he fell, he called their aunt.

Shaking his head at the memory of the time Brodie had broken his leg after taking a dare from a friend to dive into a treacherous waterfall—the idiot had grinned about winning the dare even though his femur was sticking out of his skin—Alexei went back to the front door and input multiple security codes.

His E with a temper could continue to come and go at will, but the system would now send an alert to his phone if the door was opened without his authorization. Alexei wasn't certain the little lioness was functioning on all cylinders right now. He'd found her in a prison meant for the long term. He'd also seen items of clothing in her closet that had been ragged with age and use, but too small for her petite body. As if she'd grown out of them.

His jaw knotted.

Being imprisoned in a place with no natural light, her only companion a cat, what had it done to her? That she was functional on any level was a fucking miracle—and that she had the strength to feel anger.

He wanted to pick her up and kiss her with a wolf's pride, tell her she was a goddamn ferocious wonder. But he couldn't trust that she wouldn't have a screaming nightmare and run off into the cold and the rain. He had to be ready to intercede if she was in danger of hurting herself.

His nostrils flared. He had her captor's scent, would never forget it—there'd been only one other scent apart from the E's—and her pet's—in the bunker. If the fucker ever came anywhere near Alexei, he was a dead man. Alexei wasn't a forgiving type of wolf when it came to those who hurt the defenseless.

Mind satisfyingly filled with images of rending the shadowy figure into bloody shreds, he strode to the kitchenette. As he'd expected, it was stocked with nonperishable items. The first thing he did was heat some water and make a couple of packet soups in mugs. The smell that wafted up was salty and delicious. Stomach rumbling, he put the mugs on the small table to one side.

He might be a wolf, but he had manners.

Once, in another universe, women had even considered him charming. But he'd lost his charm when he lost Brodie. He could barely remember the young lieutenant he'd been before his big brother went rogue. All those dominance fights he'd had to handle because people thought he was too pretty to be tough used to aggravate him, but he'd welcome one now. He needed an excuse to pound out his fury on a hapless opponent.

The shower shut off.

Snapping back to his task, he located a stack of ready meals that could be prepared quickly using the small unit in one corner. He took out a selection and put them on the table. Then, as his wolf was all but gnawing at his gut, he chucked in a pasta for himself and—giving up on the manners since he didn't want the E faced with a snarly wolf—was halfway through it when the bathroom door opened.

His lost E was wearing the stone-gray sweatpants he'd handed her, along with a black T-shirt. She'd also put on the dark blue sweatshirt he'd found. The front featured a maniacally grinning chipmunk with an eye patch.

Lips twitching, Alexei fought back a grin.

The demented chipmunk was the mascot of a local high school. But petite size or not, there was nothing juvenile about the woman in the sweatshirt. It wasn't so much her body, of which he'd seen little, but her eyes.

Such *old* eyes.

She'd wrapped the second towel neatly around her head. Her cheeks were flushed from the heat, a glow to them that ameliorated a bit of the sickly paleness beneath the brown of her skin. And the fire he'd spotted in her, it was there yet.

The E wasn't about to show him her throat.

Cute, he found himself thinking, then was annoyed for noticing when she was skinny from grief and traumatized. But he had eyes, and it wasn't as if he planned to lunge at her. Alexei preferred his women be tough enough to claw him back—his lovers had always been fellow soldiers. No submissives and definitely *no* healers.

Empaths fell into the latter category. Soft, gentle creatures. People who broke and got hurt and who should never be in intimate contact with a male of Alexei's bloodline. Brodie's mate hadn't stood a chance when Brodie turned. Brodie had torn out Etta's throat, spraying the forest grove a wet scarlet.

Alexei's hand tightened on his fork, the cold, hard metal anchoring him to the here and now as the soft, gentle creature he'd rescued walked toward him. She smelled of lavender soap and some kind of fruity shampoo now—*seriously, who was stocking the substation?*—but below that was her scent: warm, mysterious, with a sharp bite.

Putting aside his pasta, he nudged the soup in her direction. "Here," he said, his tone gruff because the fucking memories were haunting him today. *Brodie* was haunting him, his big brother who'd always been there for Alexei but who Alexei hadn't been able to save. When Brodie needed him, he'd been helpless.

"Which meal do you want?"

She chose in silence.

They ate and drank in that same silence for a quarter of an hour before he leaned back in his chair. "My name is Alexei," he reminded her, not sure she'd even processed the words the first time around. "My pack is SnowDancer."

Seven minutes later: "Memory." A voice rough with disuse. "My name is Memory."

Chapter 5

Kaleb Krychek, Ivy Jane Zen, Nikita Duncan, Anthony Kyriakus, and Aden Kai. The names of the five who now control the fate of the PsyNet. We are not humans, to be ruled by democratically chosen leaders. We are more akin to the changelings, who choose their alphas based on power and respect.

Power, the Ruling Coalition has in orders of magnitude. Respect? That, too, has begun to root. The question is, will it last? Or will the Ruling Coalition fall prey to the same ambition and greed that corrupted so many of our past rulers?

—Editorial, *PsyNet Beacon*

KALEB KRYCHEK, DUAL cardinal and the most powerful man in the PsyNet, finished doing up the obsidian cufflinks Sahara had given him for a birthday gift. Pure black, they gleamed against the equally deep black of his shirt, and he knew that each time he looked at them today, he'd think about how she'd kissed him when she placed them on his cuffs the first time.

Only Sahara had ever given him gifts, and hers were the only gifts he would wear.

"Strike me dead, why don't you?" Dressed in one of his shirts, the buttons only partially done up, she leaned in the doorway to their bedroom, a mug of cherry-flavored nutrient drink in her hands. "You're lethal to the female system."

He would never become used to how she saw him: to everyone else, he was a deadly cardinal telekinetic with unknown motives, but to Sahara, he was the boy who had been her friend and the man who was her love. Sahara believed, truly believed, that he would do good if offered a choice between good and evil.

Kaleb, however, had never been in any doubt about his own conscience—it was a cracked and blackened remnant. If he did good, it was for her. He'd told her that countless times. As many times, she'd smiled and said she had faith in him. He was beginning to believe they would be having this argument into eternity and he looked forward to each and every encounter. "You realize the vast majority of women are terrified of me?"

"Hah!" A wicked grin. "Guess who's featured in the 'Scary but Sexy' column in this month's edition of *Wild Woman* magazine?" Sauntering over on bare feet while he attempted to process that unanticipated piece of information, she put her drink aside on a dresser and picked up his jacket.

She went behind him, held it open. "I'm going to frame that feature and put it on our wall of memories."

Mind flashing to that wall of photographs and the bonds it represented, he slipped his arms into the jacket. "Why are you reading a magazine aimed at changeling women?"

"It's amazing, that's why." Coming around to his front, she smoothed her hands down the lapels of the jacket. "Are you doing the tie thing today?" Not waiting for an answer, she went into the walk-in closet and picked out a tie in pure black. He bent his head so she could slip it around his neck, then watched as she knotted it with expert hands.

She'd learned how to knot a tie just so she could do it for him.

"There." Hands on his chest, she rose on tiptoe to claim his mouth in a kiss that reached all the way down to the twisted dark inside him, the broken and scarred boy who would forever be a part of his psyche.

"Any plans for world domination today?" A question asked against his lips, the intimacy quiet and domestic and what they needed after the terror and the separation that had threatened to turn Kaleb into a monster.

"That's after lunch," he said, and drank in her laugh. "First I have a meeting with Bowen Knight." He and the security chief of the Human Alliance had a difficult problem to solve. "I also have to investigate a disruption in the PsyNet."

Sahara's smile faded, shadows whispering across the dark blue of her eyes. "Is the disintegration speeding up?"

"No, it's stable enough." The PsyNet was in dire straits; over a century of Silence had weakened its foundations, torn holes in the psychic fabric that kept millions upon millions of Psy alive. Cut the biofeedback provided by the sprawling psychic network and they'd die in a matter of minutes.

The PsyNet would've already failed if not for Designation E. The empaths were literally holding it together using the bonds of emotion, but even the Es' heroic effort was teetering on the edge of failure. The PsyNet was too badly damaged—it needed human mental input to stabilize, and humans hated the Psy too much to enter their network.

The current forecast was Net failure in twelve months, max.

Kaleb would survive. So would Sahara. He was strong enough to slice them out of the PsyNet with enough other minds to create a stable standalone network held together by his sheer power. The only reason he hadn't already done so was that Sahara expected him to be a good man and fight to save the rest of their people.

So he would. For her. *Only* for her.

If the world dared take her from him again, he'd annihilate it without hesitation.

Today, however, he had to deal with a different issue. "I'm getting the sense of another significant power in the PsyNet." His mind had brushed up against the wake left by that power at least twice now. "The problem is that both the DarkMind and NetMind are losing coherence." The twin neosentience was the "brain" of the Net, and as the PsyNet failed, so did it. "It's why I don't already have more information on this individual."

Sahara reached up to straighten his shirt collar, which she knew was perfectly straight. But he bent his neck so she could reach. "When you say 'significant power,' do you mean an emergent Psy? A child who was stifled by Silence?"

"No, the energy I've detected is adult. Strong and aggressive, not an awakening empath or a gifted child." What Kaleb needed to know was if they were friend or foe *and* if they had the power under control. "The PsyNet can't handle rogue power. Not now." It could collapse in critical sections, cutting the biofeedback link to tens of thousands of minds.

Those Psy would crumple where they stood, death smashing into them in a wave of agony as their minds gasped for a link that simply wasn't there anymore.

Chapter 6

SnowDancer Wolves: Tough, territorial, and perennial favorites for our "Scary but Sexy" column. DO NOT ENTER THEIR TERRITORY WITHOUT INVITATION OR YOU WILL END UP FERTILIZER. Ahem, where were we?
—From the "Pack Cheat Guide" in the March 2082 issue of *Wild Woman* magazine: "Skin Privileges, Style & Primal Sophistication"

THE BIG GOLDEN wolf who kept growling at Memory while pushing food in her direction was a young god, his bone structure clean and symmetrical, his skin holding that sunshine color that said he was a creature of the light. Though his hair was damp right now, she knew it would shine like strands of pure gold when dry.

He was beautiful.

That didn't mean much to Memory. The man who'd clawed into her mind and kept her prisoner for fifteen years was beautiful, too. In the times when he took her outside and into the world, she'd met others like him—people with symmetrical faces and pristine skin, their clothes without a wrinkle and their hair flawless.

She'd learned long ago that beautiful people could be evil as easily as anyone else. She'd felt the cold wind of their presence in her bones, her stomach revolting against the nightmares they carried within. Nightmares meant for others. Blood and death meant for others.

Beauty meant nothing to Memory.

She'd followed the bad-tempered wolf with powerful shoulders not because he was beautiful but because he didn't have the voracious black hole of *nothingness* inside him. No cold wind chilled her in his presence. No abyss howled open at her feet at his touch.

The wolf carried with him an essence far more primal.

She'd run across other changelings during her time as a prisoner who couldn't scream for help, and caught a hint of the wildness under the skin that meant she'd never mistake a changeling for human, as her captor often did—but *never* had she sensed anything this potent. An untamed energy barely contained, a presence that filled the room and was a pulse against her skin.

Her rescuer was no ordinary wolf.

When he rose from the table to grab them bottles of water, it was with a prowling confidence—as if he was a wolf in human form. She'd known what he was before he told her. She'd watched shows about the outside world during the times her captor had buried her underground, and one of her favorites had been the channel that broadcast documentaries about nature.

After her captor let it drop that her prison was in the Sierra Nevada mountains, she'd watched and rewatched the episode about the wild wolves who lived in this region. She'd dreamed of being that strong, that ruthless. But mostly, she'd dreamed about being part of a pack that would fight for her as she'd fight for them. A fantasy that could never come true, but it had helped keep her sane.

The golden wolf put a bottle of water in front of her. "A five-year-old pup eats more than that," he said, his scowl doing nothing to lessen his beauty.

Memory's fingers tightened on her fork.

While she considered stabbing at his hand in pure aggravation, the wolf sprawled back in his chair and drank. His throat moved, his muscles and tendons strong. "You know the identity of the person who put you in that hole?" he asked after finishing two-thirds of the bottle. The clear gray of his irises were edged with amber.

As if he was half wolf right now.

Memory focused on his primal nature as a renewed and enraged fear threatened to grip her throat and squeeze, *squeeze*. Renault had done that at times, deliberately cut off her air for no reason but that he could.

You can never win. A sinuous whisper that dug into her mind. *I'm inside you.*

She'd scrubbed and scrubbed in the shower before, but she didn't feel clean. She wondered if she ever would. Or had the monster's evil stained her forever, leaving an endless taint that would haunt her till death?

Plas cracked, water spraying out onto her hand.

Memory stared at the half-crumpled water bottle. She hadn't realized she was clenching it so hard. Even now, her hand was locked around it like a claw.

"Imagining it's his neck?" The growly edge in the beautiful wolf's voice was back. "Can't blame you. Personally, I prefer to just rip off the head. Blood's a bitch to wash off though—the laundry team keeps threatening to throw out my clothes."

Memory very carefully opened her fingers and flexed them. The bottle was losing water from the crack she'd caused, so she got up, found a glass, and poured the liquid into it before retaking her seat. Her movements were nothing as graceful as his, but *she* was in control of them. No one would ever again turn her into a marionette.

"Give me a name." Eyes gone even more amber held hers, the quiet words a promise of retribution.

Memory parted her lips, but Renault's name stuck in her throat, a jagged hardness that cut. Chest heaving, she gulped down half a glass of water. Her fingers clenched on her fork again afterward, the metal cold and hard in her grip. Her skin heated, her hair seeming to prickle with electricity under the towel she'd wrapped around the wet strands.

"Hate" was a hard word, a hard emotion. But Memory hated Renault with every fiber of her being. Even the idea of saying his name made her gorge rise. Yet that very hate was why she was alive. She'd survived while holding on to her own sense of self to spite him.

"Eat first," the wolf said, his not-human eyes watchful. "The talk can wait until you're not in danger of disappearing." The growl had returned. "I think a bird could take you on right now and win." A pause, then, "Not a predatory bird. A sparrow."

Memory scooped up a big bite while staring at him.

Eyes shifting to pure amber, he leaned across the table and whispered, "Stop taunting the big, bad wolf, little E."

That was another thing—why did he keep calling her an E? She knew about the newly rediscovered designation, had watched the comm reports with fascination, but she wasn't one of them. The Es were healers of the mind, and Memory was no healer. She was a monster.

The bite she'd taken threatened to get stuck in her throat, but she made herself swallow. She had to become strong so she could tear Renault to pieces. Her one vulnerability was gone. She'd buried her affectionate Jitterbug under the open sky as she'd promised. Renault had nothing to hold over her anymore, no living creature he could threaten to harm when she got too intransigent.

"Renault," she managed to get out past her ugly distaste. "His name is Erasmus David Renault and he is a murderer who likes to slowly strangle his victims to the edge of death, then bring them back, only to do it over and over again. When their brains finally shut down, their hearts dead, he hacks off a piece of their hair as a souvenir."

The golden wolf had gone motionless at her first words. "How do you know?"

"He told me," Memory lied, because while shut up in her cage for months at a time between Renault's "outings," she'd grown and educated herself. At first, she'd done so by using the teaching programs Renault had given her. He'd needed her functional and unremarkable when they were in the world, with the expected knowledge for a girl—then woman—of her age and apparent status.

It had grated on Memory that she was falling in line with his plans, but even as a child, she'd understood that education was a weapon she might one day be able to turn against her captor. Her mother had always said, "Study hard, Memory. The more you know, the more control you have over your future."

So she'd knuckled down and gone through program after program. She'd also watched everything she could find on the comm about the outside world, read every book she could download. Renault had cut off her ability to contact anyone outside, but he hadn't monitored her reading or entertainment-comm accounts—which he'd set up because he was clever enough to know she'd go insane if left with no outlet for her mind.

Her murderous captor had needed her sane.

As a result of her compulsive drive to prepare for a freedom she'd never given up on attaining, Memory knew how normal people behaved. She also knew one thing for an unqualified truth: Alexei the golden SnowDancer wolf had helped her because he thought she was a victim.

She couldn't reveal that she was a nightmare.

Chapter 7

E. DAVID RENAULT, known to his associates as Renault, had
been in a meeting he couldn't leave without causing uncom-
fortable questions when the alert hit his wrist unit. The sleek
unit didn't light up or broadcast a disruptive ping; it simply
buzzed against his skin in a highly specific pattern.

The bunker had been breached.

Memory's mind slipped from his grasp at nearly the same
instant.

Renault had forced himself not to move, not to stiffen,
though his own mind raced. He'd had no way to wire the
bunker to alert him to a rogue teleporter—Memory's presence and that of her geriatric cat would've constantly set off
the system. Given that he was ninety-nine percent certain he
was the only Psy alive who knew the location of the bunker
and had visual coordinates for it, he'd decided to focus on the
only other possible threat.

The bunker was in SnowDancer territory. That it hadn't
been found for decades didn't mean the possibility was neg-
ligible. The wolves were highly territorial—no pack rose to
be as powerful as SnowDancer without aggressively protecting what they owned. He couldn't discount the idea of a patrol stumbling on the bunker.

He'd wired the bottom of the trapdoor.

The device was tiny and difficult to spot in dim light, and

had a battery-powered transmitter. The latter had been a calculated risk, but as it was designed to only send a signal in the event of a breach, the risk was minor. Secrecy no longer mattered if a wolf was already inside the bunker.

As the endless meeting carried on, Renault's hand curled over the end of his chair arm, the brown of his skin stretched tight over his knuckles.

He was a Gradient 8.7 telekinetic with teleportation capabilities. He'd also based his head office as close to the bunker as possible while remaining under the radar—it meant he was in no danger of burning out his psychic strength even if he had to make back-to-back trips to the bunker within a single day. He'd been confident of his ability to teleport in on the heels of an alert, grab Memory, and teleport out before anyone actually got through the bunker door.

The one thing he hadn't planned for was that the breach would occur during a critical meeting with already nervous investors who would not forgive any disruption.

The discussion finally ended after night had fallen.

He teleported out the instant he was behind the closed door of his personal office.

Given the delay, he'd considered not responding to the alert. He had no desire to face off against a SnowDancer. The wolves had a well-earned reputation for being vicious—their motto was rumored to be shoot first and ask questions of the corpses. But he *had* to know. Memory was his most critical asset. He'd never found anyone else who could replicate what she did for him, and he didn't plan to lose access to her.

He chose the safest lock image he had, one that would give him visibility but obscure his body enough to guarantee he wasn't a sitting target.

A fraction of a second of disorientation and he stood beside Memory's wardrobe. No Memory. No cat. He took extreme care as he stepped out into the hallway . . . and found himself staring at a door that had been ripped off its hinges. He snapped his head right, then left, but sensed no movement. He kept his guard up regardless as he walked into the living area—wolves were premier hunters and could stand motionless in wait for prey.

As for Memory, she knew how to be quiet. He'd trained her to be quiet.

The feline, he didn't worry about. It had to be dead or very close to it by now. One kick and Renault would collapse its rib cage. Memory was lucky he hadn't done that after her pet had scratched him soon after she'd adopted the mangy thing. Overall, it had been a good decision—the creature came in useful as a leash to control her.

The living area was empty.

It didn't take long to sweep the rest of the bunker and walk out in the direction of the trapdoor. He used the light from his phone to navigate and saw that the hatch was closed. A chair sat fallen to its side on the ground, the dirt disturbed. If it had been a wolf that had entered, that hatch was probably weighed down or locked.

Not that Renault was stupid enough to crawl out into wolf territory.

Turning on his heel, he did another sweep, but he didn't find anything new. The door torn off its hinges told the whole story. As a high-Gradient Tk, he could've wrenched the door off its hinges, but he didn't believe another one of his kind had been down here. Logic stated it must've been a wolf.

Renault's mind worked with cold precision. Given her lack of compliance and continued rebelliousness no matter what he did to her, he'd considered that Memory might one day escape and had laid the necessary foundations to recover her. All he had to do was wait, and she'd be returned to him. Except . . .

He'd always worked on the premise that she would escape while outside with him.

A SnowDancer wolf, however, that altered things.

Chapter 8

Empaths are now the most critical Psy in the world. We all fall if the Honeycomb falls.

—Editorial, *PsyNet Beacon*

ALEXEI WAS CONSCIOUS of the E staying motionless in the lower bunk, could all but feel her wary attention burning through the bottom of his bunk. He'd assigned her the lower berth because her movements, while better than when he'd first found her, remained uncoordinated, and he was afraid she'd wake disoriented and tumble out of the upper one.

His own reflexes were fast enough that he could be on the floor a heartbeat after hearing or scenting any sign of a threat. But he didn't say that aloud—not when he could taste the acrid scent of her fear in the air. The idea of being helpless with a predator in the room was crushing even her lion's heart.

Claws slicing out to dig into the mattress, Alexei focused on ensuring his breathing was deep and even, of a man who had fallen into slumber. The rustle below was a long time coming. He guessed she was curling up onto her side. Her breath fell into the rhythms of sleep not long afterward, her will to stay awake no match for her exhaustion.

Alexei, in contrast, stayed awake for some time, his eyes locked on the ceiling but his mind on that bunker. He didn't have to be a psychologist to know that Memory was far better socialized than she should be if she'd spent years as a captive. She not only interacted with him, she reacted in appropriate ways—anger included. She'd definitely been ready to stab him with her fork when he'd poked at her about her bird-size portions. A bit of deliberate provocation on his part to get her to eat—if only to shut him up.

Even a woman of her petite size needed more fuel than she'd been taking in.

So yes, Memory's reactions had been about what he might've expected—in a woman who *hadn't* been caged for a long period. On the flip side, the too-small clothes he'd spotted in the wardrobe hadn't lied. He'd seen no signs of a second captive, so those clothes had been Memory's at some point in time.

The two facts didn't mesh.

A woman held captive since childhood shouldn't be as functional as Memory.

The mystery followed him into sleep, his rest the shallow one of a soldier on watch.

A scream pierced his mind. He reacted to the terror in the sound before he was awake enough to think conscious thoughts. Moving with predator speed, he jumped off the bunk to land in a crouch on the floor, his shirtless back to Memory's bunk and his attention on the door.

That door was open, as he'd left it because Memory didn't respond well to small, enclosed spaces. Nothing moved beyond . . . but there was an unknown scent in the air. A dark and coldly *metallic* scent that made his wolf's fur stand up and its upper lip curl—he knew that scent, had tasted it in the bunker.

It was so potent right now that it was as if Memory's intruder sat on her bed, but when he glanced back, he found her alone; she lay tightly curled up under the blanket, her eyes scrunched shut and her hands over her ears.

Baring his teeth, Alexei prowled out to hunt down the intruder who'd so badly abused her. But the farther he got from Memory, the more the scent dissipated. Outside the bedroom, he found only quiet. The security system showed no incursions, and he swept the entire area without finding so much as an insect.

He stepped into the bedroom . . . and the ugly scent slapped him in the face.

Memory was sitting on the edge of her bunk now, her head down and her hands still over her ears. She was whispering something under her breath that he couldn't understand. Not until he was only a foot away from her.

"Get out, get out, get out, get out, get out."

An endless, repetitive loop steeped in acidic fear underneath the cold and metallic scent that made him want to kill. The only problem was that the scent was coming from Memory.

Crouching down in front of her, he said, "Memory." When that didn't seem to penetrate, he reached out to grip her wrists. "Wake up, little lioness." Her skin was hot, her muscles rigid. He pulled gently but firmly. She resisted.

He growled loud enough to fill the space.

Her head lifted . . . and her eyes, they were obsidian.

The tiny hairs on his nape prickling, Alexei nonetheless didn't break the physical contact. "Wake up," he ordered again, dead certain she wasn't truly conscious of him.

Eyes of obsidian gleamed unseeing at him. He felt an eerie sense of looking into an endless, vast darkness. An abyss without end.

"Memory." He shook her with care not to hurt, only to awaken.

Cool curls hit his hands, her hair not yet fully dry. Those haunting eyes shimmered with color, an oil slick under the sun, and he suddenly remembered a throwaway comment his fellow lieutenant Judd, a telekinetic, had once made—that empaths were "happy rainbows" who swept everyone along in their wake.

Did Memory's psychic presence have color? Did this mean she was coming back to reality?

He stroked his thumbs over the inner surface of her wrists, the skin there soft and delicate. "Your eyes are beautiful." Deep pools of mystery that fascinated his wolf.

He didn't mention her scent, which was vacillating wildly between the ugly metallic one that made him want to snarl, and the inherent warmth of what he'd picked up from her before this waking. It was almost as if Memory were two people.

"Channel the woman who wanted to stab me with a fork," he told her. "Fight your way out."

Her breath hitching, her eyes seeming to focus on Alexei. "He's hunting me." A plea and an angry fury at once.

Alexei's vision changed, his wolf rising to the surface. "PsyNet?" He knew that, at its core, the sprawling psychic network was a lifenet. Psy minds needed a connection to a stable psychic network in order to survive. But the PsyNet also flowed with data and could be used for mental communication—or an attack.

"Yes." The single word was gritted out through clenched teeth. "Renault."

"Can you hold him off?" Alexei reached for the phone he'd kept in the pocket of his sweatpants.

Memory grabbed at his wrist. "I need . . ." Harsh breaths. "The contact, it helps."

To a wolf, touch was life. It made perfect sense to Alexei that, cut off from her own pack, Memory would reach for him. "Put your hand on my shoulder," he told her. "It'll give you skin contact while I make a call to get you help."

Her skin was cold where it met his, her hand icy. "I screamed on the PsyNet when he came at me, and he retreated, but this region doesn't have many minds. He's coming back." Rapid-fire words, jolting breaths. "I'm not strong enough yet."

"Scream again," Alexei said. "As many times as it takes. Keep him distracted." It infuriated him that he couldn't take out her attacker, but sometimes, a battle was won with clear thinking and strategic use of available options. "Just hold him off for half a minute more."

Her nails dug into his shoulder, but the small irritation was nothing to his wolf. He still held her other wrist, continued to stroke the pad of his thumb over the soft skin on the inside curve while he made the call. "Aden," he said when it was answered on the other end. "I need PsyNet help."

Aden Kai, leader of the deadliest squad of assassins and shadow operatives in the world, and a man who had a seat on the Psy Ruling Coalition, didn't question why a wolf lieutenant needed psychic assistance enough to use this emergency call code known to a strictly limited number of people. "Details," the Arrow leader said, echoes of Silence yet in his voice.

Memory began to shiver, the tremors shaking her frame.

Releasing her wrist, Alexei pulled her into his lap so she was against the naked skin of his chest. Her arms went around him, her cheek pressed to his heart. He slid his own hand under her hair, curling it over her nape. "An E is under attack on the PsyNet." He knew the psychic network was a vast place, a single mind impossible to locate without markers, but in this case, he could give Aden very specific directions. "We're in den territory, not far from the empathic training ground."

That training ground had been chosen *because* this area of the PsyNet was quiet. It gave trainee empaths room to learn control and run their psychic exercises without interference from—or to—other minds. And though the compound was on the border between DarkRiver and SnowDancer territory, it was the Arrow Squad that guarded the trainees.

The wolf watching over the lamb.

"I'm receiving multiple alerts from my people at the compound of a disturbance nearby," Aden said almost before Alexei finished speaking. "Team en route."

MEMORY screamed and screamed on the psychic plane, using her terror and turning it into a disruption that rolled through the PsyNet. Renault might still have the ability to smash through to her mind, but he'd never again bleed her dry—he needed physical contact to make the initial connection for the transfer. Once made, that connection only lasted a finite period, and he'd left her alone in the bunker for far too long.

She'd shaken off the murderous parasite.

That knowledge gave her the strength to keep on fighting, her body encircled by the primal heat of Alexei's. The physical contact made her stronger—but Renault had all the advantages on the psychic level. He'd shredded her shields a lifetime ago. She had no defenses, a turtle without its shell.

The only reason Renault wasn't already inside her mind was that she'd had a small and zealously guarded store of psychic energy that she'd released in panicked desperation when she first jerked awake. He'd been so close by then that she'd felt his breath on her neck, a fetid heat. The energy had created a shock wave. A pitifully weak one, but he hadn't expected it, and it had buffeted his mind a short distance from her own.

"Show me where you are!" he screamed at her on the PsyNet as he came closer and closer. "Give me a visual! You know you can't win! You belong to me!"

Memory had no more energy left.

But surrender was not an option. Never would it be an option.

She would fight to the death.

Blood cold at the emptiness around her, the overwhelming aloneness that would've crushed her but for the wolf who held her, Memory screamed again into the psychic space, disrupting the limited data flows around her. Then, in a final act of defiant resolve, she tore at the golden threads around her, hoping her actions would trigger an automatic alert that would send out a security team.

She hadn't been on the PsyNet in a long time. Not for years. Renault had closed his mind around hers, creating a psychic prison that had failed at the same time as the other, darker link between them. As if the latter had bolstered the former. The failure had happened seconds before Alexei tore off the bunker door.

Grief-stricken and shocked as she'd been, she hadn't immediately realized the implications of that second failure. Because from the moment Renault had caged her, her basic biofeedback connection had been her only direct link to the psychic space. A lifeline only, with no access to the Net itself.

Despite that, she knew what those golden strands represented: the Honeycomb, the empathic network that was currently holding the PsyNet together. She'd read about it in the *Beacon*.

A glimmer of awareness.

Renault was turning. He was *running*.

"I'll find a younger, fresher replacement!" he threw back as a final taunt. "You're worthless now anyway!"

No surprise that his presence disappeared in the blink of an eye. His mind wasn't anchored in this region—he'd retracted the roaming part he'd sent out to hunt her down.

Memory stopped screaming, the cold that invaded her veins this time a frigid terror.

Renault would've never run from her. He didn't see her as a threat or an opponent. He saw her as a *thing*, a possession.

Darkness. Pure darkness.

Memory focused on the horizon, on the wave of deadly black coming closer. Her eyes snapped open. "Darkness comes." She could never defeat those minds.

"Arrows," Alexei said, rubbing gently at her nape.

Her heartbeat stuttered. Renault had told her about Arrows. Master assassins, they hunted people for the leaders of the Psy, and Renault was connected to those leaders. Arrows also hunted others—murderers and monsters and nightmares.

Jerking away from Alexei, she fell onto the floor. She scrambled back from him as nausea and betrayal twisted her gut.

He watched her with unblinking amber eyes. "Arrows are affiliated with empaths," he said, his primal power pulsing in the air. "They'll protect you."

Memory's breath turned into shards of ice in her lungs.

She wasn't an empath. The Arrows *executed* those like her.

Chapter 9

Intruder has fled, but we have his psychic signature.
Proceeding to the E.

—Arrow field team to Arrow command

RENAULT OPENED HIS eyes with a racing heart, his brain working a hundred different angles. He wasn't afraid. Renault was Silent, had never felt except for the exultation that swept over him in the aftermath of the murderous ritual that he craved. He did, however, have a well-developed sense of self-preservation.

How had the Arrows discovered Memory so quickly?

He'd set it up so she'd be returned to him long before anyone affiliated with the squad or the Empathic Collective stumbled upon her. Her mind wasn't the same as an E's, but it bore a direct resemblance to it, and he'd factored both the squad and the Collective into his retrieval strategy.

Not that it mattered. Now that they'd found her—a woman who knew too many of his secrets—Renault could no longer be certain that his well-laid plan would bear fruit. The squad might be attempting to trace him even now, but Renault'd had years to prepare for this worst-case scenario.

The Arrows would find no trail, his presence a ghost in the PsyNet.

He hadn't returned to his official residence after confirming Memory was gone, had come instead to a backup property purchased under another name. The next stage in disappearing meant switching to the comprehensive new identity he had waiting in the wings. It would mean a loss of power and status, but only in the short term. He'd build himself back up again.

As for Memory, he'd have to recover her using more personal methods. He also needed to do what he'd said—locate and begin to train a replacement. It'd be a difficult task given her unique skills, but not only was her defiance becoming problematic, she was taking longer and longer to recover from sessions.

He needed to have a spare on standby before she became too worn out to use.

But he wasn't surrendering her. Memory was the most prized piece of Renault's property. He *would* claim her back, and this time, when he put her in a hole, he'd make sure she never again saw the light.

Chapter 10

An unexpected new cooperation agreement, the Trinity Accord, has been negotiated and agreed upon between major elements of all three races.

—*PsyNet Beacon* (May 22, 2082)

THE GOLDEN WOLF hadn't moved his gaze off her.

And, one hundred seconds after the Arrows spotted her, she was still alive.

"SnowDancer is allied with the Arrows via Trinity," the wolf said, and she wondered if he realized his claws had sliced out of his skin at some point. "I asked for protection for you."

Memory finally found her voice. "You called *Arrows* to help me?" It was like calling a school of carnivorous sharks to look out for a minnow.

A shrug, the muscles of his back and shoulders rippling. "Arrows are the wolves of the PsyNet."

His phone buzzed.

While he spoke to whoever was on the other end, Memory dared to peek into the PsyNet. The black wave had split in two; one mind stood sentinel on either side of her own. Protection or enforcement?

As she watched, wondering if she'd gone from one prison to another and—eyes hot—vowing to break out again if she had, the Arrows began to drop small glittering psychic constructions around her mind. She stared at them uncomprehendingly until Alexei's voice brought her back to the real world.

A kick of her heart, her skin suddenly tight. Because

she'd forgotten the predator in the room with her while distracted by those on the psychic plane. Her eyes skated away from the dangerous amber of his . . . and caught on the red marks on his shoulder.

A wave of dull heat crawling over her skin, she curled her fingers into her palm. "I'm sorry."

"For what?" He scowled. "Scrambling away from me like I'm a drunk bear with randy intentions when all I did was cuddle you? Yeah, you should be sorry for that."

Memory wanted to glare at him, but shame bit at her. "I hurt you." She pointed to the evidence.

He glanced down . . . and laughed. Threw back his head and laughed as she'd never heard anyone laugh in her whole life. It was like fur over her senses, a delicious taste on her tongue, a cascade of butterflies in her stomach. She stared, drunk on the sensations.

Astonished by his intrinsically male beauty.

Grinning afterward, he shook his head and the slightly overlong strands of his hair shimmered in the light coming from the hallway. "To a wolf, lioness, that doesn't even count as a love bite." Wickedness danced in his eyes, and she, a woman who knew nothing about courtship rituals except for what she'd seen on the comm, understood that he was a man who'd never have an empty bed unless he wished it.

"Arrows said they put warning beacons around your mind," he told her, his lips yet curved. "All stamped with Arrow markers—only a person with a deathwish would cross the threshold." He slid his claws back in, but his eyes remained wolf. "An Arrow will respond in a matter of seconds to any incursion. Squad's also attempting to track Renault on the Net—no joy with a facial lock. They tried just now when I passed on his name. He's got shields that block a teleporter from targeting him."

Pressed up against the back wall by now, Memory hugged her knees to her chest and said, "Why?" The Arrows didn't know her, had no reason to help her.

Alexei had no reason to help her.

She needed to know the price she'd pay when they discovered the truth about her. Found out she'd helped Renault commit his atrocities.

"You're an empath." Alexei yawned and stretched that muscular body, scratching absently at the ridged line of his abdomen. "And because no one has the right to cage an innocent being."

Empath. Innocent.

Shivering, Memory hugged her knees even tighter and closed her eyes, shutting out a world that would find her out sooner or later.

"You fall asleep there and I'm going to pick you up and put you in your bunk. I might even—horror of horrors—cuddle you again."

She flicked open her eyes to see that Alexei had risen to his feet in predator silence. Hands on his hips, he raised an eyebrow, and it was a silent dare. Something unfamiliar and strangely bright woke inside her, forcing her onto her feet. She wanted to spit a quick comeback, but her brain chose that moment to decide it was exhausted beyond bearing, all resources expended in the fight against Renault.

Everything went blank.

Chapter 11

Dr. Menet's fifteen-year study uncovered no common genetic markers among known rogues. However, my research has unearthed three families with at least two rogues in successive generations. Families A and B have provided DNA for further examination. Family C, with three rogues in as many generations, is currently not part of this study.

— *Changeling Rogues: Broken Minds & Broken Families*
by Keelie Schaeffer, PhD (Work in Progress)

HAWKE PULLED ON a T-shirt over his barely dry body, his hair damp from his shower, and his heart a raw knot. Not wanting to think about why, he turned his attention to the woman with cardinal eyes and ruby-red hair who stood beside the edge of their bed, attempting to pull on a pair of jeans. Other than the jeans, she wore only a white lace bra and cool-yellow panties with thin white stripes.

Sienna's breasts bounced as she jumped up and down to tug the jeans up over the curve of her butt. "What?" she demanded in the successful aftermath, the white stars on black of her extraordinary eyes as open to him as her heart.

Hawke smiled slowly—she was the best fucking thing in his life. "I think your jeans need to be tighter."

A narrow-eyed look. "I'm your mate, Mr. Alpha Wolf. You think I don't know you're feeling messed up today? Come here." She held out her arms.

He had no hope in hell of resisting.

Going to her, he enclosed her in his arms, then bent his head to press a kiss to the plump curve of her breast. Nuzzling the side of his face, she tugged at his hair and, when he lifted his head, met his lips with her own. He was the most dominant wolf in SnowDancer, used to control, to power, but this morning he let his mate take the reins, pet him, kiss him, adore him.

His wolf was no longer as agitated when they parted. "I'm going to talk to Judd." Rostered on the night shift, the Arrow-turned-SnowDancer-lieutenant had taken charge of tracking down information on the empath Alexei had rescued. "You still want to come up to the substation?"

"Of course." His mate's fingers gripping his chin, her tone unbending. "We handle stuff like this together. Don't you forget it."

"I wouldn't dare." It was a tease but it was also a truth. Sienna might be younger than him, but she was more than capable of calling him on the carpet and holding his behavior to account. "I'll see you soon."

"Hey." She rose up to rub her nose over his. "It'll be all right."

Hawke pressed his forehead to her own. "It's fucking hard knowing I hurt Alexei this badly." He'd always felt differently toward his youngest lieutenant, could remember Alexei as a shell-shocked seven-year-old boy who'd clung to a teenaged Hawke's hand the day they buried Alexei and Brodie's parents.

Brodie had come in wolf form, had pressed his furry body against Hawke's other side.

Hawke had just become a too-young alpha, one who'd been forced to make a bloody decision that had left two small boys as orphans. A year ago, he'd made the same terrible decision all over again, only this time, he'd left Alexei the sole survivor of the Harte-Vasiliev family. "I fucking broke Alexei's heart."

"I know." Sienna petted his nape, kissed his jaw. "I know, baby." Shining eyes, a thickness in her voice. "But you had no choice. Otherwise Alexei would've been put in an awful position. You know he doesn't blame you."

Thank you. I couldn't have lived with myself if I'd had to do it.

Grief-stricken words spoken by the lethally trained dominant Hawke had watched grow from a boy to a man he would have at his back anytime. "I know, but it doesn't help when I remember how long it's been since I saw the real Alexei." Though one of the quietest of Hawke's lieutenants, Alexei had always had a sly sense of humor that took others by surprise. But he rarely laughed these days, his entire being riven with anger.

Hawke was used to making hard decisions, but the one to execute Brodie, it haunted him. "I remember taking Lexie on a hunt when he was a juvenile and how proud he was to be asked along by his alpha." The age difference between them was only eight years, but when a man was twenty-two and a boy fourteen, it mattered, even more so because they were wolves and Hawke was Alexei's alpha.

Sienna ran her hand down his spine. "He loves you, Hawke. There's a reason you scheduled his secondment here at this time, and it's the same reason he didn't ask to reschedule—he still turns to you when the pain gets to be too much." A kiss on the lips, tender and soft. "I know this is the worst possible day for you to go into the bunker." Fingers stroking through his hair. "Don't let it get to you."

His mate was comforting him as he'd let only her. An alpha wolf could never be anything but the strongest person in the room—except when alone with his mate. Sienna knew his every scar, his every vulnerability. If she ever asked him to kneel down so she could slit his throat, he'd do it without blinking. Wolves didn't mate lightly, and the strongest dominants in the pack were even worse. Possessive, protective, demanding—and devoted. His every breath was hers.

"I won't," he promised. "Those bastards hurt my pack once. I won't allow them to wound us a second time."

Leaving his mate to finish getting dressed, after which he knew she had a quick breakfast meeting with another soldier, he detoured to the den's large central kitchen to grab a breakfast roll. An hour before dawn, it was mostly those on the early shift grabbing food and coffee before heading out, but their senior healer was also up and about.

"Hawke." Lara smiled, the natural dark tan of her face luminous and her high cheekbones softer than they'd been a few months earlier.

Cupping the back of her head, he kissed her gently on the

lips while putting one hand on the curve of her belly. "How is my new packmate?" This close to full term, the pup was developed enough to sense their alpha, and would be calmed by the contact.

"All sharp elbows and footballing feet." Lara leaned into him, unashamed of needing extra contact from her alpha at this time in her life. "Slowing down now though. Not much room in there."

He held her close while he touched base with the others in the room. Every single wolf gave Lara's belly an affectionate pat after glancing at her to make sure the skin privileges were acceptable. All adults in the den knew not to assume anything with a pregnant wolf; they might get their paws bitten off for daring.

Pregnant soldiers had been known to break the odd finger when a packmate got too excited and made contact without permission. The wounded winced, got the finger splinted, and accepted that it was their own damn fault, while other packmates just shook their heads at their stupidity.

Lara, however, was a healer, linked to every single member of SnowDancer through her bond with Hawke. Touch was a cornerstone of her life, the friendly touch of packmates welcome. She not only wanted the contact, she glowed under it.

Afterward, as Hawke ate his breakfast standing up, Lara said, "I'm sending Lucy with you to the substation." She rubbed the arch of her back. "I'm not exactly sprightly enough to scramble over rough terrain."

Thank the deities that watch out for wolf alphas. Hawke had not been looking forward to that argument. "I'm on my way to see what Judd turned up overnight," he said after swallowing the last of his roll. "You want to come along, see if there's anything medical Lucy needs to know?"

Lara nodded and waited for him to pour himself a mug of coffee before the two of them walked out into a hallway gray with softly dawning artificial sunlight. That technology was one of the best things to have come out of SnowDancer's research labs. Not only had sales and maintenance of the tech exponentially increased the pack's income, it had made the transition between inside the den and outside it a seamless one.

Hawke drank his coffee as he walked, his mind on Alexei and the E. If there was anything good about the situation, it was that Alexei would hopefully be too busy today to be tormented by the anniversary of Brodie's execution and why it had been necessary. Hawke would speak to Etta's family before he left for the substation, but he knew they were healing better than Alexei.

Last time he'd seen them, Etta's father had said how much they missed Alexei. "He shouldn't be ashamed to visit us, shouldn't be ashamed of his love for his brother," the older man had said, tears in his eyes. "Our Etta would never want him to lose us when he's lost so much already. Tell him to join us on the anniversary. We'll talk. Remember."

Hawke had passed on the invitation to Alexei, but as far as he knew, Lexie had kept his distance. He was too angry at Brodie to join in any day of remembrance.

"I did some reading on long-term captivity last night." Lara's tone was quiet but garnered his full attention. "If Alexei's right and the empath was kept in the bunker for years, the damage could be catastrophic."

"Chance of recovery?"

"No way to tell right now. Some captives recover with a lot of help and attention, while others spiral into breakdown, self-destructive behavior, even suicide." White lines bracketed Lara's mouth. "It also depends on what was done to her. If she was a child when taken . . ." Shaking her head, she cradled her bump with unconscious protectiveness. "I need to see her, assess her. Just . . . be kind."

Hawke didn't take offense. Lara knew that as alpha he could never trust a stranger who hadn't proven herself, but he wasn't incapable of gentleness. If the E was no threat, he'd treat her as he would a hurt submissive. "She's been with Alexei overnight," he reminded his healer. "If she's survived him, we're on the right track."

Lara groaned. "I adore him to pieces, but he's half growl these days even when he smiles."

Neither one of them spoke about the reason behind the shift in Alexei's personality. It was better to simply accept the change, accept Alexei as he was now—because some losses scarred a man forever, and you either lived with it or let it break you. Alexei had found a way to live with it. "Is he still avoiding skin privileges?"

"Never to a dangerous point," Lara murmured. "He's compulsive about ensuring he has enough skin-to-skin contact with a packmate to ward off any instability." A glance up at Hawke. "Only, I don't think Alexei allows himself to enjoy any of it. He accepts it like a pill he has to take."

Hawke shoved a hand through his hair. Wolves, like most changelings, were tactile creatures. Deprived of touch for too long, the dominants in particular tended to become aggressive—and Alexei had always been incredibly tactile. Not just in intimate situations. He might appear remote to outsiders, but he was a wolf who always had open arms for packmates who needed to be held. "He have any problems finding partners?"

"No. He sticks to friends who know him, and who're willing to give him the contact he needs without recriminations or demands. That's part of the problem."

Hawke knew what Lara didn't—that Alexei didn't *want* to find a woman who meant more to him than a friend. And his reasons weren't anything logic could overcome. Hawke's youngest lieutenant had a terrible, painful motive for chasing aloneness.

"Hawke." Judd exited the den's tech center not far in front of them. "I was just coming to find you."

"You got something on Alexei's foundling?"

Judd's gold-flecked dark eyes gave nothing away, but his words were ominous. "You need to see this."

Chapter 12

Alexei Harte: SnowDancer wolf, 6.2, blond, gray-eyed, and panty-melting gorgeous. Word is, he's won more dominance challenges than any other wolf in the pack. The wild women in SnowDancer tell us it's because outsiders see his pretty face and think he'll be an easy takedown. Most of those outsiders are still healing from various broken bones and internal injuries.

—From the "Scary but Sexy" column in the January 2083 issue of *Wild Woman* magazine: "Skin Privileges, Style & Primal Sophistication"

MEMORY WOKE TO gritty eyes, a body that ached, and a visceral awareness of not being alone. Her pulse spiked, her skin chilling as her mouth went dry. She *hated* it when Renault found her asleep and vulnerable.

Slitting her eyes open just enough to see, she—

Her eyelids flew all the way up.

A big male body, all golden skin and muscle, was stretched out on the floor not far from her bed. Why, she thought, coming fully awake, was Alexei half-naked on the floor? Her eyes snagged on what appeared to be a small tattoo on the back of his left shoulder, but she couldn't make out the pattern from this distance.

Then he pushed up on his arms, the line of his body a thing of precision and beauty, and his arm muscles rigid. He held the position for what felt like an excruciating eternity to her, then went back down.

Not making a sound, loath to interrupt him, she watched the fluid movements in breathless fascination. He was only wearing a pair of sweats that hung low on his hips, so she had an uninterrupted view of his upper body.

Her stomach felt funny, her toes curling.

An amber gaze met hers when he rose to his feet after ten more repetitions of the smooth, powerful movement. Wild energy hummed in the air, a prowling kind of patience. "Pack got in touch," he said in a voice she couldn't read. "According to allies we asked to do a surveillance check, Erasmus David Renault never came home last night, and there's no sign of him at his place of business."

Memory wasn't surprised; Renault hadn't escaped detection this long by being unprepared. "He's rich, has a lot of property."

"Techs managed to turn one of our satellites in the direction of the bunker," Alexei added. "No movement around it, no sign of an incursion."

Memory didn't flinch. She sat up instead. "He'd have teleported in to confirm my escape." Bile burned her throat as she spoke the next words. "He considers me his property and he wants me back."

Alexei's claws sliced out.

Leaning forward to grip the edge of the upper bunk, his big body far too close and the heat of him nearly a touch, he said, "Yeah? Well, I consider him prey." His voice was hard and human, but the eyes that met Memory's were a striking mix of amber and gray.

When he reached down one clawed hand to touch the side of her face, she didn't jerk back. The deadly tips grazed her skin, but instead of a spike of fear, she felt that strange fluttering in her abdomen, her breath catching. He was so close she could smell the wild warmth of his scent, catch a hint of the perspiration that had dampened the hair at his temples.

Her fingers tingled, wanting to touch his skin, feel the power of all that muscle. Gripping the mattress of her bunk to still the strange urge, she held his stare until his gaze was all amber and his chest rumbled. Memory knew that, to a wolf, aggressive eye contact was a challenge, but she didn't care.

Never again would she back down from *anyone*.

He snapped his teeth at her.

It made her jump in surprise. Eyes narrowed in sheer annoyance, she bared her own teeth at him. And, since he was looming over her, she lifted her hands and pushed forcefully at his hips. Her fingers brushed warm, hard abdominal muscles, her palms braced against the cloth of his sweatpants. The raw power of him hummed through her.

Alexei's eyes gleamed.

Though he was fully conscious that she didn't have the strength to make him move, he stepped back after grabbing the towel and fresh clothes he'd left on the upper bunk. Her heart thundered as he walked out, her skin prickling, but not in the way it usually did. The pain that was her constant companion had retreated for the moment.

The first thing she did was go to the front door and make sure her palm print still opened it. She didn't breathe until the lock clicked open. Pulling the door inward a fraction, she looked out into the hazy gray of early morning, the rain a light mist today, and just basked in freedom.

It was a bone-deep pleasure to know she could walk out at will. Because she could, she closed the door after a couple of minutes. The cold was seeping in, and she didn't want Alexei to walk out of his shower into an icy hallway.

Not that he appeared to feel the cold. He'd been bad-tempered yesterday when she'd hesitated at the doorway to this place, but he hadn't shivered once.

Wolf.

Poking around the bedroom while imagining him shifting form, she managed to find a drawer full of simple grooming supplies, and took a couple of stretchy hair bands. The small mirror on the back of the door showed her a woman with a thin face surrounded by hair that was a huge, fluffy mess.

It took some work, but she managed to corral her frizzy curls back in two sections.

That done, she padded her way down to the kitchen area and started the coffee. It wasn't the first time she'd done the task; the roots of her knowledge of such things lay in the worst darkness of her past. She'd come close to going mad after Renault first abducted her. Hours and hours she'd sat rocking back and forth, back and forth, while the visual of her mother's final moments played against the wall of her mind. She couldn't forget how Diana Aven-Rose's body had spasmed, her hand thumping on the carpet, and her face going a bruised purplish shade under the ebony of her skin.

Renault had hit Memory to snap her out of it.

Her fingers lifted to her cheek, the burn of the backhanded slap a remembrance she carried vengefully close. It was nothing in comparison to what he'd done to her kind and gentle mother, but that slap had changed her forever. The blow had been so strong it had crashed her to the floor, blood trickling into her mouth from her split lip.

When she'd opened her eyes, she'd seen the polished tips of his shoes in her line of sight, realized she was scrabbling at the monster's feet. Rage, such *rage*, had overwhelmed her, what training she'd had under the Silence Protocol in splinters by that point. She hadn't understood the emotion then, but it had made her strike out at him without warning.

It was the only time in her life she'd managed to take Renault down. He hadn't been expecting the sudden assault from a small girl he considered broken. She'd slammed her body into his legs, brought him crashing down to the floor. If he hadn't been a Tk with the attendant rapid-fire reflexes, his head might've hit the edge of a coffee table in the isolated cabin where he'd first stashed her, and his skull would've cracked open.

As it was, he'd twisted in time to avoid the injury.

When he rose, he'd brushed off his clothing and said, "It seems you need to learn your place. I'll see you in four days."

She'd been eight years old and alone in a cabin in the middle of nowhere. A cabin with bars on the windows and a door barred from the outside. Her nails had been bloody and broken and she'd had bruises all over her body from her attempts to break out when she'd realized he'd left no nutrients for her.

That particular cruelty had been accidental. Renault needed her alive and strong, not weak and malnourished— but he was also not a parent and didn't realize that small children had far fewer dietary reserves than adults.

The only things to eat in the entire cabin had been two

cans of beans that looked to have been forgotten in a corner
of a cupboard long ago. Perhaps by a former owner. She'd
found the tools to hack one can open, but had balked at eating the cold lumpy beans from the can. Her mother, a high
school biology teacher, had permitted her to watch educa-
tional comm shows once in a while, and on one of the shows,
she'd seen people cooking. So she'd poured the beans into a
dish and managed to heat them up.

By the time Renault returned, she'd eaten all the beans
and decided she'd never again touch nutrients. It was a line
in her mind. Nutrients had been for when her mother was
alive and used to work oil into her hair while Memory ate a
bar. Even at eight years old, Memory had understood that to
survive, she had to live in the now and with vengeance in her
heart.

Renault had finally given up force-feeding her nutrients
when she'd bitten him one too many times. It didn't matter
how brutally he beat her, she refused to eat and drink what
had then been accepted food items for Psy. In the end, he'd
brought her more beans, slowly adding more items once he
realized that food preparation kept her calm.

All the while he'd been digging in the hooks he'd put inside her mind after breaching her shields during the most
traumatic moment of her life. As she grieved for her mother,
lost and scared, Renault had violated her.

Memory touched her temple, dropping her hand when she
realized all over again that the hooks weren't visible, had
never been visible. But they were gone now, broken by a critical lack of physical contact. To enslave her again, Renault
would have to put his hands on her.

Memory intended to hunt him down first.

Jaw tight, she rummaged around until she located bread
sealed in packets that kept it fresh. She had the toast going
and the coffee ready by the time Alexei walked into the kitchen. His hair was damp, his body evocative of soap and a
scent that struck her as deeply masculine, intrinsically
Alexei. Her eyes dipped to his abdomen, the golden muscle
now covered by a faded gray T-shirt, and her fingers tingled.

She'd heard about attraction, had even witnessed displays
of it, but had never understood how anyone could be at-

tracted to a man. An understandable reaction when the only man in her vicinity was a psychopath. It turned out that she was, in fact, capable of appreciating a male body when it was packaged with a non-psychopathic mind.

Even if it was a body that kept on growling at her.

Now he prowled over to the coffee and poured himself a mug. His energy filled the space to bursting. It was a thing with teeth and claws, a thing that demanded her attention. Memory ignored the primal dominance of him with teeth-gritted control. She was near certain he was doing it on purpose, to see how she'd react.

The man would probably poke a bear just because.

A growl brushed against her nape when she continued to focus on putting peanut butter on her toast. Even though her spine itched at having her back to him, she didn't turn. "Do you want peanut butter?"

A long pause, followed by a grumbled "Yes."

Memory didn't make the mistake of thinking she'd won the battle of wills. That had been a mere skirmish. She passed him a slice of toast with the spread on it, then bit into her own piece. She finished half of it before she turned to face him.

His toast was long gone, and he stood leaning his hip against the counter. "I have news," he said, his eyes watchful. "It's about you."

Memory went motionless.

"I sent through your name and likely age range to the pack. Your palm print was automatically forwarded when I added you to the system."

"Did you upload to the PsyNet?" Her brain buzzed, razor-sharp knives cutting and slicing.

"No. We have hackers of our own." He took a sip of his coffee, his tone still dangerously even. "I said you were probably around twenty-three to twenty-six, though I'd say the lower end was right."

"Twenty-three," she confirmed, her hand tight around her mug of coffee.

"We found you, lioness." Soft voice, wolf eyes. "Memory Renault, adopted daughter of E. David Renault."

"*Bastard.*" The single word quivered with such violent

rage that Alexei wondered how it could be contained in such a small body.

"Fucking bastard." Memory shaped the words as if they were daggers, each one thrusting home in her captor's heart. Her body was rigid, her muscles clenched so tight that they looked about to snap.

Alexei approved. Anger could burn, could debilitate, but it could also be a weapon of survival. He was so fucking angry with Brodie, and he might stay that way forever, even as his love for his brother would never die. It stopped the grief from overwhelming him in a torrent. Especially today, when the wound was so raw it bled. "Tell me."

Her gaze sparked with fire at the order.

Alexei felt the urge to bite her. Not hard. In warning. His wolf was aggravated at being so thoroughly ignored—a predator of Alexei's power usually only had to walk into a room to get everyone's attention. "Right now, you're an unknown, a possible threat to my pack. Tell me who you are in your own words—or let Erasmus David Renault speak for you."

She slammed the coffee mug down on the counter and stalked out. He heard the front door open not long afterward. A cold wind followed. Straightening from his leaning position, Alexei prepared three other pieces of toast, put them on the same plate as her unfinished piece, then poured a fresh mug of coffee and headed down the hall.

As he'd expected, she was standing just outside the door, gulping in long breaths of the chilly morning air while a fine misty rain beaded in her hair. "You make good coffee." He took a drink, held out the mug.

Steam curled up against the cold.

"No?" he said when she remained a statue. "Back to the captive diet, huh?"

She growled at him, actually *growled*.

Alexei's wolf stood up in quivering attention. "Where did that sound come from?" It certainly couldn't have come from the petite body beside him. "Do it again."

Glaring, she grabbed the coffee mug from him and took a defiantly large gulp. She kept the coffee while snatching up her unfinished toast from the plate in his hand. Still fascinated by the growl his taunting had incited, he ate another piece of toast and waited for her to finish hers before offering her a second piece.

She took it, ate in quiet, methodical bites while her breath frosted the air. "My last name is Aven-Rose." Fierce words. "He will *not* steal that from me."

"Memory Aven-Rose," Alexei said, because some things weren't games. "I'll have the pack records updated."

"He murdered my mother. I was eight years old and she'd just picked me up from my after-school lessons." Memory's voice was flat, distant. "She helped me take off my bulky winter jacket. I was telling her about a school project when she opened the hallway closet to hang it up . . ."

Shoving the coffee into his hand, she leaned over with both her hands on her thighs, her breath harsh. Alexei wanted to pick her up, cuddle her close, tell her she was safe. Nothing was going to get through him. But that type of touch was something she'd have to initiate—he'd pulled her into his lap in the middle of the night, but only after she'd told him contact helped her fight the psychic attack.

She wasn't under attack today, hadn't asked for skin privileges.

And he had no fucking idea what her captor had done to her, what she could bear. All he could do was provoke her anger until she forgot to be scared and became a growling lioness again.

It took her long minutes to rise back up to her full height. "He was in the closet."

"Hell." That was a child's nightmare come to life. No fucking wonder Memory had nearly lost it while telling the story.

"My mother went to scream but he was too fast and he had his hand over her mouth before she could make a sound." Leaning back against the closed substation door, Memory took a deep breath, released it with slow deliberation. "He does this thing with his mind—he stalks his victims on the PsyNet and learns their mental habits, so when he attacks them, he can trap their minds at the same time."

So no one would hear a psychic cry for help. "Did he do that to you, too?"

Alexei's claws scraped the inside of his skin when Memory nodded.

"He knew she always picked me up at that time, that I'd be with her. He told me if I screamed or made any kind of a disruption that attracted attention, he'd cut my mother into tiny little pieces, but that if I was quiet, he'd let her live." The flatness broke, but not into tears. Into a red-hot anger. "That psychopath is not my father. He stole my life. He will *not* steal my identity. My name is Memory Aven-Rose. My mother's name was Diana Aven-Rose. She named me Memory because I was her most important one. The only memory that mattered."

According to the records SnowDancer had unearthed, Memory had been adopted at eight years of age, in the aftermath of her mother's death. Those records had said nothing about the circumstances of her mother's death, which wasn't surprising—Diana Aven-Rose had been murdered while the Psy Council was in power, and it wasn't to the Council's advantage to have their people aware of the psychopaths who walked among them.

Silence, after all, was meant to have fixed the insanity and violence that stalked the Psy race.

"I believe you." No one could fake such anguish, such gut-deep anger.

Memory's gaze searched his face, her body yet rigid. "Will your pack?"

Alexei considered how to answer that. "Psy," he said at last, "have harmed SnowDancer multiple times over the years." It had never sat right with the Council that the wolves were so independent and had so much power. "We have Psy packmates and allies now, and no longer see your race as a single entity, but trust with unknown Psy is still a tough road. You'll have to earn it."

Memory looked away and out into the misty gray dawn, tiny droplets of water beaded on her eyelashes. "I'm going to hurt Renault, stop him before he takes another child. He taunted me that he would, that he'd find a replacement. I won't let him do that to anyone else ever again."

A *slam* of ferocious anger.

Alexei clenched his jaw. If he hadn't known better, he'd have thought it an attack. *"Memory."*

His growl had her snapping, "What?"

"Before you turn rampaging Valkyrie," he said with a slow smile designed to infuriate her, "you'll have to learn to shield your emotions."

She blinked before he caught a sudden glow in her cheeks that he was sure was a blush, hidden though it was under the rich hue of her skin. Ducking her head, she closed her eyes and fisted her hands. The anger retreated, but it wasn't gone; he could sense it lapping at the edges of his consciousness. "Thanks," he said, and took a sip of the coffee. "I like your claws, lioness."

Memory flexed her fingers and stared at them. Alexei could almost hear her thought processes—she wanted claws like a wolf's. So she could shred her captor into tiny, bloody pieces.

Alexei's wolf watched her in primal approval, intrigued by this little E with bloodthirsty vengeance on her mind. He didn't, however, have much longer alone with her. A minute earlier, he'd caught a distant howl on the wind that would've been inaudible to Memory's ears: his alpha was on the way.

Chapter 13

Until the next life, my love.
— Tristan Snow's final words, spoken to his mate, Aren

HAWKE HAD RUN up to the substation, his skin itching with energy. Sienna was with Lucy, the two of them driving up in an all-wheel-drive vehicle that held a medical kit. Sienna was fast, but she couldn't keep up with Hawke when he ran at full alpha speed. He stayed in human form today, but he was as much wolf as man as he flowed through the forest on predator-silent feet.

The moisture-laden mist felt good on his heated skin when he stepped out of the trees.

He spotted Alexei at once. The lieutenant was seated on a large mossy rock next to the substation door, his legs sprawled out in front of him, and his back leaning up against the wall of the substation. His hair glinted gold even in the dull light, and from his pose, you'd have thought he was asleep.

A small woman who burned with anger paced back and forth not far from Alexei. Her movements were like a clock-work toy's at times, jagged and uncoordinated, while at others, they smoothed out. As if her brain was short-circuiting between one step and the next, then starting again.

A sudden jerking halt, her head whipping toward him.

Hawke lifted a couple of fingers to his temple in a casual salute. Interesting that she'd picked him up from so far away. He knew one empath very well, and Sascha Duncan made a point of staying out of people's emotions except when they were too close for her to ignore—as a wolf picked up scents, an E picked up emotions.

This E had to be wide open if she'd sensed Hawke from all the way across the clearing. Either she was scanning the area on purpose, or her shields were paper-thin. The latter would make it difficult for her to survive around a large group of people, while the former would be another strike against her status as an innocent victim.

Then there was Alexei's report about her ability to impact changelings with potent emotional broadcasts. A weapon? It was a possibility Hawke couldn't discount, not when pockets of the Psy race remained violently opposed to the Ruling Coalition's progressive decisions—including the decision to sign the Trinity Accord. To those Psy, changelings remained an inferior race that had to be brought to heel.

He braced for a barrage as he walked across the snow-laden field, but the E wasn't broadcasting. He'd made the call to go in first, with the others waiting in the trees. No point in startling or scaring the empath if she *was* an innocent, and if the time came that Hawke couldn't take on a small E who stared at him in mutinous fury, then he needed to give up being alpha.

Inside him, his wolf was too astonished by her temerity to be annoyed.

He focused on her strange courage as he walked forward, and not on the ghosts awakened by Alexei's discovery of the bunker. Not on the husky voice of a woman with sea-green eyes and an artist's hands who'd tumbled a small boy to the floor with enthusiastic kisses that made him laugh . . . and who hadn't been able to survive her mate's passing. And never on the last words spoken by a strong, tormented man who lay dying on the snow, his blood scarlet against the white while the same boy, a little older by then, clutched at his hand.

Hawke's parents were long dead, could feel no more pain. His pack, however, was vibrant and alive, and it was his task as alpha to protect each and every member. Even if that meant eliminating a threat in the form of a small empath with the grit—many would say foolhardy grit—to meet an alpha wolf's gaze.

Alexei's eyes opened. They held no surprise at seeing
Hawke coming toward him. Rising to his feet, he said,
"Hawke." A glance at the E. "Memory, this is my alpha,
Hawke."

The empath's shoulders were already stiff. Now her
hands fisted at her sides, and she shot Hawke a look full of
such anger that it battered his skull. Catching Alexei's
glance, he saw the other man give a small shake of his head.
So, the little E with the big eyes wasn't doing it on purpose—
and she was a *power*.

"Renault isn't my father!" The words were thrown down
like a gauntlet. "If you try to give me back to him, I'll stab
him in the heart right in front of you, then smash his head
open and stomp on his psychopathic brain." Her chest
heaved, her words resonant in the mountain air.

Hawke's wolf decided it liked this small, angry, bloodthirsty creature. "Never heard an E speak so violently before," he commented, crossing his arms over his chest.

"Renault is a special case." A deadly growl in Alexei's
voice that had nothing to do with the habitual grumpiness
designed to keep others at bay—not that it worked. Pack
never let anyone drown; in this particular situation, it was the
submissives who'd taken the lead—they had the advantage
over their dominant packmates. Where Alexei might snarl
and pick a fight with a dominant, he'd never shove away a
submissive who needed affection.

Hawke wondered when Alexei would click to the fact that
their plant expert Felix didn't actually *need* a hug every
afternoon and that sweet Evie wasn't morose without her
morning cuddle from him. Hawke was fucking proud of the
subtle sneak attack mounted by the gentlest wolves in his
pack. "Oh?" he said to Alexei, since the E appeared too apoplectic to form words.

"Memory and I had a 'talk' after you sent through the
information about her adoption." Alexei's slow smile caught
Hawke's attention—he hadn't seen that particular designed-
to-provoke smile for over a year. "It involved her yelling at
me for being an imbecile."

"He didn't *adopt* me!" The empath uttered a short scream.
"He stole me after murdering my mother!"

The fury coming off her was a deluge of red that threatened to incite Hawke's wolf to violence regardless of that wolf's liking for her. As alpha, he was far calmer than most of the dominants under his command, but even he was hitting a teeth-clenching edge.

He was considering how to deal with the E's violent broadcast when Alexei said, "*Memory*," in a tone that was an order.

The E glared at him.

"Want to stomp on my brain, too?" The lieutenant's lips kicked up in a genuine grin that had been missing for far too fucking long. "I've been told my head's as hard as rock. But you're doing a good job smashing at it with your mind."

The E froze at his final words. Ducking her head the next second, her shoulders rigid and her fingers flexed out hard and stiff, she inhaled once, exhaled with slow care . . . and the wave of emotion retreated. Hawke's wolf shook its fur into place while considering the empath with new eyes. This one had claws.

When she lifted her head back up, her eyes were obsidian. And they were focused on Alexei. "I wouldn't stomp on your brain," she said in a firm, sure voice. "I would tie you naked to a chair and put a small biting insect on you. It wouldn't hurt you, just bite you in places you couldn't reach to scratch. Over and over."

Hawke's shoulders threatened to shake. Alexei had clearly been irritating his mouse with a lion's mental roar for her to have come up with that particular punishment. Right now, the younger male was scowling at her. "I *rescued* you, in case you've forgotten," he snarled. "And all I get is attitude."

The E's eyes narrowed.

Curious what would happen next—he might be alpha, but he had his share of wolf nosiness—but aware he was delaying the inevitable, Hawke broke into the silent staring contest. "Lexie." He jerked his head to the left.

Prowling over with Hawke to the middle of the field, far out of the E's hearing range, Alexei pushed back his damp hair while the misty rain settled on their skin. "You found something else." Not a question, acute intelligence in the gray of his eyes.

Hawke knew Alexei was in no frame of mind to consider it right now, but Hawke and his senior lieutenant, Riley, were of the opinion that it was Alexei who should be trained as Riley's backup—the senior lieutenant needed extra time off while his and Mercy's triplets were so young. At the moment, that coverage was spread across Hawke and all the lieutenants, but it'd cause less disruption if one lieutenant could, when needed, take on the full breadth of Riley's duties.

The person who did so had to be calm, organized, and able to juggle multiple tasks at will. Alexei, despite his growling bad temper of late, was also the most controlled wolf Hawke had ever met. Which was why it was so interesting that the E had managed to niggle at him with her biting-insect threat.

The Hawke who loved Alexei wanted to abandon the lieutenant with the E and see what other reactions she could provoke in him. But the Hawke who was alpha needed to deal with a possible security threat to his pack. "We found something else," he confirmed, before taking out his phone. "Have a look at the photographs the techs were able to dig up once we had Memory and Renault's names."

ALEXEI went motionless.

On the screen was an image of a petite woman with brown skin devoid of the kiss of the sun and brown eyes, her body clad in a dark blue skirt-suit, and her hair meticulously straightened and corralled in a twist at the back of her head. Her gaze was . . . not flat, that wasn't the right description. The look in her eyes was just subtly *wrong*.

Alexei looked from the image to the Memory who stood glaring a hole in his skull from near the substation door. "It's as if she's two different women." One a wild creature, the other a being of precision and ice.

Bringing up the next picture, he felt his gut churn. She was dressed the same, but wasn't alone this time—she walked next to a tall and classically handsome man with smooth brown skin and hazel-brown eyes, his head shaven clean. He could've passed for thirty-five, though Alexei knew from Memory's "adoption" papers that he was in his mid-forties. "Renault?"

Hawke nodded, the silver-gold of his hair shimmering with the misty rain that hadn't stopped falling all morning. "The images were shot a year earlier by a news crew reporting on a merger—she's listed as his assistant."

Alexei forced himself to continue through the photos. His wolf was stiff and unmoving inside his skin, both parts of him struggling against the realization that he'd been taken for a fool. Memory certainly didn't look under duress in any of these images.

"Renault's business HQ is in San Francisco," Hawke added, folding his arms. "He's a businessman, has fingers in various pies. We haven't dealt with him, but it was worth our while keeping an eye on him."

Alexei stared at the last item on Hawke's phone: a short recording. It had been taken outside a conference center. E. David Renault was talking to the business reporter, while Memory stood only inches away—but around her moved multiple others. Including changelings and humans who would've come to her aid if she'd cried out for help.

Blood hot and his hitherto silent wolf opening its mouth in a snarl, he stalked back to her through the snow that had accumulated overnight. Thrusting the phone under her nose, he said, "You want to convince me again how he's kept you prisoner since childhood?" Not only had she fooled him, but she'd made him *like* her with her stubborn will and her ferocious anger.

Memory stared at the moving images, then glanced up at him. He expected to see fear, panic, desperation. Instead, she snatched the phone from his hand and threw it as far as she could, then—her obsidian eyes shining wet—she shoved at his chest.

He was so startled that he moved back a step.

She kept shoving at him in a wordless rage that was astonishing in a person so small. He felt slapped by the roar of that rage, but beneath the roar was something darker and heavier.

Despair.

It cut through the red of his fury, smashing to pieces

everything he thought he knew. She was an E, he reminded himself, could be using her abilities to manipulate him. But his mind flashed with images of her building the cairn for her beloved pet, the silent tears that had run down her face, the ragged determination of her putting one step after the other as he brought her to safety, the way she'd screamed and refused to surrender to Renault.

His E with a lion's heart was tough down to the bone. To see her brought so low that she'd *lost her voice*, it shook him. He put his arms around her. She continued to shove at his chest, a furious wild creature who wasn't ready to listen, who might not even hear him. Still, he spoke. "You're out of the cage." Harsh, rough words shaped by his anger at himself for doing this to her. "The battles to come are nothing to what you've already survived."

Twisting out of his hold, she put several feet of distance between them. A single moment of piercing eye contact. Her gaze was brown again and it shimmered, rain on a stormy horizon. The sight was a punch to the gut. Then she swallowed hard, fisted her hands, and turned her back to him, her spine stiff as a rod though her chest heaved.

Alexei went to step toward her when Hawke put a hand on his shoulder. "Give her time to calm down," his alpha murmured, the pale ice-blue of his gaze on Alexei's E. "When Sienna gets that mad, I risk having my head torn off if I push."

Alexei forced himself to angle his body toward Hawke. "If she's lying," he gritted out, "I'll cut off my own arm." There had been nothing controlled or manipulative in Memory's reaction. It had been the primal lashing out of a living being pushed to the end of its endurance.

"Tough little thing, isn't she?" Hawke's voice held a faint edge of respect—and coming from an alpha wolf so deadly even the most powerful Psy in the world didn't encroach on his territory, that was a big fucking deal.

"You have to trust my gut on this, Hawke." Shoving a hand through his hair, Alexei willed his claws back in before he scalped himself.

"You're my lieutenant," Hawke said, as if that was an answer.

It was.

Alexei exhaled, his shoulders relaxing. "I don't know what's going on, but I know Memory was in that hole." His eyes shifted to the wolf's vision, his blood like fire. "I found clothes that she'd grown out of—and her cat was ancient. There were signs it had been there for a long time." One sofa arm all but bare of fabric where a feline had used it as a scratching post, the cracked and faded nature of the food and water bowls, the scratches on the kitchen counter that had been weathered and worn down with time.

Alexei didn't think it had been a different cat, not with how broken his E had been by its loss. "Memory had stopped eating when I found her. I just got her started again and now I've fucked it all up." His gut churned. He was a protector; to know he'd caused her such distress? *Fuck.*

Hawke held up his rescued phone. "Your E trusts you enough to get angry with you." His alpha raised an eyebrow. "You think she'd have come at you like that if she didn't know deep down that you wouldn't hurt her? You're a fucking dominant wolf, Lexie, and you were furious with her—but she attacked you."

Alexei thought of how difficult it had been to even take her hand at the beginning, how stiff she'd been, how she'd watched him with eyes that said she was tracking a predator. "Maybe." He glanced over, saw she still had her back to them. "But right now, I'm sure she wants to throw me in a pit of biting insects."

"I can't understand why, with your charming personality."

Alexei narrowed his eyes at his amused alpha. He knew full well he'd been in a growly mood for well over a year, but it was the only way he could function, the only way he could remain a senior member of the pack on whom others could rely. Allowing the anger to fade? It'd leave him wide open to the searing agony of having lost his big brother, sister-in-law, and his chance at mating at the same time.

Never again would a Harte/Vasiliev be born. Alexei would never look into another face and see his own history reflected back.

This was it, the end of the fucking line.

Hawke's phone vibrated. Alexei caught Aden's name on the screen. The call had Hawke frowning—likely because all Trinity contact was generally through DarkRiver alpha Lucas Hunter. "He's probably looking for me." Alexei's phone had vibrated a minute earlier, while he'd been in no mood to talk to anyone who wasn't in this clearing.

"Aden," Hawke said, then nodded. "Hold on, he's with me." He put the call on speaker, listened in silence to what Aden had to tell them.

"On the PsyNet," the leader of the Arrows said, "this empath's mind is unlike any other we've come across. She has the erratic bursts of multicolored energy, but it's like light hitting a vivid dark liquid. Colors in the black."

"Is she a risk to my pack?" Hawke asked.

"Given her catastrophically thin PsyNet shields, she doesn't appear to have any martial training. Her emotions have leaked into the Net multiple times. Unless we discover anything to the contrary, we will treat her as a variant E—of an unidentified subdesignation." A short pause. "Arrows protect empaths."

Alexei's wolf bristled: *he'd* found Memory. The Arrows had no claim to her.

"This E is in my territory," Hawke responded, his voice unbending. "If she's not a threat, we won't harm her. If she's mixed up in something that could hurt SnowDancer, she loses that protection. Are you willing to go to war with us over her?"

"No. You're an ally we trust to make the right call." Given the way the Arrow Squad had silently, dangerously backed empaths, it was a powerful indicator of trust.

Hawke acknowledged it as such before he ended the call a short while later. "So, your E has a unique mind."

"A mirage on obsidian," Alexei murmured, thinking of the way Memory's eyes had changed last night, the depth and the darkness and the surreal beauty of them.

"You're point on this." Ice-blue eyes locked on Memory's distant form. "An E who isn't an E. A prison built on Snow-Dancer land. A captive who was out in the world. None of it lines up. Find the answers."

Alexei gave a short nod, his urge to go to her and offer

comfort nearly overwhelming. "I don't ever want to hurt her again, Hawke." His gut still churned from the memory of her wet eyes, her despair.

Hawke sighed. "I don't like kicking kittens, either, Lexie, but if that's just a front, if she's a Trojan horse sent to weaken us, then we have no choice." His jaw grew hard, his voice grittier. "We lost pups as well as adults in the stealth assault when we were both kids. My father bled out on the snow fighting the impulses the Psy planted inside him. We can't afford to trust her until she proves herself."

Muscles so tense it was almost painful, Alexei stared at Memory's back, willing her to turn. His alpha was right. Alexei had to be rational and cold-eyed about this, no matter how much his wolf was coming to respect his lioness of an E.

Chapter 14

Further photographs of the E with Renault just discovered by the tech team. Attached. My contact in the Net has also unearthed her original adoption papers—stamped by a telepath in the former Council superstructure. The Tp held too much rank to be involved in something this mundane unless he was doing it as a favor. We can't ask him about it though; he suffered an unfortunate accident two months after the adoption went through.

—Message from Judd Lauren to Hawke Snow

MEMORY KNEW THEY were talking about her. She couldn't hear them, but she knew. The wolf with the pale, *pale* blue eyes and hair of silver gold, his presence a pulse of power, could be deadly to Memory. She knew Alexei would follow the dictates of his alpha, even though—as the growling, infuriating wolf himself had pointed out—he'd saved her.

The alpha wolf, however . . . She shivered. He didn't know her except as images on a screen, except as words on a piece of paper. How could she possibly explain to him what it was to be a prisoner who walked the world and yet couldn't cry out for help, could *never* scream?

Today, she threw back her head and screamed up at the sky.

Startled birds flew out of the trees and she knew the two men—as well as the others who waited in the trees—must think she was insane. She didn't care. She *was* a little insane. And she missed Jitterbug. And everything *hurt*.

It didn't hurt when Alexei held you.

She paused, blinked, her breath uneven. She hurt all the time, as if tiny knives stabbed constantly at her skin. But the stabs had stopped when Alexei wrapped her up in his arms. Not just today, but in the night, when he'd tucked her against the hot silk of his bare chest. She was so used to the pain that the idea of a growling wolf banishing it had her shaking her head in mute disagreement.

One of the others she'd sensed in the trees walked out at that instant, a small rucksack on her back. She was of medium height and average build, her blonde hair in a ponytail that brushed her nape; her emotions were calm, without jagged edges, though a familiar wildness prowled under her skin.

Memory turned to watch her come closer.

The woman smiled at the alpha wolf and Alexei, but headed directly to Memory. "I'm Lucy." A cheerful smile. "Nurse from SnowDancer. I'm meant to do a physical, make sure you're healthy and don't have any deficiencies or injuries—but it's your call. Except in emergencies, healers don't go where we're not invited."

Memory's entire body, which had stiffened when Lucy first spoke, now began to relax. She didn't like the idea of a stranger touching her, but she had questions about her health. She'd seen the way Alexei moved, the way Lucy had walked across the snowy field, the way the deadly alpha flowed with predatory grace.

Memory's body didn't function the same, hadn't done so for the past year. She was uncoordinated and imprecise at times, her limbs not obeying the dictates of her mind. She hated the idea that Renault's psychic assaults had permanently damaged her, but she had to know.

"Can we go inside?" The words came out husky, her throat rough from the scream.

"Of course."

Memory led the nurse inside without further words. She was aware of Alexei and the alpha wolf coming to stand in the substation doorway—which they propped open—and knew it was because they didn't trust her with Lucy. It hurt her under her simmering anger at the world, but paradoxically, she was glad of their presence.

She had no way of knowing what Renault had planted in her head. She'd been his puppet for fifteen years. He'd dug

around in her brain as if it were his personal playground—
the only thing that had put any kind of a limit on his inva-
sions had been the risk of permanently injuring her ability.

He needed what she could do. He needed her darkness.

Once inside the bedroom, she cooperated with all of Lucy's tests, even when the other woman asked to take a blood
sample. "I want a copy of your results," she said to Lucy. "I
need to know myself."

"Standard procedure," Lucy assured her, taking the blood
sample with gentle competence. "Just so you know, changeling healers kind of sit outside the power structure of a pack."
She put the sample away in a special case. "We don't get
involved in politics and we ignore the rules, except when it
comes to the safety of the pack. Our priority is the patient."

Memory wondered if she'd fall under the single caveat.
Would her blood show a risk to the pack? She couldn't see
how. Renault's abuses and manipulations had been mental.
It was her own private darkness that lived in her blood, a
secret ugliness she could never expose to the world.

"Done." After putting away her tools, Lucy opened up
another compartment in her rucksack. "You're underweight
and slightly malnourished, but not enough for it to be dangerous. Especially if I get you on a replacement routine." She
passed over a small, sealed box. "One sachet into a glass of
water, mix, and drink with every meal."

The box had the markings of a commercial health firm
and appeared to be nothing but a potent mix of vitamins and
minerals. "Thank you," she said to this wolf who had been
nothing but kind; her throat felt thick, her eyes hot.

Lucy patted her hand with a firm, comforting touch . . .
and the tiny stabs stopped again. "I'll have our nutritionist
prepare a full meal-plan for you," she said. "Sachets are just
a stopgap."

Mouth dry, Memory held out her hand. Lucy took it as if
it was perfectly normal to have a stranger reach for physical
contact. And the tiny stabs, they stopped again. Lucy maintained the contact while the two of them spoke about pragmatic things such as protein and carbohydrates. "Touch is
important for healing, too," Lucy murmured at the end, the

comment a private one between them. "Wolves go crazy without it. I've heard Es are the same."

Memory broke the contact with a jerking motion. The tiny stabs returned alongside her knowledge that she was no E, didn't deserve this kind of sympathy and care.

Lucy didn't demand that Memory explain her sudden movement. Instead she said, "Do you have any final questions for me?"

Swallowing to wet a dry throat, Memory made herself ask. "The way I move . . ."

"All your reflexes are within the normal range," Lucy said at once. "Our senior healer is going to go over all the data I've collected today, and she'll get in touch with you if there's anything to discuss, but I see no signs of permanent damage." Kind eyes, soft voice. "Have you begun to move better since your rescue?"

"Yes, a little."

"That's an excellent sign. No M-Psy will tell you this, but the body and the soul are as deeply connected as the body and the mind." She closed her hand over Memory's again, after first catching Memory's eye in a silent request for permission that Memory couldn't withhold, not with a wolf so intensely kind that it was a song in the air around her. "It might be that the way you move was a subconscious rebellion against your captor—to make things harder for him."

Memory's eyes widened. She'd never considered that, and yet it made perfect sense that her trapped body had rebelled in the only way left to it. "Oh."

"It could also be that you have a psychic injury I can't detect," Lucy cautioned, "but again, the fact you're improving tells me it's not a deep one." She squeezed Memory's hand. "You're not alone anymore, Memory. We'll help you heal."

Memory blinked rapidly, the heat in her eyes too much. She wanted to hug Lucy's promise close, just wallow in it, but she knew the nurse couldn't have any idea of all the factors in play. The alpha believed Memory had faked being a prisoner, that she was in league with Renault.

Alexei believed that, too.

Memory's skin burned with a renewed burst of fury. She didn't know why he'd held her then, why he'd rumbled words to her she hadn't heard through the angry, hopeless, desolate haze in her head. Renault had shut every door in her face, stolen her freedom even though she'd left the cage.

No one would ever believe her, ever offer her a sanctuary where she could get strong enough to end the bastard forever. She'd wind up facing Renault weak and ragged. Memory gritted her teeth. If that was what it came to, she'd make a bomb and hide it in her clothes, take them both out in a single blast. At least it would save his future victims.

"Memory." Lucy's voice was breathless.

Realizing what she'd done, Memory throttled her violent emotions. Her blood was cold. Lucy would hate her now. "I'm so sor—"

"Hush." Leaning in, the other woman gave her a firm hug. "Stretch out your claws, find your power," she whispered in Memory's ear before she rose to her feet and picked up her rucksack.

Memory followed the nurse out of the bedroom. Lucy went to Hawke. Memory watched the alpha put one arm around her shoulders before the two of them stepped out of the substation.

Alexei met Memory's gaze, a scowl darkening his face. "I can't take you to our den."

She'd known it was coming, but the proclamation still punched all the air out of her. If she wasn't welcome in SnowDancer territory, then she'd never again see him once he drove her out of wolf lands. And no, she *wouldn't* miss him; even she wasn't crazy enough to miss a golden wolf stuck in growl mode.

Her fingers curled into her palms, her nails cutting into her skin.

She wouldn't cry. She *wouldn't*! Despite the fact she had nowhere to go, knew no one in the world. The only person who'd have taken her in was long dead, the last image she had of her mother the horrific one of her body discarded on the hardwood floor of a small home on the outskirts of Carson City, Nevada.

"Fine," she snapped, because she would not beg. All she had left was her pride.

"Simmer down, lioness—save the death stare for when I really annoy you." The damn provoking wolf put his hands on his hips while she decided she'd put *two* tiny, biting insects on him. "The pack needs to figure out if you're a threat, and you need to learn psychic control before you push a bunch of wolves into a bloodbath."

Memory's stomach fell. "I could do that?" Another horrible "gift" to add to her psychopathic résumé.

"Chances are that SnowDancer wolves are disciplined enough to grit their teeth and release the aggression in another way, but yeah, you could push deadly buttons in less well-trained predators." A ring of amber appeared around the gray of his irises. "You look like you've swallowed acid—lot of people would love that type of power."

Memory stared at him, aghast.

His lips curved into a slow smile that made things inside her curl and uncurl even as she tried to work out why they were still talking if she was being ejected from wolf territory.

"I figured as much," he said, so smug she wanted to tumble him to the ground and teach him not to taunt her.

As if he'd heard her thoughts, his smile grew deeper. "You're an E under the ferocious roar and the evil plans with tiny insects." A dark look on those last words. "That's why you need to go to the compound."

"What are you talking about, you infuriating wolf?" It came out belligerent.

"The Arrows got permission from us wolves—and from the DarkRiver leopards—to set up an empathic training area in a spot along the leopard-wolf border." He prowled closer, all heat and confidence and a physicality that compelled her to watch. "A cardinal empath will be waiting to assess you, offer you initial help."

Memory stood her ground in the face of his push into her personal space—she understood a wolfish challenge when she saw it. It severely irritated her, however, that she had to tip back her head to continue to hold the aggressive eye contact. "Sascha Duncan?" No one with access to the comm could have avoided hearing about the cardinal's defection. Not only was Sascha a cardinal, part of the most powerful and rare group of Psy in the world, she was the daughter of a *Councilor*.

Yet she'd dropped out of the PsyNet to mate with an alpha leopard—and had survived the disconnection.

"Yes," Alexei confirmed, his energy wrapping around her like a wolf's fur. As his arms had wrapped around her earlier.

She hungered for another taste of that wild warmth, the muscled heat of him making her feel like a cat herself. But asking to be held was outside her vocabulary, and it was a foolish thought anyway. She knew how she would end. In blood. Spiraling down into an abyss tenanted by monsters.

It was her oh-so-special "talent," the thing that made her irresistible to Renault.

The "psychopath whisperer," that was Memory.

Chapter 15

Pack is built on the bonds of family, of mating, of love.
—Hawke Snow

SIENNA STOOD HIDDEN in the trees that edged the clearing. Beside her stood multiple other packmates, all in wolf form. Everyone who'd been briefed on the discovery of the bunker knew the memories it'd awaken for Hawke, the pain it'd make fresh. So half of them had followed him up here, though he hadn't asked. The other half would protect the den so Hawke could do this without worry about their vulnerable.

This was what it meant to be pack. Even their alpha never had to walk alone.

As Sienna and the wolves watched, Lucy put down her rucksack by the rugged and dusty all-wheel-drive SUV in which she and Sienna had driven up. "I'm going to run down," the nurse told Alexei, her skin shimmering with the moisture deposited by rain so fine it was mist. "Tie the rucksack onto me once I've shifted. I want to make sure Lara gets the samples ASAP."

The young woman stripped with the cheerful nonchalance of changelings, put her clothing in the back of the SUV, then shifted. Light shattered the mist, and soon a sleek dark-gray wolf stood in place of the lithe young woman with a healer's hands. As she shook her pelt to settle it in place, the E who'd just circled the vehicle to get to the passenger side froze, her eyes on the wolf.

Sienna examined the woman with care. Her brother,
Toby, had a secondary empathic ability, and she'd been
around Sascha enough that she knew how Es *felt*. This
woman . . . there was something both familiar and unfamiliar about her. Sienna was predisposed to like her for
being a survivor. She'd been caged once, knew what it took
to come out of it unbroken. But that the E didn't feel like any
E Sienna knew, it gave her pause.

"That's Lucy," Alexei told the E, an amused glint to his
eyes that had Sienna switching focus. The young lieutenant
had kissed her in front of Hawke at her mating ceremony, all
teasing charm and gorgeous smile. Later that same night,
he'd stolen her from her mate and swung her into a wicked
dance.

All of it in play, in happiness for his alpha.

That Alexei had disappeared the day Brodie went rogue,
the day Alexei lost the last living member of his immediate
family. This was the first time Sienna had seen even a hint of
the dangerous but playful Alexei she'd just begun to know
before it all went to hell.

The woman with the vivacious burst of curls she'd tried
to corral with two hair ties gave him a look so suspicious that
the wolf beside Sienna opened its mouth in a predator's
laugh. "Lucy?" she asked the wolf afterward, in the careful
tone of someone who thought they were the butt of a joke.

Padding over, Lucy brushed her body against the E's legs.
Her eyes widened, her lips parting on a soft gasp. "Lucy,
you're a wolf!"

Lucy bowed her back, legs out, before rising into a standing position so Alexei could tie her rucksack on her. Designed
for wolves—in both forms—it came with the necessary
straps. While he did that, the empath walked around both
Alexei and Lucy, her wonder a soft wave in the air.

As if she were a pebble thrown in a lake, ripples circling
out around her.

Crouching down, Sienna ran her hand over the nearest
packmate's fur. "She's broadcasting again and unaware of
it," she murmured. "It's not a dangerous emotion." If anything, the sheer innocence of it made her want to smile.

The wolves around her nodded.

"There." Alexei scratched Lucy behind her ear in that one spot no wolf could seem to reach for themselves. "Good running."

Lucy loped off into the trees. The E with a face that hid nothing—the E who had the ability to crack the shell Alexei had put around himself—watched after her until she disappeared from sight. She exhaled, one hand on her upper chest.

"Come on, lioness." Alexei opened the passenger-side door. "Let's get you to the compound."

The two left soon afterward, Alexei taking the vehicle into hover mode.

As the sound of the SUV faded into the distance, Sienna looked to where her mate stood under the haze of the silent rain. Hawke held out a hand.

Stepping out, she met him in the middle of the field. "Hey, you."

She touched her free hand to his jaw. His skin was bristled, his eyes wolf. His irises were an unusual pale blue in either form, but she knew her mate, knew it was the wolf who was riding ascendant today. The rain fell soft and cold on them, but she made no move to get under cover. Hawke needed to be outside, in the wild.

One hand closing around the back of her neck, he lowered his mouth to her own. His kiss, it was fire and it was the wild, and it was home. She sank into it, into him, into the heat and the strength and the trust. Hawke could rip out her throat and she could turn this entire forest into blazing death, but together, she and her wolf were one.

When the kiss ended, she rose up on tiptoe and bit at his lower lip. He growled at her, while a primal "kiss" came through their mating bond. She smiled and kissed his jaw. And knew they'd be okay, even as they walked back into the nightmare that had made Hawke an orphan. The Psy scientists might've only experimented on Hawke's father, but they'd destroyed his mother exactly as if they'd taken a psychic hammer to Aren Snow's mind.

The two of them began to walk through the whispering

rain. Wolves flowed out of the trees to surround them, large and strong and changeling. Then came the smaller wild wolves, flanking their more powerful brethren. Yet those brethren parted for the wild wolf alpha. That alpha came to take his place by Hawke's side, and the three of them led their packmates through the snow and into the past.

Chapter 16

Silence is our only solution for a lasting peace. Our people
are going mad, killing themselves and each other with
murderous rage. We must embrace a world without
emotion, a world of perfect rationality and razor-sharp
psychic discipline. We must embrace the Silence Protocol.
          —The Psy Council (1979)

MEMORY HAD NEVER been around so much green, the
trees giants that soared to the heavy gray sky, their tips
frosted a wintry white. Space and freedom and *air*, no hard
edges, no traffic noise, no mass of humanity crushing her
with their emotions. "Renault only ever took me into cities,"
she found herself saying.

"You want to talk now? I thought I was being ignored,"
said the golden wolf in the driver's seat. "I've never been
ignored by a short-tempered lioness before."

Her sense of melancholy stood no chance against her renewed surge of irritation. "*Three* biting insects."

"Mean, mean Memory." A shake of his head that made
the damp strands of his hair slide forward. Shoving them
back with one hand, he said, "Tell me what this Renault asshole did to make you cooperative in public."

A scream building up inside her, Memory leaned her
head against the window and watched the tiny droplets of
rain settle against the windshield. The gloom of the world
suited her; she was no creature of light. "It doesn't matter
what I say. You won't believe me."

A growl filled the vehicle, a loud and primal sound that
rubbed against her skin like sandpaper but didn't hurt.
"Try me."

"Stop growling at me." She folded her arms across her chest and, lifting her head away from the window, glared at him. "It's rude."

He snapped his teeth at her.

Ugh. Wolves. Except she didn't want to scream anymore and could talk about the horror. Not that she would tell the aggravating wolf that; he'd take it as encouragement to keep on being a provoking demon.

"At first, when I was young, he controlled me with fear." Memory had only achieved Level 3 beginner status in Silence at the time of her mother's murder—she'd been behind her age group and in remedial Silence lessons after school. Ironically the very lessons from which her mother had picked her up that last fateful day before Memory's world ended. Whatever fragments of Silence she'd attained, she'd lost it all in the hallway where her mother gasped her last, frantic breaths.

Emotion had become her enemy and her leash.

"He couldn't threaten anyone I loved, because I had no one left."

"Your father?"

"It was a standard fertilization agreement, done for a fee." Psy took genetic lines seriously, and while Memory would always have access to her paternal line's medical and genetic information to ensure her health—and to keep her own genetic history unbroken—that was the extent of their contact.

"Neither my mother nor my paternal donor wanted a joint-parenting agreement. It was a strictly transactional relationship." Old enough to understand how Psy agreements worked, Memory had never expected her father to come for her. "It was worse because Renault blanketed my mind with his own soon after my abduction, cutting me off from the PsyNet. It felt like no one else even knew I existed." She'd felt *so* alone.

Alexei's hands tightened on the steering wheel. "So who did the fucker threaten?"

"Other little girls and their mothers. He'd show me pictures of them and say he'd do the same things to them that he'd done to me and my mother. Only he'd mete out more torture, cause so much pain that they'd beg for death."

Alexei was growling again, deep in his chest, but when she looked at his face, she saw that his eyes were yet human-gray. "Bastard." His free hand was suddenly on her nape, a rough warmth, while he maneuvered the vehicle with his other hand. "He knew an empath couldn't bear to cause pain to others."

Memory's mouth dried even as the stabbing pains retreated from her body to be replaced by a thick, honeyed warmth she didn't understand.

You're not an empath. You're a nightmare.

Renault had taunted her many a time, and she wasn't foolish enough to believe he hadn't lied at least half those times. But in this, he was right. From everything she'd seen on the news media, empaths healed emotional hurts and helped soothe ravaged minds. They were the counselors who could see into your soul, the healers who walked into the darkest valleys of the mind and pulled people out by the hand.

Memory didn't do that. Memory did something altogether different. Something horrible and ugly.

"What about when you got older?" Alexei continued to grip her nape, and for some reason, his rough touch felt infinitely better than Lucy's gentle hold.

"I physically couldn't ask for help." Bile burned Memory's throat. "He was inside my mind by then, moving me like a puppet."

Returning his hand to the wheel to maneuver them around a narrow and tight bend, Alexei scowled. "Current data we have says long-term mind control is nearly impossible because of the toll it takes on the controller—it literally sucks them dry."

Memory wanted to haul his hand back to her nape and tell him not to move it until she gave him permission. Clenching her abdomen against the urge, she told herself to get the tactile need under control before she became as much a junkie as Renault. "I'm a special case," she said, staring out the windshield as the tiny stabbing pains began to return limb by limb.

"Yeah?" A glance she felt. "Why?"

"I don't want to talk about that anymore." The memories of how Renault had violated her, how he'd dragged her down into the abyss, made her so angry she could barely think. To her surprise, Alexei let her be. For a growly wolf, he could be very quiet when he wanted. "Empaths don't want to kill, don't want to murder," she blurted out, her gaze on the rain-drenched landscape. "They don't fantasize about torturing annoying people with tiny insects."

A shrug of those muscled shoulders that she caught with her peripheral vision. "I dunno. Sascha scrambled the brains of the idiots who tried to come after her cub."

Memory sat up straight in her seat, angling her body so she could see his profile. "Did she truly?" Her heart raced, her lungs aching with withheld air.

A nod. "Fuckers wanted to abduct her baby. She threw them into a nightmare. Served them right."

Memory's mother had fought for her and Diana Aven-Rose had been an inmate of Silence. Sascha had rejected Silence on her defection. *Of course* she would fight relentlessly for her child. "I never heard about this on the comm."

"Not sure it was covered widely. Cats and the locals took care of the aftermath pretty fast. Couple of SnowDancers responded, too, along with several other allies." He shoved away a strand of hair that was threatening to fall into his eye. "I need a damn haircut."

"Don't." The word spilled out of her lips before she could stop herself.

A quick glance, both eyebrows raised.

Cheeks heating, Memory muttered, "It's beautiful, even if you are a bad-tempered growler."

His lips curved, the openly smug smile unexpected and devastating. "Tell you what," he said, "you let me play with your curls and I'll let you pet any part of me you like. Exchange of skin privileges. Fair and square."

Skin privileges.

Memory shaped the term inside her head, tried to understand its meaning. But she kept getting caught on one indigestible fact. "My hair is a matted nest." Renault had used his hold on her mind to force her to straighten it each time they went out, ostensibly so that she'd have the appropriate "look" as his aide, but Memory knew it'd had more to do with control and humiliation. She'd been aware and conscious while he forced her to erase a part of herself, her body a marionette and her mind caged.

"You know what hair goop you need?" As he spoke, Alexei pushed something on the dash that changed the vehicle from hoverdrive to wheels.

The SUV touched the rutted track that had appeared in the trees, the jolt that rocked up her body a pleasant reminder that she was no longer in a cage. "Yes," she said, though she'd never actually used any of the conditioners or creams; Renault had refused to supply them for her after she saw ads on the comm and asked.

In the only rebellion left to her, she'd deliberately allowed her hair to go wild the instant he was no longer forcing his mind on her own. She'd done zero maintenance on it. It had always taken hours to straighten it when he wanted her to perform, and she'd resisted him every inch of the way. It hadn't stopped him—he'd had her since she was eight years old, the pathways he'd laid inside her mind permanent tracks he could access with only minor physical contact.

But it had mattered to her that she fight.

"Here." Alexei pulled out his phone, brought up a note-taking program. "Make a list of what you need. I'll make sure you get it. Clothes and shoes, too."

Memory's hand clenched around the phone, her throat threatening to go tight. Lowering her head to hide her response, she began to make the list. It didn't take long. She'd learned to live with the bare minimum—Renault had only given her enough that she remained useful, nothing else.

"Done already?" Alexei frowned as he took a quick look at her list before returning his attention to the track. "You need to add a coat, thermal socks, and boots, for starters. It gets cold here." A rumble in his chest. "What happened to the suits you wore in the photos? I didn't see them in your wardrobe."

Memory allowed herself a small, satisfied smile. "Renault kept them in a special closet in his home after coming to get me once and finding I'd shredded every one of the suits to pieces." Her captor hadn't ever allowed her access to sharp knives or scissors, but she'd found ways to destroy the clothing. Jitterbug had assisted with glee. "I imagined it was him I was tearing into pieces."

"Bloodthirsty." Alexei smiled, and it was more than a little feral. "I like it."

Of course he did; he was a wolf.

Wondering if he looked like Lucy when he shifted, she added the coat, socks, and boots to her list. Otherwise, she'd asked for a particular hair product she'd seen advertised, a pair of jeans, underwear, and a shirt. "Should I request more clothing?"

"I'll get you a datapad so you can look at catalogs online and choose stuff you like. Phone, too, so you always have access to help."

A crushing pressure in her chest. "I'll be in too much debt." Even the small amount incurred by the clothing and the hair product edged her into breathlessness.

Alexei brought the vehicle to a stop and gave her a long, penetrating look. "You don't like the idea of debt?"

"A debt gives a person power over you."

Piercing gray eyes held hers. "In that case, SnowDancer or I won't pay for anything. It'll come out of the fund set up by the Empathic Collective, with backing by the Ruling Coalition of the Psy."

He tapped a finger on the steering wheel. "Fund was created to aid Es who come out of Silence without a supportive family network. Hawke's already told Ivy Jane Zen about you, and she'll make sure you're assigned the stipend."

Ivy Jane Zen was the president of the Empathic Collective.

Stomach lurching, Memory parted her lips to interrupt, but Alexei hadn't finished.

"It's a generous amount," he said, "but that's because the Coalition's going to try to press you into service as soon as you have the necessary training. PsyNet's coming apart at the seams and that Honeycomb thing the Es have created is apparently the only thing holding it together."

Memory's mind glowed with images of the golden threads she'd seen weaving across the blackness of the

PsyNet. "If I don't want to serve?" She'd be exposed as a fraud the instant she was assessed by a senior E, but she could live the dream a moment longer—dreams didn't ever come true for her, so what was the harm?

"Empaths heal the PsyNet simply by existing, so they'll get their pound of flesh." Alexei opened his door. "We walk the rest of the way. Rain's stopped, so you won't get wet again."

The air was cold and crisp in her lungs, the ground beneath her feet wonderfully uneven, and the *green*, so much green. The snow had faded the lower they came down the mountain, and though it was still apparent in patches at this elevation, spring had also begun to whisper its oncoming arrival here. She could imagine Jitterbug pouncing after an out-of-reach butterfly, or prowling through the underbrush like a tiny leopard.

Sadness enclosed her in heavy wings, her heart aching; she wondered for the millionth time if she'd done the right thing in taking another living being into her cage. Her only excuse was excruciating loneliness—and oh, how she'd loved him. She'd even cooperated with Renault at times so he'd take Jitterbug into the world, too.

Her captor had agreed because it meant he didn't have to waste psychic energy on forcing her actions. Not that she'd ever been free—he'd always had fingers in her mind, ready to clamp down if she stepped out of line.

Four times during those outings, she'd tried to set her pet free.

Jitterbug had always come back to her. Once, while he'd been exploring a large public square outside the meeting location, Renault had teleported Memory home. She'd cried in the chill emptiness of the bunker, but it had helped her to know that Jitterbug was free. Then Renault had taken her back to the same general area two days later, and her pet had found her. Jitterbug had remonstrated with her volubly and audibly and she'd never again tried to leave him behind.

The reminder of her pet's loyalty leavened some of her guilt, but it could do nothing for her grief.

A rough-skinned hand brushed her own.

Not taking. Asking.

Breath a knot in her lungs, she didn't look at Alexei as she slid her fingers into his, let his bigger hand engulf hers. *Skin privileges.* Hers for a short while longer . . . before the true Es discovered that she was an abomination.

Chapter 17

All historical records retrieved[1] to date support the Ruling Coalition's hypothesis that the PsyNet was never meant to contain only Psy minds. In the pre-Silence period, humans—via relationships with Psy—made up at least twenty-five percent[2] of the Net population. As all indications are that human minds cannot access the PsyNet and Psy cannot access Net-connected human minds, the humans were a passive element of the pre-Silence PsyNet.

[1] *Majority of retrieved documents are partials, resurrected then organized into coherent order.*

[2] *Conservative estimate.*
                                  —Research Group Alpha-Z, PsyNet Health

NIGHT CLOAKED MOSCOW. Kaleb stood on the edge of the terrace, his body clad only in the lightweight black pants he wore while exercising and his mind on the new damage in the PsyNet. The disintegration was increasing at multiple critical junctures, the Honeycomb strained.

"There are a lot of us Es," Ivy Jane Zen had told the other members of the Ruling Coalition an hour earlier, "but it's clear we were never meant to hold the entire PsyNet together on our own."

No, the Es were meant to *connect* the PsyNet, much like the nervous system of a living entity, so that it could live and breathe. Below that was meant to be a solid foundation, thick with muscle and bone, not a ragged and thin skeleton with an increasing number of repaired fractures.

Slender arms slid around his waist, the charm bracelet on

Sahara's wrist falling down her forearm a little as she pressed the side of her face into his back. Closing a hand over one of hers, he lifted her palm to his mouth for a kiss. "Any solutions?" She'd been on a comm conference with the Empathic Collective when he walked out here forty minutes ago.

A shake of her head. "We just don't know enough—the post-Silence Councils did a stellar job of destroying data that didn't fit the Silence worldview." Moving around to face him, she let him wrap his arm around her waist, her hair tumbling down her back. "Is Bo willing to work with us?"

"Yes." While Kaleb was the one who'd approached Bowen Knight, he'd never truly expected the security chief and effective leader of the Human Alliance to agree to offer any aid.

Humans, with their weak mental shields, had no reason or motive to help the Psy race survive—Knight himself had made it clear that he'd seen too many examples of mental rape and telepathic theft firsthand to look at Kaleb's race with anything but suspicion. But he was also a man with a soul. He wasn't willing to stand by and watch millions of innocent Psy perish in a PsyNet collapse.

Kaleb had never been certain he had a soul, but he'd never once taken a human mind. So perhaps he did have some semblance of one. Perhaps. "Knight's sent out a missive asking for volunteers willing to interact with Psy."

"It would take incredible trust." Sahara leaned into him.

"The Psy are to be empaths. Es are the only Psy that humans trust even a fraction."

Strands of Sahara's hair danced on the quiet wind. "The other thing?" she asked, the dark blue of her irises awash in hope.

"Signs of limited success." Bowen Knight had asked Kaleb to find a solution to the problem of human shields; Kaleb had responded by assembling a team of the PsyNet's brightest minds to work on the task. "Ashaya and Amara Aleine have the deepest knowledge on the topic, but they've deliberately sequestered themselves from the wider research group. Data in but not out."

"To stop unconscious bias?"

Kaleb nodded. The Aleines had created a prototype implant that had come tantalizingly close to success before failing; the twin scientists had no desire to accidentally stifle new lines of inquiry by presenting the PsyNet team with their already discovered pathway. "The Aleines have also managed to convince Samuel Rain to put his mind to the problem." Another brilliant scientist, albeit one who thought in strange patterns.

It might be exactly what they needed.

Sahara was quiet for a long moment before she spoke. "Do we have time, Kaleb?" A solemn question. "Bo's decision to ask for volunteers when we haven't been able to uphold our end of the bargain is an act of enormous compassion . . . but bonds take time to form."

And bonds strong enough to pull a human into the PsyNet would take even longer. "No," he said, because lying to Sahara wasn't something he did. "The PsyNet is failing at a catastrophic rate. Unless thousands of humans fall in love with thousands of Psy within the next twelve months, it will collapse."

Chapter 18

My daughter is a failed cardinal with delusions of grandeur. There is no such designation as E.
                    —Nikita Duncan to news media at the time of
                    Sascha Duncan's defection from the PsyNet (2079)

TWO HOURS AFTER arriving at the empathic compound, and ten minutes after eating lunch, Memory sat at a small table inside a neat little cabin. Outside, the rain had returned and become a downpour, and across from her sat a woman with eyes of cardinal starlight that tilted up a little at the corners, and skin of a dark honey brown, her black hair in a single braid.

Memory thanked the skies all over again that the rain had begun coming down hard right before she and Alexei walked into the compound. It meant no one but the Arrow guards had seen her as they ran across to the cabin Alexei said had been assigned to her. The small period of dampness while her clothes dried off in the warmth of the cabin had been worth it. She didn't want to meet the others here while dressed in ill-fitting sweats, with her badly snarled and uncared-for hair in two frizzy knots on either side of her head.

It was bad enough that Sascha was seeing her this way.

Warmth emanated from the other woman, the sense of her as deeply kind and unthreatening as Lucy, but Memory was glad Alexei was leaning up against the wall next to her all the same. He was far deadlier than Sascha, a provoking wolf on top of it . . . yet she couldn't help but remember how he'd held her hand, lent her his strength as she walked into an unknown situation.

"Did you really hurt people who came after your cub?" The question burst out of her.

Sascha's facial muscles tightened. "Yes," she said. "I'd do it again in the same circumstances, but it's difficult to know that about myself—that I have the capacity for such violence."

That was the fundamental difference between the two of them. Memory took great pleasure in imagining tearing Renault limb from limb. All at once, she knew she was being foolish in attempting to delay the inevitable—there was no way she could ever dupe Sascha. The cardinal's power was a hum in the air, an electric sensation against her skin.

Her shoulders slumped. "I'm not an empath," she whispered, speaking as much to the golden wolf who'd rescued her as to Sascha. "I'm sorry."

"Sure, lioness," drawled the aggravating wolf. "I must've imagined the ferocity of your roar."

Memory gripped the edge of the table. "Four," she said very precisely.

And the wolf laughed, filling the air with a wild humor that made her want to turn, watch him. Alexei was beautiful when he laughed, his eyes bright with light and his entire body a thing of passionate life.

Lips curving, Sascha tilted her head to the side. "My friends in the PsyNet tell me your mind expresses itself in a unique way, but there is no doubt you're one of us."

Memory shook her head. "I'm not." It came out hard and rough, she wanted so desperately for what Sascha said to be true. "Empaths heal. I . . . I can't do that." Her gut churned. "I'm not like you."

Not responding in words, Sascha held out her hand, palm up. Another invitation. Except that making contact with an empath was a dangerous risk—catastrophically so when the empath was Sascha Duncan. The cardinal would no doubt discover the heavy darkness that lived at the core of Memory's nature, the abyss she could never escape.

But what was her other choice? Memory couldn't go after

Renault with her mind wide open. She needed to learn how to shield, how to re-create the protective shell he'd systematically destroyed. Perhaps, if she cooperated, Sascha would teach her the basics before the Empathic Collective kicked her out of this compound.

"It's all right." Alexei's hand brushing her nape. "Sascha doesn't bite."

Wishing he'd maintain the contact but not knowing how to ask, Memory placed her palm over Sascha's. She was braced for a psychic intrusion, but Sascha simply closed her fingers over Memory's and said, "Who told you that you weren't an E?" Lines flared out from the corners of her eyes, her voice firm.

"Renault." Memory tried to quiet her racing heart, failed. "But I learned long ago to never take anything he said at face value. He lies so smoothly it's like breathing to him." Her captor also felt nothing as he did it; the only time he came close to experiencing emotion was when he killed, and even that emotion was twisted and wrong and made her feel dirty.

"Yet you believe he was right to deny you the label of empath."

"On the comm," Memory said, her throat dry, "the professors and Psy experts talk about empaths being psychic healers. I don't do that." Her belief was backed up by the rare opportunities she'd had to test her psychic muscles—mostly when Renault had allowed her to be "free," his psychic grip a hovering warning.

Each time, she'd seen a person in distress and reacted without thought, reaching out to try to help them. Each time, she'd failed. As she had with Alexei yesterday, when she'd caught the raw depth of the pain he carried in his powerful body. All she'd succeeded in doing was having him accuse her of trying to pet him.

"Not every E is suitable to be a healer." Sascha's voice was soothing in a way Memory couldn't explain. "Some of our kind work in large corporations, help read the other side in a negotiation." A faint smile. "We have an ongoing ethical discussion about the topic and it can get heated."

Memory wanted to grip on to the lifeline, to lie, discovered that she couldn't. Alexei, Sascha, even the lethal alpha wolf, had made the decision to help her. For no reason but that they were good people. If she kept on lying to them, what did that make her?

A shadow of Renault.

Her neck stiffened, her gut tensing. *Never* would she be Renault's reflection. "I—" She bit her lower lip, trying and failing to find the words to explain what she did. Everything felt too much, her head too full, the scream building again.

Shoving back her chair, she strode to the cabin door and wrenched it open. The wind whistled in, but not the rain, the overhang over the porch a protective barrier. Alexei had told her this cabin was hers for the duration of her training, that she could decorate it how she liked.

The wonder of having a door that she controlled, a place where *others* had to ask for entry, it was the most incredible gift she could imagine. But even as she basked in the joy of it, she'd known she'd be stealing it.

When a large, warm hand closed gently over her nape from behind, she shivered inwardly at the sweep of . . . *something* that wasn't simply a lack of pain. Her heart, it beat faster, her breath caught, and her skin, it grew hot. Her hand clenched on the edge of the doorjamb. "I should go," she said, suddenly afraid of what she might bring to this beautiful green place full of wild creatures. "Renault won't give up, will come here."

Alexei brushed his thumb over her skin, the caress turning her breath shallow. "Don't know if you've noticed, lioness, but we're predators with claws of our own." Words spoken against her ear, his breath hot, intimate. "Stop insulting us by worrying about that coward."

She felt his claws release, brush her skin—but though the hard tips lay against her carotid and jugular, Memory didn't run, didn't panic. Because deadly predator or not, this was the golden wolf who protected her as much as he infuriated her. "I don't want to bring evil here, to this bright, green, clean place."

Another brush of Alexei's thumb over her skin before he retracted his claws. "Sascha darling probably has a story or two to tell you about that."

"I'm going to smack you in a second." Despite the dark

threat, Sascha's tone was exasperated rather than angry. "Or maybe I'll just call you Sexy Lexie."

Alexei's growl made every tiny hair on Memory's body quiver in attention. Turning without dislodging his hold on her nape, she saw that he was scowling at a grinning Sascha, and she wondered why he called the cardinal "darling." Sascha was mated to another man, mother to a cub she adored enough to do violence.

Maybe she'd ask him . . . but first she had to make them understand. "I don't know how to tell you what I do," she said in a voice that broke at the end. "I have to show you." It was hard to breathe, her chest painful. "I need a monster, a murderer who kills for the thrill of it."

Alexei's jaw was a brutal line, his thumb stroking her skin again. "You're free now, Memory. You don't have to consort with bastards like Renault."

"Yes, I do," she whispered, her chest so tight she wondered if it would crack. The ugly darkness was where she walked, nightmares her home ground. "I'm not meant to heal. I'm a monster, too."

Sascha got to her feet and took Memory's hand, as if she hadn't heard anything Memory had just said, the warning she'd tried to give. "Most Es refuse to work with true psychopaths." She made a face. "I feel awful about it, but I can't even get myself to work with Amara and she's not a serial killer. It's just . . ."

The cardinal shivered. "She's better than she was before, has developed a stunted kind of emotional intelligence, but there's such *emptiness* at her core where emotion should be, an endless nothing that drags me under."

"Nothing," Memory whispered, astonished that Sascha had felt it, too. "That's what's inside Renault, too. *Nothing*." She didn't realize she'd moved closer to Alexei until she raised her free hand and fisted it in the back of his T-shirt. He didn't object, his thumb continuing to stroke the side of her neck in rhythmic motions that made her toes curl.

Sascha dropped Memory's hand—but only so she could cup the side of Memory's face. "You're an empath, Memory." No room for discussion in the cardinal's tone, Sascha's lips soft when she pressed them to Memory's forehead. "You appear to be a unique kind of empath, but you *are* one of us. I know—I see you as only another E can."

Memory's lower lip threatened to tremble at the kiss. It reminded her of her mother's gentle hands on her as Diana Aven-Rose helped her put on her coat, or did her hair. "I have to show you," she repeated; the fear of being repudiated would otherwise eat her up from the inside out. "The psychopath has to volunteer. I won't force anyone, not even a monster."

Sascha blew out a breath, her hand still on Memory's cheek. "You're certain you want to do this now?"

"Yes." Her hip and shoulder brushed Alexei's side, his body a furnace.

"Amara's a scientist. She'll probably volunteer out of curiosity—or does it have to be a murderer?" Sascha's brow furrowed, care in the hand she ran over Memory's hair. "I really don't like this, but at least Amara is safe enough if handled correctly."

Memory forced herself to think. "If she has the nothing-ness inside her, then yes, it should work." The howling abyss was the key. "I've only ever done it with a murderer, so I don't know for sure."

Alexei's chest rumbled. "Sascha, I'm not sure this is a good idea. Memory's—"

"—right here!" Spinning out and away so she could face him, she folded her arms across her chest and glared; for some reason, while Sascha's protectiveness made her feel warm and safe, Alexei's made her feral. "Don't talk about me as if I'm a dog you rescued!"

God, she was magnificent. "A dog would have more sense," Alexei said in a snarl. "You want to go party with psychopaths when you're so thin I could pick you up with my little finger." Her neck had felt scarily delicate under his touch, the unruliness of her curls the biggest thing about her.

"I'm doing this," she bit out. "Then I'm going to hunt Renault."

The wolf in Alexei approved of her single-minded need for vengeance. Hell, so did the man. The same wolf was torn by an overwhelming sense of protectiveness toward this sur-vivor who'd refused to allow a monster to destroy her. "With what?" he snarled. "You have claws smaller than a kitten's."

Narrowing her eyes, Memory looked as if she wanted to show him her claws right then and there—probably across his face—but Sascha said, "Both of you. Behave." Stepping forward, she frowned. "We have to figure out logistics—bringing Amara to a compound full of baby empaths isn't a good idea. She'll panic them."

The genuine worry in her tone had Alexei breaking his eye-contact standoff with Memory. "That bad?"

"It's this sense of being sucked into a howling emptiness that gives nothing back." Goose bumps broke out over the cardinal's arms. "I can handle it by gritting my teeth and ignoring my nausea, but untrained Es won't have a chance." She touched the side of Memory's face again, her smile holding the warm affection of an older sister. "Our Memory is far tougher than she looks if she can deal with the sensation without breaking."

Alexei saw Memory's brittle shields fracture at the words and knew he had to go along with this insane plan. It was vitally important to Memory; maybe afterward, the damn E would actually rest. "You talk to Amara, get her agreement. I'll figure out where we can do this."

As expected, Amara Aleine was in favor of being an experimental subject. "I haven't been able to dissect an E, so this will give me an insight into their function," was her unsettling response over the wall comm, her face expressionless. "I will prepare to be probed."

Memory blinked after Sascha ended the conversation. "Is she always that . . ."

"Yes," Alexei heard Sascha say as he moved out to the porch to organize the location of the test. "Her twin has the same genius IQ but only Amara is this way. It's as if her wiring got shorted out at a certain point in her development."

It took Alexei a half hour to get all the pieces in place. In a stroke of luck—if you could term anything connected with Amara "lucky"—the Psy scientist was currently at her twin sister's home in DarkRiver territory. Ashaya Aleine had balls of fucking iron as far as Alexei was concerned—he might be a big tough wolf, but no way would he choose to be alone with Amara under any circumstances. He'd never know when she'd decide he'd look better as a corpse she could cut up and study.

Turned out Ashaya's mate didn't trust Amara, either. "I have multiple packmates prowling around within hearing range of our home," Dorian told him when Alexei touched base with the leopard sentinel. "I've got Keenan with me, too—Ashaya feels better when she knows our son is safely away from Amara." A frustrated sound. "I'd rather she keep her distance from Amara, but that bond of twins . . . Ashaya is incapable of giving up on her."

"That's because your mate has a heart." Quite unlike her twin. "Look, we need a place for a psychic experiment."

After Alexei ran through the details of the proposed experiment, Dorian suggested a small, unused cabin in Dark-River territory. "It's structurally sound but old, and set to come down in the next couple of months. Anyone who uses it as a teleportation lock in the interim will end up in the middle of leopard land. Not healthy for them."

Alexei was dead certain none of this was healthy for Memory, but it was in play now. She was determined to do this. So he would stand watch and make sure she didn't hurt herself in the process. Because despite his decision to be clear-eyed and pragmatic about Memory, his gut kept telling him *she* was the one who needed protection. His damn lioness had no shell, no shield, nothing between her and the ruthless world.

Alexei's claws sliced out.

Chapter 19

My sister is like these trees. Perfect to look at, brilliant in
her design—her brain is flawless, her intellect staggering—
but all it takes to crumble that perfection is a single match.
　　　　　　　　—Ashaya Aleine on her twin, Amara

MEMORY SAT SILENTLY in the front passenger seat as
Alexei drove them to the meeting location. Sascha had taken
the backseat. None of them spoke much on the drive, and
Memory had a feeling it was because of her—she was nervy,
jumpy, all her energy on the surface of her skin. Erratic and
bouncing.

Alexei had told her that the twins would both be present
at the meeting.

"Ashaya can control Amara to a certain extent," Sascha
had added. "It's good she's coming."

Now the cardinal said, "Remember, Memory, Amara
doesn't see empaths as sentient beings. She doesn't really see
anyone but her twin as a person."

Memory put a fisted hand against her stomach. "I understand. I'll take care."

Alexei didn't speak, but she could sense his disagreement
with this entire operation in the aggressive tension humming
through his body. When she looked at the hands he had on
the steering wheel, she half expected to see claws, but his
hands were human—albeit wrapped so tight around the
wheel that the skin was white over bone.

Memory parted her lips. "It has to be done." She didn't
know why she had to poke this particular wolf, but she

couldn't help it. Alexei hadn't said a word since they'd begun the drive, and she hated the implied distance.

When he didn't respond to her comment, she literally poked him in the arm.

His growl filled the air, the look he shot her hot amber. "Keep that up and I *will* bite you." The threat was very calm, very serious, and it caused a strange flutter in the pit of her stomach.

A discreet cough from the backseat reminded Memory they had an audience. Amusement rippled outward from Sascha. Settling back in her seat on the unspoken promise that she'd aggravate Alexei again if that was what it took to breach the wall he seemed to pull around himself at times, Memory stared at the green all around her and imagined leopards prowling within.

"What was that?" She jerked, pressing her nose to the window. "I'm sure I saw a flash of gold and black."

"It'll be pack," Sascha said, as if it was perfectly normal to *actually* see leopards prowling around.

Before Memory could question Sascha further, Alexei brought the vehicle to a stop in front of a small cabin surrounded by fallen pine needles. Another rugged vehicle already sat on the far side of the cabin. Heart thundering and mouth suddenly a desert, she opened her door and stepped out.

She'd just shut the door when a glorious creature of black and gold prowled out of the trees. The leopard went straight to Sascha, pressing its body against her legs. Memory watched wide-eyed as the cardinal leaned down to run her hand over the leopard's fur. "Any problems?"

The leopard shook its head. Then it yawned, showing a whole lot of sharp teeth.

She backed up into Alexei, who'd come around the vehicle to stand behind her. "Don't bite me with your wolf teeth."

A huff of air that she thought might've been a laugh, but when she risked looking away from the leopard to glance up at him, she saw that his expression was closed, unreadable. It made her skin itch for reasons she couldn't name; she just knew she far preferred it when he was growling or scowling at her.

Perhaps she would've poked at his abdomen, simply to see what he'd do, but the first whisper of cold nothingness touched her mind at that instant, chilling her to the bone. Hugging herself, she stared at the old cabin as a battle-weary and bloody gladiator might've looked at the maw from which the lions would be released.

Like that long-ago gladiator, Memory knew that one day, the lion would be too strong and she'd end up a meal.

A hand on her abdomen, the rough warmth of Alexei's body against her back as he held her to him. "Breathe." A gravelly murmur. "Amara doesn't feed on fear, but she picks up on weakness."

As she tried to suck in air, find balance, Sascha and the leopard moved toward the cabin. The leopard curled up on the porch and put its head on its paws, a big cat readying itself for a nap. Sascha glanced over her shoulder at Memory with an encouraging smile before she walked into the cabin.

Memory exhaled, the air coming out ragged. "I have to do this. So you know what I am."

Alexei didn't say a word, but he was a deadly, protective presence at her back as she walked onto the porch. Ignoring her, the leopard raised its head and snarled at Alexei.

He said, "Yeah? Well, your fur looks ratty, you over-grown tomcat."

The leopard, its fur a gleaming and glossy coat, bared its teeth at him. She had a feeling that if she looked back and up at Alexei, he'd be baring his own back. Yet the cat didn't attempt to stop Alexei from entering the cabin with her.

The void of *nothingness* hit her like a cold scream.

Sucking in a breath that was as sharp as broken razors in her lungs, she focused on the woman who sat straight-backed in the wooden chair directly across from the door. She was aware of another woman seated on a threadbare sofa to the right, and of Sascha beside her, but her attention stayed locked on the woman with eyes of light blue-gray, and tightly curled hair of darkest brown pulled away from her face into a precise bun at the back of her head.

Her skin was an intense and rich brown, and Memory

could tell she'd be tall when she stood. She wore a charcoal gray skirt-suit paired with a crisp white shirt, her legs crossed and her feet shod in black heels.

On a purely physical level, she was striking.

But when she spoke, her voice was eerily flat. "You must be Memory. I am your experimental subject, Amara Aleine."

Memory forced herself to step forward to take the chair that sat across from the sofa—after moving it so that she faced Amara. "Thank you for agreeing to this." Her tongue felt numb from the coldness spreading over her.

"I am intrigued to discover what an empath wants with me."

None of the words evidenced emotion—there *was* no emotion in Amara; her intrigue was icily intellectual.

"Most Es tend to give me a wide berth," the disturbing woman added. "I made one empath throw up simply by shaking her hand. I would like to repeat that action to see if it was a one-time incident or has a high chance of recurrence, but no one will volunteer."

Memory's fingers were numb now, too, the nothingness seeping through her like a dark tide. "I'll need to make phys-ical contact to run this experiment."

"Excellent. Do you need to be inside my shields?"

"No." Whatever it was that Memory did, it worked on physical contact. "Sascha, you need to watch." Though her gorge roiled at having another presence in her mind, she lowered her paltry shields when Sascha knocked.

Another, infinitely colder presence immediately at-tempted to enter and was blocked by Sascha.

"*Amara*," said the woman who'd been silent until now, the woman who must be Amara's twin—Memory couldn't af-ford to take her eyes off Amara long enough to check their visual similarity.

Amara shrugged. "I couldn't pass up the opportunity." A flick of her eyes in Sascha's direction. "You're incredibly skilled in shielding."

"Sascha?" A dangerously cool question from Alexei, who stood with his back to the wall beside the open door.

"We're fine," Sascha reassured him before looking to Memory. "Are you ready?"

No, she'd never be ready. "Yes," she said aloud.

Amara held out her hand, the look on her face impossible to describe without using emotional words such as "intrigued" and "fascinated," though Memory knew without a doubt that Amara felt nothing as she or Sascha or Alexei would understand. Where emotions—or the capacity for emotion—would be in another individual was a black hole, a rapacious abyss.

She could sense nothing of the emotional growth Sascha had mentioned.

Memory girded herself to touch the darkness. Renault had never given her a choice; it was difficult to resist a Gradient 8.7 Tk when he wanted you to sit in place so that he could make physical contact.

The only thing resistance had gotten her was severe muscle bruising. Not that it had stopped Memory from fighting. To give up would've been to betray her mother's desperate attempts to save her life.

Diana Aven-Rose had fought to the very end.

So Memory had resisted, again and again. And even as a child, she'd understood instinctively that her freedom hinged on her continued rebellion. Because the instant she decided it'd be easier to cooperate, that would be the end. Even if she walked out of the cage one day, she would do so as Renault's creature. As a result, today was the first time in her life that she'd be entering the abyss by choice.

A deep breath, a slow exhale . . . and she took Amara's hand in her own. The black hole inside the other woman sucked her into a rushing vortex of sheer emptiness. As a child, Memory had screamed when Renault dragged her under, but she hadn't been a child for a long time. She stood rigid in the center of the emptiness as it took and took from her.

Once inside the void, she couldn't stop it from draining her.

She could feel herself shriveling as Amara fed off her, though she knew that in the physical world, her body wouldn't have changed. A little lost weight, but that was it. The sensation of being drunk dry, of having her bones turned to dust, it was an illusion her mind created to make sense of what was happening.

There, the stunted emotional awareness in Amara that Sascha had sensed. It was the merest flicker, and perhaps it was a hopeful thing for Amara's twin, but for Memory, the tiny flicker of warmth only emphasized the rest of Amara's cold psyche. A psyche that was attempting to bleed her to utter emptiness.

Used to gritting her teeth and riding it out, Memory didn't realize the danger until it was too late. After the first time, when Renault put her in a coma from which she'd nearly not emerged, he'd learned to stop the transfer after a strictly defined period. Memory had been too young and far too traumatized to do anything to protect herself. She figured he must have built a mental timer that caused the connection between them to short after a certain interval.

Willpower didn't come into it; the nothingness just wanted to *feed.*

The vortex of Amara's mind was blinding. Sascha had told her the scientist's Gradient level was 9.9. Memory hadn't worried because Amara was an M-Psy, an ability not considered aggressive—medical Psy worked in science, in medicine, in research labs. Only now did she realize the type of ability didn't matter here, only the Gradient level. The nothingness was a violence around her, threatening to erase her psyche.

Pulse racing so fast she thought her heart would burst, she made herself think. She had no psychic defenses . . . but Amara wasn't a telekinetic. Alongside her 9.9 strength as an M-Psy, she had a number of other minor abilities, but none of them were on the Tk spectrum. She couldn't force Memory to sit in place, maintaining physical contact. Amara also hadn't had Memory since she was a child; the other woman had no direct access to Memory's mind.

Memory tried to tear her hand from Amara's grip.

The scientist hung on with vicious strength.

Memory couldn't speak, not while caught in the center of the abyss, but she tried to wrench her hand away from the other woman a second time. Amara's body came up out of the chair as she fought to hold on.

Two large male hands gripped Amara's wrists, breaking the connection with brute force.

Amara sat back down, hard, not even seeming to notice Alexei's looming presence. Her eyes were obsidian and fixed on Memory. "I want to own you," she said breathlessly, then smiled with a brilliant delight that transformed her from striking to stunningly beautiful. "This is *wonderful*."

As Memory shivered, Amara turned toward her twin. Following her gaze, Memory blinked. Her mind took a second to correct the hiccup at seeing two such identical faces in one glance. Ashaya Aleine wore her hair loosely pinned up with combs, curls escaping every which way, but hairstyles aside, the two were indistinguishable.

The same remarkable eyes—shards of blue coming in through the gray to touch the jet-black pupil—the same skin, the same bone structure. Yet Memory would never, ever mistake one for the other. Ashaya Aleine was whole, didn't have the howling nothingness at the core of her soul.

"Amara?" the lovely woman whispered now, her gaze locked on her twin.

Smile lighting up her irises, Amara took her sister's hands in her own. "It's extraordinary," she murmured, her fingers curling over Ashaya's. Both had the blunt-cut nails of scientists, but on the back of Ashaya's left hand was what appeared to be a temporary tattoo of a caped superhero.

"I understand love now," Amara said in a voice that was no longer flat but rich, resonant. "I understand that I love you." She raised one hand to Ashaya's cheek. "The world feels deeper, more intense."

"Amara." A single tear rolled down Ashaya's cheek.

At the same time, Sascha looked to Memory with wide eyes. "How can you say you aren't an empath? I felt what you did, but I don't understand it." Wonder in every shaken word. "Not one of us has ever been able to penetrate Amara's emotional psyche, much less go this deep."

Memory didn't protest when Alexei put his hand, warm and a little rough, around her nape again. She was so cold inside. "Amara." She waited until the other woman turned to face her. "What is the most valuable thing you've gained from this interaction?"

She saw cunning flash in the other woman's eyes. Renault, too, was a terrible liar in the immediate aftermath of a transfer. As if his psychopathic brain got a little drunk and had to take a few minutes to stabilize before it could think with ruthless clarity.

"Remember," she said, "this is an experiment. As a scientist, you agreed to give me factual and correct data."

Sighing, Amara broke physical contact with her sister to sit back in her seat, her hands on the arms. "The scientist in me is suddenly a weakness." Despite her complaint, when she spoke, it was the truth. "I have gained a far subtler understanding of how to manipulate others, and I also find . . . pleasure in the act."

Amara looked at her twin again. "I do feel love for you." Wiping away Ashaya's tears, she shook her head. "I don't deserve your tears, sister-mine." The piercing intimacy of the moment hurt, and Memory had the thought that for this one instant, Amara wasn't attempting to manipulate anyone, least of all her twin.

Then the scientist sat back in her chair, though she continued to direct her words to her sister. "I understand love," she reiterated. "I also understand how I can use that love to control others. I comprehend that I have a hold over you as your twin and that you'd have to be driven to the edge of death before you'd permit me to be executed."

Amara took a deep breath, let it out with a shake of her head. "You feel you must watch over me because I'm damaged in a fundamental way. In a battle between the two of us, I know I'll have the advantage because you have emotions and I do not." A pause. "Well, I do now—but other than that, I remain who I've always been."

"Do you feel the urge to kill?" Memory dug her nails into her own thigh.

Uncrossing her legs before crossing them the opposite way, Amara took time to consider that question. "No," she said at last. "I've never been driven to kill for killing's sake. It's a waste of energy and resources. I have no problem with an experimental subject dying should it be necessary for the success of the experiment, but I am not driven to murder."

Memory's hand flexed out, her shoulders trembling. At least in this, she could forgive herself. She didn't *create* serial killers. "Do you see?" she said to Sascha, as Alexei moved his thumb over her skin in a caress that made her want to curl into him and not emerge for hours.

"I see that you've given Amara emotional depth." The cardinal was frowning, the wonder not yet gone from her voice. "No other E has ever had any success with psychopathic personalities."

"I agree with Sascha," Amara said, putting her hands around her knee and falling into a tone that was cool and pragmatic. "This aspect of my psyche has never before been available to me. You've opened the doorway."

Memory had to find the right question to make Amara reveal the truth. "By walking through that door," she said to this intellectually gifted woman who was inhuman on an elemental level, "do you think you'll become a better person? A person who doesn't believe that it's perfectly acceptable to dissect other individuals in the pursuit of scientific progress? A person who cares if her actions cause pain to others?"

Chapter 20

Twins* are a special case under Silence, the bond between them beyond emotion or a lack of it. Separating them at birth is never recommended. The psychological impact can be catastrophic, and has been known to lead to psychic collapse.

*See Coda 28 for information on triplets, quadruplets, and other multiples.

—Coda 27 to the Silence Protocol

AMARA TILTED HER head slightly to the side, a faint smile on her lips. "You're very intelligent despite your emotion-centered abilities." An edge of what might've been admiration in that smile. "The answer is no. I believe I can become better at faking empathy as a result of our contact, but I am simply an . . . enhanced version of who I was. No changes to the primary core of my personality."

This time when Memory looked at Sascha, she saw dawning comprehension darken the cardinal's expression. "You see," she whispered. "I make them better monsters."

Amara laughed and clapped her hands together. "Is this amusement?" she asked, her eyes dancing. "It is a fascinating emotion."

Flushing, Memory said, "I'm sorry, I shouldn't have called you a monster." It had been an inexcusable lapse on her part—Amara, broken though she was, was no Renault.

Amara waved away her apology. "By any objective measure, I am a monster. An ordinary twin would not have drugged, then buried her claustrophobic sister alive in a shallow grave just to see how she would react when she woke."

A shrug of her shoulders at that horrific statement. "You are also correct in your assessment. If I am a monster, you have made me a better one."

A sob caught in Ashaya's throat. Raising one hand to her mouth, she looked to Memory with bruised eyes identical to Amara's . . . yet so very different. "How long will the effect last?"

Memory frowned, realizing she couldn't use Renault as a measure. Because of how deeply he'd broken into her mind and how long he'd had access to her, the effect lasted far longer in him now than it had back at the start, when he'd first begun to use her. "Given the time we were linked," she said slowly, working through the various factors, "and the strength of Amara's psychic abilities, it'll most probably last three to four hours."

Amara sighed. "I suppose owning you is out of the question," she said with every appearance of seriousness. "I would keep you in a room where I could drink from you at will—I'd feed and water you, of course. Cruelty for its own sake serves no purpose."

"Jesus." Alexei's rough voice, his body coming close enough that her shoulder brushed against him. "It's like you're a drug."

Even though he hadn't spoken to Amara, the scientist nodded. "The effect is very similar to what I've observed in addicts," she confirmed. "Now that I've tasted Memory, I want more. Since I've only had a single hit, however, I should be able to break the compulsion with ease." Those extraordinary eyes locked on Memory. "I would suggest you not allow those like me to drink from you on a long-term basis, or you might find yourself considered prey."

Memory laughed and it held no humor. "Trust me," she said, "I know."

Uncrossing her legs, Amara turned to her sister again. "Since this is a temporary effect," she said, "and you are the most important individual in my existence, I would like to spend the time with you."

Ashaya, face stark and terribly sad, looked once again to Memory. "Once she's back to her normal state, will she be able to use the emotional knowledge she gains while with me in her current state?"

It was a smart question, and one for which Memory had a conclusive answer. "No. The knowledge gained becomes . . . colorless after the effect of the transfer fades. Amara will remember your interactions, but she'll have the same emotional understanding of those interactions as she would've had prior to the transfer."

Memory shaped her words with care, to offer what comfort she could. "To Amara, it will no longer make sense why she chose to spend this time with you rather than, for example, returning to her lab to run tests on herself." That was why Renault had kept Memory all these years; he'd needed the constant renewal to continue his meteoric rise in the business world even as he gained infinitely more pleasure from his murders.

As the fall of Silence had proven, the majority of Psy had never been *emotionless*. Their emotional core had always existed under the frigid weight of the Silence Protocol. It had made them vulnerable to a man with an instinctive and acute understanding of subconscious biases and vulnerabilities.

Renault hadn't possessed that understanding until Memory.

"So," Amara said to her twin, a genuine softness to her that Memory could feel, "it appears that today, we can be sisters, without worry that when the monster returns in all of her terrible glory, it will give her an advantage."

Curling her fingers over her twin's, Ashaya rose to her feet.

Amara came with her.

"Do you need anything more?" Ashaya asked, her voice husky.

Memory's heart ached for this woman who was forever tied to a mirror that was cracked. "If Amara could keep a detailed record of her responses and emotional reactions in the hours to follow, it'll give me further data as I explore my abilities." She made her words logical and unemotional on purpose, because in that contact with Amara, she'd gained a better understanding of how the other woman functioned.

Amara nodded. "I am intrigued myself. I will make thorough notes and send them to you once the effect fades." She held out her free hand as if to shake Memory's, smiled slyly when Memory drew back. "I *do* like this emotion of amusement."

As the two women went to leave the cabin, Memory felt a gentle knock on her mind. A polite request for telepathic contact. Wary, but aware from the "taste" of the contact that this wasn't Amara, she responded with a *Yes?*

I know my sister hasn't somehow been healed, said a voice drenched in a tangle of feelings, *and I accept that underneath it all, she remains as she's always been. But to speak to my twin and have her truly understand—even a little bit—the things that matter to me, it's a gift for which I'll never be able to repay you. Thank you.*

With that, the twins were gone.

Memory wanted to cry—Ashaya's mental presence was as warm and as giving as her sister's was cold and inhuman. Ashaya loved Amara with all of her being while understanding that Amara was incapable of loving her back.

Swallowing the lump in her throat, she rubbed her hands down the front of her thighs. And somehow, she found herself leaning against Alexei's body. He didn't push her away, didn't tell her that she didn't have the right to those skin privileges. He also still had his hand on her nape, but his silence cut at her. Did he think her a monster now?

Then he dropped an energy bar in her lap and growled, "Eat!"

Releasing a breath she hadn't been aware of holding, Memory picked up the bar that was meant to be infused with all types of minerals and vitamins. *Grouchy growly wolf,* she thought as she took a bite, her heart all tight and happy.

It was Sascha who spoke next. Dropping her face into her hands, the cardinal exhaled with force. When she looked up, her eyes were obsidian. "I *refuse* to believe that your ability to reach psychopathic individuals is only so that those individuals can become better psychopaths." A mutinous set to her jaw. "You are a gift, Memory. A remarkable E."

When Sascha held out a hand, Memory didn't hesitate to take it. Not only had the empath only ever been kind,

Memory had the feeling Sascha didn't need physical contact to divine emotions; her power was a storm. How foolish the world had been to believe her a broken cardinal for so many years of her existence.

More empathic cardinals existed now, but Sascha had grown deepest and longest into her power. She had a weight to her psychic presence that was both calming and a little terrifying in its beauty.

"The most pressing concern," Sascha said after closing her fingers over Memory's, "is your lack of shielding." Firm, practical words. "Shields happen to be my specialty and, starting today, we're going to work on building yours. You should've been able to deflect Amara—there's no reason you have to be open to any psychopath who manages to touch you."

Memory's heart thundered.

Careful not to dislodge the warmth of Alexei's hold, she shifted to fully face Sascha. "Renault was always able to get to me, no matter what." Memory had tried again and again to build on the foundations of her childhood lessons on the subject, failed each and every time. "No matter what I managed to construct, he tore through it as if it was tissue paper."

"This man had you since you were a child." Sascha's expression was suddenly fierce, and all at once, Memory could see the deadly cardinal who'd struck out at those who'd targeted her cub. "I spotted bad mental bruising during the time you permitted me in your mind. The good news is that it's begun to heal at the edges—it shows no signs of being a permanent injury."

Memory's hand curled as, beside her, Alexei's body was dangerously motionless. "Is that why my coordination is problematic? When Alexei first found me, I moved much worse than I do now."

"It's possible," Sascha said. "But, given your rapid improvement, it's also possible the coordination issues were a subconscious rebellion on your part." The echo of Lucy's words was welcome, but the cardinal wasn't done. "The bruises are a surface issue. More dangerous is that I believe your captor created back doors in your mind when you were too young to stop him—they'd give him a shortcut through any shields you had."

Alexei curled his hand further around Memory's nape, until his claws touched the front of her throat. "Can you help Memory close those doors?" His voice had a serrated edge, no growl in it, just pure, lethal focus.

Memory didn't ever want Alexei to direct that predator's tone at her.

"We have to find them first." Sascha's words contained nothing of defeat, only grim determination. "Luckily, we have access to an entire squad of Arrows—the squad knows every trick there is to subvert a mind. It means they know the reverse, too."

Memory had gone stiff at the mention of Arrows, her hand clenching on her half-eaten energy bar.

"No one will be digging around in your mind," Sascha said with the acute understanding of an E in full control of her abilities. "Any action taken will be with your full approval and participation." Eyes filled once more with stars caught Memory's, their beauty making her chest ache. "I'm lowering my shields. Look into my mind, see that I would never hurt you."

Memory sucked in a breath. Before she could speak, however, the cardinal dropped her shields. Her power roared out, a tornado that sang with strength that could not be quantified. That was what made a cardinal—they had no ranking on the Gradient.

Gripping the side of her chair, Memory fought to think. "No," she said. "It's all right." She would never violate another mind.

"It isn't a violation if I invite you in," Sascha whispered gently, as if she'd read Memory's thoughts . . . but then an empath didn't need to do that; Memory's untutored emotional responses wrote her thoughts in the sky.

"Come." Sascha smiled. "I welcome you."

Traveling back a lifetime to when she'd last entered another mind—her mother's—Memory reached up to grip Alexei's hand. His claws retracted, his fingers curling firmly around hers. Anchored in his wildness, she took a tiny step beyond Sascha's public mind. It was more than enough to tell her that the cardinal would never consciously cause her harm.

She also felt Sascha's endless love for her little girl, her passion and adoration for her mate, and her complicated emotions toward her mother. Underneath it all lay a deep sense of contentment and belonging, the purest happiness Memory had ever felt.

It was as she was withdrawing that she caught the ghost of a moment. Her cheeks burning, she scrambled out. "Sorry."

Sascha laughed, the sound warm and unabashed. "My fault—I shouldn't have let my thoughts wander." Her eyes danced. "Lucas was in a playful mood this morning."

Memory wanted to press her hands to her cheeks, but Sascha held one, Alexei the other, and she didn't want to give up, either. Especially when Alexei's threat of biting her had just taken on a whole new meaning. Sascha's mate had used his teeth on her this morning, and it'd had nothing to do with punishment or pain. The echo of Sascha's delight shivered along Memory's nerves.

"Thank you for letting me see you." *And for showing me that a male can be a source of pleasure and happiness.* She telepathed the last, embarrassed to have Alexei hear the words.

Sascha's reply was telepathic, too. *I think you've already begun to learn that yourself.* A quick glance toward where Memory held Alexei's hand. *He growls at you and you don't bat an eye, even though he's one of the most lethal wolves in SnowDancer. I've never seen anyone poke Lexie like that.* Her smile deepened. *You're an E, Memory. Trust your instincts about people.*

Chapter 21

Rogues are our curse.
  Words spoken by more than one predatory changeling through the ages. And there is a certain cold truth in it, for nature appears to have no use for these most damaged of our kind.
  — *Changeling Rogues: Broken Minds & Broken Families*
        by Keelie Schaeffer, PhD (Work in Progress)

MEMORY'S BRAIN FELT like noodles. Sascha had made the call to give her the first lesson in shielding then and there at the cabin—trainee empaths might otherwise impinge on her emotions without realizing it. Memory also needed to learn to control her own wild broadcasts.

When Memory had flushed and apologized for her erratic fluctuations, Sascha had shaken her head. "Everyone in the compound is on training wheels. Just remember they don't mean to do it any more than you do."

The idea of being ordinary in that way, just another empath finding her feet, it had made her feel good on the deepest level. Now she sat back in the passenger seat of Alexei's vehicle with her eyes closed, his primal presence wrapped around her, and practiced putting up and pulling down the basic shields Sascha had helped her construct: one to bolster her privacy on the PsyNet, the other to protect her in the everyday world.

"The more times you rebuild," Sascha had said, "the stronger each shield will become. You'll instinctively begin to fill in any holes, patch up any vulnerabilities. We'll practice more complex shields as we carry on, but a strong base shield of each type will give you a solid foundation."

Prior to the lesson in shield mechanics, the cardinal had—with Memory's full agreement—taken a careful look at Memory's mind. She'd linked them telepathically so Memory could follow her footsteps and so Sascha could directly show her the problem areas.

Memory had seen the bruises, seen, too, the healing at the edges. In the aftermath, Sascha had made contact with an M-Psy who worked in the field of Psy brain injuries, and discussed Memory's situation without specifics, while Memory listened in.

"She's a NightStar doctor," Sascha had explained to Memory before making the call. "Faith NightStar is pack. We have access to the NightStar medics through her—and they're world experts in brain trauma."

Memory knew little of the Psy who saw the future, but even she'd heard of NightStar. According to the comm reports she'd seen, its foreseers had the highest rates of accuracy in the world—and Faith NightStar was their violently gifted cardinal. To see the future . . . what did that do to a person? That the famed clan had brain trauma specialists on call was an answer in itself.

This specialist had asked to see a telepathic snapshot of the bruised part of Memory's mind, which Memory had okayed. While Sascha only had telepathy to 3.5 on the Gradient, it had been enough to bounce the scan to the medic, as NightStar had a small base right up against DarkRiver land.

Memory would ask about the politics of it all later. Today, she was simply grateful that the specialist had backed Sascha's call that her brain bruising would heal without any permanent effects.

"Hard day." Alexei's voice vibrated in her bones.

Soaking in the intimate sensation, she lifted her lashes and looked out at the falling night. Time had passed quickly in the cabin. At one point, Alexei had left to bring them food. The leopard outside had stayed, keeping watch while appearing to nap like a giant kitten.

"I feel as if I've traveled a thousand miles in the space of a single day." The Memory who'd entered that cabin was not the Memory who'd left. "Sascha insists I'm an E."

"I guess you'd better get used to being in the Collective—

word is, once you're in, there's no chance of parole." Amusement in the statement. "Es hold on to their people."

"I'm beginning to understand that." Regardless, it'd take her time to process. Going from believing herself a monster to accepting the label of an empath was no easy matter. "Ashaya's so . . . *real*, but Amara . . ."

"Yeah." Alexei shoved his hair off his forehead.

Her attention shifted, snagging on the silky golden strands.

He shot her a highly wolfish look—a highly *Alexei* look. "Remember our deal. No touching unless I can touch back."

Memory's toes curled; she was nearly certain he wasn't just talking about hair. The idea of his rough-skinned hands moving from her nape to lower down her body . . . Her abdomen tensed, the strange, fluttery feeling returning. It almost made her forget the state of her hair.

Lifting her hand to her matted curls, she shook her head. "Not yet."

Alexei jerked a thumb over his shoulder. "I picked up a few things from your list when I went to grab food. No talk of debt, lioness. It's a 'welcome to the territory' gift."

Memory went quiet. No one since her mother had ever just given her something with no expectation of a return. Renault had only fed her so she'd be strong enough to drain. He'd given her access to education only so she could pass for normal when he had use for her in the world. Even Jitterbug's food had a catch attached—Renault had brought it in only so he could use her pet to control her.

Alexei wanted absolutely *nothing* from her in return for the items in the box on the backseat—or for the food he kept giving her. Her heart felt too huge in her chest, her skin not enough to contain it.

"It doesn't hurt to let someone help you," Alexei grumbled, his hand tight on the steering wheel.

Memory wanted to open her mouth, explain to him—but how could she explain her overwhelmed reaction to a wolf who'd grown up surrounded by pack? She'd felt Alexei's intense loyalty to his alpha—and she'd felt the same loyalty coming from the other direction. He could have no comprehension of what it was like to grow up with only a psychopath for company.

He growled into the silence. "I saw you not eating most of your food, by the way." Shoving a hand into his pocket, he dropped another bar in her lap. "Granola. It's good."

Beware of wolves bearing food.

Sascha's amused voice echoed in her mind; the cardinal had made the comment when Alexei returned with their meal. He'd winked and told "Sascha darling" that she was safe. At the time, Memory had taken it to be a wolf-leopard joke, but she was no longer so sure. Narrowing her eyes, she said, "Does it mean something if a wolf brings you food?"

Alexei's eyes gleamed when he shot her a look. "In this case it means I was brought up to look after tiny starving Es who think they're lions."

Gritting her teeth, Memory reached out and poked him in the arm again. He didn't threaten to bite her, just sent her an amber-eyed glance that said her punishment would keep. Her breath caught, her toes curling inside her shoes.

"If you don't like the granola bar," he said after returning his gaze to the forest track, "tell me what you will eat and I'll make sure you have it."

Since the only reason she'd picked at her earlier meal was because it had been too close to her encounter with Amara, her stomach slightly nauseous, she opened the granola bar and took a cautious bite. Her eyes widened at the mix of sweet and salty, richness and nuttiness. Examining the wrapper, she saw it was a flavor called "Salted Caramel Almond."

The wolf in the driver's seat made a pleased rumbling sound in his throat when she devoured half the bar in a matter of seconds. Memory couldn't even be annoyed with him, not when he'd blessed her taste buds with this divine deliciousness. "Do you always have these in your pockets? I'm going to rob you if you do."

A sharp grin that made him beyond beautiful. "Heart-stopping" might be the better description. Memory wanted to sit on his lap and trace that grin with her fingers, just drink it in. Probably he'd bite her if she got her fingers that close to his mouth.

She squeezed her thighs together against a sudden deep ache low in her body.

"I usually grab a couple of different bars from the boxes the kitchen puts out. That's from yesterday. Flavor the day before was peach with dark chocolate, another day it was dried cherries and walnuts."

"Will you bring me more?" she said on a wave of wild joy in this moment with her golden wolf . . . and felt her spine lock. As an adult, she'd made it a point to never ask Renault for anything—it had only ever meant humiliation. Only for Jitterbug had she broken her rule, taken the abuse. But Alexei wasn't Renault.

He said, "If you promise to eat them." A dark look. "No granola bars if you're determined to stay a skin-and-bones lioness."

Memory glared at him. "I'm eating this, aren't I?" She took a big bite for good measure. "And why do you keep comparing me to a lioness? I'm Psy."

"You have the ornery temper and mental roar of a she-lion," Alexei said with a mock wince that earned him another glare. What he didn't add was that she had the heart of some big, wild creature, too; Memory was a survivor, a fighter, and he liked being around her, aggravation and all.

His fingers flexed on the steering wheel on a sudden wave of guilt. How could he grin on today of all days? Brodie had been fucking *executed* a year ago today. Twelve months without his brother and his sister-in-law. Three hundred and sixty-five days since the second-to-last remaining member of his direct paternal line went rogue.

Grandfather. Father. Brother.

Hell of a family history.

Then the E who kept on derailing his thoughts poked him in the biceps again. His wolf growled, wondering if it really should bite her. Just a nip to warn her not to aggravate peaceful wolves. "What?"

"You went into a dark place," was the stark answer. "It's not good for you."

"Empaths," he muttered instead of snapping at her, because snapping at her for sensing his emotions would be like her yelling at him for scenting her fear or pleasure. "Can't even let a man brood in peace."

But Memory, as he'd already learned, had a steel core to her; she wasn't about to be distracted. "What's wrong?"

Alexei's jaw grew hard, as hard as he wished his fucking heart would become. He was ready with a flip answer when he glanced at her and saw that she was holding herself very still, her eyes staring out the rain-splattered windshield with fierce concentration. Though he was no empath, he knew that she expected to be rebuffed, expected to be treated as if she didn't matter.

Fuck that.

"My brother died a year ago today." His blood boiled, his skin hot. "The bastard's in the ground and I can't fucking kick his ass for being gone." He couldn't even bring himself to visit the place where he'd buried Brodie. No marker, no headstone, as was the SnowDancer way, wolves simply returning to the land that was their heart.

Some chose to be scattered on the winds, others to rest forever beneath ancient trees.

Alexei had chosen an outlook above a breathtaking drop Brodie would've loved to rappel down while Etta watched proudly and took photos. Brodie had always shown off for his mate, like a young boy trying to impress a girl. The two of them had been inseparable despite the fact Etta was as calm as Brodie was wild.

Packmates who'd visited the couple's resting spot in spring had told him that tiny flowers had bloomed in the grass. It didn't matter. Alexei knew Brodie wasn't really there in that beautiful place; he hadn't been there since the day he went rogue. Hawke had executed a broken shell, not Alexei's fearless big brother.

And Etta . . . she'd gasped out her wish to be buried with Brodie with her last bloody breath, well aware that her mate would be executed. The pack had no other option. Not when he'd attacked his beloved Etta. Her family had accepted both her choice and Alexei's suggestion of burial site, but she wasn't there, either. Her sweet spirit was long gone.

"It hurts all the time when you lose someone, doesn't it?"

Aged pain in Memory's quiet voice. "It gets old, the pain, but it never stops."

Alexei thought of a tiny girl watching her mother's brutal murder, only to find herself in the hands of the murderer. No time to mourn as she fought to survive and stay sane. No loving arms to rock her when the nightmares hit. Alexei had been so fucking angry after they put Etta and Brodie in the earth, had refused all offers of comfort. Hawke had found him nonetheless, and they'd fought. Tooth and claw and blood. Until Alexei could think past the haze of fury. He couldn't cry, not then, not now, but he was functional again.

"Yeah," he said, brushing his knuckles against her cheek. "It hurts like a bitch."

The slightest movement against his knuckles before he dropped his hand, his E accepting the comfort offered.

"What was it like," she asked, "having a sibling?"

"He was my big brother." A constant presence in Alexei's life. "I never knew what it was like to not have a brother. He was the first person I told all my secrets and dreams." It was Brodie who'd broken their childhood trust, Brodie who hadn't confided in Alexei when the demons began to howl.

"On human comm shows, siblings fight. Did you?"

His lips kicked up. "Not much. Most of the time, I was his loyal minion in many a scheme." A faithful lookout while Brodie tried to climb an out-of-bounds tree, a small helper when Brodie decided to build a catapult to launch himself across a waterfall, a staunch ally when they got caught.

"Brodie was the one who came up with the plans, but we'd make it happen together." Alexei looked back into the sepia-toned past, saw two wild boys running through the trees. "When I got made lieutenant, then assigned to my own den, Brodie packed up and came with me." So Alexei would have family nearby if he ever needed to decompress and not be a lieutenant, just a wolf kicking back.

"You aren't based here?" Memory asked, a tone to her voice he couldn't quite decipher.

Alexei shook his head. "Three-month secondment." Ensuring its senior members rotated every so often to a different section of the territory was part of how SnowDancer kept its sprawling pack united. It was also good for Alexei to ex-

perience what it took to run the large main den at his alpha's
side—should Hawke ever need him to switch dens or temporarily take over for another lieutenant, he'd be ready.

"Brodie would've probably swung by for a visit by now if
he'd been around." Checking up on Alexei, making sure he
was settling in okay to a more senior lieutenant's duties. "He
was a good big brother."

Memory folded up the empty granola bar wrapper and
put it in her pocket. "That's why you're sad and angry. It
wouldn't hurt so much if he'd been a bad one."

"Wise little lioness," he said, because it was all getting
too deep, and soon she'd have him talking about the terrible
history of the Harte/Vasiliev family and what it meant for
Alexei.

Just as well that they arrived at the compound a bare
minute later. The only ones up and around under the wet sky
were the Arrows. "Home sweet home."

Home.

Memory didn't know what that meant anymore.

Light glowed from the windows of the cabins around
Memory's. Inside those cabins were empaths. Memory's
peers. Normal people who hadn't grown up in cages.

Her fingers curled into her palms just as Alexei came
around to open her door. Leaning both arms up against the
top of the car, he looked at her . . . and his eyes, they glowed
slightly in the dark.

"Oh," she whispered, her fingers rising of their own volition.

She jerked them back the instant she realized what she
was about to do, but then Alexei deliberately lowered his
head, just far enough that she could reach. And Memory
found that she was weak where a certain golden wolf was
concerned. Heart tight, she ran her fingers through the heavy
silk of his hair.

It was cool from the misty rain and slipped like water
through her fingers. She didn't stop with one stroke, caressing him in the same way Sascha had caressed her mate that
morning. "I like petting you," she said, because hiding it was
impossible.

When he made a rumbling sound in his chest, she found

herself exerting more pressure, and running her nails along his skull. The eyes that met hers were pure amber now, the look in them distinctly feral.

Memory shivered, but didn't stop the touch. Moving one hand, Alexei brought it to her face; her pulse kicked, her breath became shallow. He cupped the side of her face, ran the pad of his thumb over her lower lip. That lip immediately felt plumper, more sensitive.

"You have very kissable lips," he murmured in a voice that wasn't wholly human. "But I would be a very bad wolf if I took advantage of you today."

Memory fisted her hand in his hair, suddenly full of hot, burning energy that pumped her veins with fire. "I'm not a weakling to be taken advantage of," she said, her voice hard. "Not a child to have my decisions made for me." Twisting in her seat so that her feet hung out over the edge of the vehicle and she was face-to-face with Alexei, she went to kiss him to show him that *she* was the one making the decisions . . . and realized that she had no idea what to do.

Watching comm shows on which people kissed, it turned out, didn't prepare you for the reality of such intimate physical contact. A thick, dark heat began to creep over her skin, a far different thing than the fury that had erupted inside her on the heels of his words. Then Alexei rubbed the pad of his thumb over her lower lip once more, scrambling her thoughts all over again.

"If I get in trouble because of this," he drawled in a gritty voice, "I'm going to punish you." His hand slid from her cheek to her nape, the subtle pressure he exerted telling her exactly how to angle her head to put herself in perfect position for his kiss. She was in no way prepared for the brush of his lips against her own.

Sensation jolted through her, a thousand lightning bolts.

Breaking away, she sucked in a breath. Amber eyes watched her, predatory in a way that made every tiny hair on her arms rise in primal warning and her thighs clench. The tight, pulsing feeling between her legs ached and felt good at the same time.

When she didn't make any move to take her hand from

his hair, or to get out of the vehicle, he smiled slow and dangerous. "More?"

"More," she rasped out, suddenly aware that he could get away with a whole lot if he aimed that smile in her direction. She'd be putty in his strong hands . . . and under his mouth. This time, he held the contact longer, the pressure warm and firm and causing sensations in her abdomen that had her twisting in her seat. Just when she thought she couldn't bear it any longer, he closed his teeth gently over her lower lip and tugged.

Memory jerked back, bracing both hands on the seat as she gasped in gulps of the cold night air.

The wolf who'd just kissed her smiled. "Teeth are a known hazard when tangling with wolves."

Chapter 22

Unlike big, burly bears with their adorably soft hearts that us wild women have to be careful not to bruise, wolves have egos that are titanium over iron. It takes a great deal to insult a wolf, so if you manage it, kudos to you. He'll probably give you ten thousand orgasms in revenge. You poor, poor thing.

—From the December 2079 issue of *Wild Woman* magazine: "Skin Privileges, Style & Primal Sophistication"

HIS E LOOKED delicious. All huge eyes and plump lips that he wanted to devour. It had taken incredible willpower on his part to keep the kiss so gentle—and even then, he hadn't been able to resist that playful bite at the end.

He *was* a wolf, after all.

He should've felt bad for kissing a woman so recently out of bondage, but as she'd said, she wasn't a child to have her decisions made for her. Memory was a *survivor*. A fighter. A woman who looked him in the eye and dared him to make anything of it. And she'd definitely wanted to kiss him. Her arousal was a sweet, sexy musk in the air . . . but her eyes were lost now, her fingers clutching at the leather of the car seat.

She'd chosen to kiss him, but she was having difficulty processing the aftermath. As for Alexei's own arousal, it would have to remain a frustration. It still made his wolf smug to know that he'd been her first kiss, but that was where things would stay until she was ready for more.

What if your fierce lioness chooses someone else?

That a buried part of him had even asked that question had him pushing away from the door. "Let's get you inside."

He held out a hand because, bad for his control or not, he'd noticed she liked to make physical contact, was happy with it. "You need to rest."

When a frown formed between her eyebrows, he thought she was gearing up to argue with him, but she hopped out of the car. Shutting the door behind her, he grabbed the items he'd bought for her and—well aware she remained leery of the Arrow squad—kept his body between her and the guards as they walked to her cabin.

He waited on the porch while she went in to turn on the lights. After placing most of his gifts just inside the doorway, he busied himself loading up her new datapad with catalogs he thought she might like.

It was a deliberate tactic to keep himself away from her.

Tough and wild under the skin and a woman who never gave up, she drew him on a dangerous level. He could imagine walking inside the cabin, seducing her with kisses and caresses until she melted. He'd strip her with gentle care so she wouldn't shy from his touch, before taking her with a hard physicality that'd teach her that pleasure could be a delicious storm.

Even as he built the lush erotic fantasy, he knew she was nowhere near ready for what he'd demand from her. Alexei had made an art form out of leashing his most primal instincts. It was a survival strategy. Control with Memory, however, would be an impossible ask; she was so ferocious in that small body that she incited the same aggression in him.

The man she accepted as her lover would be one lucky bastard.

Claws scraping the insides of his skin, he turned to stare out at the compound cloaked in night. Memory's future lovers had nothing to do with him—the kiss the two of them had shared had been a thing of circumstance, would likely never be repeated. Alexei had to make sure it wasn't repeated. He couldn't get into bed with a woman who made him want to break all his rules, breach the walls he kept between himself and the world.

Brodie had made that mistake.

Brodie was now dead. So was Brodie's sweet, innocent mate.

Torn to pieces by the one man who should've protected her at all costs.

His neck stiffened, his shoulders rigid.

"Alexei."

He'd scented her before she reached him, but just barely. Their proximity, that kiss, it had left him brushed with her scent . . . and she wore his. The wolf inside him arched its back in unhidden pleasure—already it was beginning to fight the more rational human side of Alexei, unwilling to give her up.

"You have everything you need for tonight?" Gut tight, he passed her the datapad without taking his gaze from the rain-quiet compound.

"Yes. I feel tired." Those last words were spoken almost in a tone of affront.

Despite his attempt to maintain his emotional distance, a smile threatened to tug at Alexei's lips; she seemed to have forgotten that she'd been the prisoner of a psychopath only a day prior. His E was finding her stride and finding it quickly, with an unwavering resolve that the predator in him could do nothing but admire. All she needed was a little time, and she'd be a creature of strength and beauty courted by many.

Alexei had no right to use her current vulnerability against her. She might poke and snarl at him, but deep down, she trusted him—because he was the one who'd pulled her out of the cage. She'd had no chance to get to know other males, could make no real choice.

And why the hell was he gnawing on that when she wasn't for him, could *never* be for him?

He had to get away from the sweet temptation of her, leash himself again.

"Rest tonight." Even as he spoke, he wondered if she had enough blankets and if the heating was working efficiently; he'd check with the SnowDancer-DarkRiver supply team that provisioned the cabins. "You're seeing Sascha again tomorrow?"

"Yes." She came to stand beside him. "Will I see you?"

Alexei nodded. "Yeah, I'll be by to have a security meeting." The compound was part of his responsibilities during this secondment. "Indigo, the lieutenant who usually over-

sees things here, is looking after my den." The senior lieutenant was a stunner by any measure, but he bet no
neighboring asshole or roaming loner would dare challenge
her to a dominance fight. What the fuck was it about him that
incited idiots?

He was chewing on the sulky thought to distract himself
from the sexy, fascinating woman beside him when she said,
"Why won't you look at me? Scared by a little kiss?"

Alexei's spine stiffened, his eyes narrowing at the taunt
and his wolf insulted to the core. Oh, his E was definitely
finding her feet—and she had a mouth on her that delighted
him. This woman had teeth. To a dominant changeling of
Alexei's inclinations, that made her deliciously tempting.

"Watch how you poke the wolf," he growled, stepping off
the porch before he could give in to the temptation to scoop
her up and carry her off to his lair. "One day, you'll go too
far and the wolf *will* eat you."

MEMORY watched from the doorway as Alexei strode across
the compound toward the trees. She had to grip the edge of
the doorjamb to stop herself from going after him and finishing their verbal battle. She knew it was foolish, that he
was a wolf with strength that annihilated hers—and yet, she
wanted to fight him.

She far preferred his growling to this quiet and intense
distance. Even his threat to eat her had been oddly controlled. No snapping his teeth at her, no glint in the eye that
said he was provoking her on purpose.

Setting her jaw, she glared at his retreating form. The
damn wolf was hurting inside and rousing his temper was
the only way she could think to help him. When he was
snarling and grumbling at her, he forgot to be sad and angry
and in such terrible pain. She wished she were like other
empaths, could take painful emotions from others and soften
the edges of their hurt, but she wasn't. The only thing she
could do to help Alexei was aggravate him.

Cupping her hands around her mouth, she yelled,
"Chicken!"

Alexei turned on his heel near the tree line. He was too

far to see clearly in the rainy dark, but she knew he was glowering at her with eyes of wild amber. As she watched, he lifted his arms and tore his T-shirt off over the top of his head. A minute later and he'd taken off his boots and jeans. She couldn't see his body except as a silhouette in shadow, but she saw the flickers of light that erupted around him.

Her breath caught.

A large gray wolf stood where Alexei had glared at her. Heart in her throat, she stepped out, going to the far end of the porch in an effort to see him more clearly. The wolf seemed to shake to settle his pelt in place, then—with a final "you're in trouble" stare—it was gone, a primal ghost in the darkness.

Wonder bloomed inside her at the idea of him running as a wolf . . . and other doors opened around her, curious empaths poking their heads out to search for the crazy woman who was yelling "chicken" at a very dangerous wolf. Suddenly vividly aware of her ill-fitting clothes and matted hair, her nerves jumping, Memory melted back into her doorway until they closed their doors again. But she didn't go inside and shut her own door.

When all was quiet again, she made herself step out, even though she was afraid of the Arrows who watched over the compound. That fear angered her, but she knew it was a survival mechanism. It told her to be careful.

Reminding herself that her golden wolf would've never left her in this place unless it was safe, she clenched her stomach to quiet the queasiness, and walked quickly across the compound. Her movements had become less erratic hour by hour, but she did still have the odd jerked motion; when they came, she took a second, then carried on.

Once at her goal, she began to pick up the clothing Alexei had left in a tidy pile by the trees. He'd set his boots down sideways under the clothing, to stop the rain from getting inside. She knew people here must be used to finding piles of clothing discarded by changelings who'd shifted, but she collected everything anyway and returned with it to her cabin, holding his scent close. There was no need for his things to get wet when she could keep them dry inside.

Where the crabby wolf would have to come to retrieve them.

Her skin heated, her teeth sinking into her lower lip.

Door shut behind her, she put his clothing neatly on one of the two chairs she had around her small kitchen table, his boots just underneath, then walked into the bedroom and began to prepare for bed. A kind stranger had left soft flannel pajamas for her, as well as a simple change of clothes for tomorrow morning—a pair of jeans, a long-sleeved T-shirt, and a sweater. A set of underwear was also included, sealed inside the store's floral packaging.

She put on the bottom half of the pajamas, then snuck back into the kitchen and stole Alexei's T-shirt. It swamped her and it felt like being cuddled by him, his scent in every weave and thread. She hugged it around herself. "He shouldn't have left it behind if he didn't want me using it," she said to Jitterbug . . . and remembered too late that her pet was gone forever.

It hurt, just *hurt*.

Drawing in Alexei's scent in a desperate defensive action, she decided to distract herself by ordering more clothes. It appeared she wasn't going to be kicked out of this lovely green landscape; the least she could do was make sure she looked presentable.

After getting into bed with the datapad, she was a second away from ordering a sensible hard-wearing pair of pants when she said, "No." She wasn't a captive anymore. She didn't have to wear anything but what she wanted.

A woman who taunted a dominant changeling wolf wasn't exactly sensible anyway.

When a howl rose on the air currents, she shivered and stared out toward the silhouettes of the firs visible from her bedroom window. And she wondered if her golden wolf would find peace this night. "Don't hurt, Alexei," she whispered.

Chapter 23

"Promise, Lexie . . . you'll put us . . . together. *Promise.*"
—Etta Harte Vasiliev's final words

ALEXEI RAN UNDER the falling rain, the ghosts of his past running beside him. His big brother had never been anything but proud of Alexei's rank in the pack, not the least annoyed that his baby brother was the more dominant wolf of them. But then, when it was just them, the dominance rules of the pack hadn't applied.

At those times, Brodie was the big brother and Alexei the younger follower.

It had always been that way, the roles of childhood carrying on into adulthood, as was often the case between siblings. Ten-year-old Brodie was the one who'd climbed the tallest trees first, as younger, smaller Alexei jumped up and down below, urging his big brother on while asking him to be careful. Brodie had teased him for being a nag, but it had been gently done—because Brodie knew why Alexei worried.

When his big brother decided to try a homemade parachute, twelve-year-old Alexei had done all the research and made sure the stitches were strong, and that Brodie had a soft landing place. And when Brodie set his mind on getting a permanent tattoo at age sixteen, with ink that would last through the shift, it was Alexei who'd talked him out of the large grinning skull with one tooth.

Brodie had ended up agreeing to Alexei's choice: a small

family crest Alexei had designed in memory of their parents. Alexei, too, had gotten inked with the crest when he was eighteen. He was still too angry with Brodie to add a memory of his brother to the crest, but the two of them had been so proud of their original inkings.

"Thank the tattoo gods you were with me that day, little bro," Brodie had said to him when they were older and having a couple of beers one lazy summer evening. "Fuck, but that skull was ugly. Etta would've probably taken one look at me and walked in the other direction."

Brodie's wolf had been a darker gray than Alexei's, with a dot of white between his ears. His friends had begun calling him Skunk at some point in their teenage years, and the nickname had stuck with his peer group. Brodie had never minded, laughing and pretending to lift his tail as if to release a skunk's trademark stink.

Alexei wanted to laugh at the visual, wanted to remember how much fun he'd had with his brother and, later, with his brother's lovely, gentle mate. Etta had fit into their relationship as if she'd always been there, a slender reed of a woman who'd baked Alexei his favorite muffins and never made him feel an intruder in the couple's lives when he visited.

If he stayed away too long, she'd call him up and order him to dinner with her and Brodie. The three of them had had such good times. He should remember those, focus on those. But without Memory's spirit and warmth beside him, the wound felt too raw. Alexei didn't know if it would ever heal.

Etta was dead. And Brodie had broken his promise.

Throwing back his head, he howled out his rage at the sky, howled out his anger. In the aftermath, his wolf stood on a promontory staring out at the sprawl of dark green below him, the empathic compound a small, rain-clouded glow in the far distance. In one of those cabins slept a woman who made him crazy.

She'd called him a chicken!

His wolf bared its teeth, wanting to run down and nip at her for her insolence until she apologized and petted him with words about his bravery and strength. God, the idea of it was a pounding compulsion in his gut.

Snarling, the wolf took a step back. The force of his need to go to her had managed to get through to even the wildest part of his nature, harshly reminding the wolf of what was at stake: his sanity . . . and Memory's life.

Distance was critical.

Yet even as he turned away from the view and began to lope across the landscape again, he knew that keeping his distance would be a serious problem. *He'd* found her, and he would let no one hurt her. Until Memory could defend herself, Alexei would be her protector.

A howl sang across the mountains.

Halting, Alexei listened, then opened his mouth in a growl. He wasn't the least surprised when a big, shaggy wolf with black tips to the gray of his fur loped out of the trees only minutes later despite the fact that Matthias was based out of the den near the Cascade Range.

The other lieutenant was the last packmate Alexei wanted to see; along with Judd, Matthias was one of his closest friends. Alexei had gotten blind drunk with the other lieutenant the day of Brodie's and Etta's funerals. Judd couldn't drink without his Tk abilities going haywire, but he'd been there the entire time, and when Alexei wanted to fight someone, *anyone*, the former Arrow had put his body on the line.

Matthias and Judd had all but carried Alexei into bed and Matthias had slept in wolf form beside his bed the entire night. He knew far too much about the scars on Alexei's heart.

Ignoring Alexei's snarl, Matthias bumped the side of his body against Alexei's. He was bigger than Alexei in both forms, but Alexei was more than capable of holding his own against the other man. He didn't budge an inch at the bump. When he threatened to bite Matthias's muzzle, the surprisingly agile wolf jumped back and dropped its jaw in a lupine laugh. Stubborn asshole wasn't leaving.

Putting his head down, Alexei began to run. Matthias ran beside him. The rain faded a quarter of an hour into it, the clouds parting to reveal the silvery light of the moon. They were both panting under the moonlight when he finally brought them to a stop. Coincidentally—*yeah, right*—it was at another outlook that gave him a view over the empathic compound. Tiny cabins glowed with light below.

He shifted, then shoved a hand against Matthias's side, the other man's coat thick and healthy. "I told you to stay in your den." Matthias had called him a few days earlier, mentioned he was thinking of swinging by the main den. Well aware of the reason for his friend's sudden urge to visit, Alexei had growled at him to focus on his own den.

Judd and Hawke were already on his case; he didn't need his closest childhood friend to come poke his big snout into Alexei's current frame of mind. Now, said snout nudged at his ribs before Matthias folded himself down into a seated position on the outlook, his eyes on the compound below.

Sighing in defeat, Alexei leaned back against a nearby tree, and allowed the chill night air to cool down his body. He only groaned when Judd appeared out of the trees with a box of beer. "Seriously? How the fuck did you even find us?" The former Arrow was teleport-capable but couldn't lock on to faces.

"I will take that secret to the grave." He threw across two pairs of pants.

Alexei pulled on a pair because he knew Judd hadn't quite got to the point where he could shoot the breeze with two naked changelings. Alexei's wolf didn't understand the other man's reluctance—skin was just another kind of fur to a changeling—but what the hell, it was a small enough favor for a friend. The quick task completed, he sat down with his back against the tree.

Judd took a seat beside him, the warm body of Matthias's wolf pressing against Alexei's other side. "Fuck you, assholes," Alexei said, his chest tight.

Judd handed him a beer.

Shifting at the same time, Matthias pulled on the other pair of pants. When he was done, the six-foot-six male built like a tank took a beer, reclaimed his seat, and said, "It's almost tomorrow."

"Yeah." The first anniversary over and done with . . . and it hadn't been an awful day. His eyes returned to the glow of the compound. "Did you hear about my E?"

"Uh-huh." Matthias stretched out his arms. "Eli went up with Hawke to check out that bunker. Said she attacked you."

"Sienna mentioned that your E put her in mind of a small tornado," Judd added, his voice cool—but that meant nothing, a leftover habit from his time in the squad. "All fury and untamed strength."

"I like her already." Matthias grinned. "You think she'd be into a large wolf who resembles a bear?"

"She'd kick your beary ass." Alexei felt his lips tug up at the thought of Memory poking at him, ignoring his threats to bite her.

"From what I've heard, she's tough," Judd said quietly. "A lot of will in a small body."

Matthias yawned. "I like little things."

Well aware the big male was messing with him, Alexei narrowed his eyes. "Want me to tell Nell you're on the prowl?"

"I can wring your scrawny neck without breaking a sweat," Matthias muttered while Judd fought and failed to hide a grin.

"Try it and lose your fur," Alexei said, conscious that slender and steel-willed Nell was Matthias's weak spot.

The other man had been trying to court her for over a year, but she was having none of his rough charm. Possibly because she'd seen Matthias charm many a woman out of her panties. Between his mom and his dad, he had ancestry from the Far East, Spain, and Tanzania; it had left Alexei's friend with smooth dark skin and one hell of a face. A lot of women took one look at that face and were ready to follow him into a bedroom. Matthias hadn't ever been shy about accepting the offers, either.

"You're still celibate?" Judd asked before Alexei could broach the topic of Matthias's itchiness under the skin.

"Damn woman is going to drive me to insanity." He glared into his beer after shoving a hand through the shaggy brown-black of his hair. "I brought her a bunch of flowers today. Actual wildflowers I *picked* myself like some romantic schmuck. You know what she did? Put them in a glass of water."

Judd raised an eyebrow. "Shocking."

"Yeah, real hardcore stuff." Alexei was trying not to laugh at his poor friend's morose expression, but it was hard.

"Then she *gave* the glass of flowers I picked for *her* to Lara, who was passing by." Matthias's voice was all grumble now. "Why is she like that?"

Alexei's grin cracked his face. "Maybe because you two were in the same classes in school and she saw you work your way through the girls like a multicourse buffet?"

"Even I've heard of your teenage exploits," Judd put in. "Weren't you once discovered in bed with an entire team of cheerleaders?"

Matthias groaned. "I was *sleeping*. It just happened to be the only open spot."

"Right."

"Screw you, Sexy Lexie." Matthias punched him on the shoulder. "One time, at a high school party, Nell saw me chatting up a girl, being all smooth and charming. She raised her eyebrow and told me my zipper was undone, then left."

Alexei snorted beer out his nose he was laughing so hard, and even Judd gave it up. Matthias threatened to pulverize them both. But Alexei's shoulders didn't stop shaking for a long time. His wolf was wildly amused by the thought of a teenaged Matthias's ego being so swiftly deflated by razor-sharp Nell.

It felt strange to laugh on this day, but afterward, he raised his beer to the night sky and said, "Fuck you, Brodie. I hope Etta is kicking your ass every damn hour of every damn day." Shifting his gaze to the compound below, he thought of the woman who'd made this day far better than it should've been.

Sleep well, lioness. Dream of wolves. He scowled. *Scratch that. Dream of* this *wolf.*

Chapter 24

Progress is being stalled by the heavily encrypted protections on a large percentage of historical data. Considerable data also appears to have been scrubbed from the system, creating holes that are impossible to fill with any accuracy.

—Report to Ruling Coalition from Research Group Gamma-X, Silence & Outcomes

AS MEMORY FELL into sleep surrounded by the primal scent of a golden wolf, another Psy mind shrugged off the last of its decades-long sleep and came fully awake. The waking had been happening in fits and starts ever since the fall of Silence and the creation of the Honeycomb. It had worried him at first, his intense discipline integral to his sense of self—he'd believed the sudden influx of emotion into the PsyNet was subverting his mind.

He'd been wrong.

It was Silence that had been the trap, the prison. It had locked him up in invisible chains. As the chains snapped free one by one, he stretched out his mind and felt it grow and grow and grow. So much *power* that it made his head spin. He could take his family to the very top of the PsyNet with it, rule over an unparalleled empire.

As for the strange urges that had woken alongside the power, he'd deal with them the same way he'd dealt with the myriad responsibilities entailed in becoming the head of the family—with discipline and reason and intelligence. As he did so, he'd look for others of his kind, others who'd been in an unknowing sleep under the reign of Silence.

Would he make allies of them, or erase them so that he

had fewer competitors at this level of power? He wasn't certain. It would depend on the individual and whether they presented a threat. First, he'd familiarize himself with his own new level of power, start to work on further stabilizing the surges.

Leaving his mind to settle for now, he glanced at the report he'd received an hour earlier from the spies he had scattered throughout the PsyNet. One of them had noted the appearance of an unusual empathic mind in the training compound in SnowDancer-DarkRiver territory.

The spy had only caught a distant glimpse of her, as no one who valued their life ever encroached on that section of the Net. As a result, there wasn't really much of substance in the report, and he discarded it after a quick scan. The Es were important to maintaining the health of the PsyNet, but when it came to raw power, he had to look elsewhere.

Krychek held the alpha position, but the one who'd woken wasn't foolish enough to look in that direction—Kaleb Krychek hadn't survived all comers by being anything but deadly. The world was big enough for the two of them to share. At least for now. Until he settled into this new power that might eclipse Krychek's.

His eyes weren't the white sparks on black of a cardinal, but the power inside him felt infinite. He stilled, considered. That supposition could not be true. Cardinals were immeasurable by definition.

He commed his assistant. "Book me in with Dr. Mehra." He would have a full medical, make sure of his physical and mental health; this power was useless if it turned him into a delusional idiot.

All the while, his mind continued to expand, a sprawling vastness.

Chapter 25

All indications are that the percentage of psychopaths in the population remains steady despite half a century of Silence, though these individuals do appear to have gained more discipline in terms of hiding their kills. Most no longer fall into the trap of wanting credit.
—Fragment of a 2031 report commissioned by the Psy Council of the time and retrieved by Research Group Gamma-X

ALEXEI SECOND-GUESSED HIS decision to leave Memory even as he fell into a fitful sleep at last, haunted by images of a small woman with big brown eyes. The only reason he'd left her alone in an unfamiliar environment at all was because Sascha had pulled him aside at the DarkRiver cabin while Memory had been in the bathroom.

"Memory needs to claim ownership over her surroundings," the cardinal empath had murmured. "She can't do that if you're around."

When he'd responded with a flinty stare, she'd rolled her eyes. "I know you'd never hurt her, you obstinate wolf, but you burn with dominance. You take over a space just by being in it. Memory needs to heal and grow before she can hold her own against you."

As far as Alexei was concerned, Memory was more than holding her own against him. "Did you hear her just before?" He'd folded his arms. "Damn E doesn't know the meaning of backing down."

A dazzling smile. "No, not against you in any case." Sascha had patted his cheek. "It would be so easy for her to start relying on you, but Memory deserves better. I know she comes across as tough, but this is a big, scary world for her. And you have such wide shoulders, Alexei."

"She has no pack, no family. I can't abandon her." It went against his every instinct.

"I'd never ask that. Just . . ." Sascha's features had cleared. "Give her space to claim the cabin as *her* territory. It matters. Memory is far more than we've seen yet, and to grow into herself in a way she's never before been able to do, she needs that sense of ownership."

Alexei wasn't about to stunt his lioness's growth. So he'd given her space to stamp her mark on the cabin—but when he woke sometime around two in the morning, he couldn't stop from checking up on her.

Before he left, he raided the pack's stores. When a pack-mate on night shift poked his sandy-haired head inside and said, "Not quite your style, Lexie," Alexei gave the smart-ass a death glare.

The lanky man grinned, his amusement reaching the light green of his eyes. "What's her name?"

Fuck, now the whole pack would know; wolves were nosier than a parliament of gossipy magpies. "Go away and I won't tell Sing-Liu about the secret anniversary present you're hiding in Elias and Yuki's quarters."

D'Arn's mouth fell open. "How do you even know about that?"

"I don't see you leaving. I feel the urge to find your mate."

"I'll get you back for this," D'Arn threatened darkly before adding, "She must be special. Can't wait to tell—" The other man took off laughing when Alexei lunged at him.

Growling, Alexei packed up the very *useful* item he'd chosen for Memory, then left the den.

The Arrows didn't stop him when he walked into the compound and up to her cabin. He could scent her inside . . . could scent himself, too. Frowning, he glanced to where he'd left his clothes and boots; no rain fell to blur the darkness, the landscape clear to his night vision. His clothes were gone. A slow smile curving his lips despite himself, he put her gift beside the doorway, then stepped away and made his way back to the den. He'd just walked inside when his phone buzzed.

It was Brenna, Judd's mate and part of the den's tech team. "You said to let you know when we tracked down this Renault psycho."

Alexei altered direction, aiming himself toward the tech center. "What've you got?" Brenna's focus was meant to be on cutting-edge research, not computronic tracking, but Alexei knew the dark reason why she'd thrown her considerable brain power behind the search for Renault.

"An address beyond his official business or residential ones," she told him. "You know the cats checked out those addresses for us when you first sent us the name? Bastard was gone by then." Brenna's voice held the urge to slice and dice the man who'd kept Memory prisoner, her wolf fully on Memory's side despite having never met her.

"Yeah. Hawke told me."

"Well, E. David Renault laid an excellent false trail," she continued. "I'm finding signs of serious long-term planning. I'll say one thing—the psycho is intelligent. He exists on a superficial level, but dig below the first two layers and it's all smoke and mirrors." A pause before Brenna said, "Will she be all right?"

Having reached the tech center by then, Alexei entered and made his way to her. "She's like you," he said to this packmate who'd survived her own monster. "Tough as nails." Brenna let him run her ponytail through his hand, the silky blonde strands dipped in pink at the bottom. "She has plans to get strong, then chop Renault into small pieces."

"Tell her I'll carry her knives for her." The pinched look faded from Brenna's extraordinary eyes, the dark brown of her irises shattered by arctic blue shards. A scar she'd turned into a badge of survival. Those eyes were innocent as she said, "Did she really accuse you of being a chicken?"

Alexei growled. "Was it one of the asshole cats prowling around the compound? It was, wasn't it? Tell me. I need to know who to kill."

A giggle from the packmate next to Brenna's workstation, while Brenna herself rose and kissed him on the cheek, her own cheeks creased in a smile that lit up her whole face. After that, it was all business.

Brenna told him that her team had already ruled out two

locations—one in Arizona, one in Nevada—that had earlier come up as Renault's secret home base. She'd gotten a couple of the WindHaven falcons to fly over and double-check their assessment. "Falcons confirmed both were basically shells with some window dressing. No signs of actual habitation."

This third address was in the heart of San Francisco.

His wolf stirred.

Alexei had asked Judd how far Renault could teleport regularly given his official Gradient level. The San Francisco location was well within his range if he needed to go back and forth to the bunker. Not only that, according to the financial records Brenna had hacked, the bills paid for this property for consumables such as energy fluctuated through the seasons—as they would for a household in use.

"One of his few mistakes," Brenna said after bringing up the bills. "That, or he believed these records couldn't be hacked." A snort. "I could hack the PsyNet if only I could find a way to jack in."

She used deft movements of her right hand to manipulate the large screen. "Last automatic upload to the billing server was eight hours ago—and someone was doing things at that address that required energy. Arrogant bastard could be hunkered down there—maybe he wants to be nearby so he can try to grab Memory again."

Alexei pressed a hard kiss to her jaw. "You're a fucking queen. Send any updates to my phone. We're going to move."

It took him less than ten minutes to put together an assault team.

Hawke was a given—he needed to question Memory's captor about the bunker. Matthias because he was an extra body in the den whose absence wouldn't cause a hole in their defenses. Judd because having a Tk along seemed a good move when they were dealing with another Tk.

The fifth member of their team was Sing-Liu. D'Arn's deadly human mate could climb and move as quietly as any cat and throw a knife with pinpoint accuracy. She could also appear small and curvy and harmless, and was willing to play "simpering damsel," if necessary, to throw Renault off the scent.

"I'll take the humiliation out of your hide later," she warned Alexei.

Prior to leaving the den, Alexei called and asked to be put in touch with the leopard on patrol in the area around Renault's home. He got Emmett Schaeffer, a rough-hewn soldier with sharp eyes, who promised to keep the townhouse under surveillance and follow anyone who came out. "Can't follow a teleporter," he pointed out. "But he's probably asleep—no movement that I can see. External security lights are on, but nothing inside."

Had Emmett said Renault was there and active, Alexei would've swallowed his need to personally haul Renault in for Memory's vengeance, and asked the leopards to go in. "If that changes, you let me know."

Surveillance sorted, he and the team decided to utilize Judd's teleportation skills from the halfway point—it would speed things up without wiping him out. Judd had once told Alexei that teleporting SnowDancers had become exponentially easier for him a year after he blood-oathed fealty to Hawke and became a ranked SnowDancer lieutenant. As if the bond with Hawke created a pathway of psychic trust with all the members of the pack.

Alexei didn't care too much about the mechanics, just that Judd could get them to the location quickly. It was worth the weird split-second disorientation that came with being teleported.

Once in the city, it took them a short few seconds to make their way up to Renault's townhouse—Judd had asked Emmett to send through a photograph of the street, then used a distinctive house down the block as a visual reference for the teleport. Just in case Memory's abductor happened to be looking out the window when five strangers appeared out of nowhere.

It wasn't yet dawn, but multiple houses had light glowing from their windows as people got out of bed and downed their first coffee in preparation for the day ahead. Another half hour and some folks would start leaving for work.

Emmett emerged from the shadows as Alexei first set eyes on the target home. "I thought I smelled wolf," the leopard said, a faint smile on his face and his jaw rough with stubble.

The other man was one of the more laid-back cats in DarkRiver, but he was also a lethally skilled senior soldier. More critical to Alexei, Emmett had a mother who was currently in the midst of running the second study ever done on changeling rogues. Keelie Schaeffer had sent a message to all predatory changeling groups around the world, requesting dialogue with anyone impacted by a rogue.

The subject is a painful one, she'd written, *but we must confront it if we are to have any hope of finding an answer to why a small number of our kind succumb to such violent impulses.*

Alexei had deleted the message at the time, the loss of Brodie too close, but he hadn't forgotten it. When Dr. Schaeffer gave an interview on the subject four months ago, he'd listened to every word. Trying to find answers. Trying to not be so angry. Yet he still couldn't speak to her. Not when the wound kept on bleeding inside him.

"No movement," Emmett said, jerking his thumb over his shoulder to indicate the well-kept property. "I can watch streetside while you go in."

Technically, SnowDancer should've asked for Enforcement permission since it was a Psy home they were about to breach, but Enforcement remained full of leaks. And when it came down to it, this was leopard territory. Even many of the resident Psy now had more faith in the cats than in their own leaders. When the shit hit the fan, the people of San Francisco knew DarkRiver and its allies would come to their aid.

So yeah, no one was too worried about Enforcement.

"Thanks, Emmett." Wolf snarling inside him to begin the hunt, Alexei glanced at his alpha.

Hawke nodded, and the five of them flowed across the dark street. The first thing they did was find a window through which Judd could gain a visual. Teleporting inside a second later, he then opened the front door to let them in. All of it in silence.

A split second of warning and Renault would disappear.

Alexei's nostrils flared at the distinctive ice-metal scent he'd caught in the bunker, that scent laid down thick around him now, as he'd expect in any living creature's home. Yet nothing felt fresh, not Renault's scent and not the other smells you'd expect to find in a home. Regardless, none of them spoke as they split up to search the house in silence.

"Fucker's gone," he said to the others when they met in the large upstairs bedroom.

"Arrogant, but not arrogant enough to believe he could hide for long right under DarkRiver's and SnowDancer's noses," Judd murmured. "A pity."

"It'll have to be a different kind of hunt now." Hawke folded his arms, his pale gaze pitiless. "I'll blast his face across the Trinity network."

"We could get some pushback for playing judge and jury," Sing-Liu said with a curl of her lip, her small body held with a predator's stillness. She might be genetically human, but her heart was pure wolf.

Alexei, meanwhile, prowled around the room, his skin too full of energy and a growl building in his chest as he caught fleeting hints of a musty, unpleasant smell he couldn't quite identify.

"You know how some of the non-changeling groups can be about our laws," Sing-Liu added.

An eye for an eye, a life for a life, it was a perfectly rational law, but humans and Psy occasionally got squeamish about the brutality of changeling punishments. Alexei might've lost a brother to execution, but Brodie's death wasn't the fault of their laws. His brother had written his own death warrant the day he broke the vow the two of them had sworn as tormented young teenagers.

"Renault made this SnowDancer business when he intruded on our territory." Hawke's tone was hard as granite, the wolf prowling behind his eyes. "He's now subject to our rules—and I want the entire world to know that. Fuck with us and pay the price."

Alexei frowned at a sudden change under his feet. Moving back, he walked over the spot again, listening to the subtle difference in the sound of his footsteps. "What's below this bedroom?"

"Garage," Matthias said. "Empty except for a single spi-derweb."

"Did the ceiling strike you as low?"

Matthias took a second, frowned. "Yeah, now that you mention it. I'm used to being too tall for a lot of spaces so I didn't really think it was odd. What're you thinking?"

Alexei's claws sliced out of his fingers. "We may have a hidden compartment."

Everyone switched focus with predator speed.

It was Matthias who spotted that the carpet was only lightly pinned down along one edge. After Judd lifted the small side table sitting on that part of the carpet, Alexei peeled the carpet up and back.

"It's big enough for a person." Sing-Liu's words were quiet. "What's that smell? Bleach?"

"No, a specialized dehumidifying compound," Judd said, old nightmares in his voice. "Used to dry flesh out, halt pu-trefaction and the attendant smells."

"Looks like a goddamn coffin." Hawke's eyes didn't move off the abomination they'd uncovered. "I can scent a bare hint of decay below the chemicals."

So could Alexei, the scent a sly intruder that'd finally taken ugly shape.

Blood cold, he took hold of one circular pull, Matthias the other, and the two of them lifted the large lid open. As he did so, he tried not to wonder if the psychopathic bastard had ever put Memory in one of these boxes.

Then the lid was open.

Sing-Liu was the first one to speak. "No one is going to argue with our laws now."

Inside the space were the mummified remains of a woman with skin that looked ebony now but had probably been dark brown at death. Tucked around her were sealed but transparent packets that appeared to hold hair clippings.

When Hawke found a tissue and used it to lift out one of the packets, they saw that a name and a date were written on the label: *Hanna, December 2075.*

Alexei's gaze snagged on the corpse's hair. She'd had wild black curls, the woman who'd died in this coffin—or been placed there after death. Hair just like an empath

Alexei had pulled out of another box. And he knew in his gut that Memory's mother must've had the same hair, and that her skin had been a shade of brown.

Just like her.

He understood in that moment that Memory had been meant to die alongside her mother—two victims who fueled Renault's murderous fantasies. Then the killer had touched her and discovered what she could do.

But had he succeeded in overusing Memory to the point where her mind broke under the pressure, he'd have reduced her to a lock of hair in his sick trophy case. He'd have destroyed her vibrant light before it ever had the chance to shine. "I get to rip his head off," Alexei said very, very quietly. "He's mine."

No one argued.

Chapter 26

Jaya Laila Storm is to be the *Beacon*'s new Social Interaction columnist. In the wake of the fall of Silence, as our people grapple with emotion, we are facing questions about love, about hate, about courtship, about friendship, and the *Beacon* has always been on the cutting edge of news. In this, too, we will not fail.

As a Gradient 8.8 medical empath who survived Silence unbroken and who has psychically bonded with an Arrow, and who maintains friendships with individuals of all three races, we believe she is uniquely qualified to lead *Beacon* readers through the minefield that is emotion.

Initially, the *Beacon* senior team objected to my choice of Jaya as columnist because she has barely entered her twenties, but in the end, it was decided that this is a new age. It should be led by the young.

—Madrigal Esperanza, Editorial Director, *PsyNet Beacon*

MEMORY SLEPT DEEPLY that night, cocooned in a familiar male scent and tired from the sessions with Amara and Sascha. When she woke, it was with a delicious heaviness in her limbs. She yawned.

"Jitterbug?" She rubbed her eyes as she rose into a sitting position. "I'll get you—"

Reality intruded along with the beams of the cabin around her, the light coming through the crack in her curtains. This wasn't a prison, and her beloved pet wouldn't amble over from his position at the foot of her bed to nuzzle against her face.

Eyes hot, she touched the spot on the bed where Jitterbug would've curled up had he been alive. "You're free," she said through the tears that wanted to fall. "And so am I." Now, she had to become strong enough to take on Renault when he came after her. Because as Amara had confirmed, she was a drug to psychopaths. Renault wouldn't give up.

Rising, she took a long shower, then dressed in the fresh clothing that had been left for her. After making her bed, she folded up Alexei's T-shirt and put it under her pillow. It was hers now and tough luck to him. He could fight her if he wanted it back.

Her stomach fluttered, the sadness of the past beginning to be outweighed by the unfurling wonder of the present. She had curtains she could pull to allow in daylight, a window she could open, a door of her own. She could choose what to eat, what to wear. Her heart threatened to explode, it was so full.

As she fluffed up her pillows, she wondered when the new clothes she'd ordered would arrive. Though the Empathic Collective stipend was a generous one, she'd been careful to use only a small percentage of it. Until she knew when it would be renewed, *if* it would be renewed, she had to hoard her resources. But clothes were a necessity . . . to her body, and to her soul.

For the first time, Memory alone had made the decision on how she would dress.

Likely, delivery this deep into DarkRiver territory would take a few days at the very least; she didn't imagine the cats permitted the drone drops advertised on several of the catalogs. She could be patient. She'd wash the sweats that Alexei had given her at the substation, wear them in conjunction with this set of clothing until she had her order.

As for her hair, she'd decided to wash it again, this time skipping the shampoo and using only great helpings of the tea-tree-oil-based conditioner Alexei had found for her. The strands remained a knotted mess—she'd taken *great* pride in tangling her hair to thwart and frustrate Renault—but it did feel better than before. She'd finger-combed her wet curls as much as she could before getting sore arms and promising herself she'd have another go tomorrow.

If she tied the mass back once it wasn't so damp anymore, she could get away with it. It'd be far from pretty, but no

longer did she look like she'd taken up keeping birds in her
hair. That counted as a definite win. Smiling, she went into
the kitchen and prepared coffee and toast. Sunshine poured
in through the windows, but it was weak and soft. As if dawn
hadn't fully come.

Though the weather appeared to have a crisp edge to it,
she decided to sit on the porch while she ate. When in the
bunker, when in her prison, she'd often dreamed about small,
everyday things that would be a wonder when done in
freedom. Some dreams, however, had been beyond her comprehension.

She touched her fingers to her lower lip, still able to feel
the imprint of Alexei's kiss and the tug of that small, wicked
bite. Her skin prickled with sensation, her cheeks flushing.
Ready to battle him today until he stopped attempting to play
knight protector—she knew who and what she wanted, thank
you very much—Memory picked up her breakfast and went
to sit out on the porch. It had no railing, so she was able to sit
on the edge with her feet on the ground; her intent was to
watch the quiet waking of the compound.

She'd just taken her seat, her plate beside her but the mug
yet in her hand, when she noticed a small box sitting off to
one side of the front door. Putting down her mug on a wave
of anticipation that one of her orders had somehow arrived,
she dragged the box close.

Inside sat a pair of sparkly sneakers covered with multicolored sequins.

Her eyes went huge. They were *wonderful*.

Immediately shucking off the ugly blue trainers that Renault had forced her to wear, she pulled on the sneakers that
fit perfectly and glittered even in the washed-out morning
light. Only after she'd admired them for at least five minutes
did her brain compute that she hadn't ordered sparkly sequined sneakers.

She examined the box again and spotted a small piece of
paper that she'd missed in her earlier excitement. It was
covered by a black scrawl: *I thought you might like these.*
Brand-new. Found them in the pack stores and they looked
like they might fit you.

That was it. No signature. No other explanation. Yet she

knew without a single doubt that it was Alexei who'd left the shoes for her. Because he thought she would like something pretty and shiny and new. Even though she'd yelled "Chicken!" at him when he left.

"I'm going to kiss you again," she promised her golden wolf, "even if you threaten to eat me." Bubbles of joy bursting inside her, she picked up her abandoned coffee and took in the compound.

The Arrows were difficult to see, ghosts in the mist, but a dark-skinned woman with a lovely oval face came out of the cabin directly across from Memory right then. She looked to be close to Memory's age, but held herself with a confidence that Memory had never known.

"Hi!" A huge smile on the stranger's face, her hand rising in a wave.

Memory's stomach muscles clenched, but she waved back. She had no idea how empaths aside from Sascha would react to her.

"I'm Jaya," her neighbor said when she reached Memory. "One of the teachers here—I was part of the first intake. We're short on experience, so anyone who can teach anything is roped in."

Of course. Many of the first trainees would've been young—individuals not so entrenched in Silence that there was no hope of pulling them out. "It's nice to meet you. I'm Memory."

"Yes, Sascha told me." Jaya's welcoming smile showed no indication of fading. "You always up so early? If you are, we can get in an hour or two of drills before everyone else starts stirring and Sascha arrives for your sessions on shield mechanics."

"I'd like that." Blanketed by the warmth of Jaya's presence, Memory dared imagine the young E might one day become her friend. "It won't trouble you to wake early?" At present, the only others who appeared awake were the Arrows . . . and a slinky gray cat who came over to talk to them.

"Hello, Phantom—back from your morning prowl, are you?" Jaya reached out to scratch him behind the ears. "He adopted me about three months ago, and when a cat adopts you . . ." A sudden, quiet glance. "Oh, this hurts you."

Memory rubbed a fist over her heart. "I had a cat," she whispered through a thick throat. "He died of old age just before Alexei found me."

Jaya patted Memory gently on the thigh as she stood back up.

After rubbing his body along one of Jaya's legs, Phantom ignored Memory to pad off into the morning mist. "He's a terrible snob." Jaya sat down beside Memory. "Takes days to decide if you're acceptable and worthy of his attention—half the time, he glares at my husband for having the nerve to kiss me."

Memory gave a laugh that felt rusty and wet.

Jaya ran her hand down Memory's spine. "They get inside your heart, don't they?"

Memory could only nod.

"As for me," Jaya continued, "I tend to wake with Abbot's shifts. I've become so used to cuddling next to his body that my eyes snap open the instant he leaves the bed." She pointed to a shadow in between two cabins in the far distance. "The one with the killer sea-blue eyes and black hair is mine."

Memory bit down on her lower lip. "He doesn't seem like a cuddling sort of man," she ventured warily. Alexei knew how to cuddle. Even when he was growling at her, if she went to him, he'd hold her. Jaya's Abbot, in contrast, stood expressionless, his body at battle readiness and his eyes as cold as the Arctic.

Jaya laughed—and Memory saw Abbot's gaze turn toward her. But there was no softening in his features, nothing to betray that Jaya meant more to him than any other empath under his watch. Except . . . Jaya blew him a kiss, as if he'd made a grand gesture of love. "I had to work on him a bit," the other woman whispered conspiratorially. "But my Abbot once stayed up all night with me—playing cards very badly—just so I wouldn't be scared. I knew then that he was a keeper."

"I understand." Someone who stood with you in the worst times and who didn't take advantage of your weakness, that was a person you could trust. Like a wolf who kissed you even after he'd learned your most terrible secret.

Memory's toes curled inside her astonishingly wonderful

shoes. "Would you like some coffee?" she asked hesitantly, not sure she wasn't assuming too much in Jaya's friendliness.

"When I get back from my walk, if that works for you?" At Memory's nod, she added, "I need to shake off a few of the cobwebs from staying up late to write my first column." Jaya got up with a groan. "I don't know what I was thinking, agreeing to be the *Beacon*'s new Social Interaction columnist."

Memory made an immediate note to download a copy of Jaya's column.

"We should have forty-five minutes together after I get back. Now I have to go distract Abbot for a minute." A wink before she turned to walk in the direction of the blue-eyed Arrow.

He watched her come to him with no alteration in his expression . . . but cupped her cheek with one hand when she reached him, a piercing tenderness to his touch that was wholly unexpected in a man so outwardly martial and cold. Smiling, Memory looked away to give the couple their privacy, and finished her breakfast. She was considering whether to go inside and pour herself another coffee when her eyes widened.

Ashaya Aleine had just walked out of the trees from what Memory guessed was the DarkRiver side of the border. The M-Psy carried a small bag and at her side walked a tall man with amber-colored hair tied back in a queue and watchful eyes of near-gold, his movements subtly feline. He stopped next to one of the Arrows, an older man who appeared to be in charge of this unit, while Ashaya moved toward Memory.

The other woman's face was drawn, her body stiff.

Rising to her feet, Memory girded herself for the confrontation to come; she had no idea what had passed between Ashaya and Amara after they left the cabin, but she could guess that it had been nothing good.

Rubbing her damp palms on her jeans, she blurted out, "I'm sorry," before Ashaya could speak.

"You *don't ever* have to apologize to me." The blue-gray of Ashaya's eyes shone with emotion. "You gave me a gift I never expected," she whispered in a voice that trembled. "The effect may have been temporary, but for three hours yesterday, I saw a glimpse of who my twin might've been if she hadn't been wired wrong in the womb."

All the air rushed out of Memory. "She didn't hurt you with her new understanding of your vulnerabilities?"

A poignant smile. "I long ago learned how to conduct myself around Amara to ensure that I didn't put myself or those I loved at risk." She inhaled deeply, exhaled slowly. "Bittersweet though they were, I'd never give up those three hours." Ashaya reached back to tuck a curl behind her ear.

Memory was suddenly conscious of the state of her own hair; it hadn't dried enough to become a huge mess, but she had nothing like Ashaya's beautifully separated curls. "Would you like a coffee?" she said despite the heat in her face.

"I'd love some, and I brought a gift I hope you'll like." She lifted the bag she was holding.

Only after the two of them were seated around the kitchen table did Ashaya open the bag. As Memory watched, she took out a number of items.

Hair care products and tools designed for tight curls.

Heat crawling over her entire body, Memory looked down into the fragrant dark liquid in her mug. "My hair looks terrible, doesn't it?"

"Oh, I didn't do this to make you feel bad." Ashaya's tone was distraught. "I thought maybe no one had remembered to get you curl-specific products."

Memory looked up, her eyes burning. "Alexei did," she whispered, wanting to kiss him all over again for seeing her. Not a victim. Not a strange E. *Her*. Memory.

"Will you let me do your hair?" Ashaya's throat moved as she swallowed. "I need to do *something* for you. Please."

"Oh." No one else had done Memory's hair since she was eight years old. Her emotions got all tangled at the idea of it, her throat thick. "Yes," she managed to say.

Ashaya's face lit up.

As she got up to come around behind Memory, she said, "I kept my mate up all night telling him about Amara and our strange, wonderful afternoon." The M-Psy went on to speak about her leopard changeling mate and her Psy son, who considered himself an honorary cat and was with his adoptive father today. "Learning leopard secrets," Ashaya said with a laugh. "Important man-business."

Memory found herself wondering if Alexei took wolf pups off to learn wolf secrets. The idea of her growly golden wolf corralling curious pups made her grin.

Jaya returned while Ashaya was still detangling Memory's hair. "We can start on the drills while Ashaya does her thing," she said, her elegant features warmly affectionate. "First, we're going to do the psychic version of piano scales to warm you up."

It became clear within the first quarter-hour that the usual E exercises simply didn't work for Memory's brain. Memory fisted her fingers into her palms, her gut churning at this evidence that she didn't belong in Designation E, but Jaya wasn't about to give up. She threw out a far different exercise . . . and Memory flew through it.

"Interesting." Jaya sat back in her chair, rubbing the back of her neck. "That particular exercise was originally designed for telepathic Arrow trainees," she said just as Sascha arrived. "Abbot showed it to me."

The room was now filled with so much friendly feminine energy that Memory felt overwhelmed—in a good way. Never had she imagined she'd have this many friends around her, people who seemed to like her regardless of her dark ability. She felt shy about claiming them as friends out loud, but she hugged the thought close in her heart.

"Hmm," Sascha said, in the process of taking off her royal-blue coat with silky blue-and-white detailing at the cuffs. "Memory does have an instinctive ability to use her empathy offensively," the cardinal murmured, "so an exercise designed to teach control to a martial mind makes sense."

Stomach lurching, Memory tried not to let those words hurt.

She'd forgotten she was in the presence of two experienced Es. Sascha's eyes widened. "Memory, sweetheart, that's a *good* thing."

The cardinal came to sit beside Memory, weaving one hand through Memory's. "Do you know how many people want to use Es? Break us and manipulate our abilities for their own gain?" The stars disappeared from her haunting gaze. "If we can teach all Es to do what you do without thought, we give them a sword *and* a shield."

Jaya nodded. "You're an E we could pair with a more vulnerable one so you could protect that person."

Memory's entire sense of self altered at that instant. To be the protector rather than a victim? It filled so many broken spaces inside her. "I see now," she said through the intense tightness in her chest. "Thank you."

Sascha and Jaya both hugged her with empathic affection before stepping outside to chat about the compound's wider training schedule. Ashaya spoke into the silence broken only by the faint murmur of the other two women's voices.

"Don't let the bastard who caged you continue to mess with your head." Her voice was firm, the words an order. "I grew up with Amara—trust me, I know how subtle the manipulation can be, how it gets inside you and creates holes, weakness that a psychopath can exploit. Believe nothing he ever told you about yourself."

Memory made a face. "I need to tattoo that on my forehead." She kept falling back into old patterns, believing herself a monster—but that was Renault. Not her.

"I don't think you need to go that far," Ashaya said with a laugh as she began to pack up. "I saw the way Alexei was with you—trust me, when a predatory changeling that strong keeps expecting you to meet him toe-to-toe, strength is a given." A wink. "Don't give an inch. It's much more fun that way."

Blood hot at the memory of tangling with Alexei, Memory raised a hand and felt her curls all separate and glossy, each one full of bounce. Things cracked and broke inside her. "Thank you," she whispered. "You've given me back a piece of myself." Now, she had to claim the rest, claim the future she wanted for herself. Growly wolf included.

Chapter 27

Okay, a grumpy man. Here's the thing, it depends on the changeling. Bears, for example, can be grump monsters—but pet them and tell them they're wonderful and the best at everything and they'll smile and grab you up in those big arms and the rest, as all of us mated to bears know, is delicious history.

Wolves, however, are a tougher nut to crack. It is the opinion of the *Wild Woman* team that wolves like to brood. They are the champions of changeling brooding . . . but crack that hard shell and oh, my goodness. No one plays like a wolf—he'll charm your pants right off your body. So if you get a grumpy wolf, we suggest a sneak attack.

—From the June 2077 issue of *Wild Woman* magazine: "Skin Privileges, Style & Primal Sophistication"

SASCHA SHOOED MEMORY out around two, after offering to put together sandwiches for them. "You need fresh air— and I need to call my cub."

Fascinated by the idea of a little girl who shape-shifted into an equally little panther, Memory popped into the bedroom area first to see her hair in the mirror. Both her hands flew to her mouth. She looked like a picture from a magazine, all vibrant hair, glossy and perfect. Except that it wasn't *too* perfect—Ashaya had left her curls to go where they would, and they erupted out of her head in a burst of wild joy.

Memory all but bounced back out to the kitchen area.

"You're very smart," Sascha was saying, a tone to her voice that made Memory's heart hitch, it was so quintessentially maternal. The cardinal's attention was on the small screen of her phone, but she lifted a hand in a wave as Memory passed.

Cold air kissed her cheeks outside, the bright sun no match for the fading edge of winter. Spotting a group of people seated on a rough circle of stones in the clearing to her left, she decided to go in the other direction. Only it was too late. Jaya had seen her; she motioned Memory over.

Heart thudding, Memory reminded herself to breathe— and to remember that invisible tattoo on her forehead.

"Break from shield training?" Jaya asked when Memory reached her.

Instead of wincing at the reference to her remedial shield lessons, Memory squared her shoulders and nodded. Shields were critical and hers needed to be impenetrable. No one would ever make her feel bad about prioritizing her protective barriers against evil.

"I had to train with Sascha, too," one man groaned, while around him, his peers chuckled. "I felt as if my brain was soup after every session—but, damn, she knows her shields. You couldn't have a better teacher."

The next ten minutes passed by in startlingly easy conversation with people who weren't so very different from Memory after all. She might've been the only one who'd been physically locked up, but they'd all experienced imprisonment—their abilities crushed and stifled, not one had known they were an empath until after the fall of Silence.

Each was in the infancy of exploring their powers, and Memory realized she was far from the only one with scars on her psyche. At one point, a quiet brunette E named Cordelia mentioned that she'd been denigrated in her family group as a "useless Gradient 1.7 psychometric." Cordelia was actually a Gradient 7.9 empath.

"It's hard getting my head around that," Cordelia said in her soft voice. "I keep falling into the black hole of thinking myself worthless."

Memory wanted to kick Cordelia's family for her, bruising them black and blue. Only one thing made her hesitate in sharing her own similar stumbles into a lack of confidence. *Jaya?* she telepathed after warily requesting contact. *Do they know I was a captive?* It'd brand her as different, make it impossible for her to just be one of the group.

Dark eyes full of infinite gentleness held hers. *That's your story to share or not as you wish. To them, you're just a fellow student.*

Memory exhaled slowly . . . then caught Cordelia's gaze. "Me, too," she said simply.

And it was enough.

Buoyant in the aftermath of meeting the others, she decided to walk into the trees where she'd last seen Alexei. Annoyance simmered inside her as she passed beneath the dark green firs. Where was he? If he thought—

"Alexei." Her heart kicked at his unexpected emergence.

Golden hair messy, he was dressed in blue jeans and a black T-shirt over which he'd thrown an old black sweater. The sleeves were shoved up to bare the muscled strength of his forearms. He was beautiful—and anger raged inside him in a scalding storm. So much that it burned her senses. This was no growl to keep her at bay, no snarl of temper. This anger reached down to the bone.

She strode to stand bare inches from him, the tips of her sparkly sneakers touching his boots. "What's happened?"

A nerve ticked in his jaw. "Renault's in the wind—murderous coward did a good job of disappearing, didn't leave a trail. We found souvenirs of his kills in his home."

Pushing a fisted hand against her gut, Memory fought down the bile that threatened to rise. "He used to show me sealed packets. He had one with my mother's hair in it, and on my ninth birthday, he sat there and taunted me with what it felt like to take her life." Long-ago screams echoed inside her. "I threw a screaming fit so bad that it put me out of commission for two weeks." Days she'd spent disoriented and adrift in nightmares and grief. "He never did it again."

Alexei thrust one hand into his hair to cup her skull, hauled her close to him. She went, pressing the side of her face against his chest and wrapping her arms around his body. The primal scent of him sank into her, as wild and untamed as Renault had been an oily smoothness. His heartbeat was strong and steady under her cheek, but claws sliced out of the fingers of his free hand.

"Fucker is going to die." A flat tone rigid with fury. "We've blasted his face and details across the Trinity network and alerted Enforcement. Cops are trying to track down the identities of the other women from whom he kept souvenirs." A harsh exhale against her hair, as if he'd bent his head to be closer, as if he needed the closeness as much as her. "We found a body, too."

Memory squeezed her eyes shut as ice trickled down her spine. "After a transfer, he could become charming. He could talk women into going home with him. The victims won't all be Psy." It made her feel so ugly and dirty to know that she'd helped a monster thrive, that she was the reason many of those women had trusted him.

Chest rumbling, Alexei leaned down and bit the tip of her ear.

When she jumped, he snarled. "Don't you dare let him fuck up your head."

Pulling back to glare up at him while she rubbed at her abused ear, she said, "He'll come after me." A hard fact.

Alexei moved his hand to the side of her throat, ran his thumb over her skin. "Get strong. Get shielded. I'll give you a big knife as your graduation present so you can take the first hack at his neck before I tear it off."

It was a bloodthirsty thing to say. Memory didn't balk. Fisting her hands in the sides of Alexei's sweater, she rose on tiptoe; she wanted to kiss her angry wolf, comfort him with touch.

But he grabbed her wrists, strong fingers holding her away from him without causing her pain. "I'm not a wolf you want to play with." Wild amber eyes, claws brushing her skin. "I don't have the patience to ease you into anything."

Her chest heaved, her skin tight and a strange tension in her abdomen. "Who asked you to go easy?" she challenged, the raw physicality inside her a dark new force she could barely comprehend.

"You're a kitten when it comes to intimate skin privileges," he growled, his eyes flicking to her hair, lingering. But the stubborn wolf didn't give her a compliment, didn't play with her curls as he'd bargained with her to do. "I eat kittens for breakfast."

Memory kicked him. With the shoes he'd given her. "You're a big, fat, wolfy liar," she said, well aware she was striking a match to kindling. "My sneakers tell me so."

The nerve in his jaw began to tick again. "An attack of middle-of-the-night madness. It won't be repeated."

Her ear yet stinging and her blood afire, Memory whispered nonsense low under her breath, and when he instinctively lowered his head to hear her better, she bit him on the jaw. Snarling, he pulled back . . . but didn't let go of her wrists. "You are in so much trouble."

"I'm terribly scared," she said, batting her eyelashes at him in the most provoking way she could imagine.

Alexei's hands tightened on her wrists before he let go and took a step back. "I'm serious, Memory. I'm not a good playmate for you." Black shadows crawling across his face, the veins on his forearms standing out as he fisted his hands. "Find a nice tame human or Psy."

It turned out that she had a rejection limit, and he'd pushed way past it. "You know what?" She pointed a finger at him. "You're right. I'll get right on finding better male company." Turning on her heel even as his irises became ringed by amber, she stomped back into the compound.

Slamming into the cabin, she found Sascha seated at the kitchen table with sandwiches ready and two hot drinks waiting. "You get any angrier and you'll set your hair on fire."

Memory dragged back her chair and sat. "Alexei is treating me as if I'm a child, as if I can't make adult decisions."

Frowning, Sascha picked up her drink. "I'm usually firmly on the side of anyone coming up against dominant changeling protectiveness, but Alexei has a point." She held up a hand when Memory's head jerked up. "Before we carry on, you should know I asked him to give you space to settle into the cabin—he didn't stay away on his own."

Memory parted her lips, but Sascha wasn't finished. "You don't have a pack or a family looking out for you." Intense and unblinking eye contact. "What kind of self-appointed big sister would I be if I didn't poke my nose into your business and make sure you don't get eaten alive by a wolf?"

The deep, warm feeling at being referred to as a sister

collided against her aggressive need to forge her own path. "I can handle him."

"I'm beginning to see that." A wry smile. "But look at it from his side. Alexei can't know if you're attracted to him, or if it's only gratefulness on your part."

Memory narrowed her eyes. "I'm not a duckling, to imprint on my rescuer."

"No, you're not," Sascha said slowly. "In fact, you're incredibly well-adjusted and certain of your sense of self for someone who was held captive for fifteen years." The cardinal leaned back in her chair. "Not only that, your captor violated your mind on a regular basis."

Memory curled her fingers against the wood of the table. "Do you think I'm a fraud?" It came out a hard demand, her breath stuck in her chest and scorching flames under her skin. "Does the Collective?"

"Memory." Sascha smiled in affectionate rebuke. "I've been in your mind, little sister. I know the truth better than anyone."

Cheeks heating, Memory rubbed both hands over her face. "Sorry. It's just . . ."

"I know." Sascha took a sip of her drink. "I faced a lot of distrust when I first came in contact with DarkRiver. Trust takes time and a hundred small acts of loyalty to build—you have to be patient and so do I."

Memory knew the other woman was right, that she couldn't expect the world to just believe her, but that didn't stop her from fuming about the unfairness of it. "Why do you think I'm not mad or broken? Why am I normal enough to pass?"

"Eat first," Sascha ordered in a firm tone.

Memory picked up a sandwich with a grumpiness to rival Alexei's. "Do all big sisters think they know best?"

Cheeks creasing, Sascha said, "From what I've seen, it's in the manual. The nosiness and annoying interference-for-your-own-good is a pack thing."

Memory smiled in spite of herself as she took a bite.

Only after she was halfway through her sandwich did Sascha speak. "Part of it is you," she said, putting down her own sandwich. "You're one of the strongest personalities I've ever come across—you *shine*, Memory, this strong solid light that refuses to waver."

Memory made a face. "I came close to crumpling under Renault's control so many times."

"But you didn't," Sascha pointed out. "Own your courage."

The words rang inside Memory's skull, adding weight to the ones Ashaya had spoken. "He's slithered away. The wolves found evidence of multiple murders in his home, but no signs of where he might've gone."

"He'll be hunted wherever he lands," Sascha said with a grim smile. "I like the idea of him scrabbling for hiding spaces, don't you?"

Yes, yes, she did. "If personality is one part," she said, "what's the other?" Renault had already consumed too much of her life; now, she had to focus on learning her own strengths and weaknesses.

"The fact you're an E." Sascha took another sip from her mug. "Renault may have blocked you from consciously accessing the PsyNet, but he couldn't cut off your primitive biofeedback link without killing you, and the empathic ability works in a passive way regardless of Silence or shields. It doesn't work as well, but it works."

The cardinal tapped a fingernail against the tabletop. "This isn't common knowledge, but at one point, the Council went about trying to eliminate Designation E from the gene pool. Eugenics on a massive scale." Starless eyes held Memory's. "What use are healers of the heart in a world without emotion?"

Memory froze, black horror curdling her stomach. "What happened?"

"The Correlation Concept. Psy began to lose their minds. Violence erupted. Chaos threatened." Words that cut, Sascha's anger a refined blade. "So the Council stopped its extermination program in favor of permitting Es to exist—while erasing all knowledge of the designation from the world. They told us we were nothing, failures."

Right then, Memory saw that Sascha had lived and survived her own prison, rising to spit in the faces of those who would crush her. "You think that passive aspect worked in reverse to nurture me?"

"It explains your high emotional intelligence and innate sense of good and evil. You were raised by a psychopath and yet you're a good, whole person."

"Add spite to the list of reasons," Memory muttered. "I stayed myself to spite him."

Sascha's lips kicked up. "Poor Lexie. I think I need to look out for him, not you. He has no idea who he's messing with."

"That stubborn grouchy wolf can go jump in a lava lake for all I care."

Eyes filled with stars again, Sascha chuckled. "I spoke to Alice Eldridge, as we discussed before lunch, and she suggested that you might be one of the E-sigma."

Sascha had told Memory that Alice was the closest thing the world had to an expert on Designation E. Put into forcible cryonic suspension over a hundred years ago, the researcher had awakened to a world that had altered beyond comprehension. All her friends and family dead, her research on empaths all but erased from the world.

Memory's heart ached for the woman she'd never met.

"But even Alice only knows bits and pieces," Sascha added.

Pushing her braid behind her shoulder, the cardinal put both forearms on the table. "Apparently Es of subdesignation sigma never actually used their abilities. It was considered too dangerous."

Memory had finished her sandwich without realizing it. She took an absent sip of what she'd assumed was coffee. It wasn't. It was sweet and creamy and melted her bones. "What *is* this?"

"Hot chocolate. Food for the soul. I also brought cookies."

"I understand why Es like me wouldn't want to use their abilities," Memory said after inhaling three oatmeal raisin cookies. "I'm only alive because Renault realized my long-term utility. Most psychopaths would drain the E to death at first contact."

"It means previous sigmas didn't have the ability to cut

off the transfer from their end." Sascha put down her half-eaten cookie, her brow furrowing. "Or, more likely, since the Es blocked their own abilities because of bad historical precedent, the question never came up."

"Is it doable?"

"My mother can seed mental viruses and even she agrees I'm the best shield builder in or out of the Net." A fleeting emotion on Sascha's face, too complicated to label. "We're going to build you a shield so formidable that you can slam it down mid-transfer, slicing the feed in two."

"Then I'm ready." Alexei would keep. Next time the two of them met, Memory was going to metaphorically singe off his fur.

Chapter 28

Dear Aunt Rita,

My wolf friend has suddenly begun to bring me random gifts of food. It started off innocently enough—a piece of candy here, a sandwich there when I forgot my lunch at home. But two days ago, he left a box of out-of-season white peaches at my door. Then yesterday, he turned up with an entire trifle along with a can of whipped cream. What does this mean?

Sincerely,
Confused Human

Dear Confused Human,

Sit down, dear. I have some news for you.

—From the October 2078 issue of *Wild Woman* magazine: "Skin Privileges, Style & Primal Sophistication"

MEMORY'S PLAN TO sear off Alexei's fur hit a snag out of the gate: the damn wolf was suddenly never around when she had free hours in her intensive training schedule. Oh, she knew he kept an eye on the compound, could taste him in the air, but he was avoiding her.

It didn't take much work for her to find his comm code. Three days after their last encounter, she was standing in front of the comm, about to call him, when she thought about what she was doing. Was Sascha right? Had she imprinted on Alexei because he'd pulled her to freedom?

Every cell in her body rebelled against that idea.

"But that's not enough," she said aloud. "You have to prove it to yourself and to him." Otherwise, she might cause her wounded wolf even more pain, and that was unacceptable.

Clenching her jaw, she deleted his comm code from her system, then strode outside, off into the trees. When a black-clad form appeared a short distance from her without warning, a phantom she hadn't detected with her empathic senses, she froze.

Her mouth went dry.

Yuri, that was his name. A man with rough-hewn features and strands of silver in his chestnut hair, his jaw always clean-shaven in the morning but dark with shadow by the end of his shift. A tiny detail that had made him seem more approachable to her, but she'd never actually spoken to him. And now, alone in the trees with him, she saw only the deadly assassin who was part of the Arrow squad.

"You're aware of the perimeter limits?" His voice was ice—not because of the nothingness, but because of Silence. In his late forties, Yuri was the oldest Arrow in the security team and had spent too long under the Protocol to emerge unscathed.

"Yes." She rubbed her hands down her sweatshirt-covered arms.

"I apologize. I am causing you discomfort." He began to fade into the trees.

"No," Memory blurted out, infuriated by her reaction to this man who had done nothing to hurt her. "I'm just not used to many people yet." All the myriad personalities, all the different levels of lingering Silence.

"I felt the same," Yuri said unexpectedly, his hands behind his back. "But now I have a family, and it is good." A moment of eye contact, his irises a dark hazel against weathered skin that didn't hold a tan but was marked by tiny lines at the corners of his eyes—and what appeared to be a knife scar on his left cheekbone. "Do not allow the past to shape your future."

It was another version of what Ashaya had said to her. If the universe was sending her a message, it wasn't being subtle about it. "I won't," she promised him, and when the next day dawned, she made a deliberate effort to talk to him again.

As the days passed, they began to walk together. Yuri's energy was as calm and patient as Alexei's was wild and turbulent. Her reaction to Yuri was different, too. She felt no urge to antagonize the quiet, contained male who had lived so long in the shadows that sunlight had once seemed an enemy.

"Now, I sit in the light with the youngest and most innocent of us all," he told her one day as sunset drenched the compound in myriad hues of orange and gold. "They ask me to tell them stories, so I've had to learn human and changeling tales for children. I hope they'll never have to know the blood and pain that is the history of every adult Arrow."

Caught by the touch of melancholy he permitted to escape, she said, "Why are you worried? Arrows are free now, too." He'd told her why the squad had first been formed and what it had become, how good men and women had been used by power-hungry Councilors for their own ends.

"Arrows are Arrows for a reason," he said to her. "The children . . . they have deadly abilities. All we can do is care for them, teach them to use their strength in the pursuit of good."

"I think they're lucky to have you," Memory said honestly, and though Yuri didn't smile—she hadn't ever seen his lips curve—she thought he was pleased. She liked him so much, was glad he seemed to consider her a friend, too, but never did she feel any compulsion to know him as a woman knows her man.

But this relationship, their friendship, she treasured it in its own right.

She made herself get to know the other Arrows, too, as well as her fellow empaths—and even the leopard and wolf soldiers who swung by the compound every so often on their patrol routes. She had to understand her own heart, had to know if the fact she dreamed of Alexei night after night was more than a thing of happenstance.

In those dreams, she felt the hard muscle of his body against her, shivered at the rasp of his stubble, gasped when he bit her. Each morning she woke frustrated and alone, she glared another hole in her mental photograph of a certain golden wolf. Then one day, she opened her door and found a small sealed box outside.

Eyes narrowed, she scanned the dawn-quiet compound, but found no grouchy wolf hanging around. She took the box inside before opening it . . . to find it full of granola bars. Dark cherry with white chocolate. Salted caramel and almonds. Apricot and mango. Walnuts with nougat.

Memory emptied out the box, but there was no note. Not that she needed one.

Scowling, she put all the bars back in the box. Then, at mid-morning, she took the box around the entire compound, offering the bars to the other Es, the Arrows, and *especially* a couple of SnowDancers who'd dropped by. The dark-haired one, who'd introduced himself as Riaz, accepted a bar with a gleam in his eye, and she knew he'd scented Alexei all over the box.

Good.

This was war.

THE obstinate, crabby wolf who'd rescued Memory then rejected her left her a full-size apple pie the next morning. In a warmer.

Memory fed it to an ecstatic bunch of empaths.

Two days later, she woke to a basket of exotic fruit.

That she gave to Yuri, to share with the children at the Arrow squad's own compound.

Then came the single-serving-size blueberry cake with her name written on it in white icing that glittered with sparkles. It hurt her heart, it was so pretty. She wanted desperately to keep it.

She set her jaw: Alexei didn't get to look after her when he'd walked away from her and *stayed away.*

Picking up the small cake box, she headed outside.

No one would take it off her hands. Her fellow trainees fought not to laugh as they waved it off with cobbled-together apologies about expanding waistlines and newborn allergies to blueberries, while Jaya bit down hard on her lower lip and pressed a hand to her heart. "Oh, Memory. That's so sweet."

"Hah!" Alexei wasn't being sweet; he was just trying to win their silent battle.

Giving up on romantic Jaya—who was convinced the

damn wolf's feelings would be hurt if anyone but Memory ate the cake—Memory went to the most clear-eyed and practical people in the compound. But the Arrows solemnly stated that they didn't wish to start a war with SnowDancer.

"Very funny," Memory muttered to a stone-faced Yuri before heading toward her next target.

Riaz, his hair tumbled from his run, took one look at the cake she thrust out under his nose and whistled. "What'd Lexie do to make you this mad?"

"Do you want it or not?" Memory tapped her foot.

"While the woman I love and adore would find it highly amusing if I ate that, Lexie would tie my intestines into knots."

"Ugh!" Stomping back to her cabin, Memory slammed the door shut behind her. Then she put the lovely little cake box in the center of the table and, hands fisted on her hips, stared at it. She was going to have to eat it. Wasting food was beyond her. And such a lovely confection of a cake?

No way she could throw it away. But she wasn't going to take this lying down.

Hauling her door open, she saw Riaz finishing up a conversation with Yuri. "Riaz!"

The wolf glanced over, one eyebrow raised.

"Tell Alexei he's a big, wolfy chicken!"

Chapter 29

As the first generation born and raised in Silence comes of age, a problematic abnormality has come to light, one that appears to affect only those with abilities above 8 on the Gradient.

—Report prepared for the Psy Council (circa 1997)

THE ONE WHO had awakened stared at the papers on his desk.

Things hadn't developed as he'd planned. Dr. Mehra had found no defects in his brain, but this new power was a huge, rapacious beast that wanted to devour him whole. He'd nearly suffered an out-of-control emotional reaction to a problem the previous day, and this morning, he'd woken obsessing over the empaths.

The pen in his hand snapped, spilling blue ink across his skin.

He watched the runnels of blue as they spread out in a spiderweb, and he thought of the web in which he was caught: the Honeycomb. If he was having trouble with his Silence, it couldn't be the power at fault—he'd always had that inside him. Which left only one other possible explanation: the Honeycomb must be altering him on a far deeper level than he'd realized. He had to contain the damage.

If he didn't, he would become a slave to his power rather than a master of it.

Two hours later, as he thought over a critical business move, he didn't realize he was writing *Honeycomb-Designation E, Honeycomb-Designation E* over and over on his datapad.

Chapter 30

Hey, Lexie, I hear you have your own handpicked flowers situation going on. Unlike *some* wolves who laugh at their friends' misfortunes, I am piously sad for your disappointment.

Shut up, Matt. No one likes a gloater. And scuttlebutt is Nell sent back your handwritten letter after stamping it with Not interested *in red. Don't be too brokenhearted though—she got the stamp made special for you.*

Karma will come for you, you asshole. And if you don't steal that fucking stamp off her desk and throw it in the deepest hole you can find, I'm gonna come over there and beat your skinny ass.

You could try, you lumbering bear masquerading as a wolf. I already have the stamp—what do you take me for? I put it in the pack post for you so you can hold it hostage.
— Messages between Matthias Agrey García and
Alexei Vasiliev Harte

ALEXEI GRITTED HIS teeth and kicked the wall.

That bastard Renault had gone under so deep that he'd become invisible on every technological level. Aden had confirmed that even the PsyNet was devoid of useful data. "The man is a ghost."

Not that Alexei was about to stop hunting. Just as he wasn't about to stop his daily run to and security review of the empathic compound—even though he'd been accused of being a "big, wolfy chicken" by an E with a mouth he wanted to devour. After he bit her for the insult that had spread through the pack like wildfire.

If he found one more rubber chicken in his gear, he was going to wring the pranksters' necks. The entire pack found it hee-fucking-larious that a tiny E had no fear of one of the most dangerous wolves in SnowDancer. D'Arn the future dead man had opened a betting book on the "Memory versus Alexei Live Action Drama."

Even Lara had gotten into the act—and she had a newborn pup who'd decided he enjoyed being awake all hours of the day and night. Walker, the healer's mate, had become a familiar sight in the corridors at night, as he paced quietly up and down with their pup cradled against his chest—in hopes that the irritable little guy would decide he actually wanted to behave like a sensible newborn and sleep now and then.

Hawke had pulled alpha privilege and taken the week-old baby with him for a night shift the other day so the couple could get uninterrupted hours of sleep. Alpha and newborn had apparently had a grand old time, but so soon after birth, the pup was too little to spend much time apart from his parents with anyone other than his alpha, so the rest of the pack had to contain their champing-at-the-bit desire to pupsit.

As for Lara, she was radiant. She'd kissed Alexei on the cheek when he went to visit, and, with a straight face, requested he bring her his special wolfy chicken soup. Toby, the now-teenaged cardinal she'd claimed as her own with fierce maternal love when she mated his uncle, had protested innocence when Alexei accused him of bringing the news to her ears. The kid was a fucking terrible liar. It was a good thing Alexei's wolf liked him.

His own second-in-command, Ember, had picked Memory for the eventual winner in the game.

"I'll remember this," he threatened when they spoke over the comm, only for her to laugh and ask him to send her a photo of his E.

"She's not my E." Could never be his anything if he wanted to keep her safe.

But when he went down to the compound toward the end of a glorious mountain sunset and spotted Memory sitting on the porch of her cabin with her shoulders slumped and her eyes on the ground, he had to grip the trunk of a tree to stop himself from striding directly to her. "What happened?" he asked Jaya; the young empathic teacher had been pacing in the trees when he arrived.

Fine lines flared out from the corners of her eyes. "You know Memory and Amara are continuing to work together?"

"Yes." Alexei wasn't exactly happy about that, but Memory needed to practice cutting the feed, and Amara was the safest suitable option.

Not that anyone trusted Ashaya's twin an inch. Memory always had backup, Alexei included. He just remained out of sight, ready to offer a physical assist if Sascha called for it. "She disengaged Amara on her own yesterday." Pride burned in him, as hot and dark as it had while he stood with his back to an external wall of the old cabin and listened to her gasp at her own success.

He'd lost the battle to leave a congratulatory gift at her door.

He wondered if she'd thrown the colorful beaded necklace in the garbage. Word from the wolves who ran patrols along here was that Memory now gave the death stare to any wolf who crossed her path. His packmates blamed him for making a pretty woman mad at them, while Alexei's wolf fought not to eviscerate the assholes for attempting to flirt with her.

He couldn't stop looking after her, but he wasn't going to be the dog in the manger. Memory deserved to be loved, deserved to be adored. If Alexei couldn't do it, he had to let her choose another man.

His claws sliced into the tree trunk. "Did Amara hurt Memory?"

"No, it's not that." Jaya slid her hands into the pockets of her jacket, her lilting voice holding the cadence of her homeland, lush green atolls set in turquoise-blue lagoons. "Memory's phenomenally powerful. She won't have her new Gradient tests until she's had a bit more training, but it's obvious she's over a 9. And there's so much stubborn will there. I've never seen her give up. She just gnaws at a problem until she figures it out."

That was his E with the heart of a lioness. "Then why does she look like that?" She'd hunched her shoulders forward under a bright pink top with glittering silver shoulders, and bowed her head; her exuberant curls were restrained with a thick black hair tie.

"It's her psychic scent." Lines of strain marked Jaya's normally smooth skin. "She comes back smelling 'wrong' after every session with Amara, as if she's a different and far colder person under the skin. It's eerie and it makes the other empaths react badly."

Alexei thought of that night in the substation when she'd screamed and screamed and he'd caught a hint of a scent on her that wasn't her own. A dark and ugly scent. It had happened again that first session with Amara, but he'd shrugged it off as an artifact from Amara herself, an imprint left behind even though the scientist had departed the cabin.

"Are they isolating her?" His claws dug deeper into the tree trunk. "She needs people." His lioness had spent too long alone, was never happier than when surrounded by others.

Riaz was enjoying laughing at Alexei at present, but his fellow lieutenant also let Alexei know how Memory was doing during the times she interacted with him. "She's hardly ever alone," the other man had said after a recent patrol shift. "The others gravitate toward her porch and my wolf can feel her delight in their visits. If I didn't know better, I'd say she was part-changeling."

Alexei had seen the same on his own visits, had found himself thinking that she'd love living in a wolf den. She'd probably join up with the maternal cabal and delight in sweetly interfering in the lives of her packmates. He'd made a bet with himself that Memory not only sushi-rolled her towels and put rose petals in with her clothes, she did the same for her friends.

She shouldn't be sitting dejected, her aloneness an acute ache in the air.

"These are Es, Alexei," Jaya reminded him. "They're horrified by their behavior after they recover from brushing up against that awful cold nothingness, and then they fall over themselves apologizing, but it hurts Memory all the same."

Jaw a brutal line, Alexei said, "I'm taking her out of here

for the night." Away from people who hurt her even if they didn't mean to, and into the world of his wolf.

Jaya's eyebrows shot up. "Um, you realize she curses your name on a daily basis?"

Alexei's wolf bared its teeth inside him. "Good." Anger fueled Memory's strength.

MEMORY scuffed at the grass with one sneakered foot. She'd scared Cordelia today, and Cordelia was an intensely kind soul destined to be a medical E. Four hours ago, the other woman had made inadvertent physical contact with Memory after a session with Amara. Memory's friend had whimpered, then thrown up.

Poor Cordelia had come by again not long ago, tears rolling down her sweet round face and her creamy skin blotchy. "I'm so sorry, Memory. I don't know why I reacted that way. I'm so sorry."

Memory had hugged Cordelia to show her there were no hard feelings, but as late afternoon darkened into early evening, she faced an unpalatable truth that had nothing to do with Renault's subtle attacks on her confidence: her kind of darkness didn't fit with the sunshine and warmth of Designation E.

She was the ugly stepchild.

No, that wasn't fair to her fellow Es, her *friends*. Not one of them had been anything but mortified by their behavior. It didn't matter how Memory tried to explain that it had to do with her and the echo of her work with Amara, they still looked like kicked puppies, all bruised eyes and shame.

How could she live in this community when she gave her friends nightmares?

A kiss of primal wildness against her senses, an edgy wolfish scent.

Memory gripped one of the posts that held up the porch roof and refused to look. Not even when a pair of scuffed boots stopped in front of her. "Nice skirt."

Memory was wearing an ankle-length skirt in silvery white that was all air and clouds. She'd found it at a cut-rate price on a site that sold "seconds and remainders"—the idea of rescuing slightly blemished clothes from being discarded made her even happier than buying shiny, perfect things, and it was now her favorite site.

The "blemish" on this piece was a small drop of pink paint on the hem. To Memory, that just made the skirt even more wonderful and unique.

Her fellow Es had been agog the first time she'd worn it. At least that was one thing she'd changed for the better—the sedate Psy dress code was well on its way out of the compound. Cordelia had begun ordering colorful dresses with flared skirts and Joseph had found Hawaiian shirts, while Reema had discovered the joys of makeup.

Only the Arrows remained black-clad and unmoved by the change, but Memory was working on that. After discovering that it was Yuri's birthday a few days back, she'd bought him a long-sleeved black T-shirt, such as those she'd noticed many of the squad wore under their high-collared and bullet-proof uniform jackets—except her chosen tee had a thin stripe of silver down the outside of each sleeve.

Yuri had worn it today; it was hidden under his jacket, but he'd made a point to tell her that he'd caused a commotion among his squadmates with his "sudden stylistic prowess." He'd also asked her advice on how to respond to an understated but clear overture from a senior female Arrow.

Memory's heart had nearly burst in joy at the indication of Yuri's growing world, but her friend wasn't the male who stood in front of her, taking up all the air in the yard and blocking the last of the light.

"Hello, lioness."

"Go away," she muttered, wanting to brood alone—and definitely not anywhere near this wolf who'd ignored her for *three weeks*.

"Can you even walk in that skirt?" he asked dubiously.

She pulled up the skirt to show him her glittery sneakers. The stupid things were her favorites. Dropping her skirt when she realized she'd let him taunt her into betraying herself, she glared at the ground. "I *said*, go away."

He tugged at a curl that had escaped her messy ponytail. When she slapped his hand away, he just found another curl to tug. Hands fisting, she jumped to her feet and put a foot of distance between them. "What do you want, you big, wolfy chicken?"

The beautiful golden god of a man—who was half demon—smiled at her instead of snarling in insult. "Want to get out of here?"

It was the only thing he could've said that would cut through her morose mood. "Yes, let's go." At least she could be furious with Alexei without making anyone feel bad—it certainly had no effect on him.

Her skirt flowed around her as she strode toward the trees, the fabric as light as air. Suspiciously silent at her side, Alexei easily kept pace. When they passed Jaya coming the other way, the other E stopped to enclose Memory in the warm acceptance of her arms, not minding that Memory had stiffened in instinctive self-protectiveness.

"Give him hell," her friend whispered in her ear. "Arrows and wolves, they're the same. Show him your teeth."

Memory had every intention of biting Alexei with those teeth.

"Here." Alexei handed her his jacket.

About to snub the offer, Memory looked at his face and realized the obstinate wolf wouldn't take her deep into the forest unless she agreed to this. And Memory needed to *leave*, to get some clear air. Also, it was cold now that the sun had set. Snatching the olive-green thing from him, she shrugged into it, then rolled up the sleeves with quick motions.

The two of them had just stepped beyond the tree line when a roar of sound hit Memory's telepathic senses. Not an attack. A call for help, directed at *her*. "Yuri!" She turned on her heel . . . and a scream split the air, reverberating against the trees.

ALEXEI was moving even before he'd consciously processed Memory's reaction and the chilling scream that followed. "Talk to me!" he said to her as the two of them ran back to the compound.

"Yuri yelled for help!"

Fuck! Yuri was the most senior Arrow in the compound.

Why would a man of his lethal skills call for an inexperienced E? It had to be bad.

"Go!" Memory yelled, a sob in her voice. "I can't keep up! Yuri's mind is gone! I can't reach him!"

Alexei pounded into a ground-erasing run, his heart punching against his rib cage. He could have a catastrophic medical emergency on his hands. Sascha had briefed him on the compound when he first took over Indigo's oversight task, and one of the things he'd learned from her was that many newly emergent Es didn't know how to protect themselves against dangerous surges of emotion.

If Yuri was dead as a result of violence . . .

Memory was still standing, he reminded himself. It gave him hope. Until he scented wet iron on the air. *Blood.*

His gaze snagged on a fallen body.

Yuri was down with a bloody wound to the head. A silent weapon, because Alexei's acute hearing had picked up nothing of the attack itself, only the aftermath. Three collapsed bodies lay on the ground nearby, all of them twitching.

Empaths who'd overloaded at the close proximity to violence.

Other black-clad men and women were hauling Es out of danger. But what the fuck *was* the danger? Who had managed to not only invade this deep into predatory changeling territory, but take down an Arrow honed by decades of active duty? He dropped down beside Yuri's body, felt for a pulse with no real hope. The senior Arrow's face was awash in blood, part of his skull blown off.

Jesus!

"He's alive!"

An Arrow Alexei recognized as a trained medic slammed down beside him, already tearing off her jacket to stanch the bleeding.

Memory's voice crashed into him at the same instant. "Abbot!" She hit the edge of the chaos, her chest heaving from her headlong run and her skirt like air around her. "Alexei, it's got Abbot!"

Alexei snapped his head toward where he'd last seen the Arrow with black hair and searing blue eyes. Abbot had been grabbing Es and 'porting them out of danger, but now he stood with his weapon in his hand, and that weapon was pointed directly at a dark-eyed empath with a lovely oval face.

Jaya.

Alexei began to move, but he was too far away. He couldn't knock the weapon out of Abbot's hand faster than the man could activate it. Jaya held out her hands, palms up. "Abbot, *habibi*"—soft voice, no hesitation—"this isn't you. Fight it. Use the bond that ties us together and fight it. I'm your wife. Your Jaya."

As Alexei watched, a vein began to pulse in Abbot's temple, sweat dripping down his face. His jaw clenched . . . and the gun began to change direction. Toward Abbot. All at once, Alexei knew who had taken out Yuri.

He was close enough now to slam his body into Abbot's arm, but Abbot was a strong Arrow, and Alexei was a split second too late. The weapon went off.

Blood sprayed the air.

Jaya screamed, "NO!"

Her terror was grating claws on his skin, Abbot's blood iron in his nose.

Memory ran past him in the direction of another Arrow— one who only stepped in for the odd security shift to keep her skills sharp. Elsewise, Cristabel was one of the squad's most respected trainers. Right now, Cris was standing there, looking confused, doing nothing aggressive at all, but Alexei trusted Memory's instincts. She'd been right about Abbot.

He took off in her wake, quickly passing her.

Cristabel was just reaching for her weapon when Alexei got to her. He knocked her out with an uppercut to the jaw. He was careful to pull the punch because Psy bones were weaker than changeling. Cristabel went down, but she was very much alive.

"Incapacitate yourselves and each other!" he yelled at the Arrows. "*You* are the threat!"

The black-clad men and women were used to making split-second decisions, and they'd witnessed both Abbot's and Cristabel's inexplicable behavior. One by one, they took one another down until only one was left. Amin, who'd incapacitated multiple of his brethren with quick efficiency, nodded at

Alexei to do the same to him. But his eyes changed even as Alexei moved, a strange blankness coming over them.

His weapon was in his hand a heartbeat later.

Rather than pointing it at Alexei, he pointed it at an empath crouched on the grass, her hands over her ears as she whimpered and rocked back and forth. Alexei had only one choice. To put himself in between Amin and the E. He did so without hesitation . . . just as Amin collapsed.

Memory dropped the large rock she'd used to whack the Arrow over the back of the head. Eyes of pure obsidian caught Alexei's. "It's hunting us."

Chapter 31

The Es and the Arrows are a unit.

—Zaira Neve to Ivy Jane Zen

AS ALEXEI MOVED toward the fallen form of Jaya's beloved Abbot, Memory looked back toward Yuri. He was gone. Nerida must've teleported him out before she took herself out of the equation.

Jaya and Alexei were with Abbot.

Heart an agonized knot, Memory jolted herself toward Cordelia. Her movements were no longer those of a clockwork creature after over three weeks of healing, but today's violence was a hammer beating at her skull.

Dropping down beside Cordelia's whimpering body, Memory put her arms around her friend's soft, curvy form and rocked with her. "The darkness is gone," she reassured her in a firm tone. "It couldn't hold on to the Arrows. It's gone."

Cordelia ducked her head, tucking herself against Memory's chest, as if Memory were the taller one. Memory kept on rocking her even as she watched Alexei tear off his T-shirt and fold it into a rough pad to press against Abbot's neck. The bullet had hit the side of that neck just above his jacket collar; blood gushed, and the only other teleporter in the compound was down, as was the medic who'd first responded to Yuri.

Abbot was dying.

And Yuri . . . His mind had just *stopped*, the telepathic

disconnection a bruise inside Memory. Yuri had been meant to return home in an hour to read bedtime stories to Arrow children. They'd be waiting for him. As Jaya waited for her mate to open his eyes. Jaya, who worked with coma patients, but who could also feel the death agonies of the recently deceased.

Oh, God. Alexei didn't know that. Memory began to release Cordelia and rise. If Abbot died while Jaya was so close, her hands cradling his head in her lap, Memory knew Jaya would go with him, falling into her love's death.

Flickers around the compound, more Arrows teleporting in. Every muscle in Memory's body locked, but that horrible and *wrong* darkness didn't attempt another takeover. Ice filled the air, the Arrows focused on Alexei.

Memory found her voice on a furious wave of protectiveness. "It wasn't Alexei! Yuri and Abbot shot themselves so they wouldn't hurt us! *I* hit Amin!"

Aden Kai, the leader of the squad, stared directly at her. She'd met him once when he came to speak to the team here. He was quiet, too. But not like Yuri. Aden wasn't peaceful. Aden was contained like a storm. His friend Vasic, who'd just teleported out both Abbot and Jaya, was more like Yuri.

"What happened?" Aden hunkered down in front of her, and though he wasn't a physically imposing man in comparison to Yuri or Alexei, his body built along more slender lines and his muscles lithe, *power* lived inside him. All the more deadly for not being worn openly.

Cordelia sobbed and tried to bury herself in Memory.

Squeezing her arms tighter around the other E, Memory held Aden's unreadable dark gaze. "You need to leave. You're scaring Cordelia." She looked around. "Your Arrows are scaring everyone."

No other E in the compound was in any way functional right now. Blank faces and tears, unconscious bodies, whimpering balls, every single trainee aside from Memory had overloaded—not on the bloody violence, she realized all at once, but because of their close links to the Arrows. After weeks of interaction, they were almost all connected on the Honeycomb, Arrows and Es.

Inexplicably, Memory wasn't linked to Yuri . . . but she could see that his light, it was gone, the connection severed.

"Stay away from the Es," she ordered Aden in a harsh tone. "Find out who did this."

Aden rose to meet Alexei, who'd walked toward them—and though the squad's leader said nothing aloud, his fellow Arrows moved away from the dazed and fallen empaths. Aden's people had expressionless down pat, but Memory sensed piercing distress beneath their icy faces.

Her heart ached for these soldiers who had already suffered too much pain, but she couldn't help them, wasn't that kind of empath. All she could do was hold her brethren and listen as Alexei spoke to Aden.

"Your Arrows put their lives on the line to protect the Es." Alexei's eyes glowed amber in the darkness that had fallen while blood spilled into the earth. "Pretty sure they were being aimed like weapons at the Es, but they refused to buckle under. I didn't see Yuri shoot himself, but I saw Abbot force the gun toward himself."

"Arrows have the most impenetrable shields in the Net." Aden's high cheekbones cut against the olive of his skin. "You're saying they fell victim to mind control?"

"I'm telling you what I saw." Alexei didn't budge an inch, as powerful as Aden but in a far more primal way. "And my point is that they *didn't* crumple under the pressure—the Arrows here didn't lay a single finger on an E except to protect."

Memory realized he was trying to comfort Aden and his people. Her golden wolf understood what today's events would do to a squad of assassins who'd allied themselves with the most vulnerable Psy in the Net. Arrows were the wolves of the PsyNet, Alexei had said—but those protective wolves had broken faith and turned on their charges.

"It wasn't their fault," Memory said through a thick throat, because that was important, had to be known. "The darkness wanted the Arrows to kill us, but Yuri and Abbot and Amin *wouldn't*."

The tension in Aden's body didn't appreciably alter, his features grim.

"Memory?" A husky, broken voice as Cordelia finally

lifted her head. Her greenish-brown eyes were blurred, her pupils hugely dilated. "Yuri hurt himself."

"Yes."

"Is he . . ."

"I don't know." All connections severed, it could have only one meaning, but Memory didn't want to think about that, didn't want to imagine a world where she'd never again take a walk with her friend. Eyes burning, she brushed Cordelia's hair back from her sweat-damp forehead. "Do you want to go to your cabin?"

"No." Cordelia sat back, began to look around. "The other Arrows are sad deep inside." Her hazy gaze cleared on a wave of intense worry. "We should help."

This, Memory thought, was courage, was heart. She was so proud of her designation at that moment because Cordelia wasn't the only E who was making their way to an Arrow. Memory made sure Cordelia was up and moving under her own steam, then went to Alexei.

He was shirtless, his chest covered in a dusting of golden fur and a fine spray of red on his skin: Abbot's blood. She didn't protest when he put an arm around her shoulders and maneuvered them so that part of her back rested against the warmth of his chest, his hand splayed over her abdomen.

"It wasn't your Arrows," she reiterated to Aden. "We all know that. I shouldn't have spoken to you the way I did earlier." In her need to protect Cordelia and the others, she'd struck out at the wrong people, and the shame of it lay heavy on her heart. "I'm sorry."

"No," the leader of the squad said. "I needed to know. Our proximity at that time could've panicked your peers."

She swallowed and asked the question she didn't want to ask. "Yuri and Abbot?"

Alexei tucked her even closer to his chest as Aden's gaze went to the dark patch of grass where Yuri had fallen. "Abbot's in surgery. Yuri . . . he breathes, but we must make the decision on whether to pull the life support."

Memory pressed a hand over her mouth, a sob catching in her throat.

Wrapping his arms around her, Alexei said, "There's no hope? Judd?"

Memory didn't understand how a telekinetic former Arrow could help, but Aden obviously did. "He's in the surgery suite, but it doesn't appear that there's anything he can do." Aden looked to Memory, every line of his body held with such precise control that it hurt her to see—he was in as much pain as his men and women.

"Yuri sustained a significant brain injury," Aden told her. "He wouldn't want to live this way. We are his family and must honor his wishes."

Tears rolling down her face, Memory nodded. "The children . . ."

The tendons on Aden's neck stood out against his skin. "Yuri breathes," he repeated.

And Memory knew Aden would put off the final decision until there was no more time and he had to let Yuri go forever. There was nothing Memory could do to help her friend, but she could give Aden and Alexei information on the menace that had tried to steal Yuri's mind and turn him into a murderer. "You need to know about the intruder."

Alexei's breath brushed her temple. "You okay to talk?"

"Yes." For whatever reason, her shields had held, her mind had held. Perhaps because she was a different kind of E, perhaps because her shields were unique—Sascha had designed them for Memory alone, and Memory had built them from the foundations.

"An unknown power invaded the compound today." Grief a rock on her chest, she used one hand to wipe away her tears. "I saw it take hold of Abbot, then Cristabel, then Amin." Frowning, she struggled to articulate what she knew. "Not a vision or telepathy. It's . . . like when I work with Amara."

She straightened against Alexei, his forearm warm and hard with muscle under her palm. "There's a connection. Amara can't read my mind, but *I* seem to learn pieces of her." It was the only advantage nature seemed to have given her—with Renault, she'd spent so much time fighting his coercive tactics that she'd never consciously realized it.

"The invader's mind brushed up against mine while he was scanning for another target, and I knew he was crushing the Arrows' minds in an attempt to force their actions." A sudden shock of knowledge before the instant was past.

"He?" Aden's voice shimmered with frost.

"Yes, I'm sure." The intruder's sense of identity was strong. "A man who's powerful in some way—there was an innate confidence to him."

"He have what you call the nothingness inside him?" Alexei's voice was a rumble she felt against her back as much as heard, the rough reality of it her anchor.

Memory parted her lips to reply yes, of course, then paused. "No," she said slowly, her eyes widening. "He isn't devoid of emotion, and he felt no pleasure during the attack . . . but there is a strange 'wrongness' to him. An image seen through cracked glass."

"Insanity of another flavor?" Aden asked in that same winter-frost voice Memory hoped his mate would be able to thaw.

It was Jaya who'd told a disbelieving Memory that the leader of the squad was happily mated to a "kick-ass" Arrow assassin. "She's terrifying—but only to people who dare hurt *her* people—and she has a huge heart and Aden worships her."

The echo of her friend's smile had Memory blinking back tears as she continued. "What I sensed was . . . determination." Yes, that was the right word. "No malice. A soldier taking down the enemy."

"Not a very organized one."

Alexei agreed with Aden's icy judgment, but his mind was on Memory. It was as if she were two people. Her scent kept fluctuating between the sharp brightness of her own and an infinite and disturbing coldness. He could see how that would freak out empaths. Alexei was irritated because he hated that another man's scent had become twined with her own, but he felt no repulsion, no sense of distaste.

"Do you believe this was true mind control?" Aden asked. "Did the intruder establish an access link? Are my people compromised?"

Fuck. Alexei hadn't even considered that.

"No," Memory said at once, her voice sure. "He shredded shields and just took—pure brute force." A frown in her next words. "It doesn't tie in with the stable confidence I sensed, but that's how it was."

Aden was silent for long seconds in the wake of Memory's revelations.

"The attack didn't succeed," Alexei pointed out to this man who was as much alpha of the Arrows as Hawke was of SnowDancer. "If there's a risk here, it's to your people, not the Es."

These wolves would not maul their charges.

"I can't trust that this intruder won't try again." Aden scanned the compound, taking in the small groups of Arrows and Es who stood close to one another.

Almost all the Es were talking, their expressions earnest and anxious, while the Arrows stood with faces like granite . . . but the deadly soldiers didn't move away. Neither did they reject or dislodge a touch when an E made tactile contact.

"My Arrows need to step down from security here until we uncover how anyone got through shields that should be unbreakable," Aden said.

"SnowDancer and DarkRiver can step in." Alexei had the seniority to make that call for his pack, and he knew the cats wouldn't disagree. Not when their alpha was mated to a cardinal E.

Aden gave a curt nod and began to turn toward his people.

"Wait." Memory released a shaky exhale. "You'll let us know? About Abbot . . . and Yuri?"

Dark eyes held Memory's. "Yes." Unspoken was that the updates might not be anything Alexei's lioness wanted to hear.

Chapter 32

There are indications that Silence had an impact on the power levels of more designations than just E.
— Report to Ruling Coalition from Research Group Gamma-X, Silence & Outcomes

HE OPENED HIS eyes to darkness and the awareness that his mind ached, as if he'd overstretched his psychic muscles. Staring out at the glittering black-and-white cityscape that had been glowing orange under the late afternoon sunlight when he closed his eyes to think over a business problem, he tried to remember the time in between.

Nothing. A blank slate.

Had he fallen asleep? He'd never before done that in the office, but when he turned his chair around to face his desk, his blood ran cold.

A hard-copy contract sat there, the pages partially flipped. When he flipped back to the front, he saw notes made in his own hand. Beside the contract was a half-eaten nutrient bar. He went to reach for it and saw he wasn't wearing his suit coat and his sleeves were folded back halfway up his forearms. He stared at skin marked only by a small childhood scar.

Then he looked at his timepiece.

Four hours since his last memory.

Four hours of blankness. Four hours during which he'd taken off his jacket, folded up his shirtsleeves, eaten part of a nutrient bar, and interacted with the aide who'd brought him the contract from the changelings.

His head throbbed as he went to telepath his most senior

aide, and then his mind flatlined. He stared unseeing at his desk. He'd flamed out, used so much psychic energy that he'd fried his brain.

It could take up to a day to recover.

The only bright point in this entire clusterfuck was that his mind wouldn't have flashed red on the PsyNet, alerting enemies and opportunists that his defenses were down. His silent and secret connection to Theodora meant his shields were now feeding off her psychic energy.

Would she have noticed? He wasn't certain. The link that tied him to his twin wasn't one that scientists had ever studied. He wasn't sure anyone but those like him and Theo knew it even existed—and they preferred to keep it private. Under Silence, their bond would've seen them stigmatized.

Now . . .

Rising, his psychic senses blank, he turned back to the window and the city spread out below. All his new power, the violence of it enormous, was gone. What had he done in those lost hours? Where had he expended so much psychic energy?

His breath turned shallow, a breach of Silence, but that was nowhere near his biggest concern. The PsyNet was closed to him until his psychic energy regenerated, but he grabbed a datapad and began going through the news sites.

Nothing. Nothing. Nothing.

He threw it down.

What had he *done*?

Chapter 33

Possible sighting of Erasmus David Renault by Fisherman's Wharf. Followed up within fifteen minutes. No sign of target. Bystanders in the area didn't recall anyone matching his description.

—DarkRiver Security Log

TWO HOURS AFTER the attack and Alexei pulled on his favorite black sweater. He was already wearing a black tee, hadn't needed the extra layer until his body began to cool down. Riaz's strong and striking partner in life and love, Adria, had remembered to bring him down a change of clothes after she got assigned to the compound's security team.

Alexei and that team had worked together with the cats to clear away every last sign of violence. Two brawny leopards had turned up with shovels and literally buried the blood that had soaked into the ground. Alexei had been concerned the Es would refuse to remain near the scene of such vicious aggression, but those of Designation E were tougher than they looked. Now that the first shock had passed, they were gritting their teeth and getting on with it.

"We can't insulate them from the real world," Ivy Jane Zen had said when she and Sascha arrived to deal with the fallout, her mouth bracketed by white lines. "Es have to be able to function around pain, around death."

The two senior empaths were staying the night and had already spoken to the trainees one by one. Memory alone wasn't on their list. Sensing her emotional stability, they'd roped her into distracting those Es who'd appeared particularly shaky—she'd done so by showing her charges articles from the *Wild Woman* magazines she'd found on a bookshelf in her cabin.

Oddly, all the Es—his lioness included—had appeared fascinated by the articles, their heads huddled together as they discussed certain points in great detail. Now, at last, the rest of the Es were all settled in their cabins and Memory sat on her porch, a tough-as-a-wolf princess in an airy skirt and sparkling shoes.

Except her eyes held infinite darkness when he reached her. "Do you think it came here because of me?" she asked, her voice haunted.

Alexei told himself not to growl at her. "It wanted the Arrows, not you." The growl *really* wanted to come out. "Have you eaten dinner?" It was nearly eight-thirty at night.

When she shook her head, he clenched his jaw. "Tell me I can go into your kitchen." He would not enter her territory without her permission.

She shrugged and propped her chin on her hands, elbows braced on her thighs. "If you want."

He returned after heating up one of the ready meals stocked in all the cabins. Then he scowled at her until she glared back and took a bite. After watching her take another bite, Alexei did what he'd been itching to do all night and pulled out the band corralling her curls.

They exploded around her head.

Shooting him another death glare, she pointed her fork at him. "Who said you had those skin privileges?"

"You did. We had a deal, remember?" He was no sly cat, but "strategy" was his middle name. "You reneging?"

A narrowing of her eyes. "Fine. But don't think this'll get you kisses."

Despite his earlier thoughts, Alexei felt exactly like a damn cat as he tugged and released and generally amused himself with the wildness of her hair . . . and the ache inside him, the constant throb since he'd stopped being near her, it began to ease.

Fuck, fuck, fuck.

Yet he couldn't walk away. Not tonight. Not when Memory was so alone in her uniqueness. "I love your hair." The words just fell out of his mouth.

Pausing mid-bite, she shot him a dark look from under her lashes . . . but her lips tugged upward. The entire day got better. Going back into her kitchen, he made them both a coffee, then came to sit beside her.

His thigh pressed against her. It twisted him up how badly he wanted to touch her, how much that small contact meant to his wolf, but he didn't create distance between them. Neither did she, her skirt fluffing out over his boot. Finishing her meal in silence, she put it aside, then picked up the coffee he'd adulterated with hot chocolate after spotting the new container sitting on her kitchen table.

The heat from the mug seeped into Memory's palms, but it was the heat of Alexei's body that held her captive. Her skin tingled where his thigh pressed into her, and as for her scalp, it felt electrified from his earlier playing. He'd had such a wolfish look on his face as he touched her in a way she'd allow no one else.

"Do you think the intruder will come back?" she said, forcing herself to think about the danger rather than the pleasure of sitting with Alexei under a starlit sky. She couldn't face the subject of Yuri and Abbot again yet, but they were there always, at the back of her mind.

"You said he was out of control, so yeah." He stared out at the night. "What I don't get is why the attempt to turn Arrows? Why not attack Es directly?"

Memory sipped at the coffee . . . and tasted chocolate, too. Her stomach grew warm, her toes curling in her shoes. "I don't know if logic played a part." Shadows drifted across her thoughts once more. "The attack was a thing of chaos."

Alexei's phone vibrated before he could reply. Taking it out, he glanced at the screen. "It's Hawke."

Whatever his alpha had to say to him, it had Alexei's claws sliding out of his hands, his voice turning cold. His last words were, "Yes, I'll tell Memory."

Palms suddenly clammy, Memory wondered what fresh horror was about to descend upon them.

"You want to hunt Renault?" Alexei asked after hanging up.

The answer required no thought. "I want to *destroy* him, make it so he can't hurt anyone else ever again."

"Then get ready." He wove his fingers through hers. "The bastard's taken an eight-year-old empath named Vashti—he left a note at the abduction site that her parents should contact SnowDancer, that we had something that belonged to him."

Nausea churned in Memory's gut, but her dark rage overwhelmed it into submission. Jerking to her feet, she said, "We have to find her."

"I'm going to let my team know what's going on." He broke their handclasp. "Bring what you need."

After running into her cabin, Memory stripped out of her skirt. She had to be sleek and fast to hunt Renault. In its place, she pulled on jeans of such a deep and vibrant blue that they were midnight. She kept on her pretty top and her sparkly shoes because she refused to allow Renault to erase who she was becoming, who she'd *always* been.

As for Alexei's jacket, she didn't really want to give it back—being wrapped up in his scent was like a constant hug from his strong arms. Glancing out the window, she confirmed that none of the wolves were wearing jackets. Alexei had even shoved up the sleeves of his sweater. He and his packmates seemed all but impervious to the cold.

She kept wearing the jacket, but said, "You won't be cold?" when they met again.

A quick shake of his head before he led her to an all-wheel-drive vehicle parked on the DarkRiver side of the compound. "Kidnapping took place in San Francisco. Cats had people in the area and they've gone in first."

"Whatever helps to save her." Memory was more than willing to sacrifice her need for vengeance if it'd keep a child from being imprisoned.

Alexei got them through DarkRiver territory relatively fast, but even with the high speeds permitted on the public roads, the trip to San Francisco wasn't a quick one. "Have the Arrows had any luck locating Renault on the PsyNet?" Memory asked in an effort to find some way to help the stolen E.

"Not so far." Alexei's hands tightened on the steering wheel. "Aden's people are nothing if not relentless—they *will* eventually track him down, but it'll take time."

Time was the one thing the kidnapped empath didn't have. Not only her, but all the women who would die to feed Renault's twisted psyche; he'd murdered before Memory and she had zero doubts he'd continue to murder now that she'd escaped. "I know him," she said, turning years of forced proximity into a weapon. "It's possible that once I see the location of the kidnapping, I can work out where he might've gone."

It wasn't much, but it was better than nothing.

"I have his scent." Alexei's voice was without growl, pure focused predator. "If we can determine where he ended his teleport, I can track him."

When they got to the location of the kidnapping—a small townhouse in the Nob Hill area—it was to be greeted by a leopard changeling who confirmed Renault had teleported in and out. The DarkRiver changeling's jaw was scruffy, his eyes nightglow. "I picked up an unknown scent in only one area of the home—by the little girl's desk. It's in front of a window. Caught the same scent outside the window."

Memory gritted her teeth. "He saw her, teleported in." All Renault needed was a clear enough visual of his intended location. "He had to have stalked her beforehand, knew she was an E."

Alexei's gaze scanned the area, a steely hardness to him she'd never before seen. "Parents?"

"Single dad. Hard to read, but he recently transferred his daughter to a school that has an E on staff and runs an E training course alongside telepathy and all the rest."

Memory's heart hurt for a father who so obviously cared. "I want to go in, see if I can pick up anything." Maybe Renault had made a mistake others had missed; it was likely a fruitless hope, but she had to try.

Alexei and the leopard came with her, the two having a low-voiced discussion about the circumference of Renault's teleporting ability and how they could utilize their resources to box him in.

All Memory could think about was a scared eight-year-old girl. That girl's father sat on the sofa in the living area with his head in his hands. The pale-skinned man who couldn't have been more than thirty-five looked up when she entered. His eyes hitched on her hair. She knew without asking that his daughter had curls and brown skin.

Walking over to the delicate white desk by the window when he said nothing, Memory went to look out the window . . . and a wave of frigid cold swept over her. Not winter cold. This was the endless cold of psychopathic nothingness. It crept into her bones, chilled her from the inside out . . . and tugged her to the left.

Not knowing what was happening, she searched frantically for a door on her left, but there was only a wall. She ran outside in silence, conscious of Alexei and the leopard following. She'd been scared she'd lose the connection, but it held.

"I can feel him," she whispered, her chest heaving. "Like we're connected by an invisible thread." She saw no evidence of a bond when she glanced into the Net. Renault had probably hidden it. Or maybe . . . "I don't think this is supposed to exist." She tried to breathe, *think*, hold on to that thread. "He can't know about it or he'd have cut it."

Her mind raced. "I was under his control." Inside his shields, suffocated and isolated. "He never worried if, while he was creating pathways into my mind, he was also accidentally creating a path in the other direction." Was it possible Memory could walk into his mind as he'd done hers?

Revulsion crawled over her, but she tried.

Nothing. No sense of Renault, but the tug to the left stayed steady.

"Can he track you in return?" Alexei's eyes glowed wild amber.

"Even if he can, he needs physical contact to take control, and I have shields now." Amara was far stronger than Renault and, as of this week, Memory could rebuff her attempts at an unwilling transfer. "If I can hold off a 9.9, I should have no problems with an 8.7." Renault might be a serial murderer, but that didn't matter, not in this.

Memory also had no fear the past would paralyze her. If she'd fought back in the bunker, she sure as hell wasn't going to stop now that she'd tasted freedom, fought with a golden wolf, and made friends who liked being with her.

Alexei closed his big, rough-skinned hand over hers. "I'll

tear out the bastard's throat if he tries to lay a finger on you."
A growling promise that reminded her she was no longer
alone in the dark. "Emmett, you'll keep watch here?"

Memory barely heard the short interaction. Anchored by
Alexei's primal warmth, her brain crystal clear, she pointed
down the street. "He's somewhere in that direction."

"Jeep or on foot?"

Memory squeezed her eyes shut, attempting to gauge the
distance between her and the man she hunted without success. She fell back on her instincts. "On foot. I may lose the
trail in a car." With that, she began to run, her sneakered feet
hitting the asphalt in a rapid rhythm. Beside her ran a wolf in
human form whose wildness was a protective shield around
her as the people on the street scrambled out of their way.

She flinched, thinking she must've begun to stink of Renault, but quickly realized the pedestrians' startled faces
betrayed no disgust, nothing but wide-eyed curiosity. It was
Alexei. Of course it was Alexei. A predatory changeling on
the hunt was no unknown to these people, even if they had
to be more familiar with the cats. It was clear they recognized Alexei's changeling nature despite the fact he hadn't
shifted form.

Pain stabbed her side, but Memory blanked out the stitch
and ran on. She'd asked Yuri to suggest extra exercises she
could use to increase her physical fitness, her development
too slow under the lightweight plan worked out by the
physiotherapist who'd seen her a few days into her stay at the
compound.

Agreeing with Memory that she was strong enough to
bear more, Yuri had created an entire exercise plan just for
her. Her heart hurt at the thought of her friend, but she focused on the gift he'd given her—she was far stronger than
when she'd first left the bunker.

A low deep beat began to vibrate up her body with each
footfall. Her heart, pounding so hard that it felt like thunder.
No. There were sounds to go along with the beat. *A drum.*
And people. So many people that it was a gentle roar.

Alexei bit out a curse. "I forgot—Chinese New Year cel-
ebrations got postponed to this week because of the weather,
and we're heading right into Chinatown."

Memory didn't stop. "We can't go any other way. He's close." The signal had grown in strength. Yes, that was the better analogy—not a thread tying them together, but a signal for which she had the frequency.

Never while imprisoned could she have imagined that she would one day run headlong into a smiling mass of people while glowing lanterns swayed overhead and in the street wove a dragon created by many performers weaving and swaying the creature's colorful body.

Enticing smells filled the air. Color burst to life around every corner. Images of rabbits abounded on the lanterns, on key chains hanging from a stall doing a brisk business, and even on the walls of the buildings. Many were projected with light, others stenciled in bright colors.

At any other time, Memory would've stood in place and gotten drunk on the mass of sensation, but today she wanted the entire crowd to disappear, her mind repeating the name, Vashti, over and over again as her lungs pumped frantically.

The revelers got out of the way as soon as they spotted Alexei, but there were just too many people on the streets for them to move fast, and Memory's body kept being jostled by accident.

Growling after another bump, Alexei took the lead, his hand clamped around hers. "Squeeze my hand when we need to change direction." He began to push his way through the crowd, while keeping Memory protected behind the hard muscle of his body.

Suddenly they were moving. Paper parasols danced over her head as the attendees lifted them high to allow her and Alexei to pass. At one point, the two of them wove between what appeared to be a dance troupe, the team dressed in khaki pants and blousy shirts tied at the waist by thick swathes of colorful fabric.

The dancers also had gold in their hair, the foil applied in the pattern of a rabbit.

A male dancer jumped out of the way when he saw Alexei and bumped into a muscular woman who yelled at him in a language Memory didn't recognize. The festivalgoers were of every color and size and shape.

She made out her own people—almost always in the far

back of the crowd, but very much present in this chaotic environment that had nothing to do with Silence. A number of changelings and humans went to call hello to Alexei, but most swallowed their cries half-spoken the instant they caught the urgent look on his face.

Others shouted offers of assistance, but Alexei shook his head. The two of them were going too fast, their task too critical to stop and explain things. But Memory worried. Renault had always worked alone, but he was a telekinetic. If he still had a reserve of energy, he could throw Alexei a great distance.

As if he'd heard her thoughts, Alexei halted when one particular changeling called out, "Lexie! You need help?"

"Yeah!" Alexei called back.

The big, dark-skinned man was with a pretty woman who had old eyes and tawny-gold hair streaked with chocolate brown, a little girl who wore a bow in her hair, and a tall teenaged boy whose slouch had turned into watchful readiness in a matter of heartbeats.

Before Alexei's friend left his family, she saw him speak quickly to both the boy and a couple of other changelings around them, who had the hard-edged look she'd begun to recognize in changeling soldiers. The tawny-haired woman said something to him right afterward. He touched his fingers to her cheek and smiled at his little girl before cutting through the crowd to join Memory and Alexei.

He moved like a cat, his eyes a feline dark green.

The entire thing had taken less than ten seconds, but the delay panicked Memory. More so when Alexei took another couple of seconds to tell the leopard changeling that they were on the trail of a murderous telekinetic. Memory bit down on her lower lip—the interruption was worth it; Renault would find it much harder to control two changelings and Memory at the same time.

The DarkRiver male fell in behind Memory.

Her face was hot, her body starting to burn up in the midst of the crowd. She wanted to pull off the jacket, but there was no opportunity, no time. *Vashti. Vashti. Vashti.* She was the only thing that mattered, her life at the mercy of a serial killer.

Suddenly, the coldness inside her burned, the nothingness searing her to the bone. Her hand clenched on Alexei's. When he glanced at her, strands of his hair falling across his forehead, she pointed silently to the left—toward a small area devoid of people. It wasn't a street, but a set of steps that led down into darkness.

Chapter 34

Our working hypothesis on this point is that the increase in violence among the Psy is not a result of the fall of Silence, nor is it actually an increase—we are now simply seeing the violence that was previously hidden by those in power. At present, we do not have enough data to either verify or refute the hypothesis.

—Report to Ruling Coalition from Research Group Gamma-X, Silence & Outcomes

STOPPING AT THE top of the steps, Alexei put his lips to her ear. "Down in the basement?"

"Yes. He's there." A shiver threatened to wrack her frame, but Memory gritted her teeth and stood firm. She was no victim, wasn't Renault's prisoner. She was an E and she had the heart of a lioness.

Alexei looked to his friend. "Clay, I'll go first—you come right on my tail, take the bastard down if he's managed to use his Tk against me." Amber eyes locked with Memory's. "Chances Vashti is there?"

"High." Dissimilar to a true teleporter like Vasic Zen, a teleport-capable telekinetic had only a limited store of energy for jumps. Renault wouldn't waste his when he'd only taken Vashti to get at Memory.

"Your job is to go straight for the girl, get her out while we occupy him."

Memory nodded and the two men moved ahead of her. The locked door at the bottom wasn't powerful enough to withstand changeling strength. Alexei went in low, rolling up to his feet in a flash of speed the instant he was beyond the doorway, with Clay a split second behind him.

The nothingness pulsed and a mind reached out to grab her own. She shoved it off with violent strength . . . and the clawing nothing was gone. "He's teleported!" Memory called out as she ran into the dark space, scanning it wildly.

Terror, pain, panic.

She pounded toward the far corner, going to her knees in front of what proved to be a crumpled body. One of the men turned on a penlight, illuminating the tangled curls of the tiny girl who lay shivering on the floor, holding her hand over her stomach.

The girl whimpered and drew away before her dark gaze flew behind Memory. "Clay." Hope, relief, pain smashed into Memory's senses. "The bad man cut me."

"I've got you now, kitten." Clay ran one big hand over the girl's hair before hauling off his T-shirt and folding it up into a makeshift pad. "Call Aden, see if we can get Vasic here. Paramedics won't be able to get through—"

"No teleporters," Memory said, her head screaming with Vashti's fear. "She's so afraid."

"Shh." Clay pressed a kiss to the trembling girl's cheek. "No teleporters, then." He nodded at Alexei. "This is my friend, Alexei. He's a wolf, but I like him anyway. He's going to do first aid on you while I go get a healer I know is on this street somewhere. Okay?"

Vashti swallowed hard but nodded.

Memory saw Clay pull his phone out of his pocket as he ran up the steps. She wanted badly to comfort the small, hurt E, but that whimper at the start had held pure terror—the second-long burst of contact with Renault must've altered Memory's psychic scent. Forcing herself to back off, she went to watch the door while Alexei touched the child with conscious gentleness as he attempted to stop the flow of blood from her stomach wound.

"I have you, sweetheart," he murmured, no growl in his voice. "I have to put pressure on the wound. It'll hurt, but it's important. Ready?"

Memory didn't hear the girl's quiet response, but Alexei spoke again not long afterward. "So how'd you meet Clay? Wild party? Catnip-rolling contest?"

A small giggle. "DarkRiver had a . . . picnic." Words that

were a touch breathless. "My dad took me . . . I played . . . with . . . Noor." Sucked-in air that had Memory urging Clay to hurry. "She's younger . . . but smart. She . . . gave me her . . . hair bow."

"Next time we meet, you wear it so I can see," Alexei said. "Stay with me, Vashti. Open those pretty eyes. There you go." His voice was calm, steady. "I bet the cats tell all kinds of stories about wolves, don't they? I'm gonna let you in on a secret—they're just sore because we're better-looking. I mean those cats are covered in black spots, while we're sleek and handsome. Clear winners of the wild beauty contest."

As the little girl giggled again, the sound scarily weak, Memory opened out her senses in an effort not to miss Renault should he decide to chance a return. She didn't want him anywhere near the little girl he'd hurt for no reason but that he could—he was a teleporter, hadn't needed the distraction to get away.

A thousand emotions slammed into her the instant she lowered her first shield, the festival area bursting with minds upon minds. Gritting her teeth, she narrowed the aperture in her shield until it was on the edge of pain but bearable.

"Alexei," she asked. "Do you have a knife?" Unlike Vasic, Nerida, and Abbot, Renault couldn't teleport another person without physical contact, and at this point in the day's events, he wouldn't have enough Tk energy left to hold her in place *and* teleport out with her.

Jabbing at him with a knife would work to keep him at bay.

"Here." A metallic rasp against stone as Alexei slid across what proved to be a hunting blade. She gripped it, held watch, while Alexei fought to keep Vashti from slipping into unconsciousness.

Memory feared no one would get here in time, not with the crowd, and second-guessed her decision to veto a teleporter. But Vashti had been *so* afraid. Panic could cause her mind to short out, her heart to stop. But if there was no choice—

Feet pounded down the stairs.

The woman who entered with Clay was statuesque, with

rich brown hair to her waist and a body that was all dangerous curves and power. She was dressed in dark blue jeans that hugged her legs, black ankle boots, and a fuzzy red sweater with gold threads woven into it. On her head was a band that glowed with blue liquid and had wobbling eyes on top of it.

And inside her flowed the same deep well of wild compassion that Memory had felt from Lucy.

The healer ran directly toward Vashti, Clay following with a satchel in hand. "Tammy's emergency kit," the leopard said to Alexei, his chest heaving. "I directed her here while I ran to her car to grab the kit. You know healers—everyone in the pack is coded into her car's security."

"That's because if anyone dares take my car for a joyride, they'll be in big doo-doo with every single other member of the pack." The brunette smiled at Vashti as she got to work, her hands gentle and competent, and her voice soothing and warm.

"Doo-doo?" Alexei shook his head. "What did I tell you, sweetheart? Wolves are definitely more sophisticated and elegant."

The healer snorted. "Ignore him, kitten. He's a boy, and as I'm raising two boys, I can tell you they're mostly dirt and mischief—with a side helping of interesting bugs."

Memory knew they were joking around in an effort to raise Vashti's spirits, and it was working. The girl's joy was an innocent thing, her pain and fear forgotten for short bursts as she tried to laugh. All the while, her blood continued to flow.

Clay cradled the little girl's head with one hand, his other holding hers. "Noor can't stop talking about you," he said in his deep timbre. "She's very proud to have a 'big girl' friend. I'm going to talk to your dad about bringing her over to visit you."

Vashti's happiness bubbled again.

Memory clenched her gut and *hoped*. Vashti was bleeding out, her psychic presence weaker and weaker because Renault wanted Memory. If Vashti died . . . Memory bit down so hard on her lower lip that she tasted blood.

Chapter 35

Psychopaths who kill for killing's sake are ill-disciplined individuals who waste resources. At the core, they are driven by primordial urges that negate any assertions of intelligence.

—Amara Aleine

RENAULT'S PULSE RACED. He wasn't used to the lack of control. Neither was he used to being the one who ran, being the *weak* one. But he'd realized he was outnumbered the instant the two changelings entered the basement—he'd already stretched his telekinetic abilities; he hadn't had enough power to hold off the two aggressors.

As it was, he'd barely made it to his hiding place.

That he now lay on the floor, his cheek resting on the rough carpet, was a humiliation he would not forget. He'd punish Memory for this, for running from him, for her disloyalty after all he'd done for her, how well he'd kept her.

She would pay and pay again.

The next time he drew her out, he'd have to ensure she came alone. It could be done. He knew everything about Memory, every fear and every guilt. Something crackled in his pocket as he turned. His ace in the hole: the lock of hair that belonged to Memory's mother, a memento he always kept close because it marked the day he'd found Memory.

Yes, she would come when he called.

Chapter 36

Empaths do an overwhelming amount of good. But, as with any other group, those of Designation E have their flaws and their vulnerabilities, and these elements of their psyche can have a catastrophic impact on their mental health.
—*The Mysterious E Designation: Empathic Gifts & Shadows* by Alice Eldridge (Reprint: 2082)

MEMORY SAT IN a hard plas chair while hospital announcements echoed against the cool white walls. She was waiting for Alexei to return from the small café attached to the hospital—he'd volunteered to go down and grab coffee and food.

Two hours had passed since they'd found Vashti. Neither Clay nor Tammy had eaten dinner yet, and Memory's bones were pushing up against her skin. Whatever she'd done to track Renault, it had required huge amounts of fuel. But Memory wasn't hungry. A rock was lodged in her abdomen.

Stable at last, the small E Renault had hurt slept in a room on the other side of the wall at Memory's back. Vashti's father was inside with her while Tammy stood conferring with the medical team at the end of the hall—it turned out that Tamsyn "Tammy" Ryder, DarkRiver's senior healer, was also a highly qualified doctor who had full privileges at this hospital.

Clay kept watch close by the medical team.

There was no need to keep watch at this end; Vashti's room was the final one in this hallway, with only a wall to Memory's right.

"Empath?"

Jerking at the unexpected voice, she found Vashti's father

standing in the doorway to his daughter's room. It took her a second to realize he was addressing her. "Yes," she said, though her insides twisted at claiming the title. She'd brought a monster to this man's door.

"My daughter would like to speak to you."

A sudden cold shivered through her blood when she entered the hospital room and saw Vashti's small body in the middle of the bed, tubes and wires going from the girl to various machines. Tamsyn had reassured her that Vashti would make a full recovery, but seeing the little girl this way, knowing it was her fault, it had Memory bleeding inside.

She'd locked her guilt and pain behind solid shields for hours, not about to allow them to leak around this very young empath. If Vashti was anything like Cordelia and the others, it'd make her feel bad when Memory was the one at fault. "Hi," she said from near the doorway.

The little E's forehead scrunched up. "You don't taste bad anymore."

Exhaling, Memory dared walk closer to the bed. "I'm sorry about that. I had to connect with the man who took you to track him. It temporarily altered my psychic scent."

Expression clearing, Vashti lifted up a small hand. "Are you Memory?"

Nodding as she closed her fingers around the girl's with gentle care, Memory said, "I'm sorry the bad man took you."

"It's not your fault—he has a hole inside him. He's empty." Warm, delicate life in every breath. "He said he wanted to lock you up so you could never escape."

And this hurt and scared child had remembered and thought to warn her. "Thank you for telling me," Memory whispered, her throat raw. "I have no intention of being caught." She looked at Vashti's father. "You know you have to alter your living area so he can no longer get a teleport lock?"

"Yes. DarkRiver has moved us into one of their apartments while the changes are made." His voice was cool, but the hand he placed on his daughter's forehead gentle. "She needs to rest now."

Releasing Vashti's hand, the girl's eyelids already fluttering, Memory rose. Vashti's father wasn't Silent. Emotions seethed beneath the intense calm of his surface. Memory felt his cold fury at what had been done to his child, knew he blamed her. But she knocked on his mind nonetheless.

His eyes were hard when they met hers. *Yes?*

She's an empath, Memory reminded this man who loved his daughter so very much. *You need to learn to control your emotions beyond the surface.*

His pupils dilated. *I'll be far calmer once you're out of the room.*

Memory left at once, guilt clawing at her with vicious strength. After pulling the door shut behind her, she walked toward Clay. The DarkRiver male frowned. "Better you don't wander around while a psychopath's hunting you."

Nausea lurched in Memory's stomach. Vashti was simply the first victim. Renault wouldn't stop. He'd keep spilling innocent blood to get to her. "Toilet," she muttered.

Piercing green eyes took her in before he pointed down and to the right. "Alexei'll be back soon—wolf is right, you need to eat." A pause. "Don't worry about the little kitten's father. Man's still in shock."

Not replying, Memory headed the way he'd indicated, but when she reached the facilities, she glanced back to see that Clay had just turned to answer a question from Tamsyn. Memory kept walking. Around the corner, down a flight of stairs, and all the way out of the hospital.

Though it was well after the midnight hour, the streets still buzzed with festivalgoers heading home. A couple walked ahead, the woman carrying a paper lantern she must've bought from one of the stalls.

The red of it glowed from the light within.

On the other side of the street stood a knot of young males, all dressed to the nines, with their black hair slicked back; they laughed and talked as they shared a packet of sweets. A group of women around Memory's age wearing matching cheongsams—maybe a performance group of some kind—smiled coyly at the youths as they passed.

A quick-thinking boy offered them a sweet, and the women's bright laughter sparkled in the night air.

Memory moved on. She didn't know where she was going. It wasn't as if she could outrun her own disgust with herself. She'd never been like those laughing young women, never walked hand-in-hand with a man through the city streets, never been clean and shiny and new.

How foolish to have imagined that she could have Alexei for her own.

He was a creature of this world, of light. Memory was a nightmare.

When the couple ahead of her turned off on a side street, she didn't follow them. Their happiness made her feel even more hollow inside. Tonight, however, she couldn't avoid the happy couples and the smiling groups out for a joyous night. They were everywhere.

At one point, her eye caught on the lone figure of a man who sat in a chair on a porch just up from the sidewalk. He looked as alone as she felt, his gnarled hands clasped on his cane and his gaze on the endless night. Then the door opened beside him and another man emerged with two mugs. A smile lit the seated man's seamed face.

Hugging Alexei's jacket closed around her body, her heart a block of ice, she kept on walking. Renault wouldn't come after her tonight; his telekinetic power had to be close to flatlining. As for any other psychopaths who might be walking the streets, she could block any connection they attempted to make. The nothingness wouldn't suck her under.

But what if that's your destiny? whispered a tormented piece of her soul. *What if all this, trying to live a life, that's the illusion?*

Eyes hot, she ducked her head and continued to put one foot in front of the other, and when she scented salt air, she went in that direction. The wharf she found was bustling with stalls all open for the night. People milled around her, having conversations in so many languages that it became music in the air. She smelled things she'd never before smelled and her stomach finally woke up, rumbling in expectation. But she had no money, wasn't used to being out in the world and needing it.

That seemed appropriate for a woman who didn't exist.

Walking past the crowded area, she found a quiet spot on the sidewalk and, bracing her arms on the railing, stared at the silken dark glide of the water while her mind churned and guilt gnawed at her insides.

• • •

ALEXEI'S wolf had snarled when he realized Memory had slipped out of the hospital, but he hadn't griped at Clay, even though the other man had been annoyed at himself for not keeping a closer eye on her. Alexei knew all too well that Memory was a woman who made her own decisions. If she'd decided to go, Clay couldn't have stopped her.

"I'm sure Vashti's dad said something to your E," Clay'd told him, a muscle working in his jaw. "Man's not in a good headspace."

And Memory was a handy target.

Leaving Vashti under the cats' more-than-capable watch, Alexei had headed out after his aggravating E who needed to be held, not walking the streets alone. He'd been planning to tease her into letting him cuddle her after he got back from the café. Prior to that, he'd swept the hospital for any sign of Renault in the company of another DarkRiver soldier while Clay kept watch outside the operating room.

His wolf grumbled the entire way to her, the wildness in full agreement with the human side of Alexei: he was allowed to growl at Memory this time. At least she wasn't difficult to track—her scent was embedded inside him, until he sometimes thought he could scent her on his own skin.

But now, as he stood half a block away from her, any thought of growling at her disappeared. All he wanted to do was hold her. Head bowed and shoulders slumped for the second time that day, she looked so desolate and alone that it infuriated him. His Memory was a determined fighter, a tiny woman with the heart of a lioness.

Nothing defeated her. Not even a lifetime of captivity.

Striding across the distance between them, he put his arms on either side of her own on the railing, and pressed his chest against her back.

She stiffened. "Go away." Instead of her usual defiance, he heard tears perilously close to the surface.

"Not a chance." Closing his arms around her, he rubbed his face gently against her temple, a wolf attempting to give comfort.

Biting back a sob, she twisted; he thought she was trying

to get away, but she turned and buried the side of her face against his chest. Holding her tight, he nuzzled her curls and tried not to act the enraged wolf at seeing her in such pain. "You saved a life today," he reminded her roughly. "We would've never found Vashti without you."

Hands fisting at his back, Memory said, "Renault only took her to get to me." The words trembled. "*I'm* the reason she was taken."

Alexei couldn't hold back his growl this time. A couple of nonpredatory changelings nearby decided they'd prefer to walk on the other side of the road. The woman in his arms, however, smaller and far more bruised inside, looked up at him with a dark flash in her eyes. "Don't you *growl* at me. I'm *crying*! You can't growl at me while I'm crying!"

Delighted at the return of her fire, Alexei bent down until his nose brushed hers, her eyes locked with his. And he growled.

Glaring, she shoved at his chest without force. "Are all wolves so aggravating?" she asked, shining tracks on her cheeks but no new tears falling from her eyes.

Rising back to his full height, Alexei crowded her against the railing. "That's my E." The words sang inside him, a key sliding into a lock.

When a chill threatened to invade his veins, he shrugged it off. His fucking demons could go howl in the dark tonight. This was about Memory and about making sure she wasn't hurting. "If you're beating yourself up because a psychopath is doing psychopathic things," he growled, "then you need your head examined."

Though she had her arms tight around him, she growled back at him, doing such a good job of it that his wolf opened its mouth in a pleased grin inside him. Leaning down, he rubbed his jaw against her hair, her curls tickling his nose.

"I'm just *one* life," Memory said, so much anguish inside her that it hurt him. "Is my freedom worth the horror suffered by innocents like Vashti?"

Alexei wanted to shake her. Gritting his teeth, he told himself to think this through, to be the rational strategist and not the infuriated wolf. Which was why he bent his head and, tugging her curls aside, nipped sharply at the tip of one ear.

"Ow!" Her hand flew up to her ear, and she tilted back her head to send him a glare of epic proportions. "If you're not careful, I'll bite you back again."

"Do it," Alexei dared, his wolf in charge.

Dropping her hand from her ear, Memory poked at his chest. "I'm talking sense. If I go back to Renault—" She cut herself off. "If I go back to him, I make him a more efficient murderer." Her shoulders sagged again. "And if I stay out in the world, he's going to keep hurting others to get to me."

Alexei couldn't stand it any longer, couldn't stand that she saw value in everyone else and kept forgetting herself. Shoving his hands into her hair, he tugged back her head, intending to yell at her . . . but got caught by the pain in her dark eyes.

Right then, all he wanted was for her to know pleasure, know that the world could be better than horror and darkness and a cage.

Dropping his head, he kissed her.

Chapter 37

Wolves and intimate skin privileges? *fans face* Hold on . . .
and watch out for teeth.
 —From the November 2071 issue of *Wild Woman* magazine:
          "Skin Privileges, Style & Primal Sophistication"

MEMORY CLUTCHED AT the sides of Alexei's T-shirt, the
jolt racing through her an electric thing that threatened to
short-circuit her senses. Whimpering low in her throat, she
rose on tiptoe, wanting more of this wonderful, delicious
contact.

Alexei nipped at her lower lip.

Used to wolf behavior by now, she parted her lips and he
swept inside, stroking her tongue with his in an erotic seduc-
tion that had her thighs pressing together and her breasts
suddenly tender. "Alexei," she whispered against his lips
when he gave her a second to catch her breath.

Eyes of wolf amber looking into hers before he captured
her mouth again.

Pressed up against him as close as she could get, Memory
responded without restraint, a lifetime of need coalescing into
this one moment with a wild golden wolf. He nipped her lower
lip again, this time tugging gently before releasing her. His
chest rose and fell against her own, his mouth wet from her
kiss.

She traced the outline of his lips with a trembling fingertip. "I've never felt so alive." Every cell in her body vibrated. "Let's do it again." And again.

Groaning, he nuzzled a kiss to her temple. "Not here. My
erection's already threatening to poke a hole in my pants."

Able to feel the hard protrusion against her body, Memory rubbed against him. That got her another nip on the ear as punishment. She smiled. Alexei wasn't in any way distant tonight; he and his wolf were very much here with her. And those bites he kept giving her? Despite her earlier complaint, they startled more than hurt.

Her wolf was very careful with his strength.

Nuzzling her face against his chest, his scent delicious, she said, "What do we do now?"

"Renault isn't going to come back tonight." Growled words, but the hand he ran down her back was gentle. "Telekinetic resources aside, fucker's a coward and we scared him."

Memory's eyes narrowed. "He tried to grab my mind, but I punched him back. Hard enough that it must've hurt."

"Next time, kick him in the nuts, too."

A laugh snorted out of her before she sobered. "Vashti?"

"Fine. Cats have taken charge of her security, though I think she's safe from Renault—he didn't want her specifically. She was bait." A rumble in his chest that felt familiar now, the sound of Alexei being Alexei.

"Any time you start wondering about the value of your freedom," he added in a growly tone, "think about the young girls he would've stolen and hurt once he wore you out. Your ability is rare—he would've killed E after E trying to find another."

Memory's heart kicked. Alexei was right. Renault had been on the verge of overusing her to death; if she hadn't escaped, if she hadn't exposed his evil, he would've continued on with impunity.

Rising on tiptoe, she kissed her golden wolf's jaw. Stubble pricked her lips, the sensation making her nipples tingle. He was scowling as he wiped off the remnants of her tears. "Since Vashti is more comfortable with the leopards and Renault has run with his tail between his legs, we're free tonight—and the festival's going through the night today because a massive BlackSea-run cruise ship came in just after midnight. Let's go play."

Warmth emanated outward from Memory's heart. A different guilt cut at her—that she should feel such happiness while Yuri lay dying and Abbot was in surgery, but Yuri himself had told her to embrace life. *Freedom is a gift,* he'd said to her late one evening. *Never take it for granted. Never waste it. Live.*

Alexei took a step back and held out his hand. Swallowing the worry lodged in her throat, Memory held her friend's words close as she accepted the invitation. She and Alexei had only gone a few steps when someone whistled from across the street. "How'd you get such a pretty date, wolf?" a male voice heckled. "Bet you had to wear a catsuit!"

"Go drown in catnip, you flea-infested rug!" Alexei aimed a rude gesture at the other side of the street.

When Memory tried to twist around to see the man who'd started the small fight, Alexei tugged at her hand. "Don't encourage them," he grumbled. "Cats think they're the Casanovas of the world, can prowl their way into any bed."

"I prefer wolves."

A slow smile curving his lips, Alexei broke their handclasp to sling his arm around her shoulders, tugging her against the steely heat of his body. "Is that your stomach? Hungry?"

Memory nodded and thus began the most delicious night of her life. She ate everything that looked interesting or smelled good, until she was full to bursting. Then she had sticky, sugary rice-flour sweets that made her moan, and topped it all off with a vanilla milkshake doctored with crushed-up cookies.

"My people are deranged," she said.

Alexei raised an eyebrow at his E, even as he kept his body between her and the others on the street. They'd made their way back to Chinatown and to the festival, which showed no signs of winding down, hordes of excited human and nonpredatory changeling cruise passengers in unseasonal Hawaiian shirts and sundresses mixing with the locals. "Deranged?"

Memory held up her half-finished milkshake. "We gave this up for nutrient drinks." Shaking her head, she took another sip. "Deranged."

Alexei laughed, delighted with her. Memory saw everything through new eyes, made him feel young, too. He was ready to buy her the world—and *especially* food, but he hadn't forgotten her fear of being in "debt." So he'd channeled his protective instincts in another way.

Before hitting the stalls, he'd taken her to a twenty-four-hour automated bank and shown her how to access her Collective-linked account using her palm print. "Snow-Dancer had that in the system from when I granted you access to the substation. We sent it through to the Collective to fast-track your account. If you want, you can ask their finance person to add an iris scan for greater security."

Since she'd left her phone in the compound and didn't have a watch capable of storing financial data, he'd then walked her through how to load money onto a temporary card. Her resulting pleasure in being able to buy *him* food had melted more hard places in his heart.

He was in a fucking huge amount of trouble—and he didn't care. Not tonight.

When Memory tugged him into a girly and overstuffed trinket shop he'd usually avoid like the plague, he threatened mutiny—but they both knew he was only playing. Tonight, he was Memory's.

She came out of the shop with a pair of earrings in the shape of paper parasols. "I need to get my ears pierced like the girl who sold me these."

Alexei pointed to a sign for an all-night drugstore. "Might find a clerk trained in ear piercing there." He frowned. "But how about we put off making holes in your body until—"

But Memory was already laughing and tugging him across the street.

Five minutes later, he folded his arms and told himself not to strangle the slender male who was about to hurt Memory.

"Go glare at something else in the store," Memory ordered with a glare of her own. "Do you *want* his hand to shake?"

Growling, Alexei turned on his heel and stood by the door.

"Thanks," the clerk whispered. "I hate it when the dominants come in with their mates or cubs. Half the time I think they want to take the piercing tool and pop a hole between my eyes."

"Trust me, he's all growl and only small bites."

"Um, sure," the clerk responded dubiously, which pleased Alexei's wolf and confirmed the clerk was in possession of his brain cells. Alexei would have to talk to his E about convincing people that he wasn't scary. A man had a reputation to protect.

His muscles locked when she hissed twice.

"Alexei, it's over," she called out a second later.

He turned to see her sliding in the earrings while admiring herself in the mirror. Then she looked at him with a huge smile. Walking over, she rose on tiptoe to kiss a line along his jaw. "Thank you for not eating the clerk."

And his heart, it fell.

Hard.

ALEXEI didn't want this night out of time to end. As long as it didn't, he could ignore the voices yelling at the back of his head, the ones that reminded him of finding Etta's torn-apart body. She'd been so slender, so broken. But even magical nights didn't last forever. Daylight would come all too soon, and with it the history that haunted him.

Reaching his vehicle—still parked down the street from Vashti's home—he pressed Memory against it and nuzzled the side of her face, taking just another second, just another taste.

She curled her entire body into him. "That feels so good."

A strange ache in her voice made him raise his head, focus on her face.

The searing hunger in her eyes punched him in the gut.

"You're touch-starved," he gritted out, furious with himself for not having caught it earlier. He'd thought she was skittish, getting used to people, hadn't wanted to overwhelm her.

"It's better now." She continued to pet his chest. "My skin used to hurt like tiny things were cutting me, but it hardly does that these days."

Alexei wanted to yell at her for not telling him of her hurt, barely managed to contain the urge—and was glad he had when she whispered, "I didn't know." Eyes going obsidian with shimmers of a dark rainbow, lovely and unique. "I thought that was just the way everyone was, with that *need* inside them."

Alexei's wolf stood motionless, its anger no match for its protectiveness. For fifteen long years, his E'd had no one to ask such private questions. No one she trusted enough to reveal her pain. "Jump in the Jeep," he said, and because his voice came out harsh, he brushed his lips against hers so she'd know he wasn't mad at her.

She twisted her lips, her hands fisting on his sweater. "I suppose we have to go home."

"Not just yet." Alexei tugged a wayward curl, and the way her face lit up, it made him feel like a fucking god. "Let's go make a little trouble."

Memory pointed out myriad beauties of life as he drove: the carpet of stars in the ebony sky, the way the waters of the bay gleamed like black opals under the moonlight, the glowing windows of homes where families slept safe and warm.

"Will you take me out at night again?" she asked partway through their journey. "I always dreamed about the sun, but I never realized the loveliness of the moonlight."

"I'm a wolf." He threw in a growl because his wolf wanted to be part of the conversation. "Howling up at the moon is a favorite leisure activity."

Memory laughed and, throwing back her head, tried to howl. Shoulders shaking, he gave her pointers on a better technique and was grinning hard enough to crack his face by the time she collapsed into giggles.

He brought the Jeep to a stop in an isolated spot that should guarantee them privacy. It was too deep inside Dark-River territory to be on any patrol routes, and even if a cat *was* prowling around nearby, Alexei's scent was familiar enough that said cat would turn right around and go in another direction.

Wolves and leopards might not be natural allies, but in certain things they agreed. Intimate skin privileges were a private thing, not to be disturbed.

"It's so still, so quiet." Memory leaned forward to look out the windscreen. "I can't see the moon, but the world's all silver outside."

A wind rustled the tree leaves at that instant, and he knew it had come from the mountains, would hold the kiss of the ice and the snow. Memory felt the cold. That decided him: playtime in the forest could wait for another day.

"Backseat," he said, and when she frowned at him in an unspoken question, Alexei realized that he was leading his sweet E astray.

He smiled at her. "Please."

Eyes narrowing in suspicion, she nonetheless did as he'd asked, crawling back there between the seats. He came around the outside. After pulling the back driver's-side door shut behind himself, he put his hands on the bottom of his sweater to pull it off over his head. His T-shirt was next. Memory's sucked-in breath was loud in the confines of the car, but when he threw aside the tee and looked at her, it was to see her shrugging off his jacket, her gaze locked on his chest.

A slow smile creeping across his face, Alexei leaned close . . . and growled at her.

"Don't you *growl* at me," she said, but she was laughing.

He pretended to bite at her while she finished ridding herself of his jacket. He was aware he was crowding her, and was ready to pull back at the first sign of distress, but Memory seemed to soak in his closeness.

Jacket off, she put her hands on his chest, stroking the fine pelt there. "You have fur," she said, her teeth sinking into her lower lip as her fingers curled into him.

It was actually just a very fine layer of chest hair, but if Memory wanted to pet his fur, he wasn't going to complain. He wasn't a stupid wolf. Crowded up against a corner of the backseat, she let him pull one of her legs over his hip, then took her time learning the shape of his shoulders and chest. "Control" had long been Alexei's watchword, but he'd never been petted with such unabashed delight in his life.

He was fucking putty in her hands.

When he slipped his hands to her waist and under her top, stroking the skin on her lower back, she raised her arms. Alexei fought back a shudder and shifted them so she was straddling him, his back to the leather-synth of the seat.

He'd thought he'd have to work his way up to such intimate contact, but if Memory was ready, he wasn't going to be an asshole and puncture her confidence. His heart drumming against his chest, he tugged her top over her head and threw it aside with his T-shirt. Her body was all woman, but still too slender despite the tempting food he'd been leaving at her door, unable to stop taking care of her that way no matter how hard he'd tried to stay away.

"Did you eat the peach pie I left you?" He'd started putting her name on everything after the blueberry cake incident.

She scrunched up her nose at him. "Yes. I cursed your name with every bite."

Grinning, he snapped his teeth at her while stroking his hands up and down the curve of her waist. "As long as you ate it," he said in unhidden satisfaction before returning to his visual delectation of her body.

Her bra was fuchsia lace. It made his smile deepen, his heart fall even harder into her hands. Memory would never go for the sedate or the ordinary. Memory was fuchsia lace and sequined shoes and glitter-emblazoned shirts.

Memory was color and light and a primal joy in life.

Sliding his finger under one strap, he gloried in her shiver. She didn't tell him to stop when he leaned in to kiss her throat, and his growl this time was an uncontrolled thing that came from his wolf. Sliding her hands into his hair, she held him close, unafraid of the wolf at her throat. He made each kiss soft, slow, a little wet. Small, kittenish sounds coming from her lips, she leaned deeper into him.

Alexei's own parched body sighed at every contact, hungry for more. For *her*. He'd been worried he'd left it too long, that his wolf would be aggressive, but the two sides of his nature were in primal agreement—he had to take this slow so that Memory would come to him again and again and again.

He'd been deluding himself to think he'd ever let another man put his hands on her. That is, unless Memory asked. Then he'd back off no matter his anguish. Otherwise, he'd rip the fucker apart before the unfortunate male got anywhere near Alexei's E.

As for what his possessiveness meant, he'd deal with that later.

Tonight, he moved his hands in long, slow strokes down her back as he kissed and nipped his way across her shoulder, then back to her throat again. Arching her neck, she let him have unfettered access. Her pulse pounded at her throat, but he scented no fear, only the erotic musk of her arousal.

His cock grew impossibly harder, his claws sliding out of his hands. She didn't flinch. "Alexei." A husky whisper.

"Lioness."

She growled at him, her eyes dancing.

He kissed that wickedly lush and playful mouth, then, forcing his claws back in because he wouldn't hurt her even inadvertently, he licked and tasted his way down to the valley between her breasts.

Chapter 38

FOR A WOMAN with such a small frame, Memory's breasts were more than a handful. When Alexei cupped one, she dug her nails into the back of his neck and looked down. Her throat moved. "I don't know if I'll survive it if you touch me without the lace between us." Shallow breaths, her voice trembling. "Not there."

"We'll go slow," Alexei promised. "No rushing." Tonight was about feeding her touch hunger, stopping her hurt.

Stop lying, Alexei, this is as much for you. You need her touch.

Accepting that truth, he brushed his stubbled jaw across the exposed curve of her breast. She fisted her hands in his hair, moving restlessly on him, against him. Kissing the small redness caused by his stubble, he moved to her neglected breast and licked lightly across the same exposed area.

Memory shuddered before shoving at his shoulders.

Wondering if she'd hit her limit, he sat back, his vision such that his eyes had to be nightglow. Unfazed by the sight of his wolf, Memory bent her head and kissed his throat.

His body threatened to buck.

Alexei had his hand fisted in her exuberant curls before he knew he was about to move. He should've pulled her away, should've regained control of the situation, but it turned out he had a fatal weakness where Memory was concerned.

He was her willing sacrifice.

One hand on her hip, his thumb brushing the curve of her abdomen, he dropped back his head and let his E drive him insane. She sucked and kissed and used her teeth. Each time she did the latter, he gritted his own teeth to hold back a roughly primal sound until he couldn't. The sound of his wolf filled the Jeep.

Her nipples had already been hard points against him, but now the honeyed perfume of her arousal reached fever pitch. Clenching his jaw, he told himself to act like a man, not a fucking ravenous wolf. But since he *was* a wolf, and a starved one at that, he bent his head to her throat again and took a big bite.

Shivering against him but making no move to get away from his teeth, Memory stroked her hand down his chest once more. "Can we do this every night? I want to put my hands and mouth on every part of you."

His cock almost erupted then and there. Moving the hand he had in her hair to position her just right, he kissed her, demanding and hungry. Memory pressed her breasts against his chest, arms wrapping around his neck. Her tongue licked against his, her lush lips intoxicating.

His hand rising to grip her nape, he held her in place as he plundered her mouth. When he nipped gently at her lower lip, she parted her lips and licked her tongue against his. And every so often, she'd do to him what he'd done to her. It felt like they were in a dance and she was following his every move—while making a few of her own, turning him into her captive. He could imagine being buried inside her, the intimate dance of their hot, sweat-soaked bodies sliding against each other.

Molding one heavy breast on that thought, he deepened the kiss. Demanding more. Demanding everything. She moaned and gave it to him—while demanding the same in return.

My lioness.

She'd never be passive in bed, never be anything but a full partner. He wanted to thrust into her, brand her as his so damn much that his cock throbbed, but tonight was about pleasing

Memory. Shifting his hand from her breast, down the slope of her abdomen, he played his fingers around her waistband . . . before sliding down to cup her through her jeans.

Memory moaned and moved against him.

Grip on her nape tightening a fraction, he pressed the heel of his palm against her.

Her breathing altered to become faster, more jagged. Breaking the kiss, she buried her face against his neck, her fingers digging into his shoulders. Smile no doubt pure wolf, Alexei very deliberately pressed hard against the seam of her jeans, right where it lay over her most delicate flesh.

Her cry was short, sharp, deliciously shocked.

Cradling her against him as she trembled, her breath lost, he rumbled raw words of pleasure in her ear. "My beautiful, sexy Memory." He licked his tongue playfully along the shell of her ear. "That's what I want to do between your legs."

She stiffened against him . . . and then her entire body melted in a rolling wave. Shifting his hand to her hip, he nuzzled her through the orgasm, but when he kissed her throat in the aftermath, her responsive shiver was a touch too hard.

Protective instincts stirring, he tugged her head back so he could look at her face. She was all kiss-swollen lips and tumbled hair, and eyes of gleaming obsidian. He shouldn't have been able to read those eyes, but for him, they were no longer fathomless. He *saw* her. She was drunk on sexual sensation; any more would push her over the edge into pain.

When she cuddled against his shoulder, her hair bouncing against his jaw, he put his arms around her and indulged himself in petting her back in slow, soothing strokes. Her breath was soft and warm against him, her skin silk under his palm. And her scent, it was wild and bright tangled with the languid richness of something intrinsically soft and feminine.

He knew this was it tonight. Memory was emerging out of an enforced deep freeze. He couldn't and wouldn't force her, wouldn't rush her.

He would, however, do his best to charm her.

Careful, little bro. Remember what happened to me.

The ghostly voice was painfully familiar. His heart fucking hurt.

"Alexei?" Memory sat up in his lap, raising her hand to cup his cheek. "You're sad."

Turning his head, he pressed his lips to her palm and knew he had to tell her the truth. Because this, what was growing between them, it was a thing of truth. It held the kind of potent power that could make a man . . . or break him. "My brother was two years older than me, and he loved crazy adventures and a lovely woman called Etta, and he had this laugh that was so infectious it caught from person to person until an entire room would be rolling around on the floor."

Memory brushed her fingers through his hair, her eyes slowly shifting back to deepest brown. "You loved him a lot."

"Yeah." Brodie had been the most important person in his life for a long time. "Our folks died when I was seven, and Brodie was nine. Our aunt—our mother's much younger sister—raised us, and the entire pack was there for us, but we were brothers. That bond . . ." It had been formed of loyalty and love and grief and a stubborn commitment to stay alive.

Then Brodie had died.

Petting her hands across his shoulders, Memory said, "You love him still, but you're so angry, too." Gentle voice, an empath's knowledge. "What did Brodie do?"

"He died." The words were gritted out. "After our father died the same way, we made a promise and he broke it and he fucking died."

"*Alexei.*" She wove her fingers through his hair again. "Unless your brother took his own life"—a pause where he shook his head—"then he couldn't thwart death. At first, I was angry at my mother for being dead and leaving me alone in the world, but I knew all the time that she couldn't help it. The monster was too powerful." Her eyes shimmered. "I wish every day that she was alive, but I'm not angry at her anymore."

Alexei gripped her hips, his fingers brushing the bare skin of her back. He'd never been that alone, even at the darkest times of his life. "You will never be alone again." Would always have arms to hold her close.

She stroked her fingers over his jaw. "Why are you Alexei and your brother was Brodie?"

The question brought back memories of childhood laughter, his father's deep voice, his mother's soft arms. "I'm Alexei Vasiliev Harte and he was Brodie Harte Vasiliev." His brother's name felt so alien falling from his lips—it had been an eon since he'd spoken it aloud. "My father came from a pack in Russia, while my mother was a California girl through and through: Konstantin Vasiliev and Calissa Harte. They split the difference."

"Oh, how wonderful." Petting hands in his hair, across his shoulders, his E trying to assuage his hurt. "Tell me more about Brodie."

"Damn adrenaline junkie could make anyone laugh." Alexei's chest squeezed. "It was his way of dealing with life, with the world. The day we buried our parents, he came to the funeral in wolf form with a big green ribbon tied around his neck. Our aunt tied the ribbon for him."

"She sounds like a wonderful woman."

"She's the best." A tough-as-nails soldier, but one with endless heart. "The ribbon was for our mom, who loved the color green." Alexei swallowed the thickness in his throat. "I was always the angry one. I didn't want to go to the funeral, but Brodie used his teeth to grab the cuff of my pants and literally dragged me there."

"All your people have left you." She kissed his cheeks, his lips. "That's why you're so angry."

He exhaled a shuddering breath, took in her warmth and life on the inhale. "My family is cursed." There was no other way to put it. "You need to know about it if you're determined to be with me."

A narrowing of her eyes. "No, I get into the lap of every wolf who asks."

Growling low in his throat, he sat up. "Who's been asking?"

"Men," she said primly. "Leopards keep leaving tiny, shiny gifts at my door, and before the Arrows withdrew, several of the single males asked if I'd be interested in a private dinner, or an evening stroll."

Alexei bared his teeth. "Any man who asks now is going to get an education on the sharpness of wolf claws. As for the damn cats, I'm going to scalp their spotty fur."

She cupped his face in her hands, her smile unrepentant and her kiss tender. "What's the curse and why does it make you so angry and sad at the same time?"

Alexei's wolf lay down inside him, its head on its paws and its heart desolate. "Changelings have a single major vulnerability." It was a topic on which he'd maintained his silence with even his closest friends, the wound too close to the surface. "At times, our animal halves threaten to overwhelm our human selves." His fingers clenched on her hips. "That's not always bad. When I run as the wolf, the wolf *should* be ascendant. It's his time. The problem comes when a changeling gives up the human side of their nature forever and becomes the animal. We call them rogues."

It was so fucking hard to speak, to lay his family's pain wide open. He held on to Memory, leaned on her warmth, her affection. "My grandfather went rogue when my father was two years of age." Alexei had only ever known his grandfather as images caught on camera, a tall blond man with features startlingly similar to his own—the similarity had fascinated him as a child, but as an adult, it was a constant reminder of his ugly future. "My father went rogue when I was seven."

"Does this mean they are wolves in the wild, lost to you?"

Alexei blinked back the burning in his eyes. "I could deal with that. If I knew they lived, I could handle it." He'd have found them during his times as a wolf, run with them, been a family with them. "But rogues are so feared because they don't simply become wild wolves. They're drawn to those they used to love before they lost their humanity, and rather than just being with them—because that would be more than fine, their wolf selves welcomed—the rogues are violent. Rogues track, attack, and kill the people they once loved."

Memory's cheekbones pushed up against her skin, her expression stark. "As if they're angry at what they've lost and want to destroy it?"

Alexei shrugged. "Maybe. No one knows. I've heard rumors of rogues who made a return to being changeling, but I think they're fairy tales we tell ourselves to find hope in a hopeless situation."

For the Vasiliev family, the pain rolled down the decades

in an endless chain. "To be a rogue is to be under an automatic execution order." The packs had no other choice. "Brodie attacked his mate when he went rogue. I found Etta's mauled body when I went looking for my brother. She was still alive, died a minute later in my arms." She'd been so light in his hold, a sweet, loving woman forever gone, her family devastated, their dreams for her buried in the earth with her body.

"You should've seen Brodie with her before. He *loved* her." Alexei didn't want Memory to know his brother only as the violent killer he'd become; he needed to show her the generous and devoted mate Brodie had been before it all went horribly wrong. "Idiot once dived out of a plane above the territory with a parachute that opened out to say, 'Etta, I'm sorry,' after they'd had a fight."

Memory's smile trembled. "I wish I could've known him. Known her." She brushed back his hair, stroked his shoulder, his upper arm.

Accepting the way she touched him, comforted him, he told her the rest. "I tracked him, but when the time came, I couldn't hurt him. I would've allowed him to shred me to pieces." He'd collapsed onto his knees at seeing his adventurous, funny big brother's bloody muzzle and mad eyes, his heart broken. "Hawke knew. He'd followed me. He did what needed to be done."

"I'm so sorry, Alexei." Wrapping her arms around his neck, Memory pressed her cheek to his. The salt of her tears was wet against him, the tremor in her voice potent with emotion.

Alexei let her hold him as he hadn't allowed anyone to hold him for a long time. But he couldn't cry, the tears locked up in concrete inside his heart, the hard substance formed of his anger and his pain.

"Just because this happened to members of your family, doesn't mean it'll happen to you." Memory's voice was fierce.

Alexei wished he could grab on to the hope, hold on. "There's a stressor." He spoke against her ear, the words coming out husky and rough. "My father never said much about his father, but as a child, I once overheard him telling my mother that, according to older packmates, my grandfather began to act strange prior to going rogue. Spending long hours in wolf form and becoming aggressive toward his mate when he'd always before been gentle."

Sitting back so she could see his face, Memory frowned. "Did the same thing happen to your father and brother?"

"My father was always a little different from other changelings." Not that Alexei had consciously known that as a child—to him his dad was just his dad. "We stayed out for weeks at a time in the wilderness, and I don't think my father ever shifted back into human form except when my mother made him. I didn't know that wasn't normal."

"So he was always predisposed to it? Then why are you worried it'll happen to you?"

"After my father's death," Alexei said, "we had to know the truth. We asked our aunt."

"Why not your mother?"

Alexei squeezed his eyes shut. "She couldn't live with the horror of what he'd become. She took a massive overdose of sleeping pills right after he was executed."

Memory felt a wave of fury roar over her, directed at a woman who'd permitted her own pain to overwhelm her duty to the two small souls who looked to her for hope, for answers, for love. Forcing the anger into a tight knot in her gut, she focused on Alexei.

"I was nine by the time we demanded the truth from Aunt Min, Brodie eleven." Alexei's voice was ragged, his muscles rigid. "She said our father's DNA had been tested, but as with all rogues to date who've been examined, the scientists found no genetic red flags."

Alexei's claws slid out. "I knew there was more. I could tell. I asked and asked until she finally admitted that our father hadn't begun acting the way he did—feral, secretive, just a little strange—until he mated."

A sudden chill settled on Memory's skin. She'd been around changelings enough by now to understand what mating meant to them. She'd also felt the intense power of that bond in the glimpses she'd caught during her mental sessions with Sascha.

Conscious that Memory had gaps in her emotional knowledge, particularly when it came to a healthy and loving relationship with a man, the cardinal had been very generous with her. Never revealing intimate details, but bringing Memory into her life, as if Memory truly was Sascha's little sister.

Even when Memory was mad with Alexei and fighting with him, the idea of being bonded as deeply to him as Sascha was to Lucas, it had been her secret dream. "Mating is the stressor?" she forced herself to ask.

"Brodie and I, we made a promise to each other to never get mated," Alexei ground out. "Then we grew up and began to forget, and Brodie fell in love." A twist of his lips. "Etta was tall and slender as a reed, and as sweet and shy as Brodie was outgoing, and he adored her. When the mating bond called, he didn't resist."

Memory's heart ached for a man and a woman she'd never met, would never know.

"The behavioral changes were subtle, but I'd known Brodie my entire life. I could see it happening, see him morphing into our father. He held on for three years before he surrendered to the wolf." Alexei dropped his hands to the seat, his claws slicing into it.

His torment was a wild creature in his eyes.

Pressing her forehead to his, Memory cupped the side of his face, her first priority to comfort him any way she could. "You think the same thing will happen to you if you mate."

"Starting with my grandfather, *every* male in my direct line has gone rogue after mating—my father lasted the longest, nearly ten years, but he was increasingly erratic for at least four of those years." Alexei's jaw turned to granite under her touch. "No matter how anyone tries to spin that, they can't make it add up to any other conclusion."

Amber eyes locked with hers, nightglow in the private dark of the Jeep. "I'm never going to be able to drop my guard enough to mate. I can't, not if I want to survive." Claws slicing back in, he gripped her nape, his next words a rough whisper. "And not if I want to protect the woman who's mine."

Memory had a hole inside her, needed to *belong* in the

deepest way to her golden wolf. "Can you love without it being a risk?" she whispered.

"I don't know." Harsh words, but his hands, they stayed careful on her. "I'm not whole, Memory, not in the way you need."

Heat in her belly. "You let me decide what I need." Drawing back, she stabbed a finger into his right pectoral and said, "And I'm not certain I believe in your curse, either."

"Memory."

"Did your father spend years learning to be a disciplined SnowDancer soldier, then lieutenant? Did your brother?" It sounded as if, along with loving his mate, Alexei's beloved older brother had been an adrenaline junkie who liked breaking the rules. "You growl and snarl, but you're *always* in control." Not once had he so much as scratched her with his claws.

"It might not matter in the end—no one knows what pushes a predatory changeling to go rogue," said her stubborn wolf. "Might just be a switch in my brain that flips." Moving his hands to her back, he leaned forward so his breath kissed her lips. "When the mating song rises between a man and a woman, it's the woman who decides whether to accept or not, but it can be blocked on the male end if he wills it hard enough."

As Memory listened, her gut a knot, he told her how he'd learned about the male ability to block the bond from one of the cats. Tamsyn's mate had been forced to do it for years because of the age difference between them—Tamsyn had been far too young when they'd first found each other.

"I've never heard the mating song," Alexei said, big, beautiful, and so hurt. "If I ever do, I'll do everything in my power to block it."

Memory held his gaze, her own belligerent. "Why are you telling me this?"

"You know." A growl. "Don't you dare pretend you don't."

Huffing out a breath, Memory fisted her hands in the rough silk of his hair. "You're mine, Alexei." She was through with playing by his rules; what lived between them had nothing to do with gratefulness or imprinting. It had to do with Alexei and Memory. If she needed him, he needed her as much.

As for his vow . . .

Memory kissed him hard, shoving the shadows of the curse into the dark.

Chapter 39

Operation Scarab has launched on a wave of success. Results have been so stellar that we request permission to enroll twenty others in the trial. There is little point in wasting resources when Scarab could put those resources back into play within a relatively short period.

—Report prepared for the Psy Council (circa 1999)

THE POWER FLUCTUATIONS Kaleb had been sensing in the PsyNet were becoming dangerous. "It feels personal," he told Sahara as they walked along the edge of a Venetian canal gilded in sunshine. "Unquestionably power from an individual, not a buildup in the Net."

Her hand in his and her body clad in a red coat paired with black jeans and ankle boots, Sahara frowned. "No luck tracking it back?"

"No." Kaleb wasn't used to such failure. "It's erratic. By the time I catch the surge, it's faded at the other end." A cresting wave that didn't leave a trail. "I've dropped sniffers throughout the Net so I can react faster, but I think the mind behind the power is an intelligent one. They're deliberately erasing the trail."

"Are you worried the fluctuations might destabilize already shaky areas of the Net?" At his nod, Sahara chewed on the inside of her cheek. "If it's someone intelligent enough to wipe their trail, he or she must realize the risk."

"It's a paradox." He came to a stop in front of a Venetian residence newly painted in pale yellow with white trim, and half-submerged in water. "Are my eyes deceiving me or is a mouse watching us from that window?"

Sahara's face lit up. "You know that's Kaia's pet, Hex."

She waved up at the creature. "Come on, Kaia and Bo will be waiting—I'm so glad we were all free to catch up for coffee. Kaia said she'd make a cherry-coconut loaf."

Kaleb hesitated only for a second, his eyes on the line of her profile. She was his entire reason for existence, for waking up as a man and not a nightmare. And she was determined he would be friends with Bowen Knight. "Here." He teleported in a small bag he'd left on his desk in Moscow.

"What is it?" She took the brightly colored bag, eyebrows gathered. Two seconds later she began to laugh. "Mouse treats!"

As she tugged him down by the tie to kiss him, Kaleb felt the faint ripple of another power surge in the Net, but it was fading even as his sniffers reported it. If this emergent power didn't learn to put a yoke on their abilities, they'd cause critical ruptures in the Net.

Kaleb no longer had a choice: he had to ask Aden to unleash the Arrows, intensify the hunt. And hope the target wouldn't panic.

Chapter 40

Wolves and bears are the worst for being nosy parkers about packmates. Bears take first prize for their sheer stubborn refusal to go away if they think you need help, but wolves win on the coordinated assault front. If a single wolf doesn't have any luck getting through to a hurting packmate, he'll go away . . . to come back with ten other wolves. Being pack is being family. And wolves take family seriously.

—Essay by Dr. Gio Lantana in the 2081 *Wild Woman*
Special Edition: "Families, Packs & Clans"

MEMORY HAD HALF-EXPECTED Alexei to retreat after their passionate and painfully honest night in the forest, but he was already in the compound to run the security shift when she opened her curtains the next morning. Buoyant after the time she'd had with him, she didn't even feel tired despite having caught only a couple of hours of sleep.

Her entire soul glowed with a deep warmth at seeing him again.

She dressed in jeans, a plain white tee, and a thick sweater in a bright blood-orange color that reflected her mood. Polka-dotted socks finished off the look—she'd pull on her sparkly sneakers if she left the cabin.

When she walked out onto her porch, Alexei strode up to her and kissed her as if he had every right. He did. Memory had told him he could have any skin privileges he wanted. The growly wolf had actually ordered her to take whatever she needed from him when it came to touch—she was to never again become touch-starved.

"That's the only order of yours I'll ever follow," she'd told him with a scowl and gotten kissed for her trouble.

If that kiss had been hard and fast, this one was deep and voracious. Her wolf's possessiveness might as well have been a fluorescent flag. *Mine*, it said. *Try to court her and die.*

Another woman might've bristled. To Memory, the primal claim was welcome. Alexei might never mate with her—it still hurt to think that—but she'd heard enough from the other changelings to know that it wasn't usual for him to treat a woman with such open possessiveness.

Riaz, the golden-eyed lieutenant who'd rejected her blueberry cake, had smiled one day and said, "Never seen Lexie court a woman before. Man's apparently been hoarding his determination for you."

A redheaded leopard sentinel named Mercy had added another tidbit a couple of days later. "Entire wolf pack's finding it highly amusing to hassle Lexie over his attempts to feed you." She'd reached back to tighten her ponytail, her body sleek and tough and pure feline grace in jeans and a fitted forest-green sweater. "You know what they say about wolves and food."

Memory had thrown up her hands. "Actually I don't know! No one ever explains what they mean by that!"

A laughing Mercy'd had to leave to continue her patrol route, but that evening, Memory had received a message with a forwarded copy of the October 2078 issue of *Wild Woman* magazine. Mercy had written: *My demon brothers made me a "Wolf Survival Encyclopedia" when I mated my wolf. They printed out the Aunt Rita column from this issue. Check it out.*

The column had been eye-opening. Beware of wolves bearing food, indeed.

Smiling, she bit at Alexei's lower lip. He made a rumbling sound in his chest while stroking her spine all the way down to the lower curves of her body.

Her smile deepened. "You're in a good mood, Mr. Wolfy."

"Don't tell anyone." A mock scowl before he stepped away, a strong and intelligent male dressed in black cargo pants, an olive-green T-shirt, and scuffed black boots. His belt was obviously well loved, the buckle marked by scratches. And his hair, it was gilt under the sunlight.

Afterward, she watched him move about the compound and thought of the scars no one could see inside her golden wolf, the hurt he hid under the grumbles and the scowls. She had to force herself to pay attention when Sascha arrived to continue their work, but she did—nothing in her life could move forward until Renault was neutralized.

At the end, she clenched her abdomen and asked about Jaya's Arrow.

"Judd was able to help there," Sascha said. "Medics think Abbot will make a full recovery. Jaya's putting up a good front, but she's badly shaken—Ivy's with her. They're close."

Memory blew out a shaky breath, the nagging question of how a Tk could help heal someone shoved aside by her relief. "I'm so glad for Jaya—she loves Abbot so much." Then, fingers digging into her thighs, she said, "Yuri?"

Face soft, Sascha shook her head. "No news. Aden hasn't made the call yet."

What must it cost an alpha to decide on life or death for one of his own? Aden, Memory knew, would wear Yuri's name on his soul forever. As Hawke must wear Brodie's.

"He never really spoke to me," Sascha murmured, and when Memory looked up, said, "Yuri. He liked you, felt comfortable with you."

"It's because of the darkness in me." At that instant, Memory was grateful to that darkness; without it, she might've never come to know the intensely private Arrow. "I wish we'd had longer—I think he's the kind of friend who would've been there all my life, become an uncle to any children I might one day have."

Memory swallowed hard. "Another Arrow invited him to join her for dinner that day . . . the day he got hurt. She made it a point to mention that she wasn't inviting him as a squadmate, but as a man who intrigued her—I think he was surprised, but in a good way." Always difficult to read, Yuri had nonetheless felt quietly happy to her empathic senses. "He asked me about the 'protocol' of whether he was expected to take a gift."

Sorrow drenched Sascha's expression. Closing her hand over Memory's she said, "What did you tell him?"

"I was going to say to take flowers—I read about romantic gifts in *Wild Woman*." Her chest ached. "But then I wondered if an experienced Arrow would like that, and said he should take a small thing that related to her, so she'd know he paid attention to her."

Memory's mouth curved, her lower lip trembling. "He said he'd noticed her uniform jacket was getting worn, but that she liked the fit too much to order a replacement. He was going to take a repair kit and offer to seal up any thin patches so she could continue to stay safe while wearing it."

Sascha's eyes shone wet. "Sounds perfect."

"I thought so, too." Despite everything, Memory kept hoping for a miracle, for Yuri to get a chance to go on that dinner date and fix his date's jacket. It wasn't fair that he'd spent his entire life in darkness only to die when he'd just experienced sunlight. "I'm going to hope for him until his heart stops beating."

She expected Sascha to advise that it was foolish to do that, that false hope would only make it hurt more in the end, but the cardinal blinked rapidly before saying, "Me, too," in a husky voice. "I was like Yuri once, closed inside myself, given no choices."

Sascha's breath caught, her free hand fisting on the table. "He deserves better than this, deserves a chance to—" She broke off, staring down at the table.

Unable to see her friend in such pain, Memory jerked from her seat to go around and hug Sascha from behind, wrapping her arms around the empath's neck. She was so used to thinking of Sascha as she was now—mated to an alpha leopard, mother to a panther cub, confident in her skin— that she forgot Sascha had been the first E to break the cruel chains of Silence.

Her cardinal light had been buried for more than two decades.

"We'll be foolishly hopeful together," Memory whispered, pressing her cheek to Sascha's temple. "I won't tell if you won't."

A wet laugh as Sascha placed her hand on Memory's forearm. "Deal."

LATER, while Memory got out the ingredients for hot chocolate, Sascha called her mate at the pack's city HQ. "My cub's there, too," she said to Memory as she input Lucas Hunter's call code. "Daycare's attached to the HQ, with full access from one section to the other."

The call connected. "Kitten," said a deep male voice.

Sascha had asked to use the wall comm, but when Memory went to step out so the two could talk alone, Sascha waved her over instead and introduced her to Lucas. Green-eyed and black-haired, with muted gold skin, he had the same deadly intensity to him as Alexei's alpha. The four jagged lines that marked the right side of his face, akin to the claw marks of a large cat, just added to the sense of contained power.

"Hello, Memory," he drawled with a slow smile. "I hear you enjoy hurling insults at wolves."

"It was *one* time," Memory protested, remembering too late that she'd also once called Alexei a plain old chicken. "Anyway, he deserved it!"

Lucas's grin deepened. "Wolves always deserve it. I'm going to use 'big, wolfy chicken' the next time Hawke annoys me."

Memory found her mouth tugging up at the corners; she had zero doubts that Lucas Hunter was a deadly predator, but he was also charming in a very feline way. She could see why Sascha had fallen for him—but she felt no attraction herself. She liked her man to be a growly grouch who courted her with delicious food and used his teeth on her lips.

"I'm going to finish making the hot chocolate so you two can talk," she said. "Oh, and you can insult any wolf but Alexei. He's mine."

A sigh. "And another sane woman falls for a flea-bitten dog on steroids."

"Pay no attention to him." Hands on her hips, Sascha scowled at her mate. "He and Hawke are friends."

"Sascha, darling, we need to talk about that terrible lie you keep spreading."

Memory's shoulders shook as she boiled milk for the hot chocolate. It looked like Lucas could growl, too, when he wanted to, but Sascha was more than capable of tangling with her alpha mate. Though the two weren't talking about anything intimate, Memory felt a slight intruder . . . but she stayed. It was nice to be around such open affection.

She wondered if this was what it was like in a wolf den. Love worn openly, lives shared with packmates, care expected and given. Her stomach got all warm at the thought. Being so entwined in the daily lives of people who were her own, it was her vision of heaven.

"Naya snuck out of daycare again," Lucas said a few minutes into the conversation, his tone amused. "She likes to hide under Mercy's desk. Mercy always kicks off her shoes when in the office—prime biting material."

"Oh, Lucas, you shouldn't encourage her." Sascha's voice held affectionate laughter.

"It's Mercy you need to talk to—every time Naya launches a successful stealth attack on her toes, Mercy pets her and calls her a strong hunter." Pride prowled below the humor. "At which point, Naya runs in here to tell me of her successful mission."

"I want to snuggle her face so much right now," Sascha murmured.

"Tell me what's wrong, kitten." A voice that sounded like a purr.

Memory did step out then, to give the couple privacy. She was hoping to see Alexei, but couldn't spot him. Returning inside after Sascha ended her call not long afterward, she took the hot chocolates to the table and the two of them settled into their chairs.

"I'd like for Judd to take a look at your mind," Sascha began. "I want him to see if he can spot any back doors I might've missed. He's an expert in a way I'll never be. But, Memory, the decision is yours."

Memory's stomach churned at the idea of a stranger inside her mind, but any surviving back door was a major threat. Renault had been too panicked to exploit any holes in her defenses on their most recent encounter—he might be calmer and luckier next time. "Yes," she said to Sascha. "I want to make sure my mind is airtight."

"I'll call, see if Judd is nearby."

Only five minutes later, Alexei walked through the door ahead of a dark-eyed and dark-haired man who moved with a fluid grace that shouted "telekinetic." Memory's stomach muscles clenched.

"Forgot to give you these earlier." Alexei tugged on one of her curls as he dropped a bunch of granola bars in front of her. "I got a smack on the hand from the cook for snagging more than my fair share." A scowl. "You better eat them or I won't steal you more."

Making a face at him, Memory said, "I see the good mood was a fleeting thing."

He tugged on another curl, but shifted his gaze to the man with him. "This is Judd."

"I won't invade your thoughts," the Tk said in a cool voice. "My only aim is to check for any holes created deep in your mind by your captor."

Alexei clasped her nape in a caressing grip. "Judd's one of my best friends and I'd trust him with my life—he won't hurt you."

The rough honesty of his words helped her defeat the fear crushing her heart. "What do you need me to do?" she asked Judd.

"Lower your shields." His eyes were a deep brown with flecks of gold, far warmer than his voice. "I won't enter unless you do."

It took teeth-gritted focus on her part to force down her shields, even more focus not to shove them back up the instant a powerful mind entered hers. But he kept his word, going nowhere near her thoughts or secrets, his focus on the structure of her mind.

"I'm done," he said in a matter of minutes, and she slammed up her shields.

"Is it bad?" Sascha frowned.

A shake of Judd's head. "You two got most of them." He switched his attention to Memory. "Your captor wasn't subtle or skilled—the hidden doors are basic hacks I learned as a seven-year-old Arrow trainee."

Memory wondered if she was imagining the insulting edge to his tone—he was so icy and distant . . . but he was also Alexei's friend. Alexei, who had no ice in him.

"Don't hold back," she said with a wry smile.

No change in his expression, but his emotions held definite amusement. "Only reason Sascha couldn't see these final doors was because she's an E. Your designation isn't endowed with the gene for deviousness."

Memory and Sascha both glared at Alexei's cool-eyed friend.

Clearly not the least bit terrified by their wrath, Judd carried on. "I've tagged the locations for you. Demolition instructions sent to Sascha."

"Be any smugger and you'll turn into a cat."

Eyes gleaming at Alexei's bad-tempered comment, Judd looked at Memory again. "You realize you have a minor telekinetic ability?"

"Yes, it's worthless." Much to her disgust. "It was tagged as 1 on the Gradient when I was tested as a child." At the time, with Designation E unknown to the general populace, she'd been officially classed a 3.4 telepath. Multiple abilities weren't uncommon, but generally only on the lower end of the scale—or that's what she'd been taught.

According to Sascha, however, Judd was beyond a 9 in both Tk *and* Tp.

The ex-Arrow pushed up the sleeves of his sweater. "Your Tk's matured closer to 1.5—and nothing is useless if you know how to utilize it." He went to the counter to pick up a spoon she'd left to dry.

Placing it on the table in front of her, he said, "Nudge it."

Memory did it only so she could prove to him that this was a pointless exercise. The spoon moved a fraction of an inch.

"Do it again," Judd said.

She did.

When he asked her to do it a third time, however, she sat back and folded her arms. "Why?" It wasn't even a parlor trick when Tks like Judd could throw missiles around in the sky.

"Imagine if you had the delicate skill to manipulate the tumblers of an old-fashioned lock, or to push in the code on a computronic one. Not many prisons could keep you inside." A raised eyebrow. "Never leave an advantage on the table."

Memory sucked in a breath. "Thank you," she said. "I'll practice."

A small nod before Judd glanced at Alexei. "Ready to do our patrol, or do you want to rub your scent on your E?" Words so cool it took Memory a second to realize he was poking the wolf, his eyes alive with humor.

"One of these days . . ." Alexei growled before leaning down to kiss Memory. "Do not admire the asshole. It just gives him a big head."

As the two men left, Memory tried not to think about the wounds inside her golden wolf, scars that meant their relationship could never be like Sascha and Lucas's, or Jaya and Abbot's.

So we'll make it our own, she vowed. *I'm not about to give up on you, on us, Alexei Vasiliev Harte.* She was too far gone, his name written on her heart.

Chapter 41

It is the recommendation of this PsyMed advisory board that the survivors of Operation Scarab be placed in psychic restraints and kept away from the general populace. It has proved impossible to go backward—the survivors cannot be returned to their stable pre-Scarab state.
> —Report prepared for the Psy Council (circa 2003)

HE'D HAD THE emergency overnight brain scans done at an anonymous facility, under a false name. Had even gone to the extent of wearing an expensive disguise, a disguise he only had because his now-deceased grandfather had insisted he always have one ready just in case. He'd felt foolish doing it, but as the head of a major Psy family, there was a high chance someone would've recognized him otherwise.

It wasn't that he didn't trust Dr. Mehra. The Gradient 9.8 M-Psy was deeply loyal to the family. The one who had awakened had learned the importance of loyalty by watching not his own parent, but Kaleb Krychek. One of the most ruthless and deadly men in the Net had never—not *once*—been sold out by his own people.

It had taken time and a careful reading of rare public comments made by Krychek's employees, but he'd come to learn that Krychek had one rule with subordinates: Be loyal to me and I will be loyal to you. No capricious firings. No bad treatment. Mistakes forgiven as long as they were genuine and an attempt was made to fix them.

The simplicity of that structure had appealed to him. It'd taken time to roll it out across his own network—his grandfather had run their business units a far different way—but these days, he knew he had the loyalty of every single senior member of his staff. But he'd wanted no one to know of these scans . . . and the story they told.

The experienced neurospecialist who'd reviewed the scans, then spoken to him over the phone to get background, had made a chilling diagnosis. "There is evidence of damage in an area of the brain linked strongly with Psy abilities. High probability it's the reason behind your descent into a fugue state."

Fugue state.

A time when he was an automaton, driven not by his conscious mind but by the subconscious. A person in a fugue could do many things, become a wholly different individual. Whether he'd ever recover any memories of what he'd done was an open-ended question. Psy brains didn't always react in medically predictable ways.

The M-Psy had urged him to return to the facility within the week, have further scans, but he didn't need the scans to know the problem: his sprawling new power. He had to figure out how to turn it off, how to fix himself before it was too late and the damage to his brain had a permanent effect.

His wrist unit vibrated against his skin.

Glancing down, he froze. It was a message from Theo: *Whatever you're doing, I'd request you stop. I'm getting tired of the secondhand migraines.*

Chapter 42

It is agreed: the survivors of Operation Scarab are to be eliminated. Their psychic power surges threaten to destabilize the PsyNet, and this cannot be permitted. Death is to be by humane methods.

—Psy Council (2004)

MEMORY WAS SITTING at her kitchen table at around four that day, working on nudging the spoon along a preset path, when Alexei turned up at her door, his eyes backlit by amber. "Want to go see more of the festival in Chinatown?" Golden and strong, with a smile that hit her in the solar plexus, he could tempt her anywhere.

Rising, she slipped her hand into the warm roughness of his . . . just as his phone buzzed. "Hello, squirt," he said as he led Memory to the black SUV he was driving today. "Yeah? Well maybe I miss your face, too." He grinned at the response. "Congrats on the win, by the way. I sent you a celebratory surprise. Should arrive tomorrow."

Smiling at the happy emotions she could sense in him, Memory didn't interrupt. Alexei spoke with the caller for a few more minutes before hanging up. "My cousin, Franzi," he said after they were in the SUV and on their way. "Aunt Min's daughter. Twelve years old and smart as a whip—she just won this major computronics contest." His pride in his young cousin was adorable.

"They're based in your den?" Memory loved seeing this side of him, the dangerous dominant who made time for a little girl who wanted to hear his voice—and who'd thought to send her a gift to celebrate an achievement.

"Yeah. Aunt Min and her mate, Gustav, followed me and

Brodie when I got put in charge of that den." A roughness to his voice. "Said it was about family."

Memory already loved these three people she'd never met. "Tell me more about them."

It was a topic on which her golden wolf had no hesitation speaking. She discovered that his aunt was a senior soldier, his uncle a lighting engineer, and that they'd met while his aunt had been roaming the world on her own. Alexei, too, had roamed as a younger wolf, and he shared stories about his adventures that had her laughing.

"I have a question," she said much later, after a companionable silence had fallen between them. "How can Judd have helped Abbot if he's a Tk?" Telekinetics caused destruction; they didn't heal.

"Judd's a special kind of Tk. Can move the cells of the body." A sudden darkness in Alexei's voice. "As a child, he was taught that his only value was as an assassin. A Tk-Cell can stop the heart, can kill in undetectable ways—but it turns out you can use the same skill in the exact opposite way."

"To put the cells of the body back together," Memory whispered, her fingers clasped tight in her lap. "Do you think I could . . . be something good?"

"You already are." A scowling proclamation. "Remember Ashaya. Remember how she treasures the time you give her with Amara."

Memory couldn't argue with that. Neither could she forget what Amara herself had said to her: *You've shown me elements of the world I never before knew existed.* The scientist remained a psychopath, still spent time considering how she could use what Memory did as a tool of manipulation . . . but every so often, she'd display an unexpected humanity.

Such as when, after a session, she'd spent time fixing a scientific problem posted on an online forum by a small human community. The community could only offer naming rights to their tiny library as payment, and the work itself wasn't cutting-edge enough to tempt the caliber of scientist required. Yet Amara had sat down and solved the problem.

"Might as well," she'd said with a shrug. "It amuses me to know students will be studying at the Amara Aleine Library."

Flip words, but she'd given up hours of her time.

Memory was still considering what that meant when Alexei parked his SUV in a lot attached to DarkRiver's city HQ. "The cats are a lot more hooked into the pulse of San Francisco than us wolves," he said as they got out. "This really is a feline city."

She saw the curl of his lip, but knew by now that it was all for show. The cats and the wolves were blood allies—but they liked to pretend they couldn't stand the sight of each other. Complete with innovative insults crafted with intense care. Grinning, she took his hand and suddenly realized she was now one half of a couple out for the night. A dream she'd only hours earlier believed impossible.

Rising on tiptoe, she kissed his bristly jaw. His responding smile was devastating, and she knew she'd take her golden wolf any way he'd trust himself to come to her. She'd love him with fierce devotion and raw honesty—and she'd hunt for ways to disprove his belief in the family curse. Not for herself, but because thinking himself a rogue-in-waiting wounded Alexei unbelievably.

"Memory!"

Jolted at hearing the sound of her name, she looked across the road and saw Sascha waving at her. Hunkered down on the ground beside her was a familiar dark-haired man with wide shoulders who appeared to be doing up the shoelace of a little girl with equally dark hair. She was holding on to his shoulders with tiny hands while she lifted her boot off the ground, as if to help him.

Sascha's baby girl, not yet two years of age, wore a long-sleeved purple tunic over sparkly black tights. On the front of the tunic was a unicorn picked out in glitter. Her hair, soft but tumbled with curls, was in a jaunty ponytail. And in her hand, she carried a plas sword. Bright yellow, it matched the shield she wore on her back.

Memory waved back, not sure if she should approach or not. Alexei, however, was already stepping out onto the street, the area having been closed to traffic. "Luc," he said when Sascha's mate glanced up.

His eyes were a vivid panther-green in real life . . . and they made Memory shiver inside. Even if she hadn't known she was looking at the alpha of DarkRiver, she would've known he was deadly. Power burned inside him, a hard slap against her senses.

"Alexei." Rising to his feet, one of his daughter's small hands clasped protectively in his, he held out the other to shake Alexei's before shifting that feline gaze to Memory. His lips curved. "Ah, the creator of my new favorite wolf insult."

Memory parted her lips to reply when a small voice piped up, "I'm Naya!" The little girl bounced on her shiny black lace-up boots, her eyes as green as her father's. "I'm a danger!" She held up her sword.

"You look very dangerous," Memory said solemnly, and was rewarded by a mischievous grin. She knew Naya's physical dexterity was a changeling gift—Sascha had mentioned that changeling toddlers tended to walk much earlier than Psy, with humans also seriously outpacing Psy.

However, what she only now realized was that Naya'd also benefited from the Psy side of her DNA; the constant telepathic contact with her mother had accelerated her verbal development. The tiny girl's speech wasn't clear, but it was far more comprehensible than most children her age.

"Kitten," Lucas said to Sascha, "why don't you and Memory walk ahead, and Alexei and I'll follow with our ferocious panther."

Naya growled and showed her claws. Memory had to bite her lips to keep from laughing at the sheer adorableness of this tiny, unicorn-emblazoned, sword-carrying panther. Falling in beside Sascha, while Naya walked in between Lucas and Alexei, she said, "How do you ever discipline her? I'd have zero willpower against that face."

"Luc does most of it," Sascha admitted in a laughing whisper. "She knows I'm a soft touch." The cardinal shook her head, her lips pressed tight. "The only thing I won't bend on is anything to do with her safety, and she's a smart cat, knows that. But otherwise, half the time, she'll make me laugh while I'm trying to tell her not to do something, and it's all over."

Sascha's cheeks creased, her eyes dancing. "Yesterday, while I was in the other room for *five* minutes, she changed into panther form, managed to climb up onto the kitchen counter, and, after shifting back to human form, opened the cupboard in which I keep the special fancy chocolate Lucas gets me. It's too rich for her. I walked out to find her sitting naked on the counter, chocolate smeared all over her face and an innocent 'I didn't do it' look on her face."

Memory lifted her hands to her mouth, overcome by the sudden piercing knowledge that she'd one day like to be a mother to a naughty baby with her father's wolf eyes. "What did you do?"

"I managed to give her a stern talking-to that time." Sascha pushed her braid off her shoulder. "And my poor cub got a tummy ache later, so the chocolate stash will be fine for a little while—at least until she forgets." Tenderness in every word. "I wouldn't change her for all the world. She's growing up wild and strong, with a pack full of friends."

A small, warm body wriggled between them. "Mama."

"Naya." Taking her daughter's hand on that singsong response that made Naya giggle, Sascha said, "Where's your sword?"

"Lexie hold." Bright green eyes angled to look at Memory.

She felt as if she was being weighed, judged, and when the little girl smiled and held out a hand, the joy she felt was a wave. "I can't," she said, her voice husky, scared the darkness in her would somehow hurt this innocent child brought up in love.

Sascha's gaze caught hers. *I don't think you're a threat to her, or I would've never called out to you,* the cardinal said telepathically. *But I appreciate the care.*

Smoothing her hand over her daughter's hair, Sascha spoke her next words aloud. "Memory's a special kind of E, baby. She's still learning how to control her powers and she has to be careful who she touches. Like how you're learning not to use your claws or your telepathy while playing with your friends."

"Memi, be good," Naya instructed in a very serious tone. "No caws."

Memory nodded. "No claws," she agreed solemnly, and the five of them continued to move up the sidewalk. When Naya cried out, "Ro! Jule!" on a wave of sweet excitement

colored by pure joy, she went to follow the little girl's gaze . . .
and a curdling fear bloomed in the pit of her stomach.

Sucking in a breath, she glanced around in a frantic
search, but the crushing darkness was everywhere. It wasn't
the nothingness, wasn't the abyss. This was far worse. It had
taken Yuri, nearly taken Abbot.

"Memory? What is it?" Alexei's voice seemed to come
from the end of a long tunnel, echoing and faint.

A rough-skinned palm sliding over hers, strong fingers
enclosing hers.

Heat, a primal power, an anchor.

Her lungs expanded, the scents and flavors of Chinatown
exploding against senses that had threatened to go numb
under the deluge of darkness. "The mind behind the attack
on the compound," she said as she raced to pinpoint the exact
location of the threat. "He's here. He wants to hurt Sascha,
the other empaths."

Listening to instinct, Memory turned to the left. Her eyes
locked on a knot of Psy who'd been standing quietly together
in readiness to watch today's parade. All four had gone stiff,
their eyes black. "It has them. *Go.*"

The pressure intensified the instant Alexei was no longer
touching her.

She could barely breathe under the crushing weight of the
shadowy darkness. He'd become stronger since the assault
against Yuri and Abbot and the others. The air was too
heavy, her lungs incapable of translating it into breath. When
she felt a trickle at her nose, she lifted a fingertip to touch
it . . . and it came away red.

"Here." Sascha thrust a small pack of tissues into her
hand. "Come with me."

Alexei and Lucas were nearly at the knot of Psy—the
quartet had just begun to stride toward a group of empaths.
"Why are so many Es here?" Memory asked as she stumbled
in Sascha's wake.

In front of her, Naya was protesting and dragging her feet.
"Mama! Ro! Jule!"

But Sascha was relentless—she lifted her squirming little
girl up into her arms and ran toward a store. "Memory!" she

yelled back when Memory became distracted by another wave of violent power.

Memory got moving, stepping into the store just behind Sascha and Naya.

"Mrs. Wembley," Sascha was saying to the shopkeeper, a slender woman with Eurasian features, her hair cut into a blunt bob, the color an inky black. "I need you to take Naya into your basement and stay there."

The other woman, her face unlined but a weight to her presence that said she was at least a couple of decades older than Sascha, didn't ask any questions or voice worry about leaving her shop unattended. Her emotions, too, were streamlined—she switched modes from happy festival mood to protectively maternal within heartbeats. "Come on, munchkin," she said, and reached out to take Naya.

But Lucas and Sascha's daughter refused to go until Sascha put her on her feet, then hunkered down and pressed her forehead to Naya's. "I need you to be a good girl for Mialin's grandma, baby. There's a bad person outside. I have to help your papa handle it so this person doesn't hurt anyone."

Tiny features awash in worry, Naya said something too fast for Memory to understand. But Sascha kissed her cub and said, "Yes, I promise I'll make sure Roman and Julian and Nate and Tamsyn are safe. Go with Mrs. Wembley now."

"We'll go do some coloring in the basement room—it's very nice, with a sofa and a soft rug," Mrs. Wembley said as she led Naya away, one little hand tucked trustingly in hers. "You can help me with my latest page. It's got so many colors, I get very tired."

Naya's response showed that she was the daughter of an empath and an alpha. "Mia come base'nt, too?"

"Oh, you sweet baby, Mialin's quite all right. She's at home in DarkRiver territory with her mama and papa."

The rest of their conversation faded as Mrs. Wembley and Naya disappeared behind a door that must've led to the basement. She heard the loud slide of a dead bolt, then three other clicks.

"Basement's secured," Sascha told her, her voice grim as she moved to the doorway of the shop.

Memory was already there, attempting to pinpoint the murderous mind's next move.

"I spotted a high-Gradient E out there," Sascha added. "I've telepathed her to begin crowd control while I attempt to aim a terminal field at the ones being used as puppets—I can't spread the field far yet, so I have to target it."

Crowd control. Terminal field.

Memory had no idea what those terms meant, but that didn't matter at this instant. "What do you need from me?"

"See if you can work out if the person behind this is physically in Chinatown, or if he's attacking via the PsyNet."

Memory saw that Lucas and Alexei had the quartet corralled—all four of whom blinked as one right then and began to look around in confusion. "He's moved on from that group." Her mouth went dry, her heart thundering. "There are too many Psy here. Too many minds for him to grab, none of them as well shielded as the Arrows'."

"You let us worry about that." Sascha's eyes were pure obsidian when they met Memory's. "You focus on locating the threat—you're the only one who can sense it." The cardinal returned her attention to the street, and, a second later, Memory saw people stop in their tracks, their hands going to cradle the sides of their heads.

Squeezing her own eyes shut, she focused on the serrated presence of the huge, cracked mind. It hovered like a black cloud over the street, its intent to eliminate the Es. Hate and fear emanated from it, the toxic emotions directed at the Es. But it couldn't capture empathic minds directly, kept sliding off.

That's why it used other living beings as weapons. But there was something very *wrong* with this mind, a strange blankness where a sense of identity should be. Worse than at the compound. Then, she'd sensed his maleness and confidence both. Now even those basic elements were faded and dull.

There.

Memory caught the intruder's psychic "frequency," much as she'd caught Renault's after he took Vashti. It was *loud*. "He's here." Lashes snapping up, she ran out of the doorway before Sascha could stop her.

Memory didn't hesitate as she weaved in and out through the confused but nonviolent crowd.

Crowd control. Terminal field.

Whatever it was Sascha and the other Es were doing, it was working.

The air pressure changed again without warning, a second massive power entering the zone. Panic stuttered her heart, but this mind was ruthlessly sane, its discipline so precise that nothing leaked, not even the faintest edge of emotion. Only that sense of incomprehensible power.

Oh.

She hadn't sensed him with her abilities at all, she realized. It had been pure survival instinct that alerted her to his presence. Still running, she spotted him up ahead: a terrifyingly handsome man in a black-on-black suit, his features all clean lines and his eyes cardinal starlight. She'd seen his face on the comm while buried in the bunker, knew he could raze cities and cause earthquakes: *Kaleb Krychek.*

His presence frosted the world in ice.

And his eyes, they landed on her. Hard to miss a woman running full tilt when everyone around her was preternaturally calm. Even the huge parade dragon had laid down its head, its controllers yawning as they leaned up against the dragon's body.

Where? The single word was a crystalline telepathic contact, so pure her ears rang.

Far right of the street. Clenching her jaw against her dislike of psychic contact with unknowns, she sent him an image of what she could see—the black cloud with tendrils going from person to person, every new victim being aimed toward an E.

There were so *many* Es here. Why?

The compound—the empaths trained there see this as home ground. It was the same cold telepathic voice, frigid as winter snow, razor-sharp in its clarity and nearly painful with it.

She sucked in a breath. *Get out of my head.*

I wasn't in it. Don't broadcast your question so loudly if you don't want an answer. He was gone a split second later, his body reappearing at the far end of the street.

Chilled to the bone—what did that much power do to a man?—she continued to run in his direction. Her breath wheezed, her chest ached, and she knew her body couldn't keep up this pace. She was far stronger than she'd been, but years of bad nutrition and lack of muscle strength would take time to fully undo.

A flash of gold in her peripheral vision, Alexei racing across the street to her. With barely a pause, he scooped her up in his arms and said, "Just point."

Slinging one arm around his neck, she did. And Alexei *moved*, a predator with lightning-fast reflexes, his body primal grace.

I'm cutting off the assailant to the right. Tell the wolf to go left.

Memory winced at the icy chill of Krychek's telepathic voice, but relayed the message. "The intruder can't teleport." He would've done so by now if he'd had that ability. "I think he's trying to get out now. No more attempts to turn people."

Empaths are madness.

Memory froze; that hadn't been Krychek. It was a far less disciplined voice, a thing of fractures and need. *Empaths heal wounds of the mind,* she replied.

I had no wounds before the waking of Designation E. A kind of frothing energy against her, an attack her mind foiled without effort. *You're not like the others.* A sudden quiet. *You are darkness. You are like me.*

Yes. It was the truth, at least in one sense. *You need help. Let me.*

It's too late.

Less pressure. Then none.

"Stop." She asked her wolf to put her down, then, one of her palms pressed against his heartbeat, she searched with her empathic senses and came up blank. "I can't sense him anymore." She relayed the same to Kaleb Krychek.

"Teleporter?" Alexei's gaze continued to sweep the area.

"No, I didn't feel a sudden disconnect. It was more a . . . fading. As if he drew the darkness inside himself." Memory shoved her curls behind her ears, told herself to *think*. "How can a person disappear while physically here?"

Krychek walked down the street toward them, the starlight of his eyes speaking to her of cold, distant places where it was never warm. "Our quarry has escaped?"

Shivering, Memory backed into Alexei. "Yes," she managed to get out past her overwhelming awareness of Krychek's lethal power. Yet this man was mated, was said to be devoted to his lover. Did he show this same deadly face to—

Oh.

"Two faces," she blurted out on a wave of realization. "He has two faces." One that was normal, could fool the world, the other a creature of darkness and madness with that odd blankness at its heart.

Memory worried over that blankness, but couldn't explain it. She had, however, picked up more than she'd realized during that fleeting moment of telepathic contact—she'd never attempt to hack another mind, but his was so fragmented that his hidden thoughts had leaked through on their own. "He hates Es, wants to wipe us out of existence."

A cold wind swept down the street, raising every tiny hair on her body.

Chapter 43

Though this be madness, yet there is method in't.
—From *Hamlet*, by the human artist William Shakespeare
(17th century)

WHERE AM I?

He "woke" on an unfamiliar street in the smudged dark of night that had just fallen, his heart thumping and his body sweaty under a thin gray sweater and black pants he didn't remember putting on. He'd been wearing a suit when he left the office. The cologne he drew in with every breath was far denser than his usual crisp choice.

His pulse hammered at his throat.

Forcing himself to keep moving, he reached into his pants pockets, but there was no phone there, and his wrist was bare of his usual unit. His hands curled into fists inside the pockets, but he kept his face expressionless; from the way others on the street glanced at him before carrying on their way, he must've appeared normal enough.

No one blanched. No one tried to run.

Swallowing to wet his dry throat, he paid careful attention to the architecture and the geography. Unless he'd lost days instead of hours, he must be in his own city.

A woman laughed up ahead and opened out a lace parasol.

Next to her were several other women in pretty dresses. Nothing about them gave him a location. He could've looked in the PsyNet to orient himself, but with his mind as chaotic as it was, he didn't want to risk suffering a fugue while only partially in his body.

"Good evening, ladies," he said with a smile he'd learned to produce on cue because it put humans and nonpredatory changelings at ease.

The women looked at one another and giggled.

He deepened the smile; he knew from a lifetime of experience that he had a pleasing aesthetic appearance, one that appealed to women. He'd never had much reason to use that tool in his arsenal, but today, it might gain him some desperately needed answers. "I was wondering if you could help me," he said. "I'm a visitor just arrived in your beautiful city. I don't suppose you have recommendations about what I could do this evening?"

The women giggled again, before one said, "You're not far from Chinatown, and the Chinese New Year festival is uh-*mazing*."

"Oh, and Fisherman's Wharf is jumping," her friend added. "They've got circus performers there tonight. While we were there, one of the DarkRiver cats shifted and dove through a ring of fire on a dare!"

The rest of their words faded into the background.

Fisherman's Wharf. Chinatown. DarkRiver. He was in San Francisco. Where he kept an apartment because he flew in and out for business. Right now, that included a major deal with the SnowDancer wolves.

Many of those wolves had to be on the streets attending the festival, but no one called him out. It wasn't until five minutes later, when he passed by a glossy shop window, that he realized why: his hair was the wrong color and he was wearing the paper-thin latex mask that he'd used for the medical appointment. It altered his features beyond recognition.

Red trickled out of his nose as he watched.

His head began to pound.

Chapter 44

Project Scarab: Closed. All outstanding matters cleared.
—Psy Council (2004)

ALEXEI THUMPED A nutrient drink down on the conference table in front of Memory. He'd brought her to DarkRiver HQ for a debrief, but like hell he'd let anyone else near her until she'd gotten some food in her. "I can see your cheekbones cutting against your skin." Whatever she did when she tracked the unknown mind, she used up the same massive amount of psychic energy as when she worked with Amara.

"Drink." It came out a growled order, his wolf's chest heaving with its worry for her. "Judd says the stuff's still the best way to get a calorie hit after a psychic burn."

Memory folded her arms across her chest and refused to reach for the glass. "I swore I'd never take nutrients again."

"It's not the same as the old stuff. It's flavored—pomegranate and peach."

"I've *told* you not to growl at me."

Baring his teeth, he bent down until their faces were only an inch apart. "You have drops of blood on your shirt." His entire body trembled with his fury at her hurt. *"Drink."*

Memory unfolded her arms, her gaze softening. She leaned into him and, taking the glass, drank half before placing her palm against his cheek. "Sorry about the blood." Tender words that sought to mollify his wolf. "It was like a pressure system building inside me. He has so much power and he can't control it."

Wanting to bite off the bastard's head, Alexei pointed toward the plate of cookies and chocolates he'd found in the nearby staff kitchen. The HQ was full of changelings on a daily basis and a number of those changelings were mated to Psy—he'd known there'd be all kinds of fuel within reach. Memory had drunk more of the nutrient mix by then, but she devoured several cookies in a row.

His wolf finally began to calm down.

Only after she'd eaten four cookies and was working on a fifth did he open the door and nod at the others to come in. Lucas entered with Sascha, Krychek behind them.

Naya, her fears assuaged by cuddles from Luc and Sascha, was with Tamsyn's family. The healer's twin terrors, who'd been known to run amok through the wolf den when Tamsyn visited the SnowDancer healer, were two of Naya's most favorite people. Alexei was of the opinion the twins were secretly setting up a pint-size wolf-leopard gang. Said gang had already run a successful raid on the den kitchen.

The crew had absconded with an entire cake.

Allowing the amused thought to further calm his wolf, he took the seat beside Memory. She inched closer to him when Krychek chose a seat on the other side of the conference table—directly across from her. Krychek tended to have that effect on people; it was a wonder any woman trusted him enough to allow him close, but the man had a mate.

Then again, Alexei's fingers were currently clawed—his calm only went so far—and yet Memory had no problem with the hand he had on the back of her chair, the razor-sharp tips of those claws brushing her curls.

Love made people crazy.

Love.

It was a word he wasn't supposed to know, an emotion he couldn't afford to feel. Not for a woman who made him wish for the impossible. But it lived inside him, a primal force that had him handing Memory a sixth cookie when she finished the fifth.

"I'll explode," she complained, but took it.

His wolf settled.

To the right end of the table, Sascha ate her way through a large chocolate bar. Her face, too, looked thinner. Lucas had his hand protectively on her shoulder; the leopard alpha had chosen to stand beside his mate rather than take a seat.

"The intruder tried to grab hold of me," Memory said once everyone was settled. "He failed despite the depth of his power."

"I felt an attempt, too." Sascha lowered her chocolate bar. "It was like he kept slipping off."

"I think empathic minds must be immune to him," Memory said as Luc ran the back of his hand over Sascha's cheek. "That's why he has to use proxies to attack us."

"What did you speak of when he made contact?" Krychek asked, his expression as inscrutable as always—but not only had the man offered an assist during multiple emergency incidents, Judd vouched for him, and that was good enough for Alexei. It wasn't as if SnowDancer had a sweet and fluffy image, either.

Beside him, Memory said, "He's going mad and he blames Es—he said he had no problems before we woke up."

Silence reigned around the table.

Sascha was the first to stir. "That doesn't make sense," she said, leaning her body against Lucas's. "Without Es in the Net, our race would've long ago devolved into insanity and murder."

It was Krychek who spoke next, his midnight voice musing. "Silence was a failure because it gave psychopaths free rein, but it's possible that for a minority who were on the brink between normal function and mental fracture, the psychic discipline inherent in Silence kept them on the right side of the line."

"And the sudden influx of emotion in the Net is eroding that control?" Lucas's eyes were of his cat, the panther prowling close to the surface of his skin.

"There's now no way to avoid emotion in the Net," Krychek pointed out. "The fragments emitted by empathic minds are everywhere."

Memory felt an unexpected stab of sympathy for that desperate mind, but hardened her heart against it. He could've asked for help. Instead he'd hurt Yuri and Abbot, violated so many others.

"Murdering Es will collapse your PsyNet," Alexei said to

Krychek, his big body so hot that she wanted to crawl into his lap and wrap him around her. "This guy's clearly lost it if he's forgotten that."

"Yes." Kaleb Krychek rose to his feet. "I'll continue to hunt in the PsyNet. This individual is powerful enough to be a deadly—" A sudden chill pause. "Breaking news. Four empaths in County Cork, Ireland, injured when another vehicle plowed headlong into theirs." The cardinal teleported out.

Shivering, Memory hugged her arms around herself. "That's not going to be just a terrible accident." How many of those Es would die? How many had been irreparably injured?

Alexei petted her nape. "Bastard's getting smarter." His words weren't what she wanted to hear. "Much easier to push a single driver to make a wrong move than to force multiple single minds to murder Es."

KALEB stood at the scene of the strange crash on a country road far outside the nearest town; emergency services were on scene and working frantically, and so far, he sensed no deaths. Two of the Es had minor broken bones, the other two some bruising. No other major injuries. The driver who'd hit them was being treated for slightly more severe wounds, but he was alert and aware—and appeared distraught.

One of the Es was sitting beside him, holding his hand.

The offending vehicle was an old model, likely had no automatic collision avoidance systems. The empaths had been driving a newer model, but the avoidance system'd had nowhere to take the vehicle on this narrow road bordered by centuries-old stone walls. Not when another car was aiming itself at them.

Kaleb stared at the tire marks on the road. "It looks like the solo driver came straight at the vehicle carrying the Es, then tried to avoid it at the last minute," he said to the Enforcement officer in charge of the scene.

The stocky male with heavy black stubble against pallid brown skin didn't technically answer to Kaleb; he was human and had no allegiance to the Psy. As far as Kaleb was aware, this particular detective had never been turned by any

Psy interests. He was an honest man—and one who didn't play games.

"I have a witness who pretty much describes exactly that." The cop, his Irish accent thick, nodded toward a lanky cyclist who sat white-faced on the curb. "She called emergency services, tried to help the injured before our arrival."

A glance down at the tire marks. "Driver in the wrong claims to have no memory of the incident and I believe him—man's plain befuddled." He rubbed his jaw. "Medics say he hasn't suffered a knock to the head, so we might be looking at dementia, other mental deterioration."

A logical conclusion, but Kaleb didn't think so. Not so close on the heels of the attack in Chinatown. He reached for the NetMind and DarkMind, wondering if they'd interceded to protect the Es, but all he got was static and confusion around smaller and smaller patches of coherence. The neosentient twins were failing along with the PsyNet. They could offer him no help against this destructive threat.

Kaleb stared at the road again before sending a message to his fellow members of the Ruling Coalition, then thanked the Enforcement officer for his help. He teleported home a second later. It was empty—he knew that the instant he arrived. It only ever felt like a home when Sahara was in residence.

Taking off his jacket, he removed his tie and rolled up the sleeves of his shirt before stepping out onto the terrace of their home. The gorge fell away endlessly on the other side. Standing by the railing he'd put in when he found Sahara, his lover who couldn't teleport out of a fall, he entered the psychic vault of the Ruling Coalition chambers.

Nikita Duncan and Anthony Kyriakus were already there. Aden Kai and Ivy Jane Zen arrived at nearly the same time as Kaleb.

As expected, Ivy Jane was already up to date with today's events.

Power hummed around her, but it wasn't a power like Kaleb's—empathic power functioned on its own rules and it was defiant. Even now, the sparks of color from Ivy Jane's mind infiltrated the minds around her.

Kaleb didn't fight it—that empathic energy was part of the reason he wasn't insane. He added his thoughts as Ivy

Jane recapped the day's events, then turned his attention in another direction. "Nikita."

Sascha Duncan's mother, a woman as ruthless as Sascha was empathic, didn't pretend not to know why he'd addressed her. "Regardless of what you might believe," she said, "I didn't have knowledge of every single Council stratagem even while I was a Councilor."

Oddly, Kaleb did believe her. The previous Psy Council had been made up of seven members, each and every one hungry for power. Kaleb included himself in that assessment. So many plots had existed at any one time that no one could've been aware of all of them—however, Nikita had been on the Council for decades longer than either Kaleb or Anthony.

"You know where to dig for the Council's skeletons," he pointed out.

"True enough." No emotion in her tone, yet this woman had brought a cardinal E to term in her womb. "As it happens, I've been making use of my shovel since your first report of a careless new power in the PsyNet." She uploaded data onto the walls of the psychic vault, a rain of silver symbols against the black of the Net.

"I discovered this report in a sealed historical archive buried in what I believed was an obsolete data node—back when I first joined the Council, the oldest member at the time vetoed deleting the node. He had the vague notion we might one day need the information in it. No one cared enough to oppose him, and eventually, we forgot about it."

No one in the vault challenged Nikita's report—they all knew their race had made an art form of erasing their past.

"You can read the report yourself," the former Councilor continued, "but the gist of it is that as the first generation born into Silence came of age, it was discovered that for a small minority of Psy, Silence acted as a dimmer switch on their abilities."

A pause as the members of the Coalition scanned the report. It was too complex to absorb in a few minutes, but Kaleb was able to flip through it and find a number of interesting sections. The effect, he saw, had been most prevalent in Psy over 7 on the Gradient.

"Why did the Council allow this?" The men and women who'd ruled the Psy for more than a century had liked nothing more than power—and an army of high-Gradient telepaths and telekinetics were the foundation of that power.

"According to a later report I discovered only an hour before you called this meeting," Nikita said, "those in charge did attempt to modify Silence to eliminate the unintended side effect. It was called Project Scarab."

"It failed?" Ivy Jane Zen's warm psychic voice.

"On the contrary—Scarab was initially a wild success. The Psy enrolled in Scarab gained access to the full breadth of their abilities. Unfortunately, the subjects soon began to exhibit signs of deep mental instability—most often betrayed by erratic psychic control and emotional outbursts. Hallucinations, blackouts, increasingly violent frenzies, and memory loss were also reported."

"Nikita and I have discussed this." Anthony spoke for the first time, his mental voice as calm and measured as his presence in real life. "I did the reading on the secondary section of data, while Nikita dove deep into the first."

Kaleb wasn't the least surprised by that; whatever was going on with Anthony and Nikita, it had nothing to do with Silence. Sahara was fascinated by their relationship, and he knew she'd chew over this sign of offline interaction when he mentioned it. What Kaleb found most interesting was that both had protected a daughter who'd defected from the PsyNet.

"It appears," Anthony continued, "that Silence works as advertised for this tiny minority—it stabilizes them. The cost is loss of psychic strength."

"Silence worked for some Psy?" Ivy Jane whispered.

"At the expense of the entire PsyNet," Anthony pointed out. "Another section of it collapsed three hours ago. Even if Silence worked for these individuals, they'll still be as dead as the rest of us if the Net fails."

Kaleb and Aden had sealed that particular breach as a team. After the first wave of failures, the two of them had assembled squads of high-Gradient Psy who could, together, handle small-to-medium-size breaches. Kaleb and Aden alternated in handling the bigger ruptures—it meant one of them was always at full strength and able to respond quickly.

The only exception was where the breach was so devastating it required their combined power. The latter was occurring more and more. "Can such individuals reinitiate their Silence?" he asked—if it worked, the reversion would stop the rogue power waves while they sought a more permanent answer.

"Not with the Honeycomb in effect." Ivy Jane's voice was somber. "At this point, it's impossible to escape emotion in the Net."

"Even prior to the waking of the Es, none of the Scarab subjects were able to return to Silence," Anthony said. "Many self-terminated when they became aware of their own instability, or were killed during aggressive episodes so bad the staff had no choice but to use lethal force to defend themselves. The remainder were executed by the Council. This genie cannot be put back in the bottle."

"Such individuals must've existed pre-Silence," Nikita added. "Dangerous instability was one of the reasons our race saw Silence as our savior. But, given the degree of their volatility, many of the affected would've never made it to adulthood. Silence altered that balance."

Which meant the PsyNet would have to deal with far more dangerous and out-of-control adults than they'd ever before done in their history. It was the worst possible time for this hammer to drop on them. The Net couldn't handle any more pressure.

"There is a human saying," Ivy Jane said, pain in her voice, "that genius is tinged with madness. In the case of our race, the price for our abilities is immense mental darkness—and each time we attempt to escape that price, it gets worse."

True enough, Kaleb thought. Inside him lived a twisted and quite mad creature, the boy who'd been broken and warped before he'd ever had a chance to grow. He'd found an anchor to sanity in Sahara, the girl who'd never seen in him a monster. Take her away from him, however, and he would devastate the world.

"How big is the threat?" Aden's mind was intensely shielded, his connection to a fellow Arrow concealed either by habit or because Arrows liked to keep their secrets. "What percentage of the population?"

It was Nikita who responded. "Extrapolating from the Scarab data, less than one-sixteenth of a percent."

A minuscule number. There was just one problem. "A single insane Gradient 9 can cause catastrophic chaos."

Unspoken agreement from all the minds in the vault.

"Did the reports you unearthed offer a way to identify affected Psy before they go critical?" Aden asked with Arrow practicality.

Both Nikita and Anthony answered in the negative.

What, Kaleb thought, would it be like to wake up one day with your mind infinitely more vast than when you went to sleep? A mind strong enough to grab hold of an Arrow's and force that highly trained black ops soldier to act against his will and against his own self-interest. A mind that understood its own descent into the abyss.

Chapter 45

If a wolf invites you to play, just ask where and when. You won't be sorry. Depending on your playmate, you might also end up naked.

—From the April 2075 issue of *Wild Woman* magazine: "Skin Privileges, Style & Primal Sophistication"

MEMORY SAT SILENT and cold in the passenger seat as Alexei drove to the compound. She ached deep within, and it had nothing to do with physical pain—she felt bruised by her contact with the murderous psychic hunter. How could she feel sorry for that horrible man who'd hurt Yuri and Abbot and who wanted to murder her designation? Yet she did.

Something in that warped mind had reached her empathic core.

What did that make her?

They were nearly at the compound when Alexei went to take her hand, put it on his thigh.

Flinching, Memory pulled away.

No growl, only a distinctly wolfish motionlessness. "You going to talk to me?"

Memory shook her head.

"Yeah, well, tough luck." Alexei's primal power filled the SUV. "You're allowed to sulk, but not to hurt inside that way."

Memory bristled. "Who are you to give me orders about what I can and can't feel?"

His growl filled the entire inside of the vehicle, making the tiny hairs on her arms stand up and her heart kick. Her blood heated, a red-hot fire sweeping through the darkness. "I have *told* you not to growl at me."

He bared his teeth at her. "And if I do?"

Narrowing her eyes, she hit him with a wave of puppies and rainbows and sparkle.

He hissed out a breath. "That's just mean."

"You started it." She folded her arms across her chest and stopped the barrage of happiness. "I want to brood, so leave me alone."

The damn wolf actually chuckled.

Glaring out the windscreen, she decided to ignore him. She was so focused on the conflicting emotions inside her that it took her a while to realize they should've reached the compound by now.

"Where are you going?" she demanded.

"Wherever I want," said the infuriating man in the driver's seat.

Even the barrage of sickly sweet happiness she aimed at him just made him grit his teeth and keep going. Until at last he brought the vehicle to a stop in the middle of nowhere, the forest silvered by moonlight around them and no signs of habitation in sight. She sat stubbornly in the passenger seat even after he hopped out.

Opening her door, he let in the cool night air. "Want to see something wonderful?"

"No." She tightened her folded arms.

Pulling at her curls, he said, "Bad-tempered lioness." When she didn't respond to that provocation, he leaned in closer. "Come play." The rough-voiced request made her stomach clench, a shiver threatening to roll over her body.

He nuzzled at her curls before drawing back and beginning to strip off his clothes. Memory wasn't superhuman; she looked. And his body . . . For the first time, she understood that saying about swallowing your tongue. No one that perfectly chiseled and golden could be real. He had to be an illusion.

She didn't realize she'd reached out a hand to brush her fingers against his chest until he grabbed her wrist and brought her fingers up to his mouth to nip lightly at them. Retracting her hand, she forced herself to look away when he began to undo the top button on his jeans. Light sparked in her peripheral vision not long afterward.

Heart jolting, she turned . . . to see a large gray wolf shaking its fur into place.

A discarded pile of clothes lay on the grass and the eyes that met hers were pure amber. The wolf stretched out its body, its paws out front and its head lower than its back. *Come play*, it said.

Wonder shimmered through her, bright lights in the darkness.

Unfolding her arms while her lower lip trembled, she swung her legs out of the truck. The wolf gripped at the edge of her pants, tugged.

"Stop that," she said. "I like these jeans."

He tugged again.

Unable to bite back her laugh, she jumped down and closed the door behind her. The wolf let go at last. When she went to her knees and raised her hand with hesitant wonder, he butted his head against her chest. "Alexei," she whispered, astonished at the transformation even though she'd always known he was changeling; seeing him this way, this magnificent wild beast . . .

Fisting her hands in his fur, she rubbed the side of her face against him.

He opened his powerful and deadly jaws, pretended to grip her throat. She pushed playfully at the heavy bulk of his body and he danced away, light as air. Only to come back when she held out her hand. She stroked him, found that his coat was thick and soft. He stood in place, not just patient with her petting but angling his head or nudging at her to indicate she'd hit a good spot or that he wanted more.

Memory tugged at one of his ears, got a low growl in response, and a look that she was sure was of affront. "I guess no one dares tug a dominant wolf's ear." Her smile creased her cheeks. "What kind of game do you want to play?"

Amber eyes gleamed.

Lowering itself into a seated position, the wolf ostentatiously closed its eyes and put its head on its paws.

"A sleeping game?" Memory scrunched up her face. "That's the strangest game I've ever heard of."

The wolf opened its eyes and huffed, then got up and ran a little way into the forest before coming back. After which it folded itself back down into a seated position and placed its head on its paws.

Memory glanced at the moon-kissed forest into which the wolf had run and back at him. She'd never played games, never had a playmate, but she'd watched so many documentaries. What did wolves like to do? Her eyes widened. "Oh. A chasing game!" Pulse kicking, she rose to her feet. "I'm not very fast."

The wolf began to snore. *I'm giving you a big head start.*

She sensed that intent as clearly as if he'd spoken. The wolf's emotions were far more primal than Alexei's, but it was still him . . . and she could understand him in this form, too. That was a gift she'd never expected.

His eyes opened, a question in them.

"No peeking." She pretended to scowl.

He parted his jaws in a wolfish reply before closing his eyes again.

Trying to move as quietly as possible, she walked into the forest. She took care, unsure of her footing—but the moon lit up the world. It showed her an area with towering pines, carpeted by thick pine needles.

No cracked rocks, nothing to trip her up if she was careful.

Alexei had stopped where she could play with him without hurting herself.

Pulse a drum, she began to run. When she spotted the silver ribbon of a small stream, she took off her shoes and socks and waded upstream for five minutes before getting out. It was worth the frozen toes to give Alexei a small challenge at least. After using her socks to dry her feet, she balled them up and stuck them in a back pocket. Her sneakers fit well even over bare feet.

Ready, she began to run again.

A wolf's howl split the night sky five minutes later, raising every hair on her body, and she knew Alexei was on the hunt. Her breath hitched. Then froze in her lungs as howl after howl answered his. The wolf song echoed around the mountains, bouncing off the slopes and falling into the valleys. Memory's eyes burned at the unearthly beauty of the wild chorus, but she forced herself to keep moving.

Alexei was on her trail.

Even as she tried to keep ahead of him, she wondered what would happen if she ran across a wolf other than

Alexei. Distracted by the sudden thought, she nearly tripped on a root snaking across her path. Catching herself in the nick of time, she managed to keep her footing. Exhaling, she looked up in readiness to move again . . . and found herself eye-to-eye with a huge black wolf, his eyes vivid gold.

Her throat went dry, her muscles rigid.

The wolf angled its head in a quizzical way . . . and took a sniff at her before dropping its jaw in what she *thought* was a friendly way. She dared "sniff" back at him with her empathic senses and caught the edge of feral amusement. *Changeling.*

And he found her funny? That was fine with her. Giant black wolves with razor-sharp teeth probably didn't eat people who made them laugh.

Turning without attacking her, the wolf padded away. But just when she thought she was safe, the wolf stopped to throw her a look over its shoulder. *Come on*, that look said.

It was insane to follow a strange wolf into the dark. But this was a crazy moonlit night where she was playing a chasing game with a golden wolf—she decided to take her life into her hands and follow the amused black wolf. But something kept niggling at her . . . She took another sniff. Frowned.

The emotional feel of him was tantalizingly familiar. She just had to translate wolf emotions into human and . . . "Riaz?" she gasped with a smile.

Glancing back, the wolf gave a look of approval before carrying on through the trees.

Memory followed in silence.

Less than two minutes later, she came around a tree and nearly ran into a small Asian woman with blunt-cut bangs and jet-black hair down to her shoulders.

Memory's eyes widened, but before she could apologize, the woman—who wore black jeans, boots, and what might've been a dark blue sweater that hugged her body—scowled down at the black wolf.

"What the hell, Riaz? What are you doing with Alexei's empath?"

Alexei's empath.

The words settled on Memory's skin, sank deep. "Alexei

and I are playing a chasing game," she said, feeling as if she were in the middle of a fantastical movie where a dangerous wild creature led her to a woman who looked at her with the eyes of a friendly assassin.

"Game, huh?" The maybe-assassin exchanged looks with Riaz's wolf. "Our Lexie has a huge advantage." She looked Memory up and down. "You have a couple of pieces of clothing you can spare?"

Mystified, Memory pulled out her damp socks.

The wolf and the woman looked at one another again before the wolf shook his head. Taking the hint, Memory put the socks back into her pocket.

"Have you sweated?" The woman put her hands on her hips, and though there wasn't a visible weapon on her, Memory kept thinking of her as armed.

A lightbulb went on in Memory's brain. "Turn around," she said to Riaz.

He yawned, but did so while she stripped off her orange sweater, then took off her tee. Handing that to the woman, she pulled her sweater back on. "Sacrifice it." She nodded to the tee. "This is war."

A wicked grin. "I like you, E. Now, let's make this game a little harder for Lexie." A blade suddenly glinted in her hand. Using it to rip the T-shirt in two, she gave one piece to Riaz, held the other herself.

The wolf took off to the west.

"Follow me," the woman said. "I'll show you how to confuse your trail so it's not the most powerful of the three scent trails."

Memory went, taking mental notes as her guide ran through a list of pointers. They ended up at a rocky section of land.

"Stones don't hold scent as well," she was told. "Breeze is also going in the wrong direction to help Lexie." Another grin that lit up the dark of the woman's eyes. "Good luck."

"Thank you." Memory's heart began to race again. "Wait, what's your name?"

"Sing-Liu, and if any asshole wolf tells you to call me China Doll, stab them for me. Except if the wolf's name is D'Arn. Him, I'll handle privately."

Then the two of them were separating, Sing-Liu going in the direction where the wind would carry the scent to Alexei, while Memory went the opposite way.

The game was back on.

ALEXEI bared his teeth when he scented Riaz's path intersecting with Memory's. His fellow lieutenant should've known to leave her alone. Alexei had made sure to rub up against her until no one could mistake that she was his; the scent wasn't deep enough to hold through a shower, wasn't in her skin as it would be if they exchanged intimate skin privileges, but it was enough to warn off other wolves.

The only thing that kept his annoyance down to a slight grumble was that Riaz was devoted to Adria and would have no interest in Memory as a woman. So why the fuck had the two of them headed off together? He'd strangle Riaz if the other male had scared Memory.

What the hell? Now Sing-Liu was in this, too. He growled as he circled the area to see their next step. The trail split in two.

Oh.

Alexei's jaw fell open in a wolfish laugh.

His packmates were helping Memory.

Fair.

The human part of Alexei agreed with the wolf's determination. Memory had done a good job of slowing him down by walking in the stream, but she had no training in eluding a hunter.

Regardless of Riaz's and Sing-Liu's entrance into the game, Memory's scent was a luminous beacon to him, fresh and luscious and warm. He tracked her to the stony area where he'd often played as a trainee soldier. *That* was where it got interesting. The scent split again, then disappeared over the stone. Alexei retraced his path, went back over the stone step-by-step.

Stubborn, defiant, strong.

Teeth bared, he followed the scent of his E. But his packmates were clever. Riaz and Sing-Liu had doubled back and circled and overlapped the scent trails until he had difficulty telling which one was of Memory alone—or if she'd decided to be tricky and head off with one of the others to confuse him.

He threw back his head in a joyous howl, delighted with this game. Delighted, too, that his packmates were playing with her. That wasn't an expected thing; Riaz and Sing-Liu were powerful and high-ranking members of SnowDancer, and Alexei hadn't made a public declaration about Memory . . . except for all the food gifts he'd been leaving at her door, and the way he'd brought her deep into SnowDancer territory for this game.

As one distant packmate then another responded to his howl with their own, he ran on under the moonlight, on the hunt for an empath who retaliated against him by drowning him in rainbows and sparkle and delight. The wolf snorted. She was about as scary as a pup. And both parts of him adored her.

He couldn't wait to catch her.

Chapter 46

Intimate skin privileges are a gift never to be taken lightly.
—From the June 2079 issue of *Wild Woman* magazine:
"Skin Privileges, Style & Primal Sophistication"

MEMORY DIDN'T KNOW what warned her that she was in the crosshairs of a wolf. Perhaps her empathic senses had caught Alexei's wildness on the wind, a whisper so subtle that only her instincts understood. Those instincts told her to run or hide.

Pulse a staccato beat, she ducked down behind a large bush, and tried to stay very, very still. As far as she could tell, the breeze was working against him; it was possible he'd pass by without spotting her.

No sound but the boom of her heart.

Then the rustle of a wolf loping away.

Memory waited several more minutes before beginning to rise to her feet, her intent to run in the opposite direction. Most of the way up, she peeked over the bush . . . and came nose-to-muzzle with a wolf.

Crying out and laughing at the same time, she turned and ran. The wolf jumped the bush to come after her, and she was laughing too hard to get much farther before he caught up and ran around her to face her. He snapped his teeth at her. She snapped back. And then was laughing again as she went down to her knees.

Nudging at her with his head, he tumbled her to her back on the pine needles. The air fractured with light without warning. She froze, her eyes huge . . . and a man with wind-tumbled golden hair and eyes that glowed in the darkness was braced over her where the wolf had been. "Good game," he said, his voice so rough that she knew the wolf remained close to the surface of his skin.

Placing her hands on his shoulders—his skin was so silken and hot—she luxuriated in his closeness, his scent darkly masculine and his heat a blanket. "I'm going to get better."

He grinned and altered position so that his entire body covered hers. His lower half pressed into hers, while he used his forearms to keep his upper body off her. "I'll teach you how to trick me," he promised before dropping his head to her throat and nuzzling.

She shivered, wove her hand into his hair. It was instinct to curl one of her legs over his. Her mouth went dry. "You're naked." A startled whisper, though of course he was naked.

A rough, growly sound against her throat before he used his teeth to grip the skin above her pulse and tug. Memory's inner core clenched on a molten rush. Releasing her skin with a rumbling vibration in his chest that held definite approval, Alexei rubbed his big body against her own.

His erection was a hot, rigid rod against her stomach, his lower body heavy in a delicious way. Fire in her blood, she angled her neck to give him better access and he took full advantage—to kiss and suck and melt her bones. By the time he reached her mouth, her lips tingled, feeling swollen and sensitive.

Alexei moved one of his arms to bracket her head, buried his fingers in her hair. His kiss was primal and demanding and wet and she had her other leg wrapped around him almost before she was aware of moving. He was so strong, so sexy, he overwhelmed her and she wanted more.

Addicted to her golden wolf, she ran her hands down his back, luxuriating in the feel of his muscles moving under her palms as his mouth claimed hers with a possessiveness that filled the empty places inside her.

Sucking in a breath when their lips parted, she began to kiss his shoulders. He tasted a little of salt, and mostly of primal heat.

My wolf. My Alexei.

He made a deep sound in his throat at her kisses, at her petting of his body, and slipped one of his own hands under her sweater to lie against her stomach. Suddenly burning up, Memory pushed at him until he lifted himself up on his arms.

While he watched her with eyes gone nightglow, she reached down and pulled her sweater off over her head. Her curls bounced as they escaped the neckline, and Alexei's eyes went to them. He lifted one hand to play with her hair while she finished tugging off the sweater.

Sweater thrown aside, she caught the amber of his gaze. "Kiss me."

Devouring her mouth with the raw wickedness of his own, his body crushing hers in the most delicious way, he put one hand on her lace-covered breast, squeezed. Memory whimpered and arched against him. He was too heavy to budge, but he seemed to feel it regardless, because he repeated the erotic caress with open possessiveness before running the pad of his thumb over her engorged nipple.

The lace of her bra rasped over the sensitive skin.

Twisting under him, Memory bit at his lower lip.

He broke the kiss to scowl at her, golden strands falling around his face. "What?"

"Skin," she said, and pushed down one strap of her bra, then the other. "I want skin."

Dropping his head, he kissed the valley between her breasts, the fine strands of his hair torturous strokes on her needy flesh. But his hand was moving to her back to undo her bra. After a couple of seconds, he growled and lifted his head. "I'll buy you another one."

Lace tore.

This bra was a pretty pink and she loved it and she didn't even care that he was throwing it aside in pieces. Because he was putting his hand on her breast, his hold slightly rough. The jolt of sensation bowed her back, scrambled her brains, had her nails digging into his biceps. Murmuring roughly petting words that told her she was beautiful and sexy, he kissed his way down her throat, between the valley of her breasts, before looking up.

Amber eyes glowed at her.

Her chest heaved.

The smile of a predator who had her exactly where he wanted her. "Pretty Memory." No warning before he moved his mouth to her nipple. A single hard suck and she wanted to scream. Shoving her forearm against her mouth to muffle the cry, she clawed at the ground with her other hand.

Sliding both hands under her, Alexei lifted her up, as if for his delectation. First he sucked and teased one nipple, then the other. Just when she thought the pleasure couldn't get any better, he licked at the sensitive underside of her breast. *Oh.*

"I have you, lioness." A rumble of sound, his hands strong and protective on her body. His jaw was dark with stubble and when he rubbed it against the kiss-wet flesh of her breasts, her thighs squeezed his hips with convulsive force.

"I can scent your arousal," said the wolf who'd caught her, before he began to kiss his way down her abdomen. "Rich and dark, with a sweet bite." He ran his tongue along the edge of her waistband, then pressed a kiss to her navel.

Undone by the tenderness, she wove her fingers into his hair. *"Alexei."*

"Does it hurt, sweetheart?" A rub of his jaw against her skin before he sat up and put his hands on the curve of her waist. "Inside? Do you need?"

"Yes." She petted any part of him she could reach. "I need you."

Shuddering, he undid the button on her jeans, pulled down the zipper. He was tugging them off along with her panties seconds later. Cool air kissed her most intimate flesh. Throwing her clothes aside, Alexei looked at her with blunt appreciation . . . and unrestrained hunger.

Memory flushed.

A sudden movement and she found herself flipped so that she was on top, his hands stroking down to cup her lower curves. "No." She pushed up enough to meet the amber of his gaze. "I want to be crushed by you."

Claws brushing the bare curves of her buttocks. "Ground's too rough for you."

Memory reached out to drag her sweater and her jeans closer. "Put me on the clothes." When it looked as if he was planning to argue, she kissed his throat while slowly moving her body against his; if she loved the friction, she had a feeling he would, too. "Alexei, I'm cold."

Groaning, he shifted her onto her back again, careful to make sure she was on the clothes. Braced over her, he put one hand under her thigh, stroking up her flank until she got the message and locked her leg around his waist again. "I'm trying to look after you here." It was a dark growl.

Memory rubbed the heel of her foot against the small of his back, her brain cells not firing on all cylinders by now. "You feel so big and hard against me."

Eyes flashing, he came down on both forearms and kissed her again, all tongue and a wild affection that melted her. She wrapped her other leg around him, unembarrassed by the wetness between her thighs. He was a wolf, could scent it anyway—and he'd told her he liked it.

She kept trying to break the kiss so she could put her mouth on the rest of his body, but he wasn't done with her mouth and his kiss was so delectable that she surrendered. When he slid his hand in between their perspiration-slicked forms to caress her between her thighs, she gasped in desperate gulps of air.

Sensation rolled over her in luxuriant waves that held a piquant edge.

The wave grew and grew . . . and crested without warning. "Alexei!" Her eyes blanked, her mind a haze of pleasure contained within her shields so it was private—invisible on the PsyNet.

Lifting heavy-lidded eyes in the aftermath, she saw a distinctly smug predatory changeling above her. "That was . . ." She stroked his chest, petted his forearms.

Lips curved, he bit lightly at her throat. Used to the way he played, she wove her fingers through his hair and smiled, her entire body languid. When he nudged at her with the thickness of his arousal, she uncurled her legs from around his hips to plant her feet on the earth, open and ready for him.

His claws sliced into the earth on either side of her head. Raising his face from her throat, he said, "Are you sure?" Rough words. "You only get one first time."

Memory bit him on the shoulder. Hard.

His growl was thunder in his chest, but he made no move to harm her. Of course he didn't. Because he was a wolf who protected, not hurt. "Who taught you to bite?" It was a grumble, his nose pressed to hers.

Delighted, Memory kissed him. "Come inside me, my gorgeous, strong wolf."

Alexei pressed hard against her, the intimate friction of his erection parting her delicate flesh stealing her breath. Being so honest with her affectionate and admiring words also got her growling kisses on the throat and rough caresses of her breast with a possessive hand.

He didn't ask her again if she was sure.

Gripping her under the knee, he thrust her thigh up and outward, fitting himself even more firmly against her. Amber glowed in the night darkness as he pushed in. She moaned at the stretching sensation on the border between pleasure and pain, her body clasping spasmodically around him. Jaw clenched, he kept one hand on her knee, holding her spread for him as he worked his erection inside her with slow care.

She clutched at the earth, lifted her hips toward him.

Teeth bared, he pushed in all the way. A stab of pain threatened to derail her pleasure, a whimper escaping her throat.

Alexei stopped at once. "Memory?" Perspiration glimmered on his temples, his muscles rigid.

"I just . . ." She sucked in a breath. "You're big."

A wicked grin that flat-out slayed her, but he stayed motionless while she got used to the feel of his heat and strength lodged inside her. It made the hard little nubbin between her thighs pulse. She squeezed her muscles experimentally. Breath harsh, Alexei slid one hand underneath her to cup her bottom as he drew out, then pushed back in.

Barely able to breathe through the heavily luxuriant sensation, Memory wrapped her arms around him and held on for the ride to come. He took it excruciatingly slow, until sweat rolled down both their bodies, and she'd melted between her thighs. "Faster," she gasped.

"Only when I'm certain you won't hurt." He moved his hand to her breast, plucked at her nipple.

Memory moaned again. "I'm so ready I'm slippery," she protested, jerking up her hips at the same time.

She didn't know if it was the words or the erotic motion that did it, but Alexei braced himself with one hand beside her head and then he began to *move*. With a speed and a power that made her body shudder and electrified her nerve endings. She moved with him, able to see the precipice beyond which they would fall. So close. *So* close.

Desperate, she closed her own hand over her breast and squeezed as he'd done.

"Fuck!" Alexei's eyes on her breast, the hand he had behind her going clawed, his body thrusting into her own with a sensual aggression that pitched her over the edge. She didn't fall. She flew. On wings of pleasure so deep and wrenching that she was aware of nothing but the blinding power of it—and of Alexei.

She heard him shout out his own climax, felt the shockingly intimate heat of his release inside her, managed to open her drugged eyes in time to see his head thrown back, his arched body silhouetted against the moonlit sky. Her inner muscles clenched again, but this time, the pleasure was softer, more languorous.

When Alexei came down on top of her, she wrapped her legs around him, one hand in his hair, the other on his back. And there they lay, limp and sated as the night breeze wicked the moisture from their bodies.

ALEXEI felt a dangerous awakening inside him, a stirring he couldn't permit. But it was too late. The mating urge had woken for Memory; the wolf had chosen its other half. And wolves mated for life. Shuddering inwardly at the painful gift, he rolled off Memory and onto nature's carpet.

His skin was tougher than hers, the surroundings part of his natural habitat. Turning so he was on his side, he placed one hand on her abdomen because he couldn't stop touching her. Couldn't stop touching *his mate*.

Of course it was her.

Tough, defiant, a survivor. An empath who looked at him and saw not just the pretty face, but the darkness beyond—

and who touched him with an unguarded affection he shouldn't crave. But he'd kill any other man who dared touch her—where Memory was concerned, he was selfish and possessive and not the least bit rational.

He'd never let her go.

"I like that," she whispered sleepily. "A lot." Curling into him, she petted his chest. "Can we dance naked every night?"

Cupping her breast, Alexei pressed a kiss to her shoulder. "Every morning, too," he rumbled, both parts of his nature in favor of arousing a sleepy, warm Memory and sliding into her body as the first action of the day.

She rubbed her nose against his chest. "Can we stay out here?"

"You'll get too cold." He wrapped her up in his arms, his mate with the heart of a lioness. In his mind flickered images of Etta's mauled body, blood bubbling out of her mouth as she breathed her final breath.

Her mate had done that to her.

Brodie had done that to her.

Alexei's wolf brushed against the inside of his skin, its hunger for its own mate a visceral pain.

Chapter 47

I am losing myself piece by piece. So today, I choose to go
out on my terms, when I know myself . . . and before I can
commit the heinous crimes this madness demands.
　　　　　—Suicide note left by Scarab subject Ricky J.

THERE WERE REPORTS all over the PsyNet of an attack
against Es in San Francisco's Chinatown . . . and he'd had a
second blackout on his walk home. He'd woken in his bed
with blood dripping from his nose and his heart pounding.

At least he remembered the conversation with the women
on the street. Unless that had been a hallucination created by
his fractured mind. Maybe he'd never left his apartment, had
instead spent the lost hours locked in fever dreams.

Seated on the side of his bed, he dropped his head, rubbed
his face. It was pure luck that he hadn't made any critical
business errors that exposed his erratic sanity. Now this report of Es being attacked by an unknown mind during a
block of time for which *he had no memories*. He had to
know what he'd been doing during that time. He had con-
tacts in Enforcement, might be able to gain access to
surveillance—

His eye caught on something clinging to the edge of his
shirt cuff. A white piece of paper, possibly part of a decor-
ation. Printed with rabbits. The symbol of the new year, according to Chinese culture.

"I was in Chinatown." He had to say it out loud, had to
accept that his life was spiraling out of control. Yes, it was
possible he'd picked up the small piece of flotsam just walk-

ing the streets, but the blotter pages he kept in his bedside drawer didn't lie.

Pulling open that drawer, he lifted out the sheet: the words *Honeycomb-Designation E* crawled across the page over and over again. He had no memory of writing them, but they were in his hand and he'd discovered the pages after another lost block of time. Another fugue.

Now Es were being attacked by a powerful mind that more than one person had dubbed "ill-disciplined," but no one could identify. It was a mystery when such powers were generally well-known. The reporters had begun to theorize about "emergent Psy."

Paper crackled as he fisted the blotter pages in his hand.

He wasn't psychotic or blind to reality: the PsyNet needed empaths. Never while conscious would he assault any member of Designation E, but he wasn't conscious much these days.

He had to return to the crystalline sanity of the past, had to shut down this rogue power. There was just one problem: he'd already tried more than once and failed.

Chapter 48

MEMORY WOKE WITH a smile and an ache low in her body
that made her blush. Turning in bed, she ran her hand over the
imprint Alexei had left beside her and bit down on her lower
lip, her cheeks aching from happiness. He'd held her all night,
her golden wolf, had only left before dawn because he had
duties at his den.

"I'll be seeing you soon, lioness." A promise sealed with
a predator's demanding kiss.

Happily breathless at the thought, Memory got out of bed
and headed into the bathroom. She cherished the aches in
her body, ran her fingers tenderly over the reddened patches
on her skin. She'd gained those marks playing with a wolf.

Her wolf.

The smile held until her eye fell on a scar on her ribs. It
was small, barely there. She'd been bitten by an insect in the
bunker when she'd been about thirteen—the tiny creature
must've entered via a ventilation duct. It turned out she was
allergic to it. She'd had a fever by the time Renault checked
on her and the infection had left a scar.

Frowning, she showered, then got dressed for the day: a
button-down shirt in fuchsia-pink with white piping on the
sleeves, paired with dark blue jeans and a thin purple belt.
Her socks were blue-green with pink polka dots, and she tied
a cute purple scarf with a tiny white print around her throat.

She'd finally given back Alexei's jacket, so she picked her own out of the closet: a dark olive-green, it had epaulets on the shoulders.

Taking it out to the kitchen, she left it hanging on the back of a chair while she prepared her breakfast. Her sparkly sneakers sat just inside the doorway, where she'd kicked them off the previous night. Smiling again as a dark heat uncurled low in her body, she went out onto the porch to eat . . . and her eyes went automatically to the cabin across from hers.

Every single morning since the attack, she looked across. And every single morning, she saw a closed door. No Jaya with her huge smile and generous heart. No black-clad Arrow with "killer" blue eyes leaving to begin his shift. Just a horrible, painful emptiness.

Abbot will make a full recovery.

Memory hugged the echo of Sascha's words to her heart, a hopeful shield against the cruel emptiness of the cabin . . . and when she thought of Yuri, she focused deliberately on the things they'd discussed during their walks. She would remember her friend alive and strong and intelligent, and she'd trust in his strength and survival instinct.

When Sascha arrived not long afterward, she didn't make Memory ask for an update. "I just heard from Ivy," she said as she pulled off her coat. "Abbot's made telepathic contact with Jaya and the medics think he'll be awake within thirty minutes." Her smile was a thing of pure light. "No trace of permanent damage."

Eyes burning, and throat too thick to speak, Memory nodded.

"Yuri's still on life support," the cardinal added, the light dying. "Aden's getting consults from every neurospecialist he can. He won't make the call without exhausting all possibilities."

Memory clung to hope. And she paid attention during the session despite her turbulent emotions—she'd brought her knitting because the physical activity helped her maintain her psychic focus. She was working on a blanket for Jaya's Phantom; she needed to do something for her friend, and she'd noticed that Phantom liked to steal the blankets off

Jaya and Abbot's bed. Maybe he'd stop that if she made him his own.

Sascha admired her progress so far before the two of them settled down to hard psychic work.

"You're ready to graduate from Sascha's Shield School," the cardinal surprised her by saying after lunch. "You've worked hard and you've built on a strong foundation. Maintain what you've built and your mind will never again be hijacked."

It took some time after Sascha left for her words to sink in.

Memory had succeeded. Renault could never again violate her.

Putting on her olive-green jacket on a wave of angry resolve, she stepped out onto the porch. And there he was—her golden wolf. Dressed in a black tee and well-worn jeans, he was talking to one of the other changelings. Blonde and curvy Rina. A highly trained leopard soldier with an innate feline sensuality.

Alexei looked up toward Memory at that moment and, smile wicked and for her alone, held out a hand. It was only then that she realized a hidden part of her had been afraid last night had been a mirage, would disappear in the light of day.

When he'd kissed her good-bye this morning, she'd glimpsed a potent darkness in his eyes that made her afraid for what they had between them. It remained lodged inside him, a pain that held an edge she couldn't quite decipher, but he took her hand and hauled her in for a toe-curling kiss that had Rina clearing her throat and saying, "Jeez, get a room. Or a cave. Since you're an uncivilized wolf and all."

Giving Rina the finger with one hand, Alexei continued to kiss Memory—who couldn't hold on to her anger and sadness in the face of his wild joy in seeing her. Her entire body smiled. When he finally let her up for air, Rina had her hands on her hips and was shaking her head.

"You know they all live in a big puppy pit, right?" She shuddered. "Poking their noses into each other's business like it's a full-time job."

That sounded like perfection to Memory. To not be alone unless you chose it, to walk out night and day and find a friendly face. When she said as much, Rina groaned and Alexei looked smug.

"You want to tell Memory what your packmates spotted?" he asked.

"Drone flying overhead." Smile fading to reveal the hard eyes of a soldier, Rina folded her arms across her voluptuous chest. "We didn't even have to shoot the thing down—one of the falcons was in the area and we asked him to capture it. Smart-ass put it into my hands like it was a special delivery." A faint smile cracked her steely expression. "Anyway, the lack of damage meant we could do a full data dive."

Cold fingers along Memory's spine, a chill against her skin, but she shoved back the fear with fury. "Renault has a factory that creates drones. They were designed for use by scientists and statisticians who need to collect wide-ranging data."

"It was one of his," Rina confirmed.

"Bastard must've had one with him when he ran." Alexei was pure lethal predator now. "Our tech team's worked with Enforcement to block access to his accounts and properties— even the ones he went to great lengths to hide."

"Too many to keep watch on, use as bait?"

"The man had endless hidey-holes, big and small—and enough funds to make more," Alexei said in response to Rina's question, even as he hugged Memory to his side. "We made the call to switch off the money tap, turn him into a rat without resources. He'll make a mistake soon."

"What did the drone see?" Memory asked, wanting to know if any of her friends were in jeopardy.

"Don't worry, it never got much past our border." Rina ignored a buzz from the phone she'd tucked into a front jacket pocket. "Drone had a remote transmitter, no onboard storage. But it did have that small chip they're putting in the newer models."

"The one that tells their brains where to look?" Alexei asked.

Nodding, Rina took out her phone and brought up a picture. "Thing was set to look for this."

Memory found herself staring at a ghost: a bone-thin Memory with sallow skin and limp, tangled hair. She didn't know when Renault had taken it, but from the exhaustion on her features, the slumped shoulders, it must've been after one of the worst sessions, when he'd come close to wringing her dry.

Alexei ran his hand down her spine. "Thanks for the heads-up."

"No problem." Rina glanced at her timepiece. "I better get back to my patrol route, but DarkRiver will let you know if anything else turns up." A grin aimed at Memory. "If you're determined to hook up with a mangy wolf, he's a good choice."

Memory's lips twitched as she watched the other woman leave. Smile fading when she turned back to Alexei, she said, "I'd like to do something today if you have time."

"I've got a split shift, so I'm off now." He gripped her jaw. "You've been crying."

"Yuri," she said softly.

"Has he—?"

She shook her head. "Just the same."

"He's a tough bastard." Enclosing her in his arms, Alexei pressed a kiss to her curls. "I wouldn't count him out until they wheel him out toes-first."

From Sascha, she'd expected hope, but to hear it from her tough wolf? She rose up on tiptoe to kiss his jaw. He bent to make it easier for her, and she gave him two more kisses. When he asked about Abbot, she was happy to pass on the good news on that front.

"You doing okay with Rina's intel?"

"Yes, it's not a shock to discover he's trying to find me." Addicts didn't easily let go of their poison. "And seeing that picture . . . I'm not that woman anymore." No longer a faded shadow forced into a box.

She was color and adventure and kisses and games in the moonlight.

"Renault has no idea who I am anymore." Her captor thought he was hunting the woman in the cage. "But what I want to do, it has to do with him." She thought again of the scar on her ribs and all it represented. "I'm ready to go back to the bunker. I want to exorcise the past once and for all."

Renault would be out there until they hunted him down, but she could lay her own ghosts to rest. "I want to go back there as *me*." As the Memory who wore pink shirts, had big, exuberant hair, and was chased in the moonlight by a golden wolf.

Alexei's instincts struggled against the idea of taking her back to that hellhole, but he knew a few things about demons. His, he might never conquer, but he'd help Memory face her own, especially as there was no real risk. The pack had seeded the place with sensors the morning after he found Memory, but none had ever gone off. Her captor had no reason to come back to the bunker.

"If you're ready," he said, "we can head out now."

Memory's hug made him hers all over again. She was so tough, his E, but she had a soft heart that incited every protective instinct in his body. And the way she was with him—so honest and open in her desire and her adoration of him . . . He wanted her as his mate, tied to him in the most indelible way.

They sat in quiet for much of the drive, but it wasn't a quiet that irritated and rubbed Alexei's wolf the wrong way. This was the quiet of two people who understood each other, two people who fit together like a key into a lock.

He squeezed the steering wheel so hard that his bones showed white against his skin. "I have to tell you something." He couldn't lie to her, not even by omission.

Memory cocked her head in a listening posture, the action one he caught in his peripheral vision.

"We're in the mating dance." It was so fucking hard to get the words out when he wanted so much to finish the dance, claim her as his forever.

Memory blew out a shuddering breath. "You're fighting it."

Spotting a section of forest with delicate flowers and undergrowth, Alexei pushed the vehicle into hover mode. "I want you, Memory." The words came out feral, hungry. "More than I've ever wanted anything. But I can't." Flashes of Etta's mauled body on the wall of his mind, of Brodie's bloody muzzle, of the grief on the faces of Etta's heartbroken family.

"It's all right." Memory's voice held so much love that he

felt kissed a hundred times over. "It's all right, Alexei." She touched her fingers to his jaw. "As long as we're together, as long as I know that your wolf chose me as your mate, it'll be enough."

Grabbing her hand, he pressed his lips to her fingers. "I wish—" A harsh exhale. "I will regret not claiming you as my mate for the rest of my life." His heart twisted and broke, reformed anew. "But I will love you always." And he would protect her to his last breath.

Never would he hurt her as Brodie had hurt Etta.

Chapter 49

$60

—Price paid by E. David Renault for a street drug

RENAULT PACED IN jagged steps. It was getting harder and harder to think, his brain erratic despite the medicine he'd sourced and taken. It was Memory's fault; if she'd only stayed in place, none of this would have happened.

Shoving his hands through his hair, he stared again at the blank data feed from the drone. Fucking leopards. They must've stolen it and given it a lobotomy. It was none of their business; Memory was *his*.

Maybe he should go to the bunker and make sure she hadn't left behind anything that he could use to track her. Too bad she hadn't left that stupid cat.

He frowned, a sudden clarity in his thoughts: *Is going to the bunker a good idea in any way?* For all he knew, it was full of wolves.

The haze descended again, and with it went the clarity.

Yes, he should go back to the bunker. The wolves might've booby-trapped it, but he was a teleport-capable Tk—he'd be gone before anyone responded. He had to take action, end this now.

Memory needed to learn her lesson.

Chapter 50

Not every wolf is lucky enough to find a mate. It is a gift to be treasured and held close.
—Dalton, Librarian of the SnowDancer Pack

MEMORY ASKED ALEXEI to take her first to the resting place of her treasured Jitterbug. Tears fell from her eyes when she saw that mountain wildflowers had begun to bloom around the small, undisturbed cairn. Patting the cairn gently, she sat for a long time before rising to her feet and sliding her hand into his.

"I met Jitterbug in an alley during a time when Renault had me in the world." Always with her mind chained, her self bruised from smashing against his shields. "I was still young, and he couldn't have me with him in meetings without it appearing strange."

Alexei's voice was dark when he spoke. "He parked you nearby so he had quick access to you?"

Memory nodded. "I guess when I was younger, the 'hit' didn't last as long. He'd come out to 'make a call' or 'use the facilities,' and in reality, he'd duck in to initiate a transfer." She and Alexei walked up the rise down which they'd come what felt like a lifetime ago.

There was no rain today, the mountain sun a searing near-white brightness.

"Later on, he liked to take me as his aide so he could make the transfer right before a critical negotiation—he said the effect was strongest in the first hour." Memory shrugged.

"Personally, I think he enjoyed parading me in the world knowing I couldn't cry out for help."

She leaned into her wolf when he growled. "I'm free now and I'm going to stomp on his brains, remember?"

"That's my E." Releasing her hand to put his arm around her shoulders, Alexei nuzzled her curls with his chin.

The smug pride in him made her lips curve. "The day I met Jitterbug, Renault'd taken me to a small hotel. He'd ordered me to wait in a back room while he spoke with investors out front." She drew in the primal scent of her wolf. "Normally, I had no choice but to obey, but that day, I heard this pitiful meowing outside the window and it got through the fog in my brain."

"Your empathic instincts fighting to help a hurt creature."

Memory didn't refute his conclusion. She'd made the decision to claim her future—and in that future, she wasn't a monster. She was just an E with very disturbing patients. "It was the first time I'd been able to resist him when he had his spider legs wrapped around my mind."

Renault had utilized mind control each time he took her from the bunker, using the pathways he'd laid in her brain to suffocate her freedom. "I don't know how long it took— maybe ten, fifteen minutes, but I was able to force my body to crawl to the door, open it."

"Bastard didn't secure the door because he thought he had your mind locked down."

"Yes." A "privilege" she'd lost that day, but it hadn't mattered, not when she had Jitterbug. "The back door into the alley wasn't far from the hallway outside the back room, and I literally crawled on my hands and knees to get to it." Her palms tingled at the sensory memory of the cracked linoleum, her chest tight at the echo of how the walls in the narrow hallway had loomed.

"I fell out into the alley and into the rain. I could see Jitterbug shivering against this pipe. He was so skinny and small with raggedy fur, and I wanted to help him, but I'd reached my limit and just lay there, blood dripping from my nose to be washed away by the rain." A smile found its way from her grieving heart. "We stared at each other and it was as if he knew I couldn't go to him. So he came to me."

A tiny, bedraggled fluffball, Jitterbug had nudged at her chin as if trying to rouse her, get her to stand up. But all she'd been able to do was lift a hand and put it over the kitten's back. Jitterbug hadn't bolted. "He curled up against me and that's how Renault found us."

"Why did the asshole let you keep him?" Alexei asked as they reached the rock through which lay the trapdoor entrance.

"Renault saw Jitterbug as a way to control me."

"Behave or I'll hurt your pet?"

Memory nodded. "I was never sorry to have found him though. He was a companion through the hardest years of my life." She looked up at Alexei. "It probably sounds foolish to you—"

"No, it doesn't." A kiss that was pure predatory changeling. "He was a loyal friend when you had no one else. It's good you honor that, honor him."

Heart huge with emotion, she touched her hand to the stone. "Let's do this." Thanks to SnowDancer's extensive search, she knew this was the only entrance into her former prison.

Alexei went first. "Pack rigged the entire place with surveillance on the off chance Renault would come back, but he's never dared."

Memory's captor had to know the bunker had become a trap for him.

Regardless, Alexei dropped down first into the small tunnel, then swept the bunker. All he scented were the fading echoes of his own pack. Patrol routes had been altered to make this a compulsory stop, with the wolf on duty dropping inside to check that things were undisturbed. Other than that, it was a place that sat abandoned.

No wolf wanted anything to do with it.

After we capture Renault, we'll be filling that fucking hole in the ground with dirt and giving it back to the mountain.

Hawke's words, with which Alexei was in full agreement. These walls had never been about anything but torture and pain and imprisonment. Better to bury it and let nature cleanse the tainted earth. "It's safe." He held up his arms and Memory jumped down in a sweet trust that had him playfully nipping at her lush lower lip.

She pretended to claw at his shoulders and they both grinned. That was how they walked into the bunker, with smiles on their faces and their hands linked. When he felt her go stiff in front of the doorway, he leaned down to murmur, "You're not the child he took and abused. You're a lioness who fucking kicks ass."

"Yes, I am." Fierce words as she stepped through into her past.

She was silent as she walked around. She picked up nothing, looked at nothing but her cat's sleeping basket with sentimental eyes. "It seems smaller," she said at last. "It was always small, but now . . . I'd go mad if I came from the spread of SnowDancer territory to this. I guess it was a blessing that I was an apartment child before he kidnapped me."

Alexei's claws dug into his palms at the idea of any of this being a blessing. "You want to take anything with you?"

"I made Jitterbug's blanket—I learned to knit watching comm shows and I made that, and I'm glad it's holding him warm in the earth." She swallowed. "Other than that, nothing here is mine; even the knitting needles and the wool for the blanket were tools for Renault to control me."

Alexei forced his claws back in. "He didn't allow you to take anything of your mother's?" As an official adoptive parent, Renault would've had the papers to request the release of Diana Aven-Rose's belongings.

"I don't think he ever asked to collect." A tightness to Memory's features. "She was over and done with to him as soon as she was dead and he'd had his psychotic rush." Squeezing her eyes shut, she whispered, "I wish I could hear her voice again. I can't remember that anymore, and it haunts me."

Wrapping her up in his arms, Alexei rubbed his cheek against her curls. "I have this recording a packmate made of my parents' mating ceremony, and I watch it every year just so I can hear their voices." So young and happy, their eyes bright. "But Brodie . . . Asshole somehow managed not to leave behind any recordings, and it fucking tears me up that one day I might not remember my big brother's voice, his laugh."

They held each other for a long time before separating so Memory could take one last look around the bunker that had

been her cage for fifteen long years. "I'm okay," she said at
the end. "I was afraid I'd fall back into the nightmare if I
came here, but I'm proud of the girl who survived this."

Alexei stepped out of the doorway, turned to hold out a
hand. Memory, the tension gone from her features, had one
hand on the doorjamb, reached out the other to take his.

Renault teleported in right behind her.

His eyes widened, but he moved with reptilian speed despite his surprise. He lunged to wrap an arm around Memory's neck. Alexei was moving, too, his wolf reacting without
conscious thought. But Renault was a teleporter. Alexei's
hand sliced through empty air.

Memory was in the hands of a psychopath.

Had it been a physical abduction, Alexei would've shifted
into wolf form and hunted down the cold metal of Renault's
scent, but he couldn't follow a teleporter.

Hauling himself through the trapdoor and into the mock-
ing sunshine, he called Krychek using the direct number
SnowDancer's senior people had for the dangerous Tk. The
call went unanswered.

Fuck.

He input the number that'd connect him to the Arrows.
When Amin answered, Alexei asked for Vasic, the only
other teleporter he knew who could lock on to faces as well
as places.

"There's been a major PsyNet collapse," Amin responded.
"He and the other teleporters are on the ground shifting
people out of the destroyed zone so their minds can relink in
a healthy one. Casualties are mounting."

Alexei hung up. If Vasic was out there, then so was Krychek. He felt for the innocent Psy caught up in the disaster,
but stopping a monster from harming his mate was his priority. His wolf clawed at him, wanting to follow, wanting to
hunt, but there was no scent trail and Renault was too intelligent to have taken Memory to one of his known hidey-
holes.

Rage tore through him . . . and came up hard against the
echo of a late-night conversation in a dingy no-name bar. It
had to do with Tamsyn and Nathan, and the story Nathan
had told him about how he'd blocked the mating bond.

Alexei had gone out of state, found a dive of a bar where no one would try to stop him from getting blind drunk. He didn't need the comfort of pack. He needed to get so drunk that he forgot Brodie was dead, Etta was dead.

His plan might've worked in a pack with a less intelligent alpha. Hawke had sicced the cats on him, and Nathan had been in the area at the time. He'd slipped onto the bar stool next to Alexei's, and they'd sat in silence for over an hour, while Nathan nursed a single beer and Alexei downed three before admitting to himself that he hated being drunk, hated being out of control, and wasn't going to get shitfaced that day.

The most senior of DarkRiver's sentinels, Nathan had a powerful presence. He also had that vibe some men got when they became fathers—calm, nonjudgmental, used to misbehavior. And Alexei needed to talk.

He'd unloaded on the sentinel.

"I never want to mate," he'd said at some point. "The idea of murdering my mate when I go rogue is a fucking nightmare." He'd shaken his head, his hand tight around the bottle of beer he'd stopped drinking. "Grandfather, father, brother, it's a fucking unbroken chain of death."

Nathan, midnight-blue eyes calm, had asked Alexei if he was sure. When Alexei reiterated his vow, Nathan had told him the story of his own mating. "Tammy left me, and no one would tell me where she'd gone," he'd said toward the end. "I'd blocked the mating bond too long and it hurt her so much that she left." A roughness in Nathan's voice that said everything about his panic.

"I did the only thing I could to track her. I dropped every shield I had, and the mating bond snapped into place like a thunderclap booming in my soul. Her heart had always been open to me. I was just too much of an overprotective idiot to see it."

The leopard sentinel's words ran through Alexei's mind in the space of three heartbeats. He knew what he had to do. Memory's life over his need to stay sane? No contest. As for afterward, he'd deal with it. Even if it meant asking his alpha to execute him at the first sign of madness.

No one, and especially not Alexei, was going to hurt Memory ever again.

His wolf snarled in agreement.

He opened his heart wide, no fear, no hesitation. The shields he'd put in place after Brodie's death, they fell with a crash at his feet. The mating bond shoved its way through time and space—and there was his Memory. Her heart as open to his as Tamsyn's had been to Nathan. The visceral punch of the bond snapping into place sent Alexei to his knees, his breathing harsh gasps.

Inside him burst a kaleidoscope of emotion and color and piercing love and he knew that was her: *Memory*. God, she was even softer inside than he'd realized. The world would crush her if he wasn't around to teach her a little cynicism, a few growls.

Rising to his feet as his heart thundered, he called his alpha and told him what had happened. "Blast Memory's and Renault's faces across our network and those of our allies," he said afterward. "Make it impossible for the bastard to hide." Changelings across the world, millions of humans linked to the Human Alliance, Psy who had signed the Trinity Accord, each and every one would get the blast.

"We'll blanket the planet," Hawke promised, but Alexei didn't think Memory was in another country or even another state. Renault had been bony and hollow-eyed when he appeared, far from his full power, and the mating bond felt strong inside Alexei, not stretched thin by huge distances.

Hanging up, he began to run.

At full speed, he was faster in this terrain than a vehicle, since a vehicle could only go along certain routes. Branches whipped past his face, small creatures scurried in panic at the approach of a predator, and the wind turned into his ally, pushing rather than obstructing.

His target was the beacon of Memory's presence.

Nathan had told him the mating bond wasn't like a homing signal—it'd get him to the general area, but then he'd have to hunt by more conventional methods, using the senses of his wolf.

Erupting out of the trees halfway through DarkRiver ter-

ritory at a specific spot often used by both packs to park a car
or two, he found a familiar dusty Jeep, the keys in the igni-
tion. *Hawke*. The forest tracks were smoother from this
point, the vehicle an asset.

Shooting out onto the main highway not long afterward,
he turned the Jeep in the direction of San Francisco and
floored the accelerator.

It still wasn't fast enough.

The only thing that kept him sane was that Memory's
light burned strong and unflinching inside him; she wasn't
badly wounded or dead. He'd know. As her mate, he'd *know*.
"I'm coming, lioness. You fucking kick that bastard's ass in
the meantime."

Chapter 51

Alert. Alert. Alert. Subject lost from view.
—Alarm sounded by psychic sentries around
Memory Aven-Rose's mind

WRISTS TIED TO the arms of a heavy old chair, Memory watched her captor pace back and forth in front of her. Her heart pounded from the wild storm of emotion that had burst inside her soon after Renault teleported them into what appeared to be a warehouse.

Boxes sat neatly stacked on metal shelving against the walls, while a small hovercrane stood silent in one corner and more prosaic forklifts in another. A large number of pallets were stacked on the floor not far in front of her, blocking her view of what lay beyond. The only light came from wide horizontal windows high up near the peaked roof.

Whenever Renault spoke, his voice echoed in the cavernous space.

Either the walls had to be soundproofed or the warehouse isolated, because she couldn't hear anything from the outside. She'd also been very loud when they teleported in, and he hadn't seemed to care. At the time, he'd been focused on tying her to the chair he'd hauled out of what looked to be a back office, while using telekinetic strength to immobilize her.

His mind couldn't break into hers, but it had snapped shut around her like the deadly jaws of a great white shark. That skill of his he'd honed too well for her to counter—Memory had told herself not to panic, that she was no longer a child without resources. She'd spent hours with Sascha and Amara, had learned plenty of tricks.

And she was no longer alone in the world. Alexei would come for her.

Renault's split focus on containing her on both the psychic and physical planes was probably why he hadn't noticed her go rigid, her heart stopping for a brilliant, blinding moment of beauty that had claws pricking from inside her skin and fur brushing her senses.

Alexei. That was Alexei.

Her golden wolf had initiated the mating bond and Memory had accepted—of course she'd accepted. She'd never had any intention of rebuffing him should he ever reach out to her. But it wasn't meant to be this way—she was terribly afraid that he'd regret their connection afterward, but in that searing moment when he'd reached for her, all she'd felt was incandescent joy.

Mine, Alexei's mine. And she was his.

"The ropes aren't that tight," Renault snapped when she stayed stiff, fighting not to betray her joy. "Stop the theatrics." He walked over and, with a smile he'd learned to fake, cupped her face. "It's time for us to get reacquainted." His eyes gleamed, his tongue flicking out to wet his upper lip.

An addict waiting for his fix.

Fear threatened to close a hand around Memory's throat. But she had Alexei inside her and she wasn't the Memory who'd walked out of the cage nearly four weeks ago. She was the Memory with glittery shoes given to her by a wolf who thought she had the heart of a lioness, and she was the Memory who practiced with a high-functioning psychopath day after day.

Amara, at 9.9 on the Gradient and icily rational with it, was more proficient at attempting to breach Memory's shields than Renault. And Memory had learned to block Amara. So though the contact with Renault burned her, though the howling black hole of his nothingness tried to suck her under, she held firm. "You are not going to feed from me ever again."

Letting out a terrible scream, he *slapped* both hands to her face, so hard that her ears rang. She blinked back the sting, set her jaw, and raised an eyebrow. "Losing control already? Tut tut."

He released her with a violent jerk, began to pace the room again. Every few minutes, he'd return, touch her, try to enter her mind—and fail. And fail. And fail. Memory didn't celebrate, not with Renault's eyes bulging and his mental stabs increasingly erratic. Unstable as he'd become, he could kill her in a single burst of rage.

She also had another problem: the psychic watchdogs left by the Arrows should've alerted the squad to her disappearance in the PsyNet, her mind swallowed by another. That no one had responded to her disappearance told her a chilling truth.

"How did you move me on the Net?" A Psy's location in the PsyNet wasn't altered by temporary moves in physical location—only if the shift was meant to be permanent would the mind move its anchor point.

Renault gave a strange, jagged laugh that raised the tiny hairs on the back of her neck. She'd never heard him laugh before—even in his sickest pleasure, he'd been cool and calm. "Don't you know, little girl?"

"No," Memory said, willing to play along with his delusions if it would gain her room to beat him and escape, gain her mate time to find her. Her golden wolf had lost too many people; she would not let Alexei lose her, too. "You know I never had the usual training."

He hugged his arms around his body as he walked back and forth, back and forth, rocking slightly all the while. "No, you had *my* training." A satisfied smile. "I was in your mind long before you found your new friends." The last word was hissed out. "Where are those friends now? Hmm?"

Memory frowned inwardly, suddenly realizing that Alexei must've contacted the Arrows. One of those Arrows was a born teleporter. Yet she remained alone with Renault. "I don't understand what you did." She forced a tremor in her voice. "Why has no one come for me?" Even as she spoke, the mating bond surged inside her, Alexei's love for her a storm.

Never again, not even in the darkest, deepest hole, would she be isolated and alone, she thought fiercely. But Renault didn't know that, didn't know the beauty of a bond that wasn't Psy but changeling. A bond he hadn't been able to prevent even though he'd imprisoned her mind.

It was too primal, too beautiful, far beyond his comprehension.

"You think you're so smart to shut all the back doors into your mind." Another laugh. "But this wasn't a door. It's a path tied to your PsyNet biofeedback link. I had to make sure I could retrieve my little mouse if she got out of her hole—retrieve her and put her in another place where no one would look for her."

Clearly, he'd needed physical contact to do it or he would've taken her long ago. Memory didn't need to hear the technical details, but she urged him to speak, and he did, because she was once again his captive audience—an audience he didn't respect and considered useless in every way but one.

He took great pleasure in telling her how he'd laid the groundwork in her mind while she was recovering from the coma he'd caused during the first transfer. Laid it so deep that it was part of her core self. So deep that Judd would've had to invade her mind in horrific and traumatizing ways to discover it.

Renault's trap had survived because the former Arrow had treated her with courtesy and dignity.

"It gives me a rope," Renault boasted. "I can pull that rope and you move. Away from those nasty spies around you and where I want you." A sudden, piercing look. "You're inside my mind now and I'm keeping you there. No one will ever find you again."

Memory asked more questions about his actions, her only aim to keep him talking. And talk he did—between bursts of rage when he'd scream at her to let him in. When he raised a fist to her, she held the eye contact. "You injure my brain and that's it. No more transfer." She had to straddle a careful line between appearing too strong and antagonizing him—and appearing so weak that he'd simply ignore anything she said.

"I'll break you." Despite the threatening words, he dropped his fist to his side. "I have you now and I'll break you."

Memory's skin went cold, not because of his promise, but

because of what she saw on his face. His pupils were dilated, his skin shimmering with perspiration. She'd never seen Renault in such a state—not even when he'd left a transfer a little too late and had come to her wired. "You don't look well."

"It's the medicine," he said, stepping back from her and running his hands over the stubbled skin of his head. "I had to use it to deal with my illness, but it has side effects."

"Illness?"

"Muscle tremors, dry mouth, the inability to maintain a steady body temperature." Renault shivered hard and, hugging himself, hunched in and began to pace again. "I can't consult top-level M-Psy because your friends have made me a fugitive, and the people I considered allies have shown their true faces." A twist of his mouth. "They'll pay. All of them."

Withdrawal, he was in withdrawal. From Memory and the rush of the feed. "Do you need more medicine?" she murmured, because this was about survival, about stopping a monster, and, most important, about protecting her golden wolf's wounded heart.

Renault jerked his head toward her, hazel-brown eyes glittering. "Yes." A manic brightness to his face. "Yes, the medicine calms me and I need calm to break you." Striding over, he took a pressure injector from his pocket. It looked like the disposable kind you could buy at most drugstores.

Memory's heart kicked, her mouth like dust. "Narcotics affect my ability," she blurted out. "Remember that first time?"

He hesitated. "You were in a coma because I overfed."

"I've been tested since I've been . . . away," she said, choosing her words with care so as not to unnerve his disturbed mind. "Any trace of a narcotic in my system and I can't guarantee the transfer will work. Remember—you gave me a sedative that first time."

He'd never again bothered with the drugs, because he either had his claws in her mind, or she was in a place where no one could hear her scream.

"You're lying." He jabbed the injector against her throat, hard enough to bruise.

"Doesn't matter to me." She shrugged. "At least you won't

be able to feed off me while I'm comatose or lost in delirium."

A pause stretched thin as a wire before he shoved the injector into his pocket. Striding out of sight around a group of the tall metal shelves, he did something in the distance that made clattering sounds; then she heard boxes falling to the floor. When he returned, it was with another rope.

This one was long enough that he tied it around her entire body, pinning her legs and arms to the chair. "You won't be going anywhere," he said with a satisfied look followed by a giggle. "I'll be back soon with my medicine."

She wondered which drug he was on—it couldn't be any actual medicine, of that she was certain. Drugs had unpredictable effects on psychic abilities—that part of what she'd said was no lie. However, whatever was happening with Renault, his abilities remained razor-sharp.

"Scream as loudly as you want," he said as he walked away, tugging the hood of his sweatshirt over his head. "The local laws mean the warehouse has sound shielding. No one will hear you."

Alexei will hear me, she thought on a wave of defiant love. *My mate will* always *hear me.*

A creak of sound, then a shaft of light in the distance that soon disappeared, in time with the clang of a door. She began to struggle the instant he was gone, but it took her only a minute to realize he hadn't left any slack in the ropes.

"Think, Memory," she whispered. *"Think."*

The chaos of her thoughts narrowed down to the glint of a spoon inching its way across a table.

. . . nothing is useless if you know how to utilize it.

Stopping her struggles, Memory focused on the knot in the rope that bound her right wrist to the chair arm and reached for the tiny droplet of Tk power inside her, the one that couldn't even knock a knife from Renault's hand.

She began to nudge at the knot with her mind.

ALEXEI turned left into the Embarcadero, the pull of the mating bond a dull throb in his entire body as he drove on through the darkness that had fallen, onyx curtains eclipsing the light. Surely Renault wasn't arrogant enough to bring Memory into the heart of DarkRiver territory? One glimpse of her and Renault would be overrun by leopards.

The busy public piers passed, followed by the more utilitarian ones, the buildings hulking shadows against the night sky. And still he was pulled forward. All the way to a section of the city that held a number of large business warehouses. The tug became blindingly powerful, encompassing all the warehouses in the area and driving his wolf to a feral edge.

Parking the Jeep, he got out and took several deep breaths.

As with any city, a thousand, a million strands of scent lingered in the air, but Alexei was a wolf, designed to sift through those strands without becoming overwhelmed. Underneath the heavy mix of the city's buildings and residents, he caught faded scents of cats and wolves.

None of those scents were fresh, however, and he needed backup. Renault was a teleporter and—"You idiot, Alexei." Hauling out his phone even as he began to prowl through the area on the hunt for his mate, he called Judd. "Can you teleport to a location in San Francisco?"

"Yes. I haven't exerted much telekinetic energy lately. Send me a visual."

Alexei took a shot of a doorway festooned with creative graffiti, sent it through. When Judd arrived next to him, he was wearing a sweaty black T-shirt and workout pants, his feet in black sneakers bearing dark green stripes down the sides. "I heard about Memory. What do you need?"

"Fucker's teleported her somewhere here." Memory's presence was a song inside him, calling to wolf and man both. "I need you to hold him if he tries it again."

"Doable," Judd said. "I need a missile of some kind." After a quick search, he picked up a rocky piece of debris from a construction site where a new warehouse was being put up. "I can interrupt the teleport long enough for you to get to him."

"You pick up anything?" Judd had Gradient 9.4 telepathic abilities.

"Nothing useful. Too many minds scattered around to zero in on a particular suspicious set."

Alexei froze, his nostrils flaring. "Renault passed through

here." The cold metal twined with a hint of acidic sweat—
that was the hallmark of Memory's abductor.

He tracked the scent with icy focus, coming to a halt near
a doorway cloaked in murk. The streetlamp had been
smashed, but Alexei didn't need it to see. The scent was thick
here. As if Renault had stopped for long enough to spill the
scent like water.

"Hey, I don't want no trouble." The hoodie-wearing dealer
in the doorway held up his hands. "I follow the rules. I don't
sell to no cats or wolves or kids. Even leave the fucking Rats
alone—their alpha's a bad mofo. I don't need that kind of
trouble in my life."

The man was human, Alexei judged. A predator preying
on his own kind. There was only so much DarkRiver and
SnowDancer could do to protect people in their territories—
those who hungered for poison would find it. Brodie had
found it as a teenager, only Hawke's immediate and personal
intervention stopping Alexei's brother's slide into addiction
and oblivion.

Controlling his rage at the heavyset bearded male, who
was unlikely to have ever met his brother, he pulled out his
phone and brought up an image of Renault. "You make a
deal with this guy recently?"

"Yeah, but the asshole don't look so swish now." A curl of
the dealer's lip. "He nearly broke my arm when he used his
telekinesis shit to throw me against the wall. Stole a whole
bunch of my merchandise." He spat to one side of his alcove.
"I put out the word among my people on the street. Psy parasite's dead if he shows his face again."

One human against a Tk had no real chance, but many
violently inclined humans who knew to approach their target
with stealth? Yeah, they could win. "Which way did he go?"

The dealer nodded to Alexei's right with a grin that revealed a missing tooth and a gold one, side by side. "Hope
you tear out his guts and use them as a noose!" he yelled out
after them.

Alexei followed Renault's scent in the direction the dealer
had indicated. It wove in and out of the district, intersecting
with itself several times—either Renault was being clever

and laying multiple trails to confuse anyone hunting him, or he'd been searching for drugs for a long time before he'd finally found the dealer.

Alexei hoped to hell that meant Memory had been safe from the bastard the entire time. *I'm coming, lioness. You hold on.*

Chapter 52

MEMORY'S HEART POUNDED a rapid beat, feeling somehow more powerful than it ever before had. As if she had a wolf's heart now. Sweat dripped from her temples and her head throbbed from the constant use of her minor telekinetic gift . . . but the bond around her right wrist suddenly came undone.

She had no time for surprise or elation; she worked with desperate speed to untie her left wrist, then bent to release her feet—it was where Renault had knotted the long piece of rope he'd wrapped around her. Her fingers slipped, a nail broke, but she managed to undo the tie around her ankles. The rope tangled around her body was now the only thing that stood between her and freedom.

The door to the warehouse creaked open, letting in a shaft of streetlamp-yellow illumination. It shut with a bang. A bright ceiling light came on soon afterward.

Memory gritted her teeth and kept on working with angry calm. She was not going to let Renault win. Breath shallow but pulse rapid, she tugged off the last of the rope as she sensed Renault's twisted presence coming closer and closer.

There!

Stepping out of the pool of ropes, she padded softly away from the chair despite the heat in her blood that urged her to run toward the monster, take him down. She had to think like Alexei, like a wolf.

A good hunter stalked her prey, took him from a position of power.

She slipped behind a shelf just as Renault appeared from the other side. She examined him through the shelving, noting his slightly unsteady walk, the glittering brightness of his face. Whatever he was on, it had him hyped—it might be one of the new drug formulations aimed at Psy that had recently hit the streets.

The *Beacon* had reported on it last week.

Whatever it was, it had messed with his senses, because it took him several seconds of staring at the empty chair surrounded by ropes to realize she wasn't there. His face contorted, his mouth opening. His scream of rage echoed throughout the warehouse—she took advantage of the noise to duck around another corner, putting more distance between them while ensuring she could keep an eye on him through the breaks in the boxes stacked on the shelves around her.

Protein supplement.

Nutrient mix.

Her foot hit something.

She glanced down and had to slap a hand over her mouth to control her reflexive scream. A dead man in a security guard's uniform lay on the floor, blood oozing out of his nostrils and ears. She sensed nothing from him, no indication of a living presence, but she bent down to check his pulse. Clammy skin, nothing but death.

So this warehouse wasn't one of Renault's that he'd somehow accessed. He'd broken in—and murdered in the process. Either the place had no alarms, or he'd forced the guard to give him the codes. She was betting on the latter.

Her resolve to end him hardened. Renault would keep on killing if he wasn't stopped here and now; he'd spread pain like a cancer across the families of his victims.

No more.

"You bitch! You think I won't find you!"

Memory braced herself for a telepathic sweep—she was the only other mind in the vicinity, couldn't escape it, but Renault wasn't going to attempt to kill her with telepathy, not unless he'd completely lost it. If she kept moving, he couldn't use his Tp to zero in on her location so he could then freeze her in place using his telekinesis.

And if she managed to incite him into coming after her, she might be able to get him in a position where she could push one of the heavy shelves on top of him before he could use his abilities to block it.

She had Alexei, too.

Her mate was coming for her, his wolf a prowling wildness inside her.

Renault screamed again and Memory realized she hadn't felt a telepathic sweep. *Oh, of course.* She was *inside* Renault's own shields; he couldn't attempt to find her mind without first releasing her.

It had to be the same reason her attempts at swamping him with negative emotion weren't having any impact—her energy was being trapped inside the shell he'd placed over her mind. The next thing she felt was a slam of power against her mind that had her gritting her teeth, her eyes watering.

"Run! Run! I'll smash your shields open!" He kicked over the chair so it fell to the floor with a clatter, all the while battering at her mind.

He was a stronger telepath than her, and he'd had decades longer to learn aggressive tactics than she'd had to learn defensive ones. In a blunt-force fight, she'd lose. So she had to be cleverer, had to outthink him. Aware from past experience that she could telepath him while locked inside his shields, she said, *Shatter my mind and you kill the part of me you want.* No lie. This kind of savage and violent breaching often led to severe brain damage.

She watched through the shelves as he paused, the muscles in his jaw and neck bulging. *Come out and I won't hurt you.* His eyes moved in jittering sweeps.

Damn it, she'd made a strategic error. Now he knew for certain that she was nearby. *I want an agreement,* she said, stalling while she looked for anything that would work as a weapon.

An agreement?

I'm not a child any longer. I'm an independent contractor.

An incredulous look on his face. *An independent contractor?*

Yes. Memory crept toward the door. If Renault stayed where he was and didn't pursue her into the shelves, then she'd slip out and wait for Alexei, and they'd take down the monster together.

One way or another, this ended here, tonight.

I like having money and being able to buy pretty clothes, she 'pathed him. *Pay me and you won't have to spend energy trying to keep me caged. I'll appear as scheduled for regular sessions.*

Renault stared around the warehouse before leaning down to calmly right the chair. "If you're attempting to get to the door, don't bother. I twisted the lock with Tk. I'll have to untwist it to let you out."

Memory had no intention of just believing him. She'd see for herself.

"As for paying you . . ." Taking a seat on the chair, he propped one ankle over his other knee, a CEO at rest. "How about your new allegiance to the wolves and the Empathic Collective?"

Sascha, Jaya, the stipend provided so Memory could live a free life, the open embrace of her divergent abilities . . . Renault couldn't hope to understand the bonds she had with her fellow Es and she could use that to her advantage. *Where was the Collective when you had me in the cage?* She considered what to say next, what he'd buy. *I won't betray the wolves, since they let me out of the cage, but you don't do business with them anyway, so there's no conflict.*

Another pause, just as she reached a spot with a sightline to the door. Not only was the lock twisted, but so was the security bar across the doorway. No one but another telekinetic would be getting through that door. She wished she had her phone, some way to warn Alexei, but Renault had smashed it to pieces after first tying her to the chair.

Not about to give up, Memory searched the walls of the warehouse for another exit.

All she could see from her current position were the high windows and the huge roller door used for deliveries. That door wasn't an option—the access scanpad was just visible to her, and she knew it had to be secured against unauthorized use.

"An intriguing proposal," Renault said aloud, and she knew he wanted to push her into a mistake. A single spoken word and he'd know her general location in the warehouse. "How do I know you're telling the truth?" he added.

Memory tried to think like a smart monster. Because under the influence of drugs or not, Renault was smart. But Amara was smarter. Never could Memory have predicted that she'd one day tell herself to think like Amara, but that might just be the ticket here. Amara would no doubt be highly amused when Memory shared that fact with her post-transfer.

You are the only person I know whose motives are crystal clear to me, she said. *We have a relationship. Others in the world want to use me, but there is a risk they'll overuse and break me. You know how to control the draw.*

"Yes," Renault murmured, the sound barely reaching her. "That much is undeniable. You are helpless against a transfer."

Not anymore, you pathetic psychopathic coward.

Can I ask you something? He appeared rational at this second, and it might be the only chance she had to get this information for Alexei's pack. *How did you know about the bunker?* she said, directing her next words at his ego. *It's so secret.*

"I bet your wolf friends are going crazy trying to find the answer," he said, conceit in his laughter. "My father was a teleporter who worked with a bunch of scientists. He got paid to create that bunker, and once he was done, he took me there to show me what he'd made. He had some ridiculous notion that I would follow in his footsteps—as if I would waste my energy on manual labor. But I filed away the visual references just in case."

Memory dared another question. *Oh, so other people do know about the bunker? It's not just our place?* The words made her want to throw up, but they got results.

"Everyone else who knew is dead. Probably killed by the wolves." Renault's tone said he didn't care. "I eliminated my father when I began to indulge in my hobby. Couldn't have him deciding to teleport into what he considered his best work, could I? Not when it was my special secret place."

A crackle of sound that sent a chill down Memory's spine.

"Your mother had such thick ebony hair," he said in a honeyed tone. "It's one of my favorite souvenirs."

Memory bit back her scream and stayed silent. The monster would pay for her mother's death and the deaths of all the others.

"You don't want to see? I've kept it nice all these years for you."

Keeping a tight grip on her rage, Memory forced herself to say, *It means nothing to me. Do you want to make a deal or not?*

"It is a nice surprise to see you've absorbed my business acumen."

I have no problem with allowing you to use my abilities, Memory said. *But I want an apartment and pretty clothes and the freedom to go out in the world in between.*

"How much?" The words were clipped, cool, business-like.

Memory had no idea what to ask for, so she went for ten times her stipend from the Collective.

Renault snorted. "You have a high opinion of yourself." He offered a far lower number, and they got down to negotiating.

Memory went along with it while intensifying her search for a weapon. *That's too low,* she said at one point. *Designer clothes cost money.*

"This is my final counteroffer." Renault named a figure and a schedule of expected visits.

Memory took her time forming an answer. *I'll take that if you organize an apartment for me,* she said, forcing a hint of fear in her voice, though she wanted to—as Alexei had suggested—kick him in the nuts. *A small place. I don't like wide-open spaces.* That would please Renault. Even when Silent, he'd fed on the pain and fear of others.

She didn't know how else to explain it—he was a psychopath, but to an empath like Memory, psychopaths *did* have the facility to feel pleasure, though their version of pleasure wasn't anything a person with normal emotions would understand.

"Of course, of course," he said, his voice modulated into the soothing tone he'd used with her when she'd been younger.

Memory had never fallen for it; in the forefront of her mind was the memory of the same voice saying ugly things to her mother as he hurt Diana Aven-Rose. At times, she'd pretended to listen, but only because she had to survive so she could get her revenge.

"We'll make it a quiet place," Renault said in that same rage-inducing voice. "You know you'll be more comfortable that way."

Memory's eye fell on a wrench sitting on the shelf in front of her. Sweat broke out on her spine as she stared at it. Forcing herself forward, she tried to close her hand around the tool, but her hand trembled, froze. Before, vengeance had always been an idea, a future concept that made her bare her teeth in relish. The thought of doing actual violence, however, of causing bloodshed, made her gorge rise.

Damn it! This was the exact wrong time to discover she was very much an E.

But . . . Es fought back when monsters threatened their own. And Alexei was on his way to her. She wasn't about to stand back helplessly while her mate took on a psychopath who would never fight fair. Setting her jaw, she closed her fingers around the wrench and held it firmly to her side.

Renault did *not* get to hurt her golden wolf.

Once again, she thrust destabilizing emotions at Renault while watching him from her hiding spot. He frowned and touched his temple, but remained otherwise unaffected. Memory's own head ached.

"Enough talking." A punch of telepathic power.

Memory bit down so hard on her lower lip that she tasted blood. Barely able to breathe past the pain caused by the attempted breach, she began to make her way back toward Renault. The mating bond surged inside her, a protective thing with claws and teeth. Pressing her hand against her heart, Memory tried to convey that she was all right.

The idea of Alexei frantic for her made her hand tighten on the wrench.

Stop, she telepathed to Renault. *Stop. I'm coming.* All the while, she told herself to think like the most dangerous, most calculating person she knew. The facts hadn't changed—she couldn't win physically against a Tk of Renault's strength. Not in a fair fight. But the way he'd set up the chair in an open space in the warehouse meant she couldn't sneak up behind him and whack him over the head.

Memory, Memory, Memory. A sigh from the ghost of Amara in her head. *Have you learned nothing? We don't whack people over the head. We make them whack themselves.*

Memory's gaze fell on the rope at his feet.

Smile slow, she squared her shoulders and focused her tiny amount of Tk to nudge the rope around his ankle. *Gently. Gently. Tie the knot.*

A keening sound in her ears, her telekinetic ability burning out.

Shaking in the aftermath, she went to stall again somehow . . . and sensed a piercingly familiar wildness in the air. Her heart kicked. Alexei was here. That changed everything. She had to put herself in position to help him and stop Renault from teleporting.

You hurt me again. Once more, she tried to infuse her telepathic voice with fear instead of anger and protective fury. *How do I know you won't put me in the hole?*

"I own you!" Renault yelled, his cool demeanor cracking under a wave of red-eyed rage; whatever drug he was on, it was seriously destabilizing his psyche. "Come here right now or I'll teach you pain!"

Memory looked again at the wrench in her hand as Renault began to assault her mind with warning strikes that were shallow but still bruised. She had no way of knowing if Alexei was ready, but she had to take action before Renault lost it and launched a deadly assault.

He'd be sorry afterward, but she'd still be dead.

She sent her determination and readiness down the mating bond, not sure if it would work. The returning wave of feral resolve nearly had her growling. Teeth bared in a primal smile, she hefted the wrench and threw it as far from herself as possible. It clanged loudly against a bookshelf.

The sound had Renault jolting to his feet, his eyes glimmering. "There you are." He went to move.

His foot hooked on the rope and he fell onto his face.

She heard the crunch of his nose breaking.

Even as rage contorted his bloody features, a wolf launched itself at him with lethal fury.

"Renault!" Memory yelled and stepped out of her hiding spot.

Turning his head toward her, he pushed up to his knees. Ugliness twisted his face. "I'll make you pay—"

The wolf hit him hard, taking him to his back.

That wolf had its jaws around Renault's throat before the man could recover enough to teleport. It was over in seconds, blood spilling onto the warehouse floor, the wolf's muzzle drenched dark red.

Memory collapsed to her knees. Right in front of her lay a blood-splattered plas packet, a lock of hair within. Memory didn't pick it up; that wasn't her mother. Diana had been smart and gentle and protective. Memory would not reduce her to a memento kept by a psychopath.

"He's dead," she whispered, her mind free; the PsyNet was alive around her once more, stars appearing in the darkness in an endless carpet. "Finally, he's dead."

When the wolf turned to her, she held that amber gaze without fear, with love. "He deserved to die." She felt no pity for Renault, felt nothing but the ache of justice long denied. "My mother, all his other victims, they can rest in peace now."

The wolf padded to her. Fisting a hand in his fur, she buried her face against his warm body and she cried. For all the years lost. For all the lives taken. For the battle won.

Chapter 53

Shoot first and ask questions of the corpses.
                    —Rumored motto of the SnowDancer wolves

THE WOLF THAT was Alexei glanced up at Judd as the other man walked up to the scene of the execution. Taking in the blood and Renault's lifeless body, his friend said, "You want to disappear this?" He placed Alexei's discarded clothing to one side.

While Alexei hadn't needed Judd's help to keep Renault from teleporting out, his fellow lieutenant had helped him get inside. Alexei had given him a boost up so Judd could look in a small window at the far end of the warehouse, gain a visual inside the space. They hadn't been able to see Memory from their spot, but Alexei had scented her, his wolf prowling under his skin.

Judd had teleported them both inside.

And Memory had thrown the wrench after warning him of her intent. Alexei had never known the mating bond could be used that way—and perhaps only an empath could communicate with emotion with such specificity—but regardless, he loved it. Knowing his mate could reach him via the bond if she was ever in danger, it satisfied his every protective instinct.

Waiting until she'd cried herself out and was taking deep, steadying breaths while petting his back, Alexei shifted. He knew he was splattered in blood and that it appeared even more savage in human form than in wolf, but Memory just undid her pretty scarf and used it to wipe his face, his hands. "There," she said quietly, and he knew deep inside that she accepted all of him, the primal and the human.

Alexei regretted nothing of what he'd done—but he regretted having done it in front of his E. Cradling her close, he nuzzled her curls. "You okay?" It came out a growl, his wolf yet at the surface.

"Yes. He was only pain, only horror. He gave nothing good to the world." A grim smile. "It had to be done."

"Sorry I acted too fast to let you get your licks in." He felt bad about that, though not about saving his empath from carrying a death on her conscience. It'd have eaten at her. His wolf, on the other hand, had zero trouble with dispatching a serial murderer.

The human side of him was also fine with it.

"It's all right." Memory's smile was pure lioness. "I made him break his own nose and that gives me great pleasure. Amara would be proud."

When he raised an eyebrow, she shrugged. "I had to think tricky and sly."

"Got it." Rising after a hard promise of a kiss, Alexei pulled on his pants while Judd examined the scene.

"There's another body," Memory said as she got to her feet, her tone sad. "Security guard."

"We'll make sure he's treated with dignity." Renault on the other hand . . . Alexei knew that if he wanted, Judd, Hawke, and the rest of his pack *could* and would disappear all evidence of the psychopath's death. The cats would help. But he narrowed his eyes and said, "I think the world needs to be reminded what happens to people who attempt to take a SnowDancer's mate." He held out his hand.

Memory took it. Her eyes were red but her spirit bright. His lioness. His mate. His.

"It won't cause trouble for your pack?"

Alexei shot her a surely feral smile. "We don't exactly have a sweet and fluffy public image." Wrapping his arm around her, he cuddled her against his bare chest. "All else aside, Renault was a serial killer who'd taken you prisoner and was threatening to murder you." A shrug. "I'd like to see Enforcement do anything but say thanks for taking out the garbage."

• • •

ENFORCEMENT all but shook his hand.

Then Hawke called to say SnowDancer had shifted Alexei to quarters for a mated pair. Of course his alpha knew he'd mated. And the asshole wasn't shy about showing off his knowledge. Yet the call wasn't about that—it was about acceptance. Though Memory remained in the PsyNet, she was Alexei's mate, and as such, she was welcome in the den.

ALEXEI was painfully conscious of his mate's quietness on the way back to her cabin, but said nothing until they were inside. It had begun to rain again, the sky as heavy as his heart. "You're going to have nightmares, aren't you?" He'd torn out a man's throat in front of an empath—what the hell did he expect?

"What?" A shake of her head. "No, it's not that." Eyes turning obsidian, she shifted to stand toe-to-toe with him. "We're mated. Are you sorry?" It was a scowling challenge.

He growled at her, his wolf adoring her beyond life. *"Never."* Thrusting his hands into her curls, he nipped at her lower lip before admitting the depth of his selfishness. "I should be sorry that I've put you at risk, but I'm not.

"You're inside my heart and you're shadow and light and beauty and the best part of me." It terrified him that he'd hurt her as Brodie had hurt Etta, but his fear was no match for the depth of his joy. "Before, I didn't know what I was missing. I'll never give it up."

Smile fierce, Memory turned and pressed her lips to his palm. "You won't go rogue, Alexei. I work with the worst kind of darkness and you have nothing even remotely similar to that kind of damage inside you." She saw from his grim expression that he didn't believe her; that was all right—she could be as stubborn and she was inside him now, as he was inside her.

Another worry continued to niggle at her, however. "Are you sure your pack wants me in the den?" she asked. "I'm still in the PsyNet."

"You see us there?" Alexei asked, a deeply wolfish curiosity in his eyes.

Memory looked and felt her breath catch, her heart stop. "Yes," she whispered. "We're connected by a bond of wild amber." Aggressive, primal in a way that would probably fascinate and terrify in equal measure, it was a bond with teeth and claws. "But you're not in the Net." Her brain couldn't make sense of it. "The bond disappears at a certain point, but I *know* you're at the other end." She poked at the stunning wild amber of their bond.

A growl from Alexei. "Whatever you're doing, it's making my wolf snarly."

Laughing, Memory deluged him with flowers and rainbows. He groaned. "I'm a big, scary wolf. Have some respect."

She laughed and blew him a kiss.

Brows heavy, he scratched his jaw. "You've met Mercy, right?" At her nod, he said, "She's mated to a wolf and their bond does the same thing. Connects them across the DarkRiver and SnowDancer networks."

All at once, Memory remembered an article she'd read in *Wild Woman*. "Silver Mercant's bond with her bear mate does the same thing! Everyone's theorizing it's because Silver's too important to the PsyNet for it to let her go."

"There you are, then." A tug on her curls. "PsyNet's definitely not willing to let go of any more empaths."

Memory pressed the heel of her hand over her heart. "It's bad, Alexei." Ripples from the latest collapse continued to rock the Net. "Hundreds dead despite an immediate emergency response. I wish I could help."

Enclosing her in his arms, Alexei rubbed the bottom of his jaw over her hair. "You help by being an E, by being strong and a fighter."

Biting down on her lower lip, she admitted the shameful truth. "All the other Es are nodes in the Honeycomb. Even the trainees—they all link into and feed the Honeycomb, keep it strong. I'm the only one just kind of floating inside the network." No one knew why.

"Is it hurting you?"

Memory shook her head. "I just . . . I'm not giving anything back. Only taking."

"*Never* say that about yourself." One hand in her curls, he pressed his forehead to her own. "You're a new sub-designation. No one knows all the answers of you. Have faith."

Memory held on to the confidence of his wolf, her own shaky on this point. "I can do that."

"Good. Now, let's get you packed, so I can take you home to the den tomorrow morning." A possessive kiss. "Because yes, I'm sure. My entire pack is sure. Mating is the first loyalty, the loyalty on which a pack is built. Welcome to Snow-Dancer, lioness."

"My wolf," Memory whispered, seeing the apprehension he hid deep inside, the fear that stole his breath in the midnight hours. Alexei was so afraid he'd hurt her that he was hurting himself.

Well, it was time he stopped.

She set her jaw. She'd find a way to be the wolf—and tear out the throats of Alexei's demons.

Chapter 54

Fractures. Cracks. Scars.
We are all broken eggshells sewn back together.
In a madness of courage.

—Adina Mercant, poet (b. 1832, d. 1901)

HE STARED AT the carnage in the area of the PsyNet rupture.

Powerful and highly trained, he'd responded to the emergency, but even as he finished helping to suture the Net back together, he considered causing a deliberate rupture to break off part of the Net, a section free of empathic influence. It'd allow him to return to Silence, reverse his increasing instability.

Then, however, he'd be stuck in a small psychic network without access to the huge dataflows and connections of the PsyNet—and every piece of data he'd been able to unearth backed up the Ruling Coalition's insistence that without empaths, the Net went mad. There was no way to maintain a sane Psy system with no empathic influence.

That was when it struck him that *he* was acting mad, thinking about breaking off a piece of an already badly damaged psychic network. Dropping out of the psychic space after completing the repair, his brain tired from the work, he shoved up the sleeves of his gray sweatshirt and stared out at the rainy skies beyond.

Madness howled at him from every side, no answer in sight. The only "bright point" in the situation was that he'd begun to remember some of what he'd done. He'd attacked the *Arrows*. It was the most dangerous and frankly ill-advised thing he could've ever done—the squad would never stop hunting him. *Never*.

Especially if his memory of an Arrow shooting himself in the head to avoid the compulsion to kill empaths was correct.

Finding information about the squad was all but impossible, but he'd had a stroke of luck. The doctor who'd done his neural scans was a world-class neurospecialist. Said doctor also happened to be in a great deal of hidden debt. Enough debt that it created a hole in his ethical boundaries and cut through his fear of the squad.

When asked by an anonymous benefactor if he'd treated an Arrow at any point recently, he'd cracked under the offered financial incentive and shared that he'd been called in to consult on a comatose Arrow who'd suffered brain damage. "He's on life support and I'm fairly sure the squad is readying itself to turn it off. I wanted to help him—who wouldn't want the Arrows in their debt? But there's nothing man or machine can do for him. Not with that kind of damage."

At least with the squad, he could justify it. Surely the comatose Arrow had killed in his life? He was no innocent. But there was no justifying his attack on the empaths in Chinatown. He'd crossed a critical line. He lived by very few "human" rules, but not taking out innocents was one he'd never broken.

Not for the first time, his mind flashed with split-second images of an unusual empathic mind. It was the first memory he'd recovered after the Chinatown incident, and he'd been able to track down the owner of that mind—it hadn't been difficult given her unusual appearance on the PsyNet. Others, too, were fascinated by the "midnight empath."

Slipping back into the Net, he made his way to her as he'd been compelled to do over the hours since he'd found her . . . and saw the primal bond that tied her to another. In his room in San Francisco, his hands curled into fists in his pockets. Her mind was anchored at the empathic compound in

DarkRiver-SnowDancer territory, so chances were she'd mated either a wolf or a leopard.

Abducting her wasn't an option, even if the madness whispered at him to take her. *Use her.* That the insane thoughts were now filtering into his everyday life . . . His time was running out.

Chapter 55

I live in the den. The den is gynomus. It has a lot of rooms.
Even mor than one hundred! My frends and I like to run in
the grass outsyde and stawk the groanups. It is fun. Some
days we go to the kichin and steel extra cookies and eat
them. We love the den. We love pack.

—Composition by Benjamin Stone (Age 7)

DESPITE ALEXEI'S REASSURANCE that his packmates
would accept her not just because she was his mate but for
herself, Memory's nerves were in a thousand knots by the
time she stepped out of the trees and into a wild grassy area
in front of what Alexei said was the den.

It was now nine-thirty; she'd had a prearranged session
with Amara at seven-thirty and she'd kept to it. In her own
way, Amara was trying, and Memory didn't want to interrupt
any progress she'd made. Because something very weird had
begun to happen: Amara's lab mates and twin had reported
instances of normal empathy at random times *between* sessions.

One time, she'd noticed when a colleague cut his finger
and gotten him a Band-Aid.

Another time, she'd helped a pregnant colleague move lab
equipment.

In neither case had her actions helped Amara in any way.

Renault had never shown any long-term changes. Whether
it was because Renault had been a murderous psychopath and
Amara wasn't compelled to murder, or because Memory was
working voluntarily with Amara while she'd been forced by
Renault, no one knew. It was also possible the effects were
blips that'd never be repeated, but Memory wasn't about to

give up if there was any hope. Especially as she had Amara's full agreement.

"I have never seen a lack in me," Amara had said. "But I cannot evaluate a life of which I have no comprehension. As a scientist, I must experience both, then make the call. If the effect of your ability sticks, at some point, I will reach an equilibrium where I will see both sides with equal clarity—that moment is far distant, and so we continue."

Memory had also shared how thinking like Amara had helped her escape Renault. As she'd expected, Amara had been overcome with amusement. "I'm glad the wolf tore out his throat," she'd said later. "An individual stupid enough to get between a wolf and his mate is clearly no loss to the genetic tree."

No matter what, Amara was still Amara.

Memory would continue to both work with her and attend sessions at the compound, even though she was moving into the den. Right now, she couldn't see anything beyond the clearing but for a mountain overgrown with plants and moss. The snow had melted away at this elevation and the grass in the clearing was tall and green under the brilliant morning sun, only the odd droplet of dew still clinging to the blades.

Despite the sense of emptiness, she knew other wolves were around, their wild emotions music in the air. Many were distant echoes but a couple seemed so close and so *bright* that she felt as if she was right on top of them. Frowning, she glanced at Alexei . . . to see he was grinning. As she watched, he put two fingers to his mouth and whistled.

A small wolf pup who'd been nosing around in the long grass popped up his head, ears pricked. Delight emanated from him, but he didn't race over. Instead, he glanced to his left.

"Oh, my goodness." Memory raised a hand to her mouth as an even *tinier* wolf pup tried to poke her nose up out of the grass. She was too little to truly succeed, but her delight in spotting them was as innocent and shining a joy as his.

She began to run over—more enthusiasm than coordination.

The bigger pup ran beside her, holding himself back to her slow pace. Loyalty, love, protectiveness, exasperation, his emotions were so clearly of a big brother that Memory laughed a little, her heart so full it could burst. The tiny pup, her sides heaving, flopped down to rest on reaching them, while the other one bounced up on Alexei's boots, his paws small and perfect, and growled up in what appeared to be a hello.

Memory's hands itched to pick up the little one, but she held back, not sure if it was allowed, or if a stranger's touch would scare the tiny girl-wolf. She knew the tiny one was a girl the same way she knew the other was a boy. It was in their emotional scent, both very certain of their sense of self already.

"Hello, Ben," Alexei growled back before crouching down to pick up the tiny ball of brown fluff that was Ben's sister. "I see you've escaped school again." He nuzzled the ecstatic pup in his arms. "Did you break Elodie out of the nursery?"

Ben gave a tiny, happy howl, then ran around them both before stopping to stare up at Memory with eyes of pale, pale amber. As Memory's heart thundered at the wonder of being so close to such a small wild creature, the pup angled his head sideways, then back to center, and took a sniff of her.

When he reared back, her heart fell.

The pup was shatters of light without warning, and a naked little boy with hair of deep mahogany, his skin gilded by the sun and his eyes brown, was looking up at her with a scrunched-up nose.

"You smell like Lexie," he declared.

"I'm his mate," she whispered, just as light shattered in her peripheral vision.

A gorgeous girl who couldn't yet be two sat in Alexei's arms. Her hair was as dark as her brother's, but fell in big fat curls where his was silky straight. She also hadn't tanned as much, her skin creamy with rosy patches on the cheeks.

Her eyes danced with unhidden glee. "Curwy!" She held up a hunk of her own hair, then pointed at Memory's.

Cheeks aching from the depth of her smile, Memory nodded. "We're both curly girls."

Laughing, Ben's sister held out her arms.

Memory's heart thudded. "Alexei?"

"Elodie here doesn't bite anymore, do you?" He nipped playfully at the tip of the pup's nose, sending Elodie giggling, then glanced up at Memory, his eyes telling her she didn't have to question herself; she was worthy of this precious trust.

Memory opened her arms and Alexei passed Elodie over—who settled onto her hip with the practiced ease of a child who expected affection, expected love. Neither child had any shame about their nudity—wild creatures at home in their skin.

"No pulling her hair, Dee," Ben instructed his sister sternly.

When Elodie stuck out her tongue at him and laughed, Ben slapped a hand to his forehead. "I can't take her anywhere."

Memory's poor heart was mush by now. Then Ben took her free hand, his own soft and warm, and she just melted. No matter what anyone else in the pack said to her, this joyful welcome would carry her through.

"You smell weird, too," Ben said conversationally as the four of them began to walk across the clearing. "Under the Lexie smell."

"Bad smelly!" Elodie echoed after a sniff . . . but she kept her arms wrapped around Memory's neck.

Memory took her cue from the pups' open and friendly demeanor. "It's from my work," she said. "It makes me smell weird sometimes." This was also why she hadn't canceled her session with Amara—better she know now how the wolves would react.

Alexei had said they'd shrug it off as no big deal, but he was her mate. He loved her. She couldn't forget how the other Es—such kind, gentle people who'd never hurt her on purpose—had reacted.

"Like after I fell into stinky mud," Ben commented, while a small hand patted Memory's curls with gentle curiosity. "Mama made me have a bath and it was better."

Chest aching at the simple acceptance, she was about to reply when Elodie twisted out of her arms in such a sharp movement that she couldn't hold the little girl in place.

A cry left her lips, but Elodie didn't fall, shifting midjump into her wolf-pup form.

When she glanced back at Memory, it was with pride in every line of her tiny furred body. Memory's heart, in contrast, was racing double-time.

"Dee! You can jump-shift!" Ben did a little dance before throwing back his head to emit a small howl.

Memory jumped when he was answered by a far stronger howl from next to Memory—and then the sound was taken up all around them from wolves she couldn't see, the wild song carrying across the mountains.

The tiny hairs on her arms stood up, the haunting beauty of wolf song rippling in her blood. When her own wolf nipped playfully at her ear, she shivered and slipped her free hand into his. The three of them followed the tiny pup to what turned out to be a door hidden in the side of the mountain.

Beyond that door lay a stone corridor painted with scenes of wolves in the wild. The detail in the paintings was so exquisite that she knew she'd come here again and again, her brain absorbing it a piece at a time. But first she had to set foot inside the den. Her mouth grew dry, her skin hot.

Putting his lips to her ear, Alexei told her she'd already been authorized to enter and exit as she wished. "This door's hardly ever locked anyway." A growly kiss that made her feel at home. "Only ones who've ever breached the den are the cats, and they're allies now." She wanted to laugh at his pretend-scowl. "If the worst ever happens, we have ways to evacuate our vulnerable from deep inside the den, while the dominants fight on the front line."

Memory trusted Alexei with her life, but she still had to clench her stomach to step inside; her abdominal muscles hurt from the tension.

"We can live outside," Alexei rumbled. "My den is set up pretty much the same, but—"

"No." Memory gripped her fear in an unforgiving fist. "I want to be part of a family, live in a big puppy pile." A place where small pups might run up to her at any moment expecting a cuddle, and where passing packmates would wave hello.

Like the tall redhead currently heading toward them, her walk fluid and unmistakably feline. "Congratulations," Mercy said, a wicked glint in her eye. "Guess the wolf food fetish paid off."

Memory felt a giggle form in her throat. "I'm going to frame that *Wild Woman* column."

Mercy winked, her grin wide.

Alexei, meanwhile, was sending the two of them a distinctly suspicious look. "Are you two friends? How did you end up friends with a cat? Have I taught you nothing?"

"I'm a lioness," she reminded him. "Which means you're mated to a cat."

"Dear God."

Ignoring his aghast words, Mercy kissed him on the cheek, then did the same to Memory. "I can't wait to dance at your mating ceremony."

"She smells bad because of her work," piped up a small voice from beside Memory, while Elodie ran back to stand between Alexei's booted feet, annoyed at missing out on the fun.

"We've all been there," Mercy said. "One time I walked into the middle of a juvenile battle and ended up drowned in homemade concoctions that smelled like rotten socks and putrid fruit." She shuddered. "It all wears or washes off."

And so it continued, with little Ben announcing to everyone who would listen that Memory's smell was temporary—as if he wanted to ensure no one would judge her for her odd dual-layered scent. Memory wanted to cuddle her small defender to death.

The SnowDancers, her new packmates, made commiserating faces at her and, as with Mercy, shared their own scent disasters . . . and Memory began to understand that to a wolf, a temporary unpleasant scent was just bad luck. "They really don't care," she whispered to Alexei after they'd escorted Ben back to class and dropped Elodie at the nursery.

One arm around her shoulders, he raised his eyebrows. "You should listen to me when I tell you these things, lioness." A snap of his teeth that made her want to kiss him. "Assholes *will* tease you though—but only because they sense you can take it. I'd tell you to feel free to dish it back, but you don't need the encouragement." A scowl. "I found another goddamn rubber chicken in my stuff the other day. Some genius had drawn a wolf face on it."

Memory's shoulders shook. "I love you," she said, throwing her arms around him.

"Grr."

She went to rise on tiptoe to bite at his stubbled jaw when her nape prickled. Primal power licked the air. Shifting on her heel, she found exactly who she'd expected: *Hawke*. The alpha wolf's pale eyes were even more striking today, his hair an extraordinary silver-gold. Holding her gaze, he lifted a hand.

Memory stood motionless, her heart thunder—but she didn't flinch when he cupped her cheek. A deep sense of acceptance, primal protectiveness, wild affection, it sank into her soul. *This* was why he was alpha. Because he had the capacity to hold every member of his pack in his heart.

"You're one of mine now," he said, brushing back her hair with his other hand before leaning down to kiss her cheek. "Wild, a survivor, a fighter, you do this pack proud."

Eyes stinging at the unqualified acceptance, Memory hugged him.

Wrapping his own arms around her, his scent familiar to her in a way she couldn't explain, he said, "For a big wolfy chicken, you did good, Lexie."

"I'm going to murder you," Alexei muttered, but a minute later, he accepted his alpha's back-slapping embrace with a grin.

"Hey! Russian Bridegroom!" yelled an unknown male voice just as Hawke and Alexei separated. "What's this I hear about you going off the mail-order market?"

Alexei threatened to punch the big, dark-skinned, and shaggy-haired male who dropped a rucksack on the floor and fought him off with a grin. "Out of my way," the other wolf said. "I'm here to meet the pretty half of this pair."

When the big man held out his arms, a laughing Memory allowed him to enfold her in them. His friendship with and love for Alexei might as well have been written in neon against the stone walls of the den. "Hello, Matthias," she said, recognizing him from the description Alexei had given her last night of his childhood best friend.

Then another friend stepped into view, and Matthias released her so Judd could touch his fingers to her cheek. The blonde with him bounced up and down before opening her arms. "Do you hug?"

"I'm an empath." Contact with people as openly happy to see her as Alexei's friends and alpha . . . it was like sunlight to her. She flowered under the affectionate attention, and she flowered most of all in the light of Alexei's love.

Her wolf made no effort to hide his smug pride in having her for a mate. Below that, however, was a screaming tension that refused to snap. Alexei, her beautiful golden wolf, was waiting to go rogue. Was waiting to start hunting her. Was terrified of looking at his claws one day and seeing her blood.

Chapter 56

The shield vulnerability has been identified. It is limited to a small number of Arrows who came of age during a specific outdated training regime—it was unfortunate chance that four of them were in the compound at the time of the attack. Yuri was one of the first to be taught under that regime, Amin in the final class.

The only outlier is Abbot. He came into training at a later age and was taught the older technique because it was faster. No other Arrows under the age of thirty-five bear the shield flaw. All Arrows with the shield flaw, whether on active duty or retired, are in the process of building new next-generation shields.

We are ready to resume our duties as the guardians of Designation E, but we understand if empaths no longer feel able to trust our presence.

> —Aden Kai, leader of the Arrow Squad, in a report to Ivy Jane Zen, President of the Empathic Collective

My Es have missed your Arrows. Welcome back.

And tell the squad to forget about brooding or stewing in guilt. Because you know what my Es saw? That even under vicious mental duress, your men and women will not hurt an E—no matter the cost. Arrows and Es have become an even tighter unit, one that nothing and no one will ever tear apart.

> —Ivy Jane Zen to Aden Kai

Axl is going to read bedtime stories to the children today. I want you two to take some personal time. Honor Yuri's joy in the squad's freedom to live and love, and step away from his bedside. Nerida's more than ready to stay with

him—she's half in love with him, in case you haven't figured it out already.
—Personal message from Ivy Jane Zen to Aden Kai and Zaira
                                                              Neve

We hadn't figured it out. Thanks for the intel. We'll leave her to spend time with him.
        Fuck, Ivy, we just played our last card and failed. No one can help Yuri. Aden's going to have to make the call to pull life support and it's breaking him apart.
                                        —Zaira Neve to Ivy Jane Zen

Take care of him, Zaira. Vasic and I will hold the fort.
                                        —Ivy Jane Zen to Zaira Neve

IT WAS THREE days after the PsyNet collapse that Kaleb noticed something. Actually, the NetMind and DarkMind noted it in an unexpected but encouraging display of coherence, and nudged him in that direction. "It's the new E," he told Sahara, holding out a psychic hand so she could join him at the same coordinates.

"She's different," Sahara said after a long moment.

When he asked the NetMind and the DarkMind about the discrepancy, the twin neosentience showed him images of running water, crashing rivers.

"Ivy Jane needs to see this," Sahara said.

Kaleb made the contact.

. The president of the Empathic Collective appeared on the PsyNet beside them not long afterward, with Vasic by her side. Given recent events, the other man's protectiveness was understandable.

"Can you tell what she's doing?" Kaleb asked Ivy Jane.

"No, and we should stop spying on Memory and bring her into this discussion. She's at the empathic compound. Give me five minutes to warn her we're coming, then teleport in."

When Kaleb and Sahara arrived, it was to find Memory and the SnowDancer lieutenant, Alexei Harte, waiting with

Ivy Jane and Vasic near the tree line. Folding his arms, Alexei set his booted feet apart in an aggressive stance. "What's this about?"

Ivy Jane took the lead, explaining what the four of them had seen on the PsyNet. "There's a . . . I don't know what to call it . . . a kind of *motion* in the PsyNet around your mind," she said to Memory, and undulated her hand to show the wavelike pattern. "It's slow but constant."

Lines formed between Memory's eyebrows. "Am I causing a problem? Further disintegration?"

Kaleb saw Alexei's jaw go hard, the other man's arms opening. He curled one around the empath's shoulders, tucking her close to his body. "If she's doing anything, she's making your network stronger." He growled. "Memory does that. She takes the bad out of things."

Eyes shining, the new variant of E rose up on tiptoe to kiss the wolf's jaw.

He gave her a stern look in return. "I'm trying for an attitude here."

The E's laugh faded when she faced the rest of them. "I can't see the motion."

"Possibly because you're inside it." It made sense that her own viewpoint was static—else she'd find it impossible to get a stable sightline when she entered the PsyNet. "There's also a bond." Keeping one eye on the wolf—despite how he treated the E, Alexei Harte was a deadly predator who could not be taken lightly, even by a Tk—Kaleb explained what else he'd spotted. "The NetMind and DarkMind are hiding it from view."

Memory scowled. "Why? It's beautiful, just like Alexei."

Kaleb felt a certain sympathy when the wolf lieutenant groaned. He, too, had a lover who kept puncturing his deadly reputation. "The director of EmNet, Silver Mercant, is also mated to a changeling."

"Yeah, StoneWater bear alpha." Alexei's gray eyes had developed a rim of amber. "You saying the Net's hiding their bond, too?"

Not just a predator, but a very smart one. "Yes. Silver is not a woman to hide her allegiance." His former aide *and* her mate were alpha personalities who dared anyone to try to interfere with their bond. "She's curious to know what the NetMind and DarkMind are doing, but she doesn't have a direct communication line with them. I do, but they're being coy on this point."

"Es can talk to the NetMind," Ivy Jane explained to Memory. "And because this is *your* mind, if you ask, it might tell you why there's motion around it—and why it's hiding your bond." A smile. "Do you want to try?"

MEMORY had put her hand on Alexei's lower back, now clenched her fingers in his T-shirt. Part of her didn't want to know, didn't want to find out what was happening. She already knew she was designed to work with the most twisted psyches on the planet, and that she contributed nothing to the Honeycomb—which was pretty much all that was holding the PsyNet together at this point.

She'd accepted those truths, even begun to see that perhaps she could help people no one else could reach, but she didn't know if she could take more. Learning that she was hurting the Net, it'd be one blow too many.

When Alexei took her hand and said, "Give us a minute," to the others, she didn't resist, and they walked off a short distance into the shadow of the trees.

"What's got you tense?"

Her answer had him growling. Before she could tell him to stop it, he said, "Sometimes, mate, you make me want to bite you." He put his hands on her hips and tugged her close. "Why would the PsyNet hold on to you if you were bad for it?"

She parted her lips to growl back at him . . . and realized he was right. Why *hadn't* the PsyNet dropped her like a hot potato when she mated Alexei and had another available network to which to link? Why had it held on to her when she was a strange E who worked with psychopaths and couldn't do much to heal the Net? Who just took energy and gave none of it back?

"I'm not saying you're right," she said, poking Alexei in the abs, "but I'm going to do what Ivy Jane said and try to talk to this NetMind."

Her wolf smiled a smug smile. "I'm right."

Glaring at him had no effect. She loved that about him—she didn't think she could bear it if Alexei ever actually got mad at her. The growling and the snarling, she could handle any day of the week. It was all a front, Alexei trying to keep people at bay because he believed he'd eventually let them down.

Memory had an idea of how to take care of that problem, but first, she'd deal with this. Walking out of the trees, she came to a stop across from Ivy Jane and the woman with dark blue eyes and a warm smile who'd arrived with Kaleb. Memory had seen her on the comm while in the bunker: Sahara Kyriakus. A woman linked to Kaleb by a devoted love no empath could fail to sense.

"Show me how to talk to the NetMind," she said to Ivy Jane, whose bond with Vasic was as intense but had different colors to it.

"Just ask. It really likes Es."

Squaring her shoulders, Memory tightened her grip on Alexei's hand and, closing her eyes, peeked out into the PsyNet. *Um, NetMind?* Braced for silence, for failure, she physically staggered at the joyous welcome that poured into her mind.

Flashfire images of flowers, of rain, of bright splashes of light, of rushing rivers, of stars glittering in the sky, of a waterfall slamming into a pond.

Her eyes snapped open. She pressed a hand to her heart, her breath rough.

"Memory?"

"I'm fine." She reassured her mate through their bond. "It's just . . ."

"I should've warned you." Ivy Jane winced, her lovely eyes penitent. "It can be a little enthusiastic the first few times. Just tell it to go slow. Use images."

Nodding, Memory returned to the PsyNet and *felt* an eager, curious presence around her. She slowed down all the images it had sent her and fed it back to the neosentience. The response she received was slower . . . but it wasn't from the original presence. This being was darker, colder, infinitely deadly.

Memory didn't push it away. It was like her. If the other Es were the NetMind, she was this darkness. "I see the DarkMind," she murmured without opening her eyes.

"It's never caused harm to an E." Kaleb Krychek's midnight voice.

"No, it won't hurt me." She sent out her greeting again, this time to both presences. They were, she realized, not quite separate anymore, even if they'd once been; one merged into the other at the very edges.

What am I? she asked, trying to send the question in images.

??? The lack of comprehension was followed by more images of water. Rain, fresh and ozone-rich on her skin, the cool ripples of a lake sliding against her body, a river sending up spray as it broke around a rock.

Are you cleaning me? Blood suddenly scalding in her veins, she showed them an image of her under a shower, scrubbing. Her expression was angry. She might not be perfect, but no one had the right to change her!

But the image was returned to her, with her scrubbing the walls of the *shower*.

Memory opened her eyes. "I'm cleaning the walls of the shower." She scratched her head.

Vasic said, "Will you telepath us the image?"

Since Memory had imagined herself clothed in that shower, she had no problem doing so. While they considered the meaning of the exchange, she described what she'd seen to Alexei. The aggravating wolf actually rolled his eyes at her. "Lioness, like I said—you take the bad out of things. Obviously, you're taking the sickness out of the PsyNet. Like a purifying filter."

Everyone else went still.

Memory's heart kicked. "A filter." It was such a clear way to describe what she did, especially if she factored Amara's erratic displays of empathic behavior. It could be said that Memory had filtered out enough psychopathy that a droplet of emotion was able to fall through.

This time, when she entered the PsyNet, she sent out an image of herself on the PsyNet, scrubbing at a badly damaged section. The NetMind returned the image back to her, altered slightly. She now saw cracks in the area she'd "scrubbed"— but the section was whole again. The crack was a scar, strong, not weak.

Show me, Memory said. *I want to try.* She projected an image of herself standing with cleaning supplies, in a ready stance, and when the NetMind and DarkMind tugged at her, she went. "I'm running an experiment," she said aloud.

Two other Psy minds appeared in the Net—Ivy Jane and Kaleb Krychek.

The two followed her as the twin neosentience took her to a part of the Net that was in danger of fatal collapse. It had been cordoned off, no minds anchored inside it, and though the golden threads of the Honeycomb crisscrossed it in a thick mesh, it was barely holding together. Kneeling beside it, Memory realized she had no idea what to do, and went with the image she had; she put a scrubbing brush in her hand—and began to clean.

She didn't know how long it took, but she was leaning up against Alexei's chest by the time she finished. The damage hadn't been erased . . . but it was better. Scars had begun to form. Two or three more scrubs and she might be able to return it to a level of strength viable enough to support Psy minds.

A pulse along the mating bond, her mate calling her back.

She went, because she would always answer Alexei's call as he would hers. That's what it meant to love. Opening her eyes, she would've swayed if he hadn't been holding her tight. "It takes a lot of energy."

Alexei shoved a granola bar into her hand and muttered that he was going to start carrying around nutrient bars if she kept losing weight in front of him.

"Flavored," she reminded him as she tore open the granola bar.

He kissed her temple.

"Checks and balances," Sahara murmured. "The Net-Mind has always kept the PsyNet stable—even when Psy were going insane a hundred years ago, the Net itself was stable. We broke that stability with Silence. The NetMind couldn't keep up."

Ivy Jane nodded, the soft dark of her hair glinting in the

sunlight. "Pre-Silence it makes sense that it had a few Es like Memory, who could consciously or subconsciously repair any damage."

"The ability to filter psychopathy is the secondary ability," Alexei said with his usual clarity. "It's the one that freaked out Es in the past, but it's not an E-sigma's primary function."

E-sigma. That's me. Wonder made her float for a glorious second before despair crashed her to the ground. "It's too big." Memory took another bite of the granola bar, swallowed. "The damage is too much. I can do small areas, but I can't do the entire Net." The task needed hundreds of thousands of her. "I feel on the edge of flameout. It may take days to recover." Her psychic veins were sluggish, the energy not even trickling in at this point.

"Show me what you saw when you cleaned." Krychek, in that cold dark voice that made her nape prickle.

Frowning because he'd been right there, Memory nonetheless telepathed him the image. "It's not even the size of a room."

Ivy Jane stared at her, then glanced at Kaleb. It was the cardinal who spoke. "Your mind must telescope the sections to make it easier to visualize. Ivy and I witnessed a vast section of the PsyNet ripple with black light. An area big enough—and now nearly strong enough—to support a thousand minds."

Memory actually squeaked. "A *thousand*?" She leaned back into Alexei, needing his solid warmth as an anchor.

Ivy Jane nodded. "It's the most astonishing thing I've ever seen." Her voice was breathless.

A thousand was amazing, but the PsyNet held millions of minds.

As if reading her bleak thoughts, Kaleb said, "Triage. If I work with the Arrows to give you a map, can you attempt to strengthen the most critical areas with the largest populations?"

Memory nodded even as her throat closed up. "Yes, I'll help." She'd seen the true scale of the problem during her time connected with the NetMind and DarkMind, the horror of it. "Millions could die, couldn't they?"

Alexei's arms tightened around her as Krychek said, "We're holding on, but it's going to become critical sooner rather than later."

"You've just bought us an incredible amount of time." Sahara's gaze held a fierce hope. "Even another year could mean everything."

Memory's heart ached for all the lives that hung in the balance. She would survive, she knew that—Alexei's wolf would haul her into the SnowDancer network that held Judd and his family, but so many others had no option but the PsyNet. "I forgot to ask about why the NetMind's hiding the mating bond."

"You're exhausted," Alexei said with a scowl. "It can wait."

"Yes, that's not critical," Sahara reassured her. "It's more a curiosity."

Overcome by the scope of what she'd learned about herself today, Memory stayed quiet for the rest of the conversation. After the others left—Krychek and Sahara teleporting out, Vasic and Ivy going to speak to the other Es—Memory turned into Alexei's chest and burrowed in.

He slid one hand to her nape, his other arm like steel around her. "If I hear you question your abilities ever again, I'll bite you twice."

She laughed, the sound a little wet. "You already bit me twice today." It had been in bed, her wolf in a wickedly playful mood this morning. He'd done it lightly, left no marks, but she could still feel the brush of teeth on the underside of her breast, and at her throat. "But . . . can we go do that again?"

Alexei brushed back her curls. "You're exhausted."

"Psychically, not physically." She kissed her wolf's throat, the intimate area he'd allow no one else to touch. "Today was a good discovery . . . but I feel unsteady, off-center. I never feel that way when we're naked together."

Chuckling, he grinned. "Come on, then, lioness. Let's go play."

Chapter 57

Skin privileges are a core necessity to any changeling. Without tactile contact, the dominants become edgy, irritable, bad-tempered, while others get depressed. But you know who're the worst? The predatory dominants. Good grief. Talk about snarly.

So if you're with a wolf, or a leopard, or a bear, or any of their dangerous brethren, we highly recommend a daily dose of skin privileges—intimate and not. We know, we know, it's going to be a *great* sacrifice on your part, but think of the good of the pack or clan and you can get through it.

—From the February 2083 issue of *Wild Woman* magazine: "Skin Privileges, Style & Primal Sophistication"

THE TWO OF them snuck into the den like naughty children, on a mission to avoid being stopped. Of course that proved impossible. Memory tried to keep a straight face when a packmate flagged them down to ask Alexei about a border incursion issue. She just barely managed to hold it together until the packmate had moved on and they were around a corner.

Giggles erupted inside her.

Leaning into Alexei, her hand linked to his, she tried to stop it, but the delight filled her bloodstream. That was when they ran into Mercy, who was on the hunt for Alexei to talk about something else. She took one look at them and shook her head, her lips tugging up at the corners. "I have no knowledge of your whereabouts for the next hour and I feel the strange compulsion to cover your shift for the same period." She glanced pointedly at her watch. "Time's ticking."

"I owe you one!" Alexei called back with a grin as he and Memory took off.

"You can babysit the triplets in return!"

"Mercy has triplets?" Memory's eyes widened.

"We call them pupcubs." Alexei ducked into a corridor to avoid a group of passing packmates, then tugged her back out after the risk passed. "Alphas say her two boys will shift into wolves, her baby girl into a leopard."

He winked. "Babysitting's actually a hotly contested item among the two packs. Last week, Mercy's brothers absconded with all three of them, so this week, Riley's sister's staked a claim. And we're here."

Hauling her inside their quarters, he shut the door behind her and pressed her up against that door. One hand at her throat, he kissed her with the slow deliberation of a connoisseur. Shivering, Memory slid her hands under his T-shirt and kissed him back the same, tasting her golden wolf, lick by lick, touch by touch.

He shifted back at one point to tug off his T-shirt, then her top, then lifted her up so she could wrap her legs around his waist, her back to the door. Arms around his neck, she drew him back into their languid playtime of a kiss, her breasts crushed against his chest. Big hands curved around her rib cage, moved down to the dip of her waist.

She was beginning to fill out under the care and attention of not just her wolf but her pack. Food appeared in front of her any time she was seated somewhere for five seconds. The other day, little Ben had broken his muffin in half and given it to her. Well aware by now what food meant to a wolf, Memory had sat down next to him and shared the gift in the spirit it was given.

As for Alexei, he tempted her with treats every single day. "I love you." She spoke against his lips, her smile bone-deep. "My gorgeous, growly wolf."

"Grr."

Grinning, she arched her throat so he could kiss it, and he took full, voracious advantage. She petted the muscled silk of his shoulders, moaned out his name, tugged up his head for more kisses. Slow and languorous, they took their time, the slide of skin on skin a pleasure to be savored. Alexei traced the scalloped edge of her striped sea-green bra at one point and smiled. "I have something for you."

Memory ran her nails through the fine hair on his chest. "I know. I can't wait to have it inside me," she said, feeling young and naughty and confident.

Dipping his head, he sucked her nipple into his mouth without warning. Her back arched, her fingers clenching in his hair. A scrape of teeth through the satin of her bra before he released her. "You'll get that, too," he promised with a slow grin that melted her bones, then carried her to the bed and dropped her onto the mattress.

Turning over onto her stomach, she watched him open the built-in closet and pull out a small delivery bag. "You're not the only one who knows how to use the Order button," he said with a smug smile as he walked back.

Memory wanted to pounce on him, but he was so proud of whatever he'd bought her that she sat up on her knees and accepted the bag. He watched her with wolf eyes as she tore it open to retrieve a box marked with the emblem of a lingerie brand. Teeth sinking into her lower lip, she opened the box . . . and grinned so hard her face ached.

"Told you I'd replace it," said her wolf.

Memory picked up the pink lace bra, identical to the one he'd torn off her their first time together. He'd even gotten the size right. Just like he had with her sparkly sneakers. Because her wolf noticed her and what mattered to her. Not only had he found the right bra, he'd gone one step further and ordered the matching panties, which she hadn't originally bought because the bra on its own was splurge enough.

The froth of pink held in one hand, she looked up and crooked a finger. When he bent over, she nipped at his lower lip. "Want me to model it?"

His eyes gleamed. "I thought you'd never ask."

And that was how Memory found herself exiting the bathroom a few minutes later dressed in the new pink bra and matching panties, and nothing else. Unless you counted her hair, which was doing its usual crazy thing.

Alexei wolf-whistled as she strode across the length of their bedroom as if on a catwalk, one hand on her hip and breasts high. "Twirl," he called out.

Giggling, she turned, gave him a sassy look over one

shoulder, then swiveled back to blow him a kiss . . . before running to the bed to pounce on him. Never, never had she thought she would ever feel this young and carefree. The idea that she'd one day be tussling in bed with a golden wolf who thought she was beautiful and sexy and told her so hadn't even been a dream.

They laughed and played and she kissed him all over and told him he was wonderful.

"I know," he said solemnly.

Grinning, she bit his throat. One hand in her hair, he held her close, arching his throat so she could do what she wanted. And what she wanted was to adore her wolf. This time, she got him naked first, then ran her hands over every hard ridge and hollow, pressed her mouth to delectable inch by delectable inch.

He groaned when she closed her hands around the thick hardness of his cock. "Take the bra off or I'll be putting in a repeat order."

Reaching back, Memory unhooked the bra, then tugged it off her arms and put it carefully at the end of the bed. Alexei's hands were on her waist before she finished turning, and she was flat on her back seconds later. He hooked his fingers into her panties, pulled them down the heated skin of her legs.

Lifting her arms above her head, she stretched her body as she spread her thighs, enticing her mate.

He slid one hand under the curve of her thigh, squeezed. "Pretty lioness." Kisses across her navel, lower.

Memory gasped and clutched at his hair. "*Alexei.*" It came out a touch shocked.

A rumble in his chest, he kissed her inner thigh. "Yes?"

It took her no time to make her decision. "Yes." She had no secrets from Alexei, no part of herself she wouldn't share.

Claws slicing out, he pushed her legs open wider, then he devoured her like the wolf he was. Memory lost count of her orgasms at some point after three. By the time her very satisfied wolf mate finally pushed his cock inside her, she was pure boneless female. Eyes heavy-lidded, she watched him move above her, this wolf with the face of a young god and a heart so big it loved too hard and hurt too much.

Today, however, his emotions were as young and as playful as her own. When he kissed her it was with a smile. Wrapping her lazy limbs around him, Memory held on to her mate as he took her with an erotic slowness that had her gasping his name again at the end.

Chapter 58

While twins are not to be separated at birth, so-called Harmonies are to be curtailed. Though most prevalent in twins, this rare phenomenon has, through Psy history, occasionally been found in unrelated individuals who share an unusually close bond.

Regardless, Harmonies go against every tenet of Silence by forging a deeper emotional tie between the pair with each use. Twins who display this propensity—or twins born into a family with a history of it—should be separated and alienated from one another as soon as they turn seven years of age, and are no longer at risk of psychic collapse.

—Classified rider to Coda 27 of the Silence Protocol (to be disclosed only to trusted individuals in affected families)

HE COULDN'T GET to the comatose Arrow. The squad's minds were all but invisible in the PsyNet and they'd no doubt surrounded their injured squadmate when the male's own shields failed. Even if he *had* been able to find the dying Arrow, he couldn't do this alone. He needed the cooperation of the one person who had no loyalty to him.

His twin opened the door with an expressionless face. "Pax," Theodora said. "What have I done to merit your presence? Come to hand me another headache?"

He looked into that blonde and blue-eyed face that so strongly echoed his, except that her bones were finer, her lips softer, her hair longer, and he knew he would fail. But he had to try to fix this. "I need your help."

A raised eyebrow. "What can I, a lowly 2.7 Tk, do for my Gradient 9 brother?"

That had always been the problem. He was stronger by

magnitudes and thus groomed for leadership, while his twin
was relegated to working as a tech who moved tiny comm
components using her mind. He'd been educated at Eton and
then Cambridge in the UK, while she'd been comp-schooled
on her own at home, then sent to a community college. He
lived in a penthouse suite, Theo in a small one-bedroom
apartment in the same building.

In a final insult, the family had spent a large amount of
cash to obscure her birth and place her at a different point in
the Marshall family tree. As far as the world was concerned,
Pax had been a single birth, his sister born a year later. "Better for you if the PsyNet doesn't see you linked with such a
weak mind," their grandfather had said to Pax while Theo
was standing right next to him. "Perception shapes power."

It had been their seventh birthday. He and Theo hadn't
lived in the same home since.

Pax kept an eye on her, made sure she was never out of
funds and that no one was abusing her because of her low
status in the family, but the two of them weren't siblings, not
really. "I need you to Harmonize." It had taken him years to
find the official word for what they did; it had been buried in
moldy historical documents in the family archives.

Turned out twins in the Marshall line had a history of the
phenomenon.

Her eyebrows came together, the nascent frown another
sign of her "weakness"—per their parents' relentless pro-
nouncements when they'd been children. Pax had tried to
defend her, but that only led to more punishment for her, so
he'd stopped. Instead, the second he could hide it from their
parents, he'd begun to boost her shields so no one would see
that her Silence was fragmented. It was a fact the two of
them never discussed.

Now Silence had fallen and his twin no longer needed the
one connection between them.

"Harmonize? What are—" Eyes widening, she stepped
inside, holding the door so he could follow. "What is your
problem?" she said in a hard tone after they were behind the
privacy of the closed door. "You broke Silence, learned what
it means to be amused, and decided to come play with poor,
pathetic Theo?"

"I need help because I'm going mad." She deserved the truth.

Theo stared at him. "Pax, you have a mind like a razor. Remember?"

Another wall between them, their Psy Councilor grandfather castigating her while praising him. "Look. See." It was the first time since early childhood that either one of them had invited the other in.

Theo balked. "I don't know what game you're playing—"

"*Look*, Theo. Please."

He actually saw a tremor run through her at the last word. "Fine." Teeth gritted, she made mental contact, slipping through his shields because he let her.

He showed her all of it.

Her face was bloodless when she emerged. "The Arrows can't help you," she whispered. "That's not what they do."

"I know." Pax found the words to explain. "I think a certain E might be able to help, but she needs to know I'm not a monster."

Theo's lips twisted. "Always the manipulator."

Pax didn't correct her. He did always think five steps ahead . . . except in madness. "There's also a chance no one can help me." If so, he'd no longer be around to protect Theo. "I've set up an account for you. I'm telepathing you the details. I'll warn you before I terminate myself so you can get out." Their vicious family would massacre her otherwise, simply for being born into the direct line of power, even if she didn't want that power.

Theo ignored everything he'd said. "How do we know if the—what did you call it?—Harmonizing, still works? We only did it a couple of times as children."

The first had been when they'd discovered a dying bird on the lawn, the second after they'd escaped their parents while in a care facility; their mother and father had gone there to check on the status of a badly injured relative. Pax and Theo had ended up in the room of a coma patient.

They'd been separated for a month after each incident—because Theo's psychic abilities had flatlined dramatically, and so had *Pax's*. Their parents didn't know what they'd done, but they knew the twins needed to be together for it.

After that, Pax and Theo were monitored constantly on the PsyNet to ensure no connections ever took place.

"I don't know," he answered. "But I have no other option. Will you help?"

Theo stared at him for a long time before nodding. Because when their conscience had been divided in the womb, she'd gotten the lion's share.

ADEN'S direct call code was one he shared rarely with those outside the squad. However, since signing the Trinity Accord, the squad had provided a way for others to contact them. Trinity was about building a stable world that was a true triumvirate, Psy, humans, and changelings working as a unit. That couldn't happen without open lines of communication.

Pax Marshall had never taken advantage of that contact option until now. Neither had he ever asked to meet with the squad. But Aden knew who he was—the head of the Marshall empire. A powerful business unit, but one with no obvious military ties since the assassination of their last patriarch. Below the surface, however, Pax had access to a very well-trained black ops team.

"Pax," Aden said when he met the Gradient 9 telepath on an isolated outcrop above the crashing ocean. "This is unexpected."

The arctic blue of Pax Marshall's eyes held his. "I may be able to assist the brain-damaged Arrow in a coma."

Aden went motionless. Marshall had no reason to know of Yuri's injuries and the heartbreaking decision Aden planned to carry out tomorrow. "Were you behind the attack?"

"Yes."

Aden was leader of the squad partially because he was so calm, but at that moment, he came within a split second of executing Pax Marshall where he stood. "Why are you here?" Because no one ever admitted to harming the squad; it was a death sentence.

"My mind is failing." Pax's voice, with its crisp English accent, was steady, his eyes on the distant horizon. "When I attacked the compound, I did so without conscious volition—

I am too intelligent to make an enemy of the squad. Right now, however, I'm sane and may be able to offer recompense."

Aden had no way to know if Marshall was lying, but he couldn't discount the offer on the minute chance the telepath could make good on it. "What's in this for you?" Pax was too ruthless a negotiator for it to be otherwise.

"I need help from the dark E."

"That's not my call to make." Memory Aven-Rose was very much her own person.

"I know. I'll help Yuri first. Then . . . we'll see if she decides to assist me."

"Come to these coordinates in one hour," Aden said, his murderous urge toward Pax under brittle control at best. "Yuri will be there." He strode toward Abbot; the teleport-capable Tk was on light duty and had brought Aden to this meeting. The teleport distance to their next destination was also well within the capacity of his healing body. "Take me to Yuri."

WHEN Pax Marshall arrived at the private hospital to which Abbot had shifted Yuri from the medical facility in their home valley, it was with a woman Aden didn't immediately recognize, though she bore a startling resemblance to Marshall. *Tamar,* he telepathed to the surveillance and data expert he had on standby. *Identify the woman.*

Marshall's younger sister, Theodora, Tamar telepathed only thirty seconds later. *Gradient 2.7 telekinetic. Works as a comm tech, specifically shifting miniature components using Tk.* A short pause before she said, *Wait. Wait. There's something shifty in these files. A whole lot of folks went to considerable trouble to hide the birth records, but Tenacious Tamar is on the case. Hell.* No levity in her tone when she added the next words. *Aden, she's his twin.*

Aden had never heard of twins with such divergent abilities. "Why is your twin present?" Especially since she appeared terrified of Aden and the Arrows on guard outside Yuri's room.

She also swallowed hard at being ID'd as Marshall's twin,

while he remained unmoved. "This ability only works when we're together."

Aden gave nothing away, but hope flickered to life inside him. He'd heard of such abilities; his parents had mentioned them when he was a child. The "Harmonies" had disappeared with Silence, but prior to that had emerged in people who were closely linked. Like twins.

Aden had a distinct memory of his father mentioning how his grandmother had once told him a strange tale: "She swore that a non-twin Harmony pair in her home village once brought her brother back to life after he drowned. According to her, he had no pulse for at least fifteen minutes and the resident M-Psy pronounced him dead, but the Harmony pair said his mind wasn't gone and they were able to revive him."

Aden's father had made a dismissive noise. "Of course, she wasn't exactly fully compos mentis at that point. I accept Harmonies existed—there are rumors of a classified coda to the Protocol dealing with them—but if these paired abilities are so powerful, why have they disappeared? Why hasn't the Council done everything in its power to locate and draft Harmonies into service?"

"Maybe the ability demands a base emotional connection?" Aden's mother had suggested, before the two of them got interrupted by another Arrow and the subject was dropped.

Very young at the time, Aden had forgotten the entire conversation until this moment when he stood face-to-face with twins who appeared to have an ability that only worked in concert.

"I need to act now," Pax Marshall said. "I don't know how long I'll be rational."

Aden stepped aside so the two could enter Yuri's room. There was no need to warn them their lives hung in the balance—they knew. Though the sister wouldn't be hurt unless she did direct harm to Yuri.

Arrows were no longer monsters.

Marshall put one palm on Yuri's temple. His sister echoed him on the fallen Arrow's other side. Then the two connected hands over Yuri's chest. They didn't speak as they closed their eyes, but on the psychic plane, Aden saw energy sparking through Yuri's mind.

The other man wasn't brain-dead—if that had been the case, Aden would've made the hard call the very first day. No, the senior Arrow was in a gray no-man's-land between life and death, the damage done to his brain catastrophic, but not enough to kill him. Aden and Vasic were maintaining his shields.

And because they were, Aden could see what the twins were doing.

Pax was the more powerful by far, but he was only the conduit—and the source of the raw material. It was Theodora who was somehow taking Pax's psychic energy and using it to weave something from nothing. She was building neural material with a delicacy Aden hadn't ever seen. Only Judd came close. Another Tk who could move minuscule components with his mind.

Clenching his gut, he maintained the shield. When Vasic joined him in the hospital room an hour later, they switched on and off as per their plan to ensure the shield was never less than impenetrable.

The operation took hours.

The sister collapsed first, Marshall a second later. Both were caught instinctively by Vasic using his telekinesis. He lowered them gently to the floor just as Yuri's mental activity spiked so sharply across the neural monitoring system that it set off an alarm.

Chapter 59

Long-sleeved black shirt with fine silver pinstripes.
—Order placed by Memory Aven-Rose

MEMORY COULDN'T BELIEVE she'd allowed Aden to talk her into this. "I don't know Pax Marshall and he hurt people I care about," she said to Alexei. "I don't want to help him." She'd tried that one time in Chinatown, but she'd changed her mind in the interim, her anger growing with each hour Yuri'd spent fighting for his life.

"Okay. Want to go home?" No sarcasm, just wolfish acceptance of her anger.

"Ugh." She kicked at the grass on the outskirts of Dark-River territory. "Aden says Yuri is awake." Joy had her eyes burning all over again.

The senior Arrow apparently had some memory loss. About a month's worth. As a result, he didn't remember Memory. That was all right—she'd make friends with him again, starting with when she went to visit him with her gift of a stylish new shirt. She'd also remind him about the whole being-asked-out-on-a-date situation, to nudge the romance back into gear.

All that mattered was that Yuri was awake. It was a miracle—but it still didn't make her feel positive toward this Pax Marshall. "I don't even know what I'm meant to do."

Alexei hauled her close for a kiss. "Want me to tear the asshole's head off?"

Memory considered it for long enough that Alexei's eyes

gleamed amber. "No," she grumbled at last. "But only because of his twin—*she* helped Yuri, even though she had nothing to do with hurting him. I'm doing this because we owe her, not him."

A sleek black vehicle turned into the meeting spot. Pax Marshall, aristocratically handsome with an expression like ice, emerged from the driver's side. From the passenger side came Theodora Marshall: half a foot shorter than her brother, slender where he was muscled, with more delicate features and longer hair.

The clear blue eyes, however, were identical.

Memory flinched at Pax's psychic presence, so dark and familiar. "What do you expect me to do for you?" she demanded.

"I don't know." His English accent took her by surprise. "But if this fails, my only other option is a planned and smoothly executed suicide." Memory was concentrating on Pax, but it was Theo's jolt of pain that had her throat closing up. "I won't take Theo down with me. She's already suffering bad migraines and nosebleeds."

It was hard to keep on fully disliking a man who appeared to love his twin. His shields were locked down so tight she couldn't feel the emotion, and it could be that he was a world-class manipulator. But Theo wasn't. And it hurt her to think of Pax dying.

Memory held out a hand. "I need physical contact."

The telepath touched his hand to hers. Braced for the nothingness, she was startled by the subtle "wrongness" in him. He wasn't a psychopath, but neither was he normal in the psychic sense. Not sure this would work, she gave him some of her empathic energy—what Amara drew from her in a session.

Hissing out a breath, he dropped her hand.

When she flicked open her eyes, it was to see that Pax had his eyes scrunched shut, one hand at his temple. His twin was close to him, her features stark. "Pax?"

Pax's lashes lifted . . . and Memory realized belatedly that the twins were connected on an emotional level. It was hidden deep, so deep they might not realize it, but it was very much there. That was why Theo was getting headaches and nosebleeds. Pax's brain was automatically reaching out to her during the episodes.

He must've telepathed his sister because her breath eased. Then he looked at Memory. "The sudden clarity took me by surprise." His pulse thudded in his neck. "I hadn't realized exactly how cloudy my thinking had become."

"Is the effect permanent?" Theo Marshall asked on a wave of naked hope.

"No, I don't think so." Memory didn't know how to heal Pax or if it was even possible. Her entire ability was one unknown after another . . . but things were becoming clearer with each day. "I suggest," she said to Pax, "that you form a strong emotional bond with your twin." It wouldn't be difficult, not with what already existed. "She'll know when the regression begins and you need another dose." As good a word as any, she supposed.

Pax Marshall looked to his twin. Neither spoke except to thank Memory, though Memory knew the constant vigilance would wear on them both. She wished she could comfort Theodora in some way, but right now, this was the best she had.

It wasn't until after they'd driven out that Alexei said, "Has it struck you that an incredibly powerful man in the PsyNet is now in your control?"

"No." She poked him in the abdomen. "And it's not going to strike you, either. This is between me and Theo. Don't you dare use any of this to lean on Pax during negotiations."

"Empath." Alexei scowled and shook his head. "Soft as butter."

"I am not." Turning on her heel, she gripped the front of his T-shirt. "Talking of which, we need to have a conversation."

"Yeah?"

"I'm tired of you jerking awake in the middle of the night." Furious at his pain and the way he continued to hurt himself imagining the worst.

"I thought the honeymoon period would last longer." It was a grumble. "But if it bothers you, I can sleep on the couch."

"Ugh!" Memory grabbed hold of his hand. "You're coming with me."

He didn't resist, a slight curve to his mouth. "So no separate sleeping?"

"Just try to go to the couch and see what happens," she threatened. "Today, you drive where I tell you to drive." She hadn't yet learned the skill, though she was down to do so in two months' time in Alexei's home den. Alexei had introduced her to the packmates in that den via the comm, and the teens were delighted that she and another older packmate were going to be joining their driver's ed class.

He'd also introduced her to his aunt and her family. Clementine "Min" Harte had arrived at the Sierra Nevada den a day later. "To welcome my Lexie's mate properly." The honed SnowDancer soldier's hug had been fierce, and she'd brought with her the gift of a sparkling bracelet. "I heard your abductor allowed your familial history to be destroyed." A lopsided smile. "No secrets in a pack."

Memory had no argument with that; she wanted to live her life in the open, in the light.

"I can't bring back that history," Alexei's young aunt had said, "but I can start you off on creating your own history to pass on to your pups. This bracelet belonged to my sister, Lexie's mother." Warm hands cupping Memory's face. "I saved it for Lexie's mate."

Memory's eyes had filled, spilled over. "It means so much." Clementine Harte could have no idea of the depth of her joy at being so deeply accepted by Alexei's family. "Thank you." She knew without asking that Clementine had given another piece to Etta. It hurt her heart that she'd never meet the lost young woman, but she would get to know her from Alexei's stories of his brother and Brodie's mate.

"There's no need to thank me." Clementine had kissed her forehead. "We're family now. You two are expected at the dinner table every week once Lexie's back in our den."

In her, Memory had seen where Alexei got his stubborn will and calm control. Today, however, she was the one who planned to be stubborn. "Go left," she instructed. "There's another path to the right after that."

"Bossy mate," Alexei grumbled, but he followed her instructions . . . until he brought the vehicle to a sudden halt.

"Memory." His hands clenched on the steering wheel.

"You have to go." She put her hand on his forearm, loving but determined. "Keelie Schaeffer is the closest thing changelings have to an expert on rogues."

ALEXEI knew that. He'd been ignoring it for years.

Grinding his jaw, he squeezed the steering wheel even harder. "I don't want to know what she might tell me." A confession he could make only because Memory was his mate, his lioness who loved him without boundaries. "As long as I don't know, I can have hope."

Keelie Schaeffer had apparently managed to track down the records of over a hundred rogues across three generations and had come up with multiple commonalities among all of them. If anyone could predict who would go rogue, it would be her.

Memory put her hand on his thigh as she leaned across the seat. "You tell me to trust my instincts and abilities. Now, my wolf, I'm asking you to trust them." Obsidian eyes full of stubborn conviction. "I know you don't have it in you to go rogue."

She spread her hand over his heart. "I *know*, Alexei. I feel your connections with your family, your pack, your friends. You might try to keep your distance, but you always fail. Your life is full of those you love, who love you, while rogues inevitably shut out the world."

Alexei dropped his head back against the seat. "Brodie didn't come to my birthday party." It had been thrown by the senior soldiers in his den, a laid-back event involving pizza and beer—and a huge-ass chocolate cake.

When Alexei didn't see Brodie, he'd asked a friend if they'd told his brother.

"Yeah, of course," had been the answer. "He's probably running late. I bet he gets here in time for the cake."

But Brodie hadn't come at all. Worried something was wrong, Alexei had tracked him down. "He'd forgotten birthdays, other events before, was nearly late to his own mating ceremony." If Alexei hadn't dragged him out of bed after a drunken party with friends the night before, Brodie would've been lucky to survive Etta's wrath.

"But then, he'd laugh and cop to flaking, and we'd share a beer and it was all good. I never expected Brodie to be anyone but who he was." Not always reliable, but always loyal. "That day, however . . . the way he looked at me, it was so flat and emotionless."

"The one thing your brother had never been."

"Looking back, that's the day I'd pick out as the critical turning point, but back then, I was just hurt." He blew out a harsh breath. "Stupid, huh? I was a lieutenant and I was hurt by my brother not bothering to say happy birthday."

"No," Memory murmured. "You were a lieutenant, but you were also Brodie's younger brother. He was your big brother. It mattered."

Alexei wove his fingers through hers, his wolf brushing up against the inside of his skin. "I miss them, Memory. Every fucking day." His eyes burned with all the tears he'd never allowed himself to shed. "I miss how much Brodie loved Etta. I miss how she'd giggle and kiss him. I miss her sweet smile when she'd come by with cookies just because. I miss her out-of-nowhere hug attacks."

It was getting hard to talk, but the words kept tumbling out. "I miss his lunatic, infectious laugh. I miss knowing I could turn up at his door day or night and he'd haul me inside. I miss hearing about his latest death-defying stunt. I just . . . I miss my big brother and the woman he loved beyond life." He swallowed again and again.

Maneuvering her way over to his seat, Memory straddled his body, then wrapped her arms around his neck. Locking his own arms around her, Alexei buried his face against her neck. Then, for the first time since his brother had been lost to him forever, he cried.

MEMORY'S heart was breaking, but she knew Alexei had to get this out, this horrible pain he'd kept inside for far too long. She cried with him, and then she just held him. They sat there locked together for a long time after he went quiet, while she murmured sweet, soft words to him, rubbed her cheek against his, and stroked her fingers through his hair.

Along the bond, she sent all her love, speaking to the wolf as much as the man.

Alexei let her pet him, and when he leaned back, he cradled her jaw and took a kiss that tasted of salt and of Alexei. Afterward, he got out and used a bottle of water to wash off his face, while she used a damp tissue to wipe off the remnants of her own tears.

Drying his face on the bottom of his T-shirt, Alexei got back in the passenger seat and started up the truck. "Let's go see Dr. Schaeffer."

Five minutes later, they came to a stop in front of the Schaeffer house, deep in DarkRiver territory. They didn't have an appointment, but Memory had asked around and knew the doctor was working from her home office today.

A slender woman with thick hair that held tones from ash to gold, and whiskey-colored eyes, opened the door before they got to it. "I thought I scented a wolf," she said with a gentle smile that held not even a pretense of leopard-wolf antagonism. "Alexei, isn't it? And you must be Memory."

Alexei shook Keelie Schaeffer's hand, while Memory returned the older woman's genuine hug. As the three of them walked in, an unsmiling Alexei said, "I need to know if I have the indicators for going rogue."

Keelie Schaeffer took the abrupt comment in stride. "I was hoping you'd come to me when you were ready." She waved them into a large office dominated by an old and battered wooden desk set by a huge window that brought the forest inside. Family photos played across the computer screen—and the current one included a face Memory knew: the rough-edged DarkRiver soldier with wide shoulders who'd met them at Vashti's house.

Oh, of course. He'd had the same striking eyes as Dr. Schaeffer.

That familial link wasn't visible in the photo. Wearing a checked shirt, his jaw dark with stubble and his sleeves shoved up, the leopard male stood looking down at a tiny baby cradled in one arm—a baby who was staring up at him in equal fascination. One day, that'd be Alexei, she whispered inside her mind. A big, tough changeling holding their baby with protectiveness, tenderness.

Below the screen, a black cat napped on the doctor's touch keyboard. The projected letters and numbers glowed on its silky fur.

"Midnight's favorite spot," the doctor said with a laugh before picking up her pet and dropping him to the floor after a stroke. Midnight's expression displayed disgruntled affront at being so summarily impeached from his spot.

Memory smiled when the imperious cat came to wind himself through her legs. Jitterbug had done the same while she was on her feet. She bent and held out her fingers for the cat to sniff. After a thoughtful pause, he decided she was an acceptable individual and reached up to place his paws on her shins. She gathered him up in her arms and began to pet him while Alexei stood rigid beside her.

"Please sit." Keelie Schaeffer indicated a U-shaped seating area beside her computer station. When Alexei went to refuse, Memory shot him a look. He scowled at her, but followed her onto a sofa, while Keelie Schaeffer sat across from them in her computer chair. Midnight immediately sprawled over Memory's lap, a liquid creature.

Able to sense the coiled tension in Alexei, his wolf a growl at the back of his throat she could almost hear, Memory wove her fingers with his again.

Emotions turbulent, he accepted the touch—and the loving affection she sent him through the mating bond. "Do you need to do a blood test?" he asked Dr. Schaeffer.

"No, my research isn't focused on DNA." The doctor brought up a document on her computer. "It's a psychological profile validated by blind tests set up by colleagues—my task was to predict which profiles were of rogues. The paper hasn't been published yet, but my success rate in separating rogues from non-rogues was one hundred percent."

She leaned back in her chair. "The problem arises when I look at those who have the markers for going rogue, but haven't yet done so—only a minuscule minority of possibles ever actually go rogue."

Alexei tapped their clasped hands on his thigh. "You're saying all rogues share certain traits?"

"Every single one I've studied, and I threw a wide net." The doctor picked up a pad of paper and a pen. "Consider this a representation of every changeling in the world." She drew a large circle. "Now these are the people with the indicators." A much smaller circle within. "And these are the rogues." A dot within the smaller circle.

Memory knew why the doctor was belaboring this point—she wanted Alexei to know that even if he had the markers, that didn't mean he would ever go rogue. Memory also knew Alexei wouldn't see it that way. But while she might be an atypical E, she *was* an E, and she sensed no hint of instability in Alexei. She wouldn't have brought him here if she hadn't already been certain of the answers.

"I want to know, whatever the answer." Primal energy along their bond, Alexei's wolf brushing up against her. "Let's do it."

The interview took two hours. Afterward, Keelie Schaeffer asked Alexei if he'd be willing to talk about his brother. Alexei's skin pulled tight over his cheekbones, but he gave a curt nod. Though Memory listened with care, she couldn't see what it was Keelie Schaeffer was looking for in the brothers' profiles.

The doctor included a number of questions about their father, too, but Alexei had limited information on the man who'd died while he was only seven years of age.

At some point, Memory rose to make sandwiches and coffee.

Midnight supervised.

Darkness had fallen outside, the trees whispering under moonlight. Dr. Schaeffer's mate was working late leading a training session on strategy for senior soldiers, so it was only the three of them—and Midnight—in the house. Memory was glad of that; she knew in her gut that Alexei wouldn't have been as open with another male in the area, especially when that male was a DarkRiver soldier.

He hadn't remained seated for long, prowling the room while answering the doctor's questions. Midnight had paced with him for a while before curling up on the sofa to nap again.

"Thank you for that." Keelie Schaeffer put down the datapad on which she'd been taking notes, though she'd also asked Alexei's permission to record the interview. Rubbing the back of her neck, she stretched out her spine, then asked Alexei if he'd like to walk outside while they talked about the results.

Alexei's response was immediate. "I just need to know." He gripped the back of the sofa behind Memory.

"You don't have the markers."

The air hung in silence, but inside Memory, the mating bond *surged*. Throat thick, she jumped up and ran to throw her arms around her golden wolf. His own clamped around her, his scent in her every breath and his claws so careful against her body.

"I told you so," she whispered, rising on tiptoe to kiss him.

"No one likes a know-it-all," he grumbled, but he was kissing her back.

Dr. Schaeffer's smile was wide when the two of them looked back at her at last. "I'm glad to be able to give you good news."

"My brother?" Alexei asked, a roughness to his voice that was crushed gravel.

The other woman's smile faded. "I'm sorry, Alexei. Brodie did have the markers." She rose then, and the three of them, plus Midnight, walked outside into the moonlit forest while Dr. Schaeffer talked them through her conclusions.

She explained that the signs of possible rogue status were many and subtle, but a major one was a lack of impulse control, or other thrill-seeking behavior. "It's a blunt hammer indicator." The researcher put her hands into the pockets of her long cardigan. "On its own it means nothing—*especially* in a pack of predators. It must be accompanied by myriad other factors, and even that isn't a guarantee a person will go rogue."

Stopping beside a stream, she watched the ribbon of water for a long moment before saying, "That's partly why I haven't published my paper. It could do a lot of damage, mark people as being in danger of going rogue—and maybe turn it into a self-fulfilling prophecy."

"Yeah, I can see that." Alexei shoved a hand through his hair. "Brodie would've probably killed himself if he knew ahead of time." Stark words. "My big brother, the brother I grew up with, would've never taken the risk. Not after seeing what happened to our father."

Memory could see him struggling with his love for Brodie against all that had happened, because Brodie *hadn't* known. Hugging him from the side, she drenched him in love. He crushed her close as he said, "What will you do?" to Dr. Schaeffer.

"I plan to make my research known to a small, tight circle, people I trust to follow the rules—the main one being that we only profile adults who come to us. I'll keep on trying to work on the question of why a minority of people with the markers go rogue, while others live a full life. I'm missing something, and until I know it, it would be negligent of me to spread the information."

Dr. Schaeffer shifted on her heel to face them. "Creating a usable profile has only ever been my initial goal. My true objective is to find a way to stop the process before a changeling goes rogue—or to at least be able to reverse it." Echoes of old pain in her gaze. "Our pack's lost people, too, and the scars of such a loss, they linger."

"What you've been able to do for me, it's a gift." Rough words from Alexei. "Thank you."

"Live your life with your mate, Alexei. Fear has no claim on you."

Epilogue

Thank you for making a special trip to introduce us to your mate. You don't know how much that meant to us. When we lost Brodie and Etta, we lost a son and daughter. Then it felt as if we'd lost you, too. We're so joyful that's no longer true.
—Note from Etta's parents to Alexei

THREE DAYS AFTER returning from Matthias's den to visit with Etta's warmhearted and loving parents, and two weeks after the meeting with Dr. Schaeffer, Memory sat with Lucy. She and the nurse were sharing a small plate of pecan sugar cookies while they watched over pups playing in the safe area in front of the den.

The two of them were present to make sure the pups didn't hurt each other or get into accidental trouble. Memory had already petted and comforted one who'd tried to climb a tree only to suffer a fall on his furry butt. As she did so, she'd noticed that her skin had darkened after so much time out of the cage and in the light of the sun. It had a glowing depth to it now, a rich health.

"Other than nursing, this is one of my favorite jobs." Lucy finished off a cookie. "Watching these hellions is a blast." She growled back at a pup who'd bounded over to growl at her.

Elodie threw back her head in a wobbly howl before racing back to join her playmates—some in human form, some in wolf.

"Mine, too," Memory said. "Being with them, feeling their happy emotions, it just whisks any stress away." She was on a constant rotation of PsyNet cleaning sessions, followed by recovery time, then E studies. Rinse and repeat.

The bonus was that she could stuff her face with as many cookies as she wanted; her psychic burn was huge.

"Memory, look." Laughing, Lucy pointed to a pup who had the tail of another pup in his teeth and was mischievously dancing around behind the second pup as the pup tried to see what his tail was caught on. It was obvious the first pup wasn't hurting his friend, just playing a game, so they let it be.

"Thank you for being my friend, Lucy," Memory said, the words just bubbling up inside her. "It means a lot to me."

Lucy's gaze was soft when she glanced over. "You say things like that and you wonder why I—and so many of the pack—like hanging out with you." She tugged on one of Memory's curls, as the wolf pup had pulled on his friend's tail. "You're kind and funny and you take no shit from Alexei and I like being around you."

Memory hugged the words close to her heart. And when she felt a kiss of wildness inside that heart, she smiled. "Alexei's coming."

"Ugh." Lucy pushed at Memory's upper arm. "You have that goofy just-mated look on your face. I'm going to throw up any second now."

Grinning, Memory got up off the rock on which she and Lucy had perched. "Can you hold the fort while I go say hello?" Alexei was on a security shift, likely only in the vicinity for a short period.

"Shoo. Go make kissy faces." Lucy waved her hand. "I'll manage the rampaging horde."

Memory navigated her way through said horde—surviving with only a couple of "attacks" and playfully threatened bites—and made her way into the trees. She knew her mate was nearby. However, when he walked out of the trees, she was surprised to see him wearing his jacket on such a bright, sunny day. Not only that, he had it closed over his chest, his arm kind of cradling one side of it.

"Did you hurt your arm?" She hurried closer.

Unzipping his jacket, Alexei brought out a tiny ball of orange-and-white fur he'd had tucked inside.

Memory froze.

. . .

ALEXEI hoped like hell he'd done the right thing.

Stepping toward his mate, he held out his palm—on which sat the tiniest kitten in the fucking universe. "Runt of the litter," he said, running his fingers over the damn thing's body because it cried if he didn't. "Got sharp claws though. Tiny beast did this." He pushed aside his jacket to show her the drops of blood on his white T-shirt from where the kitten had clawed at him.

When Memory didn't make any attempt to touch the kitten, Alexei said, "You're right. He's probably too much trouble for a pet. I'll drop him off in the forest. If he survives, he survi—"

Memory rescued the kitten from his palm and held it close to her body, her fingers already stroking the creature. The azure of her nail varnish was bright against the kitten's fur. The ungrateful brat began to purr. Alexei scowled. "That rat with orange fur didn't purr for me."

Memory glared at him. "He knows you don't like cats."

The kitten rose up to put its paws on Memory's chest. She looked down . . . and her body, it went motionless again.

Alexei held his breath.

And the kitten meowed and rubbed its head against her chest. She laughed that unique, lovely laugh full of emotion that tangled around him, and began to scratch the spot the kitten had demanded.

Her curls bounced around her head.

Wolf and man both relaxed. It had been a calculated gamble, bringing her the kitten. He hadn't considered it until he'd seen her petting Keelie Schaeffer's pet. Her grief over Jitterbug wasn't gone, but it had been tempered. These days, when she spoke about her pet, it was to tell him sweet stories of the fun she and Jitterbug'd had together.

He'd also become aware of the growing pet population in the empathic compound. Jaya was back with Phantom—and both had fallen in love with the blanket Memory had knitted for her friend's pet. The cat had been known to drag it out of his basket and onto the sunny porch so he could lounge in comfort.

While Phantom was, at present, the only resident cat, Ivy Jane dropped by often with her energetic mutt, three other trainees had dogs, one had a bird that followed the E around of its own free will, and another one had a hamster. He'd also heard that a family of wildcats regularly visited Sascha, each member waiting patiently for their turn to be showered with attention.

Es and pets seemed to go together.

"You keeping the little monster, then?"

Another glare that made the wolf inside him grin. "He's too small to be out in the forest."

"I don't know. He's a feral thing." He growled for good measure.

The kitten hissed back at him before cuddling up to Memory. The tiny creature seemed not to realize it was all bone and a bit of fur. Alexei had picked him out of the litter exactly because of that. That litter had been in DarkRiver territory, but he'd been given first pick when he'd told the leopards why he wanted a kitten.

The runt might be tiny, but he'd also been the most ferocious.

Now, the kitten jumped out of Memory's hands to land on the forest floor. Tail in the air, it began to prowl around. "Thinks he's king of the forest instead of a bite-size snack."

Putting her hands on her hips, Memory glared at him again . . . then ran over without warning to throw her arms around him. He lifted her up with a grip on her waist, smiling smugger than the cat as she kissed him again and again. The wolf inside him rubbed up against his skin. "I guess this means you want to keep the tiny beast," he said darkly.

"I know you like him, so stop pretending." Pressing her nose to his, she gave him a stern look, but she was stroking his nape with her fingers while he held her with her feet off the ground. "What will the rest of your pack say when I bring a kitten into the den?"

"*Our* pack," he said, "will say it's all Riley's fault. He went and mated a leopard, and now we're inundated with cats."

"Oh! Beast, come back here!" Memory wiggled down and went to collect her pet—who was about to wander off into the forest.

"Beast?" He grinned. "I like it. And don't worry about him getting lost. I've got his scent."

But the kitten was curled up against Memory's chest, purring like an old-fashioned motor, so he put his arm around his mate and they walked back to the den. The pups gathered around them in astonishment when they reached the play area. Memory put Beast down and all parties stared at one another for a long time.

"No biting Memory's beast," was the consensus before the pups returned to their play.

Beast stayed back, watchful and probably planning world domination.

Picking the kitten up again, Memory turned to Alexei. "I love you."

"I know." He laughed when she elbowed him, sunlight in his soul. "I love you, too, lioness. Even if you do let me get mauled by tiny beasts." Reaching out, he scratched the beast on its head.

It threatened to bite his fingers.

Memory leaned up and kissed his jaw. "You're not on security shift, are you?"

"No, I went to get your ferocious beast."

"Then come inside and I'll kiss your sorely mauled body better."

Alexei's vision altered, his wolf rising to the surface. "Come on, mate, let's go scandalize the beast."

IT took a month for Kaleb to notice the change. The PsyNet area around Memory Aven-Rose's mind was healthier, stronger . . . solid.

Much more so than could be explained by her fledgling abilities.

His eyes went to the place where the wild amber bond disappeared into nothing. A bond the neosentience of the PsyNet continued to protect with an intense and strange secretiveness. And a bond that connected the PsyNet with a changeling pack. Not just any pack, but the biggest and most powerful in the world.

Kaleb couldn't access SnowDancer minds via the link

that appeared to go nowhere, but was it possible the invasion was occurring in the other direction? Primal wolf energy entering the PsyNet? It would do the wolves no harm—choice underlay a healthy PsyNet, else Psy would've forced humans into bonds long ago.

To test his theory, he checked the area around Silver's mind. Healthy. Extremely so. And his former aide and current director of EmNet wasn't an empath, so that eliminated one possible factor. In point of fact, the two women had only a single similarity: each was mated to a dominant predatory changeling who was part of a sprawling pack.

Whatever was happening, it appeared to be a passive transfer that no one else had noticed. Kaleb would tell only Sahara. These bonds could not become political. They were too important.

"The wolves, bears, and humans of two deadly packs might help save tens of thousands of Psy lives," he said to her that night.

"Kaleb, we have to tell the alphas at least." Her blue eyes asked him to choose the side of right, of conscience.

She was his lodestar.

He made it a conference call with Hawke Snow, Valentin Nikolaev, Silver, Memory Aven-Rose, and Alexei Harte.

The big bear alpha let Silver ask the questions, "since my Starlight's the expert."

Hawke raised his eyebrow at that and pulled his own Psy mate into the conversation.

The final conclusion was the same as Kaleb's: nothing was flowing back through the bond. Hawke's cardinal mate was actually able to enter the wolf network to check and confirm that. "We're also at usual levels of biofeedback and psychic energy. Far as I can tell, we've lost nothing."

In the end, the alphas made the call to allow it to continue. Each would monitor their pack for signs of trouble, but Kaleb didn't think they'd ever find any. This was how the PsyNet was always meant to work. "To be a living, vibrant network with multiple kinds of psychic input," he said to Sahara after the call ended.

She chewed on her lower lip. "Did you notice Memory

and Silver's stable sections are similar in size, even though SnowDancer is much bigger than StoneWater?"

Kaleb checked, saw she was right. His blood cooled. "It's not only about numbers." Else, the SnowDancer connection alone should've gained them a healthy section of the PsyNet equivalent to California.

"No," Sahara whispered. "I think Psy have to make human or changeling connections through the world. An even spread." She thrust a shaking hand through her hair. "How do we change a hundred years of division and isolation and pain across an entire planet?"

Kaleb cupped her jaw, ran the pad of his thumb over her cheekbone. "In the space of a few weeks, we've gained a working E-sigma and an entire pack of wolves. Tonight, we celebrate by confusing seismologists around Russia." Control became a foreign concept when he was with Sahara—the best he could do was ground his enormous telekinetic power.

Sahara's panicked expression fractured into laughter. "You know, you're right." She grabbed his tie and tugged. "Kiss me, Mr. Krychek."

AS Kaleb kissed Sahara under a Russian sky, and Alexei chased Memory through a Sierra Nevada forest, minds across the PsyNet began to throw off their shackles and wake to new powers that dazzled and blinded. None were as disciplined as the first of their kind. The initial rogue power surge was a mere ripple. More built on the horizon, ominous weights about to crash onto an already fractured Net.

Anarchy took its first breath.

Keep reading for an excerpt from
Nalini Singh's new novel

A MADNESS OF SUNSHINE

Available now from Berkley!

Chapter 1

SHE RETURNED HOME two hundred and seventeen days after burying her husband while his pregnant mistress sobbed so hard that she made herself sick. Anahera had stood stone-faced, staring down at the gleaming mahogany coffin she'd chosen because that was what Edward would've wanted. Quiet elegance and money that didn't make itself obvious, that had been Edward's way. Appearances above everything.

His friends had looked at her with sympathetic eyes, believing her grief so great that she couldn't cry.

And all the while, Edward's mistress sobbed.

No one knew her.

Anahera hadn't explained who the woman was.

And she hadn't cried. Not then. Not since.

Now, she drove the dark green Jeep she'd bought sight unseen over the internet and arranged to have delivered to the airport that had been the last stop in her long plane trek from London.

Christchurch, New Zealand.

A land at the bottom of the world. So far south that she'd felt no surprise when their pilot pointed out a cargo plane being loaded with freight bound for an Antarctic research station.

How many hours had it been since she walked through the departure gate at Heathrow?

Thirty-six? Thirty-eight?

She'd lost count somewhere between yesterday and tomorrow. Between the gray drizzle of a city full of theaters and museums and the cold sunlight of a barely civilized land adrift in the ocean.

Edward had liked cities.

He and Anahera had never driven through such a primal and untamed landscape together, the trees born of ancient seeds, and the ferns huge and green and singing a song of homecoming.

Tauti mai, hoki mai.

And this moment a whisper from the end of her journey, she stood on a jagged cliff looking out over the crashing sea below as fog wove through the treetops, a light misty rain falling and dissipating before it ever got to her.

Dark gray water smashed against unforgiving black rock, sending up a frothy white spray that disappeared under the violence of the next crashing wave. The water went on endlessly, a tumultuous vastness that was nothing like the European beaches she'd visited with Edward. You couldn't swim in the water below, not unless you wanted to be swept out into the cold arms of the ocean, but its beauty spoke to Anahera's heart, made it ache.

She could watch it forever, might just do that once she reached the cabin. Josie told her it was still standing—and that no one had smashed in the windows.

Maybe it had been out of respect. Perhaps out of fear.

To some, the cabin was a place of ghosts.

To Josie, it was where she and Anahera had once sat on the porch and laughed, two nineteen-year-olds with their whole lives ahead of them. Her best friend from high school was the only person with whom Anahera had kept in touch after she left Golden Cove, and she'd told Josie not to bother worrying about keeping an eye on the place.

After all, Anahera was never going to come back.

Turning away from the cliff, she got into the Jeep and started it up.

Driving inland and away from the crashing sea—it was

an illusion, the sea still there, just hidden by the trees—she drove the last ten minutes to the edge of forever. The sign startled her. Golden Cove hadn't had a sign when she'd left. Only an old gumboot on a fencepost that Nikau Martin had put there when they were eleven.

For some reason, the adults had never taken it off.

But it was gone now, and in its place stood a gleaming sign that said: HAERE MAI, with GOLDEN COVE lettered in swirling font below, and WELCOME below that. She went past, then stopped and looked back to see that, from this side, it said, HAERE RĀ, with GOLDEN COVE below, and under that, FAREWELL.

Shrugging off the disquiet of the unfamiliar after a long moment, she continued on down the otherwise empty road.

Her car hiccuped, then jerked.

"Don't you crap out on me now," she said, hitting the dashboard. But the Jeep was in no mood to listen to her. It spluttered and hiccuped again before going dead.

Managing to guide it to the side of the road, Anahera put it in park, then turned off the engine. Well, at least it wasn't a total disaster. From here, it would only take her about twenty minutes to walk into Golden Cove. She'd have to leave her two suitcases in the back or maybe not. They had wheels, didn't they? It just seemed appropriate that the angry girl who'd left this town in her dust would return dusty and travel worn.

Fate sure had a sense of humor.

A car engine sounded in the distance, growing increasingly louder. Before she'd left the stark emptiness of New Zealand's West Coast all those years ago, Anahera would've thought nothing of jumping out and flagging down that truck or car or whatever it was.

Despite her childhood and the chill darkness of her fourteenth summer, she'd grown up thinking of this entire wild landscape as safe, those who lived within it all people she knew. But the wider world had hammered it home that no one could be trusted. So she stayed inside her locked vehicle and watched a large SUV approach in her rearview mirror.

It was white, with a bull bar in the front. That wasn't unusual—what was unusual was the distinctive blue-and-yellow-check pattern along its sides, a pattern she could see because the SUV had come to a stop right alongside her, though it stayed far enough away that she could easily open her door should she need to.

The word POLICE was written in solid white letters against a large blue piece of the pattern. Since when, she wondered, did Golden Cove deserve any kind of a police presence? It was too small, the residents relying on the police station in the closest big town, Greymouth, to supply their needs, though "big" was a relative term on the West Coast. Last she'd heard, the population of the entire coast had been hovering around thirty-one thousand.

She cautiously lowered her window as the other driver lowered their passenger-side window so that the two of them could talk. A man. Thirty-something, with a hardness to his jaw and grooves carved into his face, as if he'd seen things he couldn't forget—and they hadn't been good things.

His hair was dark, his skin that light-brownish tone that made it difficult to tell if he was just tanned, or if he had ancestors on her side of the genetic tree. She couldn't see his eyes behind the opaque darkness of his sunglasses, but she imagined they'd be as hard as his jaw. "Everything all right?" he asked.

She noticed that he wasn't in uniform, but then, if he really was stationed in Golden Cove, it wasn't as if any of the locals would report him for breaching protocol. "Car trouble," she answered. "I can walk the rest of the way into town." She had no intention of getting into a vehicle with an unknown man on a deserted road surrounded by dark green native forest and not much else.

"Let me have a look at it." Pulling ahead of her car before she could answer, he got out and she saw immediately that he was a big man: wide shoulders; strong, long legs; equally strong arms. But everything about him was hard, as if he'd been smelted down until all softness was lost.

Gut tight, she raised her window a little farther, but he didn't come around to the door. Instead, he indicated that she should pop open her hood. Figuring she had nothing to lose, Anahera went ahead and did so.

As he disappeared behind it, she tried to imagine what it

would be like to walk into the cabin after all this time. She couldn't. All she could see was her last glimpse of it, the floor scrubbed of blood and the ladder taken away to be crushed in a compactor.

The cop looked around the side of the hood. "Try it now."

She did so without hope and the engine caught. Not smiling at her shouted thanks, he unhooked and closed the hood before finally coming around to her window. "It doesn't look like anything major," he said, "but if you intend to drive through more of the West Coast, you should have a mechanic check it out."

It was good advice; these roads were exacting. It wasn't that they were in bad condition—for being in the middle of nowhere, the roads were just fine. But they were empty. Long stretches of nothing but wilderness and water; break down in one of those areas and there was no guarantee anyone would come along for hours. As for cell signals, the mountains played havoc with them.

"I'm going to the Cove," she told him. "Does Peter still work in the garage?" Maybe her old schoolmate had gone on to bigger and better things by now.

Raising an eyebrow, the cop nodded. "It's not tourist season. You here to do a retreat with Shane Hennessey?"

Josie had told Anahera about the famed Irish writer who'd relocated to Golden Cove. "No," Anahera said. "I'm coming home. Thank you again." She rolled up the window before he could ask any more questions.

But this man, he wasn't someone she could simply ignore. He knocked on the glass politely after taking off his sunglasses to reveal slate gray eyes as dark as the clouds gathering on the horizon.

When she lowered her window a fraction, he said, "I'll follow behind you, make sure you get in okay."

"Knock yourself out," she said, not certain why she was being so antagonistic to someone who'd helped her.

Maybe it was knowing she was driving back into the past.

She pulled out.

In the rearview mirror, she saw the cop take his time getting into his vehicle. Then she turned the corner and he was gone. But his SUV reappeared behind her soon enough, and then their party of two made its way into a town founded on a golden illusion.

The miners had thought they'd find gold here, find riches, find a future. Instead, they'd found nothing but a harsh and unforgiving landscape with water as treacherous as the rocks that crushed so many of them one after the other.

Chapter 2

WILL FOLLOWED THE unfamiliar vehicle through the heavily tree-shadowed road that led into Golden Cove. There was nowhere else to go from this point.

The town's self-appointed business council might have managed to get up a few signs, but come winter and even those signs wouldn't help those new to the area find the place Will had called home for the past three months. It wasn't surprising that he didn't recognize the dark-eyed woman with wavy black hair and striking cheekbones that pushed against skin of midbrown.

The skin was smooth but the eyes old.

Late twenties or very early thirties, he guessed, likely a child of Golden Cove who'd lit out of here the instant she was legal and who was returning to pay a visit to a parent or grandparent. You'd think with the town's younger residents almost universally restless, just itching to leave, the place would be a retirement village—but that was the strange thing with Golden Cove. It seemed to draw back its prodigals.

Peter Jacobs, the garage owner she'd mentioned, had spent six years working for a Formula One team and traveling the world before he landed back in the Cove. When asked why he'd given up his glamorous life in favor of running the family garage with his aging father and resentful younger brother, he just shrugged and said that a man got tired of Ferraris and wanted to return to the ocean.

Peter, however, had only been back for less than a year, and yet the woman with the car trouble had asked if Peter was "still" working in the garage, which meant she'd last been in Golden Cove at least seven years earlier.

Will's eyes narrowed: the woman and Peter might even be the same age or close to it. Could be they'd been school-mates. And what, he asked himself, did it all matter? It wasn't as if he'd been dumped in Golden Cove to be a de-tective. He might hold the rank, but he'd been placed here as the community's sole policeman because he'd become a problem for the force—but was too decorated and senior an officer to simply fire. So instead, they'd put him out to pas-ture in Golden Cove and forgotten about him.

That was fine with Will. Prior to being offered this job, he'd been planning to quit. Since his plan after quitting had involved any remote job he could get his hands on, he'd thought why the hell not just bury himself in a sole-charge station that covered a sprawling geographic area but in-volved only a very small number of people?

There were far more trees in his patrol area than human residents.

Most of the folk in Golden Cove let him be, and the odd time that he did have to step in, it was usually to break up a bar fight or calm down a neighborhood dispute. Yesterday, he'd had to handcuff a drunk to a chair until the other man was sober enough to be dropped home.

Will didn't have a jail.

And so far, no Golden Cove problems had justified formal charges. Come summer, with tourists pouring in for various adventure activities thanks to the region's advertising cam-paign over the past couple of years, and he'd probably have more trouble. Which was also why the town now had a po-lice officer. The regional tourism bodies had apparently gone apoplectic about a couple of tourists who'd gotten beaten up in Golden Cove after dark.

Bad for business to have visitors posting photos of black

eyes and broken ribs instead of the bleak scenery, dangerous cliff climbs, or local cuisine.

So now Golden Cove had Will.

The first small home appeared on the right, complete with a white picket fence and hardy wildflowers in a neatly tended garden. Mrs. Keith sat on her rocker out front, her girth overflowing the white wood of it and her face a pale moon surrounded by a halo of teased black. Pink lipstick slashed across her mouth, her plump fingers bejeweled when she raised her hand in a wave.

Will didn't know if the curt woman in the Jeep waved back, but he raised his hand.

The next house was on the left, this one as ramshackle as Mrs. Keith's was immaculate. Peeling blue paint, a wheelless car rusting in the front yard, grass as high as his calves. On the front stoop sat a good-looking man with nut-brown skin, a cigarette in hand and his face tattooed with a full *tā moko* that might've been traditional, but that tended to make strangers wary. It didn't help that Nikau Martin consistently wore ripped black jeans, shitkickers, and T-shirts imprinted with the Hells Angels logo.

Right now, the other man's dark eyes were following the green Jeep.

Will paused in front of the rickety gate.

Nikau got up and sauntered over to jump the gate. Leaning his arms on the open window of Will's SUV, he said, "I never thought I'd see Anahera back in this town."